A PLACE OF SAFETY

Helen Black was brought up in a mining town in West Yorkshire. She moved to London in her twenties and trained to be a commercial lawyer. On qualification she shifted lanes and has practised criminal and family law for over ten years. She specialises in representing children in the care system. She now lives in Bedfordshire with her husband and young children. Her debut novel *Damaged Goods* has sold across Europe.

For further information on Helen Black, visit her website at www.hblack.co.uk and go to www.BookArmy for exclusive updates.

Praise for *Damaged Goods*:

'A fantastic first novel.'
Jane Elliott, author of *The Little Prisoner* and *Sadie*

'A dark and gripping read that will have you on the edge of your seat . . . this terrific debut novel is full of intrigue and a real page-turner.' *Closer*

By the same author:

Damaged Goods

HELEN BLACK

A Place of Safety

AVON

AVON

A division of HarperCollins*Publishers*
77–85 Fulham Palace Road,
London W6 8JB

www.harpercollins.co.uk

A Paperback Original

1

First published in Great Britain by
HarperCollins*Publishers* 2008

Copyright © Helen Black 2008

Helen Black asserts the moral right to
be identified as the author of this work

A catalogue record for this book is
available from the British Library

ISBN-13: 978-1-84756-071-1

Set in Minion by Palimpsest Book Production Limited,
Grangemouth, Stirlingshire

Printed and bound in Great Britain by
Clays Ltd, St Ives plc

Mixed Sources

Product group from well-managed
forests and other controlled sources
www.fsc.org   Cert no. SW-COC-1806
© 1996 Forest Stewardship Council

FSC is a non-profit international organisation established to promote the
responsible management of the world's forests. Products carrying the FSC
label are independently certified to assure consumers that they come
from forests that are managed to meet the social, economic and
ecological needs of present and future generations.

Find out more about HarperCollins and the environment at
www.harpercollins.co.uk/green

Acknowledgments

Before I wrote my first novel I thought authors were solitary beings, chained to their old-fashioned type-writers for months on end. Now of course I know that any book worth reading is a collaborative affair and I for one am grateful for that.

First shout goes to Peter, Rosie and Jessica Buckman who continue to champion me and my work.

Huge thanks are also due to everyone at Avon, particularly Kesh, who goes that extra mile for me.

My fellow HUG members, David and Mike, have once again offered red wine and positive criticism for which I continue to be grateful.

A big virtual wave goes to the community of writers on www.writewords.org.uk. Wit, wisdom and general blather are always only a keyboard away.

And I know she's going to be mortified but I'd like to single out my mate, Sarah S, for keeping me sane with our morning walks. My thighs salute you.

Then there's the family. The noisy, messy lot of us. We don't lead a normal life, but then again, who wants to?

There are 9.2 million refugees worldwide.

The UK offers a home to 3%.

Of those seeking a place of safety in the UK, a fifth are unaccompanied children.

For Mum

Prologue

Things, as Luke Walker's mother is fond of saying, are getting out of hand.

The voices of his friends jar his ears as they stumble through some song by Lily Allen, clapping out of time, urging her on. Tom whoops with glee like a small child at Christmas, saliva dribbling down his chin. Charlie digs Luke in the ribs and shouts something in his ear but the words are lost in a fit of giggles.

The girl is in the middle of their ramshackle circle, her laughter almost hysterical. She says something none of them understand and spins round and round so that her skirt flares up and the boys can see her knickers.

Tom reaches out to touch her. 'Yeah baby,' he brays, but the momentum makes him lose his balance and he falls over, bringing Luke down with him.

Tom gropes the ground and swears.

Luke feels sick. He wants to go home. He would go home but he's boarding tonight, and if the house master catches him in this state he'll be in detention for a month.

And anyway, the field is spinning and he doesn't think he can stand.

'You like?' the girl asks them.

The other two applaud but Luke can't even nod his head. He doesn't like, not at all.

That night had started the same as any other. With prep finished and Mr Philips dealing with one of the homesick new boys, Luke and his friends sneaked out of school to mooch around the village. They pledged how different their lives would be when they could drive.

Charlie's the eldest and is getting lessons for his seventeenth, but that's not for over two months.

Luke should be next, but every time he mentions it his mum gives him the look and talks about how many young people die in road accidents.

Tom is the youngest of the group but will probably still be first to pass his test. His dad already lets him drive an old Jeep across their land.

They wandered down to the off-licence. Luke didn't know why they bothered because Mrs Singh knows they're all from the boarding school and under age. Tom called her a 'fucking Paki' and knocked over a rack of crisps. Luke hates it when Tom does stuff like that.

They finally dragged Tom out with Mrs Singh threatening to call the police, and there was the girl, leaning against the Post Office window opposite. She was one of that lot from the hostel. You could tell by the way she dressed, the way she wore her hair. And she stood like they all do, hunched in on herself, as if trying to disappear.

'Hey you,' Tom shouted.

She looked startled at being spoken to and was about to move on when Tom dashed across the street and caught her arm.

'Do you want to earn some money?' he asked.

She didn't answer, her face a blank canvas.

'Money,' he repeated, rubbing his thumb and fore-finger together as if she were deaf or an imbecile. So they paid her five quid to get them some bottles of cider and headed to the park.

It was built for the local kids but they're all at home on their Nintendos. Only the boarders use it when they manage to slip out of evening prep. It's cold and deserted, but at least they can get pissed in peace.

Luke doesn't know why the girl came with them. Maybe she liked the look of Charlie, who's tall and dark – all the girls fancy him. Or maybe Tom talked her into it. He's ginger and has a big gap in his front teeth, but he has a way of getting people to do what he wants. 'Leadership qualities' his mum calls it.

Either way, she sat on the swings and shared their booze. She barely said a word, except that her name was Anna. Luke thought she was very pretty in a weird sort of way.

When she started dancing you could tell she didn't really know what she was doing, that she was drunk. He should have told her to sit down. Why hadn't he told her to sit down?

Now things are going pear-shaped. Tom has managed to pull Anna onto the floor. She's still laughing but trying to push him away.

'No no no,' she says.

Tom mimics her accent. 'Yes, yes, yes.'

She tries to push him away but she's not very strong, and Tom's the captain of the rugby first eleven. Luke notices how tiny she is and Tom easily holds the sticks

3

of her arms above her head. Her sweater has ridden up and Luke can see her ribs protruding through her skin.

'Come on, Tom, leave her alone,' he says.

Tom's breath comes in hard pants. 'Fuck off.' His forehead is greasy with sweat and the unmistakable bulge of Tom's cock pushes against his trouser leg.

Luke feels the acid burn of bile in his throat and tries not to retch.

The girl struggles to free herself.

'Give me a hand, Charlie,' says Tom.

Charlie seems unsure and hovers above them.

'Hold her arms,' Tom grunts.

When Charlie still doesn't move, Tom snarls at him. 'Hold her fucking arms, you queer.'

Charlie steals a glance in Luke's direction. He's terrified of what's about to happen, but more terrified of defying Tom. Luke wills him to walk away, to make a joke out of the whole thing. He doesn't. He kneels above Anna's head and presses firmly on her wrists.

Luke realises now that she is screaming. The air shatters around him.

Tom clamps one hand over her mouth and uses the other to pull at his flies. Luke tries to get to his feet to help the girl but falls sideways and ends up flapping like a fish in a net.

Tom laughs. 'Don't worry, you'll get your turn, Lukey boy.' He thrusts his hips forward and Anna's eyes shoot open. He knows he has to do something. Anything. So why doesn't he move? Why is he still lying on the hard autumn ground? He closes his eyes, disgusted at himself and wishes for tomorrow morning.

Chapter One

The sky outside the office was clear and welcoming. The pale October sun attempted to make its presence felt and Lilly longed to take her lunchtime walk. She'd instituted a daily turn around Harpenden Park after a four-week contested divorce case that had frazzled her mind. She found that the fresh air calmed her, and it stopped her from wolfing more than a sandwich for lunch.

She turned her gaze from the window back to her client and sighed. Mr Maxwell was so absorbed in his story he had failed to notice his solicitor's evident lack of interest.

'I simply cannot justify another penny,' he said. 'And I cannot see why she should be allowed to sit at home all day while I work my socks off.'

Lilly wondered why a man with such a profound lisp would choose so many words beginning with 's', and pretended not to notice the spittle that was accumulating on his tie.

'She has three children to care for,' said Lilly, 'and they are your children.'

'We have an au pair for them.' He fixed Lilly with

eyes that bulged like marbles in an otherwise flat face. 'You have a child, Miss Valentine, yet you seem to manage to work without too much trouble.'

Lilly thought of her ridiculously complicated childcare routine, involving her ex-husband, friends, and anyone prepared to offer a lift to school.

'What do you think she could do to earn some money?' Lilly asked.

Mr Maxwell gave a dismissive shrug. 'She used to be a model.'

Lilly tried to hide her shock. What beautiful woman would go for this unappealing specimen of manhood? Mr Maxwell gave a tree-frog blink. The sort who would be happy to sit on her bony arse all day and count his money was the obvious answer.

'As galling as it seems, Mr Maxwell, the court has ordered you to pay maintenance to your wife and children,' said Lilly.

'Ex-wife.'

Lilly nodded. 'So you will have to pay.'

Mr Maxwell shuffled his whinging backside out of Lilly's office, his eyes pulsating.

As he left the building she watched him limp up the road. Lisp, blinking eyes, a limp – maybe she was being too harsh on the poor man. Then a blonde bounced towards him, her plastic breasts fighting to escape. She covered his bald head in tiny kisses and squealed.

Mrs Maxwell Mark Two was waiting in the wings. Some men never learned.

Lilly checked her watch and groaned, realising that her next client was due any minute. She tried to leave a gap between them but divorce cases always overran. These people paid by the hour, so it was their funeral if they blabbed over their allotted appointment, which invariably they did. When it came to splitting up the marital assets, this lot would argue over the contents of the hoover bag.

Lilly missed her care cases. Stroppy teens who might spare you ten minutes between shoplifting in Tesco's and meeting their mates in the arcade. Sometimes they didn't turn up at all but left convoluted messages about ASBOs, social workers and pregnancy tests.

God, she missed it.

She pulled a Kit Kat from her bag. Chocolate and no exercise, a double whammy. As sugar and hydrogenated fat entered her system, she realised that the only thing keeping her sane was the weekly trip to Hounds Place. At least there she could do some good. Some real good.

'Might pop over there after this client,' she mused.

'Don't even think about it.'

Lilly turned to the door, where the ever scowling secretary-cum-receptionist, Sheila, had appeared.

'You don't even know what I was talking about,' said Lilly.

Sheila crossed her arms. 'You want to go running off to the Dogs' Home.'

'It's called Hounds Place,' said Lilly. 'As you bloody well know.'

Sheila scooped up some papers fanning the floor and slid them back into their file. 'Do you keep your house as tidy as this?'

'Did you just come to annoy me or did you get bored with filing your nails?'

Sheila tried to put the file back in the drawer but the runners were jammed. She pushed and pulled, the metallic groans matching her own.

Lilly sighed. 'Do you actually want something, Sheila?'

'The powers-that-be want to take you for a drink after work,' she said, without turning around.

Lilly put her head in her hands. 'Bloody marvellous.'

'Stop whining,' said Sheila, and thrust her arm into the cabinet. It disappeared like a vet's arm in a cow. 'They probably want to thank you for your hard work and good attitude.'

'In my new role as advisor to the rich, ugly and divorcing I make them shitloads of money. Good attitude is not part of the package.'

Sheila was now virtually inside the cabinet, her shoulders and chest lost in its recesses, her face pushed against the handle.

'I don't know why you're so miserable. You're making good money, aren't you?'

It was true. Lilly's wage had increased by fifty per cent since the firm had reallocated her caseload.

'The root of all evil,' she said.

Sheila's cheek was contorted by the pressure of the metal. 'You weren't saying that when you didn't have any, you just moaned endlessly about the state of your house, how your car was knackered and you couldn't afford Sam's school uniform.'

'But it's so boring.'

'Grow up,' Sheila grunted. 'It beats the bunch of

no-hopers that used to come here thieving the staplers.'

'Vulnerable kids,' Lilly sniffed.

'Junkies, most of them,' said Sheila. 'Like that bleeding nutter who drank the bleach.'

'Kelsey was not on drugs,' said Lilly. 'It was her mother who was addicted.'

'Whatever.' Sheila shook her head as if the details were unimportant. 'The point is it nearly bankrupted the office.'

'We got paid,' said Lilly.

'Legal Aid scraps, and you know it,' said Sheila. 'And as for those scroungers at the Dogs' Home, I don't know why you bother.'

'Because it stimulates my intellect,' said Lilly. 'Something you wouldn't understand.'

'I understand that having kids means making sacrifices.' At last Sheila withdrew her arm, bringing with it a battered book. 'This was stuck at the back.' She threw it onto Lilly's desk. *The Art of Positive Thinking.*

'Something to stimulate your intellect.'

Lilly put her head on the desk. 'Do I really have to go for a drink?'

Sheila's laugh was nothing short of cruel. 'Rupinder says it's a three-line whip.'

It's been a horrid day. A nightmare. Mr Peters had bawled Luke out for not paying attention in Latin. He'd said he was wasting his talents, and that it was nothing short of criminal. Luke had wanted to tell him how close to the mark he was.

During Information Technology he'd surfed the Net to see how long people got for rape, how old he'd be when he got out of prison. He couldn't breathe when he saw life was an option. He'd seen a politician on the telly saying the government were cracking down, that 'life should mean life'. He'd bitten his lip until it bled, terrified he'd burst into tears in front of the whole class.

Worse still, Tom had been acting like nothing was wrong. He'd even boasted in the common room about meeting a 'right little goer'.

The other boys had laughed at him, said he was talking bollocks.

Tom leaned over the snooker table and potted the black.

'Ask Lukey boy, he'll tell you what she was like,' he said. 'Gagging for it, wasn't she?'

Luke smiled weakly, but he could still hear the girl screaming and see her slender wrists being held so tightly that they seemed to turn blue-black. A bit like the sky before a storm.

Now the bell is ringing and Luke can finally escape. Thank God he's not boarding tonight. He wants to go home, to throw himself onto his Arsenal duvet and let it all out. Maybe he should tell his mum. Maybe she could help. Even if she can't it would stop the whole thing running through his head like a bad film on a loop.

He sees her car parked by the cricket pitch and bolts towards it. Inside it smells of clean washing.

His mum smiles. 'Had a nice day, love?'

He can't answer and squeezes his eyes shut.

'Is everything all right, love?' asks his mum.

He stirs his pasta with a limp wrist.

'Luke?'

Her voice is so very gentle. He feels wrung out like a damp cloth, all the moisture down the sink.

She lifts his chin and looks into his eyes. 'You would tell me if something was wrong?'

He sees in her familiar face a lifetime of wiped noses and birthday teas. This isn't a broken window or a bad school report. How can he tell her what he has been part of, what he has done? She can't make it better. No one can.

He forces some words out. 'I'm just tired.'

'You look peaky,' she says, and presses a cool palm against his forehead. 'You're not hot but you're obviously coming down with something.'

He pushes his bowl away. 'Yeah. I feel sick.'

Relief plays at the corner of his mother's mouth. This is her territory.

'Better lie down, love,' she says. 'Will you be all right while I collect your sister?'

The thought of Jessie, a year younger than Luke, fills his mind. What if some boys took her to the park . . . held her down . . .

He runs from the room, his hand over his mouth, acid bile running through his fingers.

* * *

His bedroom is spinning and Luke concentrates on a small brown water stain on the ceiling.

'I'll be twenty minutes,' his mum calls from the bottom of the stairs. 'How about I call at Waitrose for some Lucozade?'

Luke doesn't answer.

When he hears the front door close he lets the tears spill. He curls into a ball and weeps, snot pooling under his nose, sliding onto his lips, until it becomes clear what he has to do.

He wipes his eyes on the back of his hand and packs a bag.

Lilly had tried, she really had. She'd put on her coat and fully intended to head to the bar where her boss and the other partners were waiting for her. But when it had come to it, Lilly had made a sharp right turn and jumped into her new Mini Cooper. Sheila was right about some things. A car that started first time, every time, was a joy on a par with a night with George Clooney.

As she sped down the A5 she pulled out her phone.

'Rupes, it's me. Sorry I couldn't make it to the pub but I need to collect Sam. He said he'd leave home if he had to go to after-school care again.'

It was true that Sam preferred not to stay late at school with the boarders. He said the common room smelled and tea in the refectory was always the same. 'I don't know how they do it, Mum, but whatever day you go it's always some sort of mince,' he'd said. 'They give it different names but it doesn't fool anyone.'

To say he hated it was perhaps an exaggeration, but extreme times called for extreme measures.

Rupinder said nothing. Lilly could imagine her pursed lips and tried to make light of it. 'You can give me my bollocking tomorrow and save yourself the price of a pint.'

'Just get your backside over here.'

Lancasters had changed hands again. Now a franchise of a famous chef who had never stepped out of the West End, it had restyled itself as a gastropub. What this meant in reality was sage-green walls by Farrow & Ball and steaks costing fifteen quid a pop. As usual, it was almost empty.

Rupinder and the others were congregated at the far end of the bar. Lilly heard the pop of a champagne cork and her heart sank. Had she missed something important? Whose birthday was it?

'What's the occasion?' she called, all faux bonhomie.

Rupinder held out a glass of bubbly. 'Your application for rights of higher audience. You passed.'

Earlier that year, Rupes had come under pressure from her colleagues to give Lilly the boot because of her propensity to speak her mind and take on cases that would add little to their pension funds. Rupes had resisted but had agreed to improve her bottom line. One suggestion was that money should stop being wasted on barristers and that Lilly should handle her own advocacy wherever possible.

'Wow,' said Lilly. Drowning in the sea of divorce cases, she'd forgotten all about the exams she'd taken that summer.

'Wow indeed.' Rupinder's tone was cold. Lilly was obviously not forgiven for her attempted escape. 'Congratulations.'

Sheila drained her glass and helped herself to a refill from the jeroboam. She didn't tilt her glass, and the expensive froth flowed down the stem.

'I suppose you'll be in the office even less now,' she said. 'And muggins here will get all the extra paperwork.'

'Every cloud,' said Lilly.

'Perhaps we could all put our differences aside and pull as a team,' said Rupinder, 'just this once.'

Lilly girded herself for a lecture but was saved by her phone. 'I told you Sam would get the hump.'

Rupes looked gratifyingly crestfallen so Lilly didn't mention that football training wouldn't finish for another hour.

She stood away from the others.

'Miss Valentine?'

'That's me,' she said.

'I'm from Hounds Place. I wonder if you have any time to speak to one of the residents.'

Lilly looked over at Rupes and gave her best contrite parent face. 'I'll be right there.'

This 7 message thread spans 2 pages: [1] 2 >>

The People of Britain Have Had Enough! Blood River at 15.05
This country used to be something to be proud of.

14

It used to stand for something around the world. Its people knew who they were.

Can we say that any more?

The People Of Britain Have Had Enough! Skin Lick at 15.12

No we can't.

The country has gone to shit with all the bending over backwards for immigrants.

The People of Britain Have Had Enough! Snow White at 15.15

What really annoys me is when you walk down the street and every other person is a foreigner. I went on a train to London last week and heard about twenty different languages. I began to wonder where I was . . .

The People of Britain Have Had Enough! Skin Lick at 15.22

I know what you mean, Snow White. My home town has three mosques. Three!!!

We truly are living in Englastan.

The People of Britain Have Had Enough! Snow White at 15.26

I read that some schools are forced to celebrate Eid and Diwali but the children aren't allowed to send Christmas cards to one another. I don't want my children bringing up that way.

<u>The People of Britain Have Had Enough!</u> Skin Lick at 15.38

It's a scandal.

The white indigenous population of this country will soon be in the minority and then we'll lose all our heritage and culture.

Prepare to say goodbye to Easter, New Year's Eve and Bonfire Night.

<u>The People of Britain Have Had Enough!</u> Blood River at 15.46

I for one am not about to surrender everything I hold dear.

Mass immigration has been a disaster and it's got to stop.

We are at saturation point.

Write to your MP saying you will no longer tolerate being a second-class citizen in your own home.

Boycott shops owned by in-comers.

Fly the flag of St George with pride.

Snow White closed the lid of her laptop. She hated to leave a live discussion but she needed to pick up her husband's shirts from the dry-cleaners'. She checked the clock. If she didn't dilly-dally she'd still have enough time to pop into the butcher's and get home in time for the live podcast.

A hostel had recently opened in Manor Wood, within half a mile of Sam's school. The building, Hounds Place, had previously been a police-station house but had been bought up by a professional landlord who saw the potential for squeezing five desperate refugees into each room.

The influx of nearly thirty foreigners into a small village like Manor Wood had not been greeted with over-whelming delight. The infamous hospitality of the English countryside did not, it seemed, extend to the raggle-taggle bunch of young men and women who had risked everything to leave their wartorn homelands.

Lilly had begged Rupes to let her represent two fourteen-year-old boys who had fled the Taliban. Without any relatives in the UK care orders had been made without fuss or objection so the use of Lilly's time had been negligible. Two had become four, then a teenager from Bosnia arrived and another from Uganda. Although she kept the increasing numbers quiet, particularly from Rupes, Lilly now represented at least half the kids in there. It didn't take up too much of her energy, she told herself, as she checked her watch.

As soon as she crossed the threshold a young man in a checked shirt and denim jacket sidled over.

'Hello, Artan,' said Lilly.

He should have been a good-looking boy with his full pink lips and the blackest of lashes, but something about him always unnerved Lilly. His entire family had been killed in Kosovo, but he never seemed angry or sad or even confused. He was cold.

'How are you?' she asked.

Artan shook his head to indicate that things were not good. 'I need to speak to you.'

'I've got twenty minutes,' said Lilly.

They went to the kitchen and the few residents who had been sitting around chatting got up and left. Something was very wrong.

'Have you been arrested again, Artan?' Lilly asked. A month ago she'd got him off with a warning for shoplifting.

'It is nothing like that.' His eyes were vacant, devoid of any clue as to what lay beneath.

'Are you in trouble?' she asked.

'Something has happened to my friend,' he said.

'Something bad?'

'Very, very bad,' said Artan.

Alarm bells started to ring. 'Has he been hurt?'

'It's a girl,' said Artan. 'And yes, she has been hurt.'

The alarm bells were pounding out now. The three-minute warning.

'Go on,' said Lilly.

'Some boys from the village have taken advantage of her,' said Artan.

'You mean she's been raped?'

Artan nodded.

'Has she been to the police?' asked Lilly.

'It is not so simple,' said Artan. 'She doesn't trust them.'

Lilly nodded. Despite special suites and task forces, most rapes continued to go unreported, and refugees were even less likely to take their chances with the authorities.

'She doesn't think the police will believe her,' he said.

'Why not?'

'She drank alcohol with these local boys and went to the park with them,' he said. 'They will say she wanted to have sex.'

'Why did she go with them?' asked Lilly.

'Because her mind is not clear,' he said.

The silence was thick between them. Lilly knew all their stories were horrific. That none of them were unscathed.

'Can you promise these boys will be convicted?' he said.

'No one can make a promise like that.'

Artan leaned towards her, his voice dropping. 'Is there a good chance?'

Lilly weighed her words very carefully. 'Rape is one of the most difficult offences to prove, and in a case like this where it's one girl's word against three presumably squeaky-clean schoolboys it would be even more difficult.'

Artan closed his eyes, his breathing slow and heavy.

Lilly shivered. 'But that's not to say she shouldn't report it.'

'Why?' His voice was barely above a whisper. 'So that she can be humiliated again and again?'

When he opened his eyes they seemed even more desolate than before.

'I'm sorry,' said Lilly.

She thought she saw a flash of anger skitter across his face.

'We are not animals,' he said. 'These boys must be punished.'

* * *

Twenty-four pounds.

It was daylight robbery.

Still, it was the best organic beef from cows allowed to roam freely around their farm in Sussex. Mr Simms even had photos of 'the girls' above his counter, all doe eyes and bell collars. Some thought that was a step too far but Snow White saw nothing wrong with it. Grandpa had kept chickens and had slit their throats in front of her for Sunday lunch. She could still hear the damned squawking.

People these days had no respect for the provenance of their food. They wanted everything clean and shrinkwrapped.

She had taught her children that life just wasn't like that. When a fox had killed every last one of their pet bunnies she had told them to stop crying and let them sit up with her until midnight when she took him out with her shotgun. 'Sometimes you have to get your hands dirty.'

She put the meat in the fridge and logged on to her laptop.

Welcome, Snow White – today's live podcast will start in five minutes.

Excellent. She hadn't missed it.

Humming to herself, she made a pot of Darjeeling.

Lilly's mind was still heavy with what she had heard. When she pulled into her son's prep school she almost hit a Mercedes and its driver hooted. Lilly was tempted to give her the finger, but such a gesture would be considered rude and vulgar, an unforgivable sin for the middle-class parents among whom Lilly already had few friends.

She was about to berate herself once again for giving in to her ex-husband on the subject of schooling when her mobile rang.

The voice was Irish honey. 'Hello, gorgeous. Got time for a natter?'

Lilly got out of the car and smiled. 'For you,' she said, 'I've always got time.'

It was Jack McNally, a copper Lilly had known for years, and had flirted with for nearly as long before he'd finally made a move.

'What are you wearing?' he asked.

Lilly laughed. 'I'd like to say a basque and fishnet stockings.'

A passing parent wrinkled her nose. Lilly wanted to stick out her tongue.

'But,' said Jack, 'I'm sensing a "but".'

'To be honest, I'm at school, and even I'm not brazen enough to parade around here in my undies.'

'You wouldn't want to make all those yummy mummies jealous,' he said.

'Now I remember why I like you.'

She sauntered to the football pitch where Sam, in goal, was in position to save a penalty. Lilly hardly dared watch, even though it was only a practice session. 'So how're things?'

'Same old, same old,' he said.

'Oh,' she groaned, as Sam batted the ball clear of the

goal, the slap of the leather against his skin audible even from the touchline. Though it was undoubtedly uncool for a nine year old to show any pain his middle-aged mother couldn't help herself.

'You okay?' he asked. 'You sound a bit distracted.'

'I had a funny meeting just before you called.'

'Funny ha ha, or funny peculiar?'

'Funny disturbing,' she said. 'A girl from the hostel has been raped.'

'One of the asylum seekers?'

'Yeah. Her friend wanted to know what would happen if they got the police involved.'

'And?' Jack asked.

'And I told him the truth.'

The referee blew his whistle and ten boys ran towards Sam, who had clearly saved the day.

'I've got a bad feeling that he might do something stupid,' she said.

Ever the professional, Jack's tone was serious. 'Like what?'

Lilly waved at her son, who shook hands gravely with the other side and then scampered towards her, wind-milling his arms.

'I don't know, it could be nothing. Ignore me.'

'It doesn't sound like nothing, Lilly.'

Sam was almost upon her. 'You know how I over-react. He was probably just upset. Anyone would be.'

'Lilly, you don't overreact,' said Jack. 'You have excellent instincts, and if you think something is going down you need to tell someone.'

'I will, well, I might. I need to think it through.' Sam jumped into her arms, nearly knocking her off her feet. 'Look, I have to go, Peter Shilton needs his tea.'

* * *

Welcome, members. Today's discussion will feature regular contributor Nigel Purves.

Snow White helped herself to a Garibaldi and settled down. Nigel was always good value.

. . . I want to talk to you all about diversity and I want you to think about whether this is a good thing.

Snow White dunked her biscuit and smiled at her screen. Nigel was such an articulate man, able to make his point with a clarity and conviction that was sadly lacking in most politicians. And he knew how to work a suit and tie. The Des Lynam of the Far Right.

. . . On the face of it we might find difference a good thing – after all, who wants everything to be the same? Diversity makes life interesting, no?

But pause for a second and ask yourself what makes family so special.

Snow White reached for a ginger snap. Nigel was on top form.

Isn't it the fact that everyone is cut from the same cloth? That you have things in common? That you are a homogenous group?

Nigel ran a hand through his hair, still thick with flecks of grey.

23

Whatever anyone tells you, it is perfectly natural for each of us to want to be with our own kind. Some might call that racist. I say it's just common sense . . .

'Mum, I'm starving.'

Bugger. Snow White shut down the podcast.

'Is there anything to eat?'

The girls were home early. Nigel would have to wait.

'I have scones,' she said. 'Or crumpets. You choose.'

'I know a man who knows a man. He'll get you what you need.'

Artan nods and hands the money to the Albanian.

He doesn't ask any questions. Knows he wouldn't get any answers. He's thought about this and nothing else since he met with the solicitor.

These boys must pay.

Chapter Two

'You will be there, Mum?'

Lilly looked up from the washing-up bowl and smiled at her son. 'Yes, Sam.'

He stuffed the last spoonful of porridge into his mouth and beamed. 'Sometimes you get held up at work.'

'I've already squared it with the office and marked myself out in the diary with a fat red pen.'

'But stuff comes up on those big children cases,' he said.

'I'm not doing those any more, as well you know,' she said. 'And would I miss the semi-final?'

Placated, Sam collected together his kit bag and three bananas. 'For energy,' he said.

Unable to find a tea towel, Lilly wiped her hands down her jumper. Suds accumulated across her chest. She tried to rub the bubbles away with her elbow but only managed to smear them around. 'Damn it.'

'Why don't you get a new dishwasher, Mum?' asked Sam.

'I will,' she said, and grabbed her car keys. She pulled at the front door with both hands but it wouldn't budge. A wet November had swollen the wood of both it and the frame. Superglue couldn't have attached them more firmly. She braced her foot against the wall and heaved. The door opened about a foot and she ushered her son outside.

'We need a lot of stuff doing to the house, don't we?' said Sam.

Lilly squeezed through the gap then braced herself again, this time with the heel of her boot against the stone of the cottage. She slammed with all her might. The door shuddered to a close, showering plaster from the roof of the porch.

'One or two odd jobs,' she said, and shook the masonry from her hair.

'When I play for Liverpool I'll be rich,' he said. 'But I suppose we need the money now.'

They threw their bags on the back seat and got into the Mini. 'Don't you worry, big man, these divorce cases pay well.'

'You don't like them though, do you, Mum?'

Her new car purred. 'I like them well enough.'

'What about all those children you used to help?' he asked.

Lilly sighed. 'Someone else will represent them.'

'And you really don't mind?'

Lilly smiled and set off down the lane.

When she dropped Sam at school, he turned to her again.

'I'll be there,' she laughed. 'And I have something for you.' She handed him a small plastic bag and watched the joy on her son's face as he unpacked a pair of brand new Nike goalie gloves.

* * *

The bench is hard and cold but Artan is prepared to wait all day. Anna leans against him, her cheek against his chest, her bony arm around his waist.

They watch for the telltale green blazers that separate the boys from Manor Park from the local kids.

'Tell me if you see them,' he says.

She nods slightly, her cheek grazing the zip of his jacket.

The air buzzes with lunchtime chatter. Two boys in hoodies spar in the road, pretending to land karate kicks. Their friends shout encouragement and shower them with sweets and crisps. When they spot the strangers on the bench and whisper to each other.

'What you looking at?' shouts one.

Artan doesn't reply, but the look on his face sees the boys off.

He feels Anna's body tense against his own.

'What?'

'There,' she says, her gaze directed towards four boys in green.

'Are you sure?' he asks.

Anna nods. 'The dark-haired one and the redhead.'

'I thought you said there were three.'

'I did,' she says. 'He is not there.'

They let the boys buy some drinks and follow them at a safe distance.

The boys lark about all the way back to school. The redhead is in charge. His voice is the loudest and he punches his friend on the arm just a little too hard. When the other cries out, he laughs in his face and calls him 'gay'.

'He reminds me of Gabi,' says Anna.

'Don't ever say that name.'

Anna leans against him. 'Sorry.'

He pushes her away and wraps his hand around the handle of the gun. Its feel is familiar, like an old friend.

Jack pounded forward, the rhythm of his feet beating in his head. One, two, three, four. It was relentless. Yet oddly comforting.

He'd taken up running six months ago, when the doc told him his blood pressure was borderline dangerous. He'd also been told to curb his drinking – but you could only do so much.

He surged through puddles and oil slicks, oblivious to the mud catapulting up his calves, concentrating instead on his breathing. One, two, three, four. He thought it would lose its attraction once the summer skies had disappeared but oddly he found the grey streets and lanes even more enticing.

He'd lost nearly a stone already, which was no small feat considering how good Lilly's cooking could be. He smiled at the thought of her licking cake mixture from a spoon.

He'd call her later, see if she and Sam fancied catching a film. She'd sounded distracted yesterday, worried about the boy at the hostel. She was always so committed to these kids she worked for. Took it all to heart. It would do her good to do less of that kind of work.

He remembered that Sam was playing a footie match at the school this afternoon. Maybe he wouldn't call her. Maybe he should surprise her . . .

* * *

Jack watched Lilly stamping her feet against the cold. Most of the other mothers were dressed in green Hunter wellies and puffer jackets, cashmere scarves wound around them. Lilly, however, had obviously come straight from work and was in her suit and leather-soled boots. She looked freezing and jigged from side to side. The playing fields were exposed on all sides and the wind ripped across unchecked.

'For the money you lot pay, you think they'd give you better weather.'

Lilly smiled at Jack. 'How did you know I'd be here?'

'Sure, I've been tapping your phones.'

She laughed, her breath swirling around her face.

'I hope you don't mind,' he said. 'Me coming, not tapping your phone.'

She tucked her arm through his. 'Of course I don't mind. And Sam will be thrilled to see you.'

'Where is the wee man?' he asked.

'They'll be on in five minutes. If we haven't all died of hypothermia.'

He took off his leather jacket and wrapped it around her shoulders. 'You need a proper coat in this weather, Lilly.'

'Yes, Dad.'

Now Jack was freezing but he couldn't have cared less. He was here with his woman, and a fine one at that, watching her son play football. It felt like . . . he hardly dared to think it, but it felt like a family.

More parents arrived and boys from the senior school, come to cheer on the little ones. A couple were larking about, braying like donkeys. The biggest really fancied himself, despite his frizzy orange hair. He puffed out his chest like a robin, arrogance tattooed across him. Jack hoped Sam never turned out like that, but he said nothing. Lilly already tortured herself over the whole private school thing, but her ex-husband insisted. Jack knew better than to get involved.

The hedge is thin, autumn having stripped it down to its spindly skeleton. They push their way through it easily and head across the lawns.

Artan glances up to the main building. A mansion house of smooth brown stone, ivy-clad. Each wooden sash window is freshly painted white. Could this really be just a school?

To the left, three beech trees are losing the last of their leaves, the ground below carpeted in bronze and gold.

A man in uniform holds out a machine to suck them up.

'What is that?' whispers Anna.

'A vacuum cleaner.' Artan shakes his head. 'A vacuum cleaner for leaves.'

Still this country can amaze him. Back home, his mother didn't even have one for the house. She swept with an old broom, as her mother before her had done.

'These people,' he says, 'they have no idea how lucky they are.'

'Quick, before someone sees us,' she says.

They march towards an outbuilding, but it's too late.

'Oy,' the man shouts. 'Oy, you two.' He throws down the leaf machine and stamps over to them. 'What d'you think you're doing?'

Artan opens his arms. 'Sorry. English no good.'

'I see,' says the man. 'You're from the agency. Well, you're late.'

Artan and Anna freeze. What is an agency?

'You're here to work?' says the man, and pretends to sweep up.

Artan thinks again of his mother and laughs.

'Right,' the man points to some sheds, 'grab some rakes and get yourselves back out here.'

'Rakes,' repeats Artan.

'That's it. Now get a move on.' The man shoves Artan in the small of his back. 'Bloody foreigners.'

Artan continues to smile, but his right hand has tightened around his gun.

The crowd cheered. Not exactly a roar, more a cheerful smattering of clapped hands, but it made Sam smile all the same.

Lilly waved at her son across the pitch and his face lights up at the sight of Jack beside her.

Was it her relationship with Jack that had finally put to rest all the arguments with David about who had done what to whom? Or was it the sight of his girlfriend, bleary-eyed and exhausted from their baby daughter's teething, that had seen off dusty resentments?

Things felt right. New, somehow.

Lilly laughed aloud at her flight of fancy.

The opposing team from the village school won the toss and the match began.

'Come on, Manor Park,' Lilly shouted.

'Yeah,' shouted one of the boarders, 'let's show these chavs what we're made of.'

Lilly pretended not to hear but saw a few Manor Park parents smirk. Why did these people have to be so bloody self-important? Why did they have to look down on others just because they had less cash?

'The ball wasn't that bad,' said Jack.

'What?'

'A mistimed pass, I'll grant you, but they're only nine.'

It was a blatant attempt to divert her. Lilly laughed and pressed her cheek against Jack's shoulder.

At the far side of the grounds some parents were walking towards the pitch. They were late and would get it in the neck from their son after the match. As they came nearer, Lilly could see that they were both in overalls. Not parents, ground staff. The school had an army of them to trim and mow. Never before had fifteen acres been so well manicured, and never before had Lilly seen a woman among their ranks.

'Great save,' shouted Jack, and Lilly tore her eyes back to the game.

'What happened?'

'Number eight made a great run up the wing and chipped it in the left corner, but Sam just got his fingers to it.'

Lilly smiled. 'Since when are you into football?'

'Thought I was a rugger bugger, did you?'

Lilly spluttered. 'Definitely not.'

'What then?'

Lilly pretended to appraise him with an earnest eye. 'Fly fishing?'

'Go on with you, woman,' he said, pushing her away with one hand and pulling her back with the other. 'I'm too sporty for that.'

'Sporty?'

Jack flexed a non-existent bicep. 'Pure muscle.'

'From lifting pints,' said Lilly.

She was about to make another remark when she again caught sight of the couple in overalls. They had stopped about one hundred metres away and were deep in conversation, heads bent together. Their hair was the same dark chestnut, thick and shiny, dancing in the wind. Suddenly the man pulled the woman into his arms. Not like lovers, but proprietorial, like a father with his daughter. Or a brother and his younger sister. He embraced her tightly, as if he were holding the pieces of her together. In turn she surrendered to him, wishing to be engulfed.

When the woman turned her head to the side, Lilly saw she was very young, very beautiful, and very, very frightened.

Jack felt the electric current of tension ride through Lilly's body.

'Are you okay?'

'I don't know,' she said.

He followed her eye-line to a couple of teenagers moving towards them. The girl was striking, with creamy skin and almond-shaped eyes. He noticed the boy too, his face grabbing Jack's attention with its complete lack of expression.

'Do you know them?' he asked.

Lilly nodded. 'From the hostel.'

'What are they doing here?'

'I don't know.'

But she did know.

Maybe they had got a job at the school? It made sense, didn't it? They lived nearby, and anyone could cut grass, sweep up leaves.

She swallowed her alarm and waved in their direction. 'Artan.'

He didn't look up, but whispered something to the girl and kissed her cheek. Then he strode off, not towards Lilly but over to the group of noisy boarders. The girl stumbled after him.

Jack looked from Lilly to the couple and back again. 'Speak to me, Lilly. What's going on?'

She looked into his eyes, her own shining with fear. 'Something very bad.'

They ran towards the couple until they were almost upon them. Only then did Lilly see the gun.

The shot rang out, incongrously clear in the graphite sky.

Jack quickly assessed the situation. The girl had a gun, which she held out at arm's length, both hands shaking around the handle. The boy held his above his head and whirled around, trying to regain his footing from the recoil of the gun and the panic that had clearly grabbed him. A kid was down. One of the boarders.

Someone screamed, then someone else, and soon the air was teeming with the horrified cries of parents surging from the sidelines towards their boys.

'Stop,' the boy screamed, but they ignored him and swarmed forward.

The boy pointed his weapon towards them. 'Stop.'

'Everyone stay still,' Jack shouted.

One of the dads reached out to his son, caked in mud and weeping.

'I said be still. Now.'

Everyone froze. Silence fell, punctuated only by the muffled sobs of the injured boy.

Jack opened his arms, his palms to the sky, and approached the girl.

'I'm the police,' he said. 'Put down the gun.'

She panted hard. Her body convulsed. Her arms could barely hold up the gun, yet she kept it trained on a boy in the crowd. His eyes were wide in his freckled face. Not so arrogant now.

'Put down the gun,' Jack said.

She shook her head.

Jack held out his hand. 'Please.'

He laid his hand under the gun and wondered if he was about to die.

He held his breath.

She dropped it into his palm.

Slowly, very slowly, Jack turned towards the other assailant. 'And you too, son.'

The boy laughed. It was harsh. 'Do you know what they did?'

Jack glanced towards the group of boarders. 'Why don't you put the gun down and tell me?'

'She knows,' said the boy, pointing the gun at Lilly.

Jack heard the sharp intake of her breath and terror coursed through him.

'But she said nothing would be done.' He looked at

Lilly with pure venom. 'That the police would do nothing.'

Jack inched between the gun and Lilly until his chest was in the firing line.

'Maybe she was wrong,' said Jack.

The boy shook his head and wheeled the gun back towards the boarders, his sights on the largest. The redhead.

'This piece of shit does not deserve to live,' he spat.

A stain spread across the redhead's groin. 'Don't shoot me.'

'Put the gun down,' Jack shouted.

The boy shook his head again. Almost imperceptible, but Jack caught it. There was a shift. Conversation was at an end.

Jack watched the boy's finger touch the trigger as if in slow motion. He knew what he had to do. He raised the gun in his own hand, conscious of its weight, its girth. He closed his eyes and discharged two rounds. When he let the light in, the boy lay on the ground. His shoulder gaped, blood and bone splattered over his overalls. An ugly wound, enough to disarm him, not fatal. But the boy didn't move until Jack turned his lifeless head and saw the second wound, clean and perfect at the left-hand side of his temple.

'Are you okay?'

Lilly stood in the doorway of her cottage, bewildered.

Penny Van Huysan stood in the dusky shadows and pushed her carefully highlighted hair behind her ears.

'Are you okay?' she repeated gently.

Penny was another Manor Park parent. She was girly, giggly and chichi. She knew what everyone's husband did for a living and could spot a Christian Louboutin pump at two hundred yards – yet she chose to spend her time with Lilly rather than the other Yummy Mummies.

They had formed a bond during the Kelsey Brand case, when Lilly's life imploded and Penny had proved an unlikely form of support. She was flanked by Luella, who had all Penny's shallowness but none of her charm or compassion.

'Lilly?' said Penny. 'Can you hear me?'

When Lilly didn't reply, Penny and Luella exchanged glances and ushered her inside.

'Is Jack here?' asked Penny.

Lilly shook her head.

Penny ran a glass of water and pushed Lilly into a chair. Lilly gulped it down. She hadn't even realised she was thirsty.

'He had to go back to the station, to explain what happened.'

'And what did happen? People are saying a gang from the hostel tried to shoot everyone?' said Luella.

'No, no,' said Lilly. 'There were two, a boy and a girl, just kids.'

'But there was a shooting?' Luella asked.

Penny put her hand on Luella's knee.

'The headmaster specifically told us not to gossip about this.'

'We're not gossiping,' said Luella.

'He doesn't want the press getting hold of this and descending on us.'

37

'No one wants that,' said Luella.

Lilly could see she was desperate to extract information. That was the only reason she had come.

'Is Sam in bed?' said Penny.

'Yeah, he didn't really see what happened, but he was shaken all the same,' Lilly replied.

Luella persisted. 'So what did happen?'

Penny frowned a warning but Luella waved her away. 'We've a right to know.'

Lilly sighed. Luella would not be put off, so Lilly might as well fill her in before the school bongo drums went into overdrive.

'Like I said, they were just kids.'

'But they were armed,' said Luella.

'Yeah. Jack disarmed the girl, but the boy wouldn't . . .' She paused, unsure how to explain. 'Jack had to shoot him.'

'Dead?' Luella almost screamed.

'I don't suppose Lilly took his pulse,' said Penny.

Lilly smiled. 'You're right, I didn't, but I'd say he was dead. The wound to his head was too serious to survive.'

'Jack must have thought the situation was pretty grave,' said Penny.

'It was. The boy might have shot someone else,' said Lilly.

Luella could barely contain herself. 'Someone else! You mean he'd already killed someone?'

'I don't know. They took someone off in an ambulance.'

'Who?' asked Penny.

Lilly squeezed her eyes shut, picturing the boy, white and still on the stretcher. 'A pupil. One of the boarders. Charlie Stanton.'

Silence fell on the three women as the enormity of what had happened at their children's school sank in. At last, Luella stood up and dusted down her skirt. She had obviously processed the information.

'I'm sure we're all agreed that something must be done.'

'The police are dealing with it,' said Penny.

'I mean about that hostel,' said Luella.

Lilly was puzzled. 'Whatever do you mean?'

Luella's jaw was firm. 'I mean we must get it closed down.'

Lilly didn't know whether to laugh or cry.

'It's nothing to do with the hostel or the other people staying there,' she said.

Luella's eyes were glinting. 'How can you say that when those animals went up to our school with the sole intention of murdering our children?'

'That's not how it was,' said Lilly. 'I don't think the girl intended to hurt anyone.'

'You're being ridiculous,' said Luella. 'People don't carry guns unless they mean to do some damage.'

Lilly looked to Penny for help but she shook her head. 'It's a fair point, Lilly. I mean, how would you have felt if Sam had been hit?'

'I know what you're saying, but you can't lump the other residents together,' said Lilly.

'They sound dangerous,' said Penny.

Lilly was shocked. She expected reactionary politics from Luella, but Penny?

'There were only two involved and they had their own reasons,' said Lilly.

Luella's nostrils flared. 'Like what?'

Lilly knew she could not mention the rape. That information had been given to her in confidence and, anyway, she didn't know for certain that it had anything to do with what had happened today.

'You see,' Luella lifted her chin in triumph, 'there is no explanation for what happened, other than the obvious. Those people are not like us. They hate us. And I for one am not going to stand around while another gang of them does any more damage.'

Jack was still shaking when he got into bed.

He'd been over and over it at the station. With a man down and the boy still wielding the gun, he had had no choice.

'Couldn't you have disabled him?' asked the investigator.

Jack shook his head. 'I couldn't take the chance. If I'd missed he would have killed me.'

On and on it had gone, until they finally let him go at two in the morning.

'You're lucky,' said the investigator. 'He doesn't have any family so no one's likely to complain.'

In the dark, his duvet wrapped around him, shivering uncontrollably, Jack didn't feel bloody lucky.

Chapter Three

Snow White came from a long line of brave soldiers.

Grandpa had fought in the Second World War and Father had worked bomb disposal in Northern Ireland for over ten years. Taking difficult, often unpalatable, decisions was in her blood.

By her father's sixth posting and her corresponding move to the sixth different school she had stopped blubbing and discovered that a swift smack in the mouth made the loudest of tormentors keep their distance. Her transition to boarding school had been softened by this knowledge.

Whenever one of Daddy's platoon was blown to smithereens he would get as pissed as fart and sing at the top of his voice: 'No surrender, no surrender, no surrender to the IRA.' He'd go back to work the next day nursing a sore head and throat, and a new man would be learning the ropes.

She turned on the local radio station and went on to the Internet. The home page told her that a singer, whose head reminded her of a round sweaty cheese, had overdosed on drugs, a wildly talented footballer had been found in bed with an eleven-year-old boy, and the Chancellor was warning of another hike in interest rates.

The Manor Park shooting had not made the headlines. In fact, Snow White could find no mention of it anywhere. It had been well and truly hushed up.

No doubt it was better for all involved if matters remained as they were. Questions from the press would only be painful and intrusive for the parents involved.

She logged on to her favourite site and started a new post.

<u>Asylum Seekers Gun Down Children</u> Snow White at 8.10
Yes, you heard correctly.
    Yesterday afternoon, two asylum seekers armed themselves and shot at pupils at Manor Park Preparatory School in Hertfordshire.

She sat back and waited for the thread to start buzzing. Sometimes, for the greater good, difficult decisions had to be made.

The noise was overwhelming. At least fifty clients, solicitors and barristers were crammed into the narrow corridor, and every single one of them seemed to be shouting. Lilly grimaced and searched for a clear space to devour the sandwich that was burning a hole in her pocket.

Only the prayer room was free.

'Figures,' she muttered, and slipped inside.

She pushed the Qur'an to one side and laid out her

bacon butty. She wished now that she'd gone for cheese, but hunger dispelled her guilt. She opened her mouth for the first salty bite when the door opened.

'Are you looking for Jesus?' asked Jack.

'I think the poor man's got enough on without Luton County Court.'

Jack looked old and sad and tired.

'Jesus, I'm starving,' he said.

'If you think I'm sharing you're hoping for a miracle,' she replied. 'And the man in that line of business is out.'

'You're a heartless woman.'

She looked from Jack to the sandwich and back again and split it in half. 'This is a true mark of our friendship.'

They chewed in silence until Jack wiped his hands on his jeans.

'Everything okay?'

'Yes,' she said. 'You?'

'Been better,' he answered.

She touched his thumb with her own. 'You had no choice, Jack.'

He nodded. 'Doesn't make it any easier, though, does it?'

'He was out of control,' she said. 'Anyone could see that.'

He gave a doubtful shrug.

'Seriously, Jack, I was bloody terrified.'

They sat in silence while Lilly racked her brain for something positive to say. How did you make someone who had just killed a child feel any better about themselves?

'At least the press haven't got wind of it,' she said.

43

'And how long do you think that will last?'

'They can't criticise you, Jack,' she said.

He shrugged. She understood Jack well enough to know he didn't care less what the newspapers might say. He had spent the night asking himself what he could have done differently. Hadn't she been asking herself the same question about her conversation with Artan?

'What happens now?' she said.

'Got to get back to the station,' he said. 'More questions, more reports.'

'Then what?'

'I'll be suspended pending the outcome of the investigation.'

'That doesn't seem right.'

'I did shoot someone, Lilly.'

'He would have killed you,' she said. 'Or maybe me, or maybe Sam.'

Jack scratched his chin, his nails making a rasping sound against the stubble. 'It's standard procedure, and I'm on full pay so it's not all bad.'

Lilly knew he was playing it down and felt obliged to join in. 'You won't know what to do with yourself.'

'I'll take up a hobby,' he said.

'I hear stamp collecting's fun.'

He gave her a wink. 'Or you could keep me busy.'

She pulled him towards her by his lapels and kissed him with greasy lips. 'I'll tell you what you can do for me.'

'Is it dirty?'

'Oh, yeah,' she said. 'You can start by fixing my dishwasher.'

'Miss Valentine?'

Lilly and Jack looked up. A man in his mid-twenties stood in the doorway and fixed them with the greenest eyes Lilly had ever seen. They were beautiful yet startling in their intensity.

'I'm sorry,' he said. 'I'm looking for Lilly Valentine.'

Lilly was mesmerised.

'Lilly?' said Jack, one eyebrow raised.

She coughed. 'Yes. That's me.'

The man moved towards her, hand outstretched. She took it in her own, felt the cool smoothness of it.

'And you are?' said Jack.

'Milo,' said the man, still holding Lilly's hand and her gaze.

'And what can we do for you today, Milo?' asked Jack.

'I need to speak with Miss Valentine.' He didn't even glance in Jack's direction. 'In private.'

'So, Milo,' said Lilly. 'How can I help you?'

'I work with the residents at Hounds Place.' He spoke with the deep clipped tones of an Eastern European.

'Social services?'

He shook his head, hair falling into his eyes.

'I'm a volunteer,' he said. 'I offer advice, and help with the language. A shoulder to lean on, I think you call it.'

'I see,' she said. But in truth she didn't.

He opened his arms as if to explain. 'When I came here there was no one to help. No one to explain. And so.'

And so, thought Lilly, this strange and dazzling man did what he could for those that needed it the most.

'What is it you need me to do?' she asked.

'Charles Stanton is dead.'

'Shit.'

'Anna Duraku is at the police station.'

'The girl up at the school?'

Milo gave a single nod.

'And?' asked Lilly.

'She needs a good lawyer.'

Lilly scribbled the name of a firm in Luton who specialised in criminal law and handed it to Milo. He took the piece of paper and folded it in half.

'She would like you to represent her.'

'I can't.' Lilly shook her head. There were a million reasons. 'I'm full to bursting with cases,' she said, 'and my boss would literally kill me if I took this on.'

Milo put the paper in his back pocket.

'And I'm a witness. I mean, I was there at the school, I saw the whole thing,' said Lilly.

'Then you know she didn't kill anyone.'

Lilly squeezed her eyes shut. 'I'm sorry.'

The step is cold and hard, but the light spilling from the shop is comforting. People glare as they enter, stepping around him like he was dog shit, but their hard faces make him feel safe.

Luke spent last night wandering around Oxford Street and Leicester Square. The rain lashed down and the wind got up. Luke got wet and cold, but it was nothing compared to the fear that burned through him.

They say London never sleeps, but on a midweek night with shocking weather, Luke discovered it certainly went home to rest. And after the last revellers dashed their way through the puddles to the night buses at

46

Trafalgar Square, the others came out to play. They emerged from the bins like rats, from behind the cinemas and the side streets in Chinatown. The homeless, the winos, the junkies. This was their time.

Luke had been up to town loads of times. Calf-aching visits to the British Museum with school, birthday jaunts with Tom and Charlie when they'd tried to pick up foreign-exchange girls in the queue for over-eighteen movies. He'd seen down-and-outs, as his mum called them, in their huddles, but he'd passed them by, secure in the knowledge that she would be waiting at Harpenden station. She'd grumble about being a taxi service, but she would never not be there.

He'd made his way into Burger King in Leicester Square and ordered some fries and a Coke, planning to sit and dry off. And he had, until a man sat opposite him, hands buried deep in his leather bomber jacket.

'Do you want to earn some money?'

'Sorry?' said Luke.

The man pulled out a hand, the top coarse with black hair.

'Money,' he said, and rubbed his finger and thumb together.

Luke's stomach lurched as he remembered that Tom had done the exact same thing to the girl.

'Twenty quid,' said the man.

Luke was puzzled. Why was this stranger offering to give him money?

'I don't know what you mean,' he said.

The man put his hand over Luke's. It was gross, like a werewolf's or something.

'You give me some relief,' said the man, 'and I'll give you twenty quid.'

Luke was frozen to the spot, he didn't even dare pull away his hand.

The man smiled. 'If you'll suck it, I'll make it thirty.'

'I'm sorry.' Luke didn't know what else to say. 'I'm sorry.'

As Luke made his way to the door, the man called after him. 'Thirty-five if you'll swallow.'

Luke walked and walked all night, too terrified to stop.

But now he is exhausted. He sits on the step, hugging his rucksack to him, and hopes the time will pass slowly until night falls again.

Maybe he could explain to his mum, tell her what happened. She could call the police and make them understand.

He pulls out his mobile phone and scrolls down to 'HOME'. The word makes his eyes sting.

He presses select.

'Hello.'

Luke's heart leaps in his chest at the sound of his sister's voice.

'Hello,' she repeats.

Everything he wants to say gets stuck in his throat, like a ball of cotton wool, all thick and dry.

'Luke?' Jessie's voice rises. 'Luke, is that you?'

The televisions in Dixon's window flash beside him. The constant stream of pictures is hypnotic.

Jessie is shouting now. 'Say something, Luke.'

He hasn't slept in forty-eight hours and his head feels

weird. The last time he'd stayed up all night had been at Harriet Mason-Day's party. They'd all chipped in for some Es and he'd ended up getting a blow job from her little sister in the laundry room.

That had been fun. This is something different entirely.

'Luke Walker, you are a selfish little prick. Mum is completely beside herself.'

Luke wanders into the shop, mobile still pressed to his ear.

'You can't come in here,' the assistant shouts from behind the counter.

'Just tell me where you are.' Jessie's still angry but a sob escapes. 'I'll get Mum to pick you up.'

A security guard approaches. His face is so black it shines. 'Come on now, you know you can't come in here.' His tone is kind but firm. Like he feels sorry for Luke.

For a second Luke is puzzled, until he sees himself as they do. Dirty, wet and pale with fatigue. They think he's from the streets.

He leaves the shop without another word, shocked at how quickly he has made the transition from public schoolboy to scumbag.

Jessie is crying into the phone. 'Luke, please come home.'

He hangs up and drops the phone through a grate into a drain.

When he turns to retrieve his place back on the step a girl has taken his spot. She peers out at him from the hood of an oily parka.

Luke is lost as to what to do next. His mind is fit to explode.

The girl scratches her face with bitten nails. Each one is down to the quick, yet painted a luminous orange.

She gestures to the grate. 'You could have sold that.'

Luke points to his rucksack. 'Can I get my bag?'

'You shouldn't leave it hanging around.' Her voice is loud with a strong Liverpudlian accent.

He nods. Of course he shouldn't have left it. Anyone could have nicked it.

She passes it up to him. 'Got any ciggies in there?'

Luke shakes his head.

'Anything to drink?'

'No.'

'You're not much cop then, are you?' she says.

Luke laughs in spite of himself. Hers is the first half-friendly face he's seen since he left home. 'I don't suppose I am. Much cop, that is.'

The girl pulls herself to her feet and adjusts her over-sized coat. It makes her look pitifully small, hidden in its folds. When she's a few feet away she turns back to him.

'If you're hungry I'll show you where to get some scran.'

Luke is not the least bit peckish, but he races after her all the same.

'I'm Luke,' he says.

The girl smiles. 'Everyone round here calls me Mad Caz.'

'Do you want counselling?' asked the Chief Super.

Jack raised an eyebrow.

The Chief Super put up his hands. 'I have to ask.'

'I'd rather put all this behind me,' said Jack. 'Get back to normal.'

The Chief Super nodded. 'If you change your mind the offer's there.'

Jack thanked him, but he knew it wasn't something he'd take up. Yapping endlessly about how he felt wouldn't change the fact that one of the boys from the school was lying in intensive care and the shooter, Artan, was on a slab.

He'd been down this road before, in Northern Ireland, and he knew the best way to recover was to look forward, not back. You couldn't change the past, but you could shape your future.

And what was Jack's future? What did he actually want? If you'd asked him a year ago he wouldn't have known. A bigger flat? A pay rise? For Liverpool to win the double? Now he had no hesitation. He wanted Lilly and Sam.

He drove to their cottage knowing everything he needed was inside. For too long he had pussyfooted around, flirting, complimenting, letting Lilly get away with murder on his cases. He never imagined a woman as sorted as she was would have time for a loser who had never held down a relationship for longer than six months. Now he had her there was no way he was going to let anything stop him from making this work.

Lilly answered the door. She smiled with her mouth but not her eyes.

'What's happened?' asked Jack.

'The girl's been arrested.'

'The other shooter?'

He saw her shoulders tense. 'She didn't shoot anyone.'

'And your man went all the way to court to tell you that?'

'Milo asked me to help her,' she said.

He didn't like the way she said his name, as if there were magic in it.

'And what does this *Milo* expect you to do?'

She turned away and walked towards the kitchen. 'He wants me to represent her.'

Oh, no. She wouldn't – would she? She was bloody pig-headed, but even she would see this was madness.

'You can't do it,' he said.

'I know.'

'You were there, Sam was there.'

'I know.'

'Mary Mother of God, I was the one who shot her boyfriend.'

'I know.' Lilly threw up her arms. 'I bloody well know all that.'

'So you told him no?'

'I told him no.' She didn't meet his eyes.

Alexia Dee stretched out a smooth leg and admired her shoes. Purple suede with a high square heel. A small hole at the toe allowing a flash of nail of the same colour. Pure sex.

'Busy, are we, Posh?'

Alexia pursed her lips. Her boss was in a foul temper, stalking around the office like a lion waiting for a kill, leaving his usual trail of stale smoke and sweat.

Steve Berry hated quiet days, unable to settle, pouncing on the phone like an addict on his drugs. Well, everyone hated the quiet days, didn't they? Alexia hadn't studied for three years in the backwoods of Bristol to spend her time drinking coffee, but any decent journalist knew that it's part of the job. You sit. You wait.

The phone rang. Alexia yawned.

'You gonna get that?' said Steve.

Alexia sighed. No doubt another tip-off about the Harvest Festival at Mary of the Sacred Heart. Only the fourth that day.

'Alexia Dee,' she said.

'Go on a website called *The Spear of Truth*,' said the voice.

'Can I take your name, sir?' she answered.

'Just do it.'

The line went dead.

'Charmed, I'm sure,' said Alexia.

Steve leaned over her, his breath raspy. 'Well?'

'Crank call,' she said.

He moved even closer, grimacing, and she could smell the onions he'd eaten earlier on his mid-morning kebab.

'Jesus,' she muttered, and went into her search engine. *The Spear of Truth.*

It was a white-power site, all black and white pictures of 9/11 and ugly close-ups of Abu Hamza. She scrolled past the edited highlights of 'The Nuremberg Rally' until she reached the daily discussions forum. Then she saw it. A post from someone calling themselves Snow White.

'Bloody hell.'

'What?' shouted Steve.

'If this is true,' said Alexia, 'we've just got a fantastic story.'

Chapter Four

Lilly pushed open the door of Luton East Police Station. The reception was bare except for three metal chairs bolted to the tiled floor.

She turned to Milo. 'Not very comfy, I'm afraid.'

'Have you ever been arrested in Sarajevo?' he asked.

'That's a pleasure that has so far eluded me.'

'Trust me,' he said, 'this is palatial.'

A WPC in her early twenties ushered them through to the custody suite. Her skin was clear, her hair sleek, pulled back into a neat ponytail. Lilly's hand instinctively went to her own messy bird's nest.

'It's chaos in here,' said the WPC. And she was right. The benches were full of prisoners waiting to be processed. Coppers milled around waiting for interview rooms to become free. Two men pushed against the sergeant's desk and clamoured to be heard. One had a gash across his forehead, blood running down the bridge of his nose.

'Luton Town at home,' said the WPC by way of explanation.

The desk sergeant was trying to note down their

details but the injured man was waving his hand in front of his face. A few fat drops of blood splashed onto his friend and he howled in protest at the red stains on his cream jumper.

'Fucking Stone Island, this is,' he shouted.

'River Island, more like,' said the injured prisoner.

The sergeant shifted in his seat. He was trying to keep his patience but Lilly could see it was wearing thin.

'How long are you going to keep us here, mate?' The man pulled on the sleeve of his jumper. 'I need to get this in the wash.'

The sergeant didn't even look up. 'As long as it takes.'

'I'll sue you if it don't come out,' said the man.

The sergeant sighed. 'I'm sure you will.'

'And I need to get up the hospital,' said the injured man, sending another arc of blood across the desk.

'The FME will be here in five minutes,' the sergeant said.

'I ain't seeing no fucking police doctor.'

The sergeant shrugged. 'Then you'll bleed to death, mate.'

The man turned towards Lilly and she could see that half his face was ferrous with blood. 'Did you hear that?' he shouted at her. 'You're a witness. He threatened to kill me.'

Lilly smiled. 'He didn't actually say that.'

'He fucking did.' He turned to his friend. 'Didn't he just say that?'

'Call yourself a brief,' he shouted at Lilly. 'Whose fucking side are you on?'

55

Milo placed a protective arm in front of Lilly. 'Leave her alone.'

The injured man leered at him, his face grotesque. 'You want some, do you?'

If Milo didn't understand the term, he certainly appreciated the tone and stood firm, keeping direct eye contact.

'Don't abuse this lady. None of this . . .' Milo spread his arm towards the man's wound, 'is her fault,' he said calmly but firmly, threatening them with his eyes.

The man with the stained sweater patted his friend on the shoulder.

'Leave it,' he said. 'It ain't worth the bother.'

The injured man shrugged off the hand, his shoulders still square, his neck pulsing.

'He's only a fucking Polack,' said his friend.

This did the trick and the man turned back to the desk, bleeding once more over the sergeant's paperwork.

When at last the men were bailed, Lilly stepped up. She looked at the blood still in gelatinous pools and tried not to think about hepatitis and HIV.

'Get a cleaner in here,' shouted the sergeant to no one in particular. 'What can I do for you, Miss?'

'Anna Duraku,' she said.

The sergeant pointed to the whiteboard. 'That her?'

Lilly saw the girl's name had been misspelled.

'There's a mistake,' she said.

'Oh, yeah?'

'Her name is incorrect.'

The sergeant shrugged. 'They're hard ones, aren't they?'

The sloppiness annoyed Lilly. 'Not really.'

'Does it matter?' asked the sergeant. 'We all know who we mean.'

Lilly sighed. There wasn't much point arguing.

'Can we at least talk about bail?' she asked.

'Not a chance,' said the sergeant.

'I'm glad we talked about it,' said Lilly.

The sergeant smiled and leaned forward on his elbows. 'Well, I'm interested in what you've got to say, considering she's in here for conspiracy to murder.'

'Can I speak to the DI?'

'This is bullshit and you know it is.'

Lilly and the policeman were only inches apart. She could smell his aftershave. Pine, lemon and grass.

'She was at the scene with a gun,' he said. 'Someone got killed, end of story.'

Lilly took a step back and appraised DI Moodie with a cool eye. Double-breasted chalk-stripe suit and starched shirt. A silk striped tie, not the splattered horror from BHS that most of the coppers favoured.

'Look, Officer, I understand that what happened was a terrible thing and that the world and his wife will be baying for blood. I can see the headlines now. "Children gunned down in Columbine-style massacre."'

'I don't give a monkey's about the press,' said DI Moodie.

The hell you don't, thought Lilly.

'As I said, I get it, my own son goes to that school.' Lilly ignored the raised eyebrows and pressed on. 'But the person responsible is dead. You got him. The girl

57

you have was dragged along for the ride and gave it up before anything got serious.'

DI Moodie nodded and she thought he might be convinced.

'They went together. They had guns together. They pretended to be staff together. They were in on it together.' He opened his arms. 'In my book that's the best description of conspiracy to murder I've ever heard.'

Lilly turned to leave, but at the door shot him a glance. 'You'll never make it stick, and when it unravels you'll be left explaining why you wasted so much time and money.'

DI Moodie laughed.

'Something funny?'

'DI Bradbury told me all about you.'

Lilly put her hands on her hips. 'And what did he say?'

'That you were difficult, intransigent and bloody-minded.'

Lilly was smarting but refused to show it. 'Did he also mention that the last time we crossed swords I won?'

Lilly slammed the door behind her, leaving DI Moodie staring after her.

'Sadly, he did.'

The cell was cold.

Lilly stepped over the tray of fish fingers and beans and made her way to the bench at the far end. She patted the girl's arm. Her clothes had been taken for examination and her police-issue white paper suit rustled like dry leaves.

'Can't blame you for leaving it. I wouldn't feed it to a dog.'

Lilly looked into the girl's face. So very beautiful and so very sad. Her full lips were already set with lines. Where nature had been generous, life had not been kind.

'I'm Lilly Valentine.'

'I'm Tirana Duraku,' she said. 'Everyone calls me Anna.'

Lilly nodded. 'Milo asked me to come today. To help you.'

'To help me.' Anna rolled the words around her mouth as if trying them out for the first time.

'I can get you an interpreter,' said Lilly, 'if English is a problem.'

'No.' The girl's tone was sharp. 'Sorry. I do fine with English.'

Lilly wasn't sure – but the girl's English was pretty good.

'The police intend to charge you with conspiracy to murder.'

'I didn't kill no one.'

Lilly held up her hand. 'I know that, but they're saying you and Artan had a plan together, and that plan was to kill those boys.'

Anna shook her head and wisps of glossy hair whipped her translucent cheeks. The contrast in colours was unnerving.

'There was no plan,' she said.

'Artan didn't tell you what he was going to do?' asked Lilly.

'He don't tell me anything.'

'And you didn't wonder,' Lilly asked, 'why you both needed a gun?'

Anna shrugged and Lilly felt her impatience begin to rise. 'Not good enough, Anna. People don't find themselves with guns for no reason. Where did you get it?'

'Artan give it to me.'

'Where did he get it?'

Anna shrugged again.

'Why did he need a gun?'

'Protection.'

'From what?'

Anna's eyes filled with tears. 'From everything.'

'Why on earth did you take it, Anna?' asked Lilly. 'Why didn't you refuse?'

Without warning, Anna fell forward, clutching at the neck of her suit.

'Anna?' Lilly fell to her knees. 'What's wrong?'

'Pains,' the girl barked like a seal. 'Pains in chest.'

Lilly leapt to her feet and banged her fist against the cell door. 'We need a doctor here, now.'

The automatic gates of the station car park began their slow arc. Normally Jack would be tapping his finger against the steering wheel, revving the accelerator, but today he idled in neutral.

There was no prisoner awaiting interview, no custody sergeant breathing down his neck to get on with it and free up a cell. No urgent statements to be tweaked and mailed out. No impatient colleagues needing access to his notes. For the first time, for as long as he could remember, Jack had nothing to do. He'd only come in this evening to collect his photos of Lilly and Sam and to clear his desk of anything that could decompose.

He pulled into his usual spot and contemplated how to spend his free time. His flat could do with a clean. He hadn't been able to take the jam out the fridge this morning, so firmly set was the jar to the now-opaque shelf.

And there was the paper. When had he last read more than the headlines?

He had to look on this suspension positively. He could double his running and lose more weight. Maybe get a body like your man Milo.

Then he saw the Mini Cooper.

Lilly cringed when she saw Jack lumbering towards her. She felt like a naughty schoolgirl caught smoking by her dad. 'I was just holding it for my friend, honest.'

'What are you doing here?' he asked.

She hedged her bets. 'A case.'

He stood, arms crossed, his face giving nothing away.

'A client in custody,' she said.

'I'm a copper, Lilly, I'd worked that much out for myself.'

Lilly put up her hands in surrender. 'I just came down to give her some advice. I'm not taking on her case.'

'Mary Mother of God,' Jack yelled. 'I thought we'd been through this.'

They stood looking at one another for a moment. Lilly reached out and stroked the leather of his jacket. It was warm and creased from years of wear.

'She's in a terrible state, Jack. The doc says she's having horrendous panic attacks.'

'You can't take on the case.'

Lilly nodded. 'I'm not taking on the case.'

Steve's car smelled as bad as the man himself, and Alexia wound down the window. She shifted in her seat, her skirt sticking to the plastic. And who the hell still owned a manual?

She supposed it was better than the bus. The salary of a junior reporter on a local rag didn't stretch to her own transport, so she grudgingly accepted the use of her boss's and tried to ignore the ash that clung to her black wool suits.

'I bet Kate Adie doesn't have to put up with this.'

As she crunched into third, she banished from her mind the Alfa that Daddy had bought for her twenty-first. A gorgeous little red number with tan upholstery and a walnut dash. It had broken her heart to give it back.

She pulled in front of the gates of Manor Park and admired the floodlit countryside that flanked it on all sides. It reminded her of Benenden, her own alma mater, with its tennis courts and clock towers.

Until seconds ago she had remained sceptical that the report was true but the multitude of press vans and cars stationed at the foot of the sweeping drive made her heart pound. A shooting – in a place like this? Fantastic . . .

She parked the battered Honda and entered the throng. All the nationals were here and the main TV stations.

Alexia smiled at a man fiddling with the boom on his camera.

'What's the story?' She tried to sound as casual as she could.

'Police won't let us in,' he said. 'No one's saying anything.'

'So we don't even know if it's true?'

He shook his head and went back to his boom.

Alexia squeezed past the mighty power of the media until she stood in front of three policemen who were blocking the gate.

'Can you confirm whether a pupil has been shot?' she said.

'Nope,' said the nearest. The others simply looked over her head.

'So you're prepared to say nothing about a terrible crime which presumably happened on your patch?'

'Yep.'

Alexia sidestepped them and craned her neck up to the school. She held out her hand to lean on the wrought iron gates and peer through.

'I wouldn't do that if I were you, Miss,' said the policeman.

'What?'

The policeman nodded at the gate. 'They've taken out an injunction preventing anyone so much as touching their property.'

Alexia laughed. 'They can't do that.'

'They can and they have.' He pulled out a piece of paper. 'And you'll see that we're empowered to arrest anyone who fails to comply.'

Alexia skim read the document and flicked it with contempt.

'So much for freedom of speech.'

She headed back to her car where the cameraman was still adjusting his sound equipment. 'Like I said. No one's saying anything.'

Alexia's phone rang.

'Well?' barked Steve.

'The world and his wife are here but we can't get in,' she said. 'And the police refuse to give a statement.'

'Some bloody story that'll make.' She could hear him dragging on his cigarette. 'May as well get your arse back here.'

But Alexia was not ready to give up. 'I'll have a scout around first.'

'You've got half an hour,' said Steve and hung up.

She pocketed her phone and jumped back in the Honda. The main entrance might be guarded, probably as well as any other official routes into the school – but her years in boarding school had taught her that there was always a way for the pupils to sneak out. And when she found it she would sneak her way in.

She drove along the entire flank of the school grounds shielded by a high wooden fence with nettles growing to waist height. Nothing. Maybe she was out of touch and kids these days finished their prep and were tucked up by nine.

She turned the car around to head back when she saw it. A small patch of nettles well trodden down. She parked close by and inspected the trampled weeds. Then she checked she wasn't being watched and pushed the plank of wood nearest to the ground. It fell with ease, as did the one above and the one above that. Alexia

64

smiled at the small opening to the Magic Kingdom and ducked inside. She found herself within two hundred yards of the main building.

The sound of a cello floated from a window but apart from that all was quiet. She sneaked around but still nothing. No police tape, no sign whatsoever that anyone had been killed. Maybe it was a hoax.

Alexia was about to go home when she saw a white tent flapping in the wind on the far edge of a football pitch. It might just have been a marquee left over from Speech Day, but it was very small.

Her pulse quickened as she got closer and she pulled out her phone.

'How are things in the country?' asked Steve, phlegm rattling in his throat.

Alexia pulled a clod of earth from her heel. 'Wet.'

Steve let out a laugh that soon gave way to a barking cough.

'Those fags will kill you,' she said.

'Not before you do, Posh,' he replied. 'Got anything for me?'

'I'm inside the school.'

'Ain't it closed at this time of night?'

'It's a boarding school.'

'Poor little rich kids whose parents don't want 'em,' he said.

'Do you want to know what I've found?' she asked.

'Go on then.'

She tried to keep the excitement from her voice. 'From where I'm standing I can see something that looks distinctly like a forensic tent.'

Steve let out a low whistle. 'So it's true.'

'Can we help you?'

Alexia looked up. Three women were striding across the field, their breath white in the dark air. The leader had a fierce look in her eyes, frizzy hair and a wax jacket. The other two looked like they'd fallen out of a Boden catalogue.

'I said "Can we help you?",' Frizzy stomped towards Alexia. The accent was cut-glass and Alexia followed suit. She usually took the edge off for Steve.

'I thought I might lay flowers.' She rhymed 'flowers' with 'vase'.

Frizzy raised a bushy eyebrow.

'My niece, Emily, said we simply must do something,' Alexia continued.

'Emily?' asked Frizzy.

'Royston-Jones,' Alexia was banking on Frizzy not knowing everyone in the school. 'She's been very upset and her parents are in the Maldives.'

Frizzy gave nothing away, her shins solid in their tan tights.

'I came straight here when she called.' Alexia turned to the other two. 'What do you think? Is the school organising a tribute?'

'I think they're waiting to see what the Stantons want to do,' said the first.

'Of course,' said Alexia. 'They must be devastated.'

The second pursed her lightly glossed lips. 'They're beside themselves. Charlie was such a treasure.'

'Appalling, isn't it?' said Alexia, careful not to push too much and risk giving her game away.

Glossy Lips threw up her hands. 'Those people have to be stopped.'

Frizzy glared at her. 'We're under strict instructions not to discuss this with anyone, particularly outsiders.'

'She has a niece at the school.'

'Loose lips sink ships,' said Frizzy.

'I'm sorry if I caused any offence. I fully understand your position.' Alexia tucked her hair behind her ears. 'I deliberately came out of hours. I mean, one doesn't want to be showy.'

Frizzy gave a curt nod and turned to leave. 'I think we've all said enough on the subject.'

Too late, love. Charlie Stanton. Bingo.

The air was redolent with the smell of rubber and chalk dust as forty feet beat out their muffled rhythm on the mats.

'Sorry I'm late,' said Lilly, and squeezed onto the bench beside her friend. 'Had to drop off the boy wonder at his dad's.'

'Good day at the office, darling?' said Penny. Lilly stuck out her tongue and they waited for their turn to warm-up.

After Lilly had been attacked by a maniac and had managed to save herself only by the fortuitous use of a vase, she had decided to take up self-defence. Penny had suggested Tae Kwon Do, and the pair came to practise each Tuesday evening.

Penny crossed her legs, toned calves peeping out from her karate suit: smooth brown skin against white cotton. Each toenail was round and pink, a shimmering shell.

Lilly looked down at her own legs. Red indentations from her socks made perfect circles around each hairy shin. A plaster peeled away from her ankle.

Lilly wondered if she could ever look like her friend.

'Fine feathers make fine birds,' her mum used to say, but Lilly never seemed to have enough time to keep up with the preening.

'How's life on the domestic front line?' asked Lilly.

'Bonkers,' said Penny. 'We've got a new boy coming at the weekend.'

'How many's that now?'

'Four. Two come for respite care one weekend a month, and Rachel comes every Thursday.'

'Is she still traumatised?'

Penny see-sawed her hands. 'It has got better, but I'm still stripping and washing the beds till Saturday.'

'Have I ever told you how much I admire you?' asked Lilly.

'Only twice a week.'

The sensei called them to the dojo and they began their stretching.

'I should do something like you,' said Lilly.

Penny stamped hard with her left foot and punched with her right. 'You don't have time.'

'But all I do now is commercial stuff. I don't make a difference to anyone's life.'

'Oh, Lilly, stop beating yourself up. Everyone has to make a living.'

Lilly kicked out and grunted hard.

'I just wish I could do something to help those that need it most.'

'We can't help everyone,' said Penny. 'And frankly, there are a lot of people who should jolly well help themselves.'

The sensei clapped his hands. 'Ladies, you may spar.'

The two friends turned to one another and bowed deeply in respect. Then they proceeded to kick the shit out of each other.

Lilly plotted the rest of her evening with precision and relish. Sam was at his dad's, torturing the new baby, so she would bathe at length and make the most of the unopened basket of Jo Malone oils that Jack had bought for her birthday. At the time she'd thought it a ludicrous extravagance, but she had to admit they were so much better than the cheap crap she usually picked up in the supermarket. She would paint her toes a glamorous shade of crimson and then cook herself a feast. Steak Béarnaise. Blood oozing from the meat into the eggy sauce, the tang of tarragon vinegar piercing its unctuous blandness.

She would not give a moment's thought to Anna Duraku.

When the bath was run, she lit a candle and sank into the oily heat until only her nostrils cleared the surface. Bliss.

Ring ring. The phone. She'd ignore it.

Ring ring. Worse than the phone, it was the bloody doorbell. Who the hell could it be? Jack was still mad at her for going down to the station and had gone out for a drink with an old mate who'd quit the force to open a dry-cleaners'.

Lilly pulled a towel around herself and padded downstairs.

Ring ring.

'Keep your hair on, will you,' she shouted, and yanked at the door handle. After three firm tugs the door opened a few inches.

'You need a new frame.'

It was Milo, his breath white against the cold.

Lilly dripped and blinked. 'How do you know where I live?'

'Everyone knows everything in this village.'

Milo looked her up and down. From her ragged toenails to the towel barely covering her arse and back down to the pool of water gathering on the floor below her.

'Sorry,' he said. 'I needed to speak to you about Anna.'

Lilly cringed with embarrassment and ran for the stairs.

In her bedroom she threw open her wardrobe doors in search of her good jeans. They were snug at her hips but not at her thighs, and the style magazine Penny passed on each week had declared them the hottest jeans of the season. Lilly had found a bargain pair in TK Maxx and they looked great with a black V-neck jumper. She scraped her wet hair into a knot at the base of her skull. No time for makeup, maybe just a slick of mascara. At least she smelled good.

Lilly stopped in her tracks. What the hell was she doing? Why was she in a tailspin because an attractive man had turned up at her house? She reminded herself that she had Jack. A good, kind and decent man. A man her son adored. A man who thought oral sex was part of the deal and not just for anniversaries and birthdays. A man who had stood between her and a bullet.

Deliberately, she put her jeans back in the wardrobe and pulled on the lumpy jogging bottoms that lived on a wicker chair in the corner of her room. She zipped a beige fleece over a thermal vest and pulled on slipper socks.

The message was clear.

She found Milo in the kitchen, tinkering with the buttons on her dishwasher.

'It's broken,' she said.

He laughed in the direction of the sink, where a mountain of crockery tottered. 'I can see that. Do you have a screwdriver?'

Lilly opened a kitchen drawer and rummaged. She pulled out a knife, a hammer and a can of Mace.

'My safety kit,' she said, in answer to Milo's puzzled look. She handed him a screwdriver. 'I had some trouble on one of my cases.'

He simply nodded and went to work.

'You've come to ask me to take on Anna's case,' she said.

'Of course.'

No flannel, no spin. Lilly smiled. 'I really can't, you know.'

Milo twisted a screw. 'There.'

'It's fixed?'

He shrugged a shy confirmation.

Lilly couldn't hide her delight. 'I could kiss you.' She had spoken without thinking and needed to backtrack. 'Don't worry, I won't.'

'I'm not worried.'

71

They looked at each other, their connection a fraction too long.

Lilly was the first to break away. 'I'll make you some dinner.'

Milo sank back in his chair. 'So much food.'

Lilly cleared the plates. 'There's lemon tart if you want some. I made it at the weekend but it should still be good.'

Milo shook his head and rubbed his stomach. 'Are you trying to kill me?'

'Oh, you know – lawyer, cook, murderer.'

'A person of many talents.'

Lilly stroked her dishwasher and felt its soft rumble. 'As are you.'

'My father taught me many things.'

The sadness was unmistakable.

'Where is he now?' Lilly asked.

'Gone,' he said.

'I'm sorry. I didn't mean to pry.'

'You English people are so funny. Everything is private business, you don't care about anybody else.'

'That's not true,' she said. 'We just don't like talking about painful things.'

He fixed her with the jewelled glint of his eyes. 'If you don't talk, how are you going learn?'

Lilly closed her eyes, willing herself to pull away.

'I can't take on Anna's case.'

Milo stood to leave with a half-smile. 'You are a very strange woman, Lilly Valentine.'

When he had left, Lilly noticed a package on the work

72

surface. She opened it up and began to read Anna's statement from her application to remain in the UK.

TIRANA DURAKU

My name is Tirana Duraku and I was born in Glogovac, some 25 kilometres from Pristina, the capital of Kosovo.

I lived with my parents, and my three sisters and one brother. We stayed in a small apartment in the Albanian section of Glogovac.

When I was a young child I was happy. I went to school and was commended for my studies. I wanted to be a teacher when I grew up.

I recall that there would be trouble sometimes from the police. They would round up the menfolk and take them away. When they came back they would have black eyes or bloody mouths.

My mother told me she paid them, which was why they didn't come for my father or brothers.

In January 1999 our neighbours were arrested. This time it was not the police who took them but the paramilitaries. There were about six of them, each with an automatic rifle. When our neighbours came back they packed up their apartment and left. I never saw them again.

My mother said they didn't have enough money to pay the police.

A few weeks later they came to us. They wore green uniforms with red bandanas. I was very frightened. My mother tried to pay them the usual amount but they laughed in her face. In the end they took all the money we had in the apartment.

The next day they forced my mother to take off her rings. She couldn't get one of them off and had to put soap round her knuckle and force it.

That night my oldest brother, Brahim, and my father decided to stand up to the soldiers. My mother cried and begged them not to make a stand but my father said Allah would provide.

The next morning they came at six. We were all still in bed but no one was sleeping. My father told them calmly that he would pay them nothing more. The captain nodded and I thought he was agreeing to leave us alone, but he snatched my little sister and put his gun to her head.

'Give me the keys to your car,' he said.

My father did not want to give in, but tears were pouring down the face of my sister and my mother.

Two days later we went to stay with my father's brother and his family. There was not enough room in the house but the menfolk said there would be safety in numbers.

Throughout March and early April we girls hardly left the house. We would take it in turns to sleep. There was almost no food available and we lived on boiled corn and wheat.

My uncle's neighbour had forty people staying in his house, and his wife called to my mother through the window saying that their houses had been burned by the paramilitaries.

On 22 April they came early in the morning. They pointed their guns in our faces and forced us outside. The men were ordered to step forward with their hands on their heads, then they were led away. We thought for sure they'd be shot and we cried all day. That afternoon they returned, but we could not throw our arms around my father because he had been beaten with the handle of a shovel and his collar bone was broken.

That night a local Serb policeman came to the house and told us the paramilitaries were out of control. He told us to leave.

'There is no safety for you here,' he said.

As soon as it was light we were once again forced into the street. This time the men were ordered to sing the Serbian national anthem. I saw my brother's jaw jut out in refusal. The soldier poked him in the back with his gun but still Brahim refused.

My mother screamed at him to sing but he would not.

'We'll make you do what we say,' they said, but Brahim would not even answer.

The captain walked back to his car and pulled out a can. He shook it so we could all hear the petrol inside. Then he poured it over my mother's head. He pushed her and my sisters back in the house, threw the can in after them and locked the door.

In terror my brother began to sing, but the captain would not listen. He lit a cigarette and smoked it.

Brahim sang for all he was worth.

When the captain's cigarette was finished he tossed the butt into the house.

The noise was unbearable. The whoosh of the flames, my brother's singing and the screams of my mother and little sisters as they were burned alive.

That night my father paid a man to take my brother Brahim and me away from Kosovo. To take us to a place of safety.

Chapter Five

Luke is a clever boy. Everybody says so. Ten straight A's at GCSE. His reports always bring a smile to his mother's face:

> Walker is a model student with a firm grasp of Latin grammar. A bright pupil who fully comprehends the importance of Tudor history.

Well, I'm failing bloody miserably on the streets, he thinks.

'A bit slow on the uptake,' Caz always teases.

Thank God for Caz. She sussed straight away that he didn't know his arse from his elbow and has taken him under her wing. Why she did that is still not clear to him. Tom always says that nothing in this life is for free, that everyone is on the take, but Luke can't for the life of him see why Caz is being so kind to a basket case like him.

'I like a challenge,' she says.

Whatever her reasons, he's bloody grateful.

Hot meal – she knows where to get it. Dry place to sleep – she'll put you right. And if you need some gear she'll do a deal with Sonic Dave, who everyone says is a bit of a nutter but likes Caz because she reminds him of his baby sister.

This morning, when he woke up in a squat on Brixton High Road and she was gone, her sleeping bag rolled into a fat sausage, Luke was overcome with panic, gut-wrenching, sickening panic. He didn't dare move, afraid to go anywhere without her, afraid that if she came back for her bag he'd miss her. He sat in that spot for two hours, staring wildly around him.

It had been dark when Caz had blagged them a space in the squat last night, but now he can see as well as smell the damp patches spreading across the walls and the black sack of rubbish in the corner. There's someone else in the room, buried deep under a green blanket. Luke can't see who it is but he can hear the coughing.

He needs a pee. It started as a vague pressure in his bladder but it's built to a searing pain. But he's not moving, he'd rather piss himself in his bag.

The door opens and Luke's heart leaps at the sight of a female figure silhouetted in the doorway. 'Caz?'

She shakes her head and Luke can see now that she's at least ten years older. Luke thinks he might cry, and a weird strangled sound comes out as he tries to swallow down his tears.

'You okay?' says the woman, the accent thickly Eastern Bloc.

'I just wondered if you know where Caz went?'

The woman shakes her head, then almost as an after-thought shouts behind her in a language Luke doesn't understand. A voice shouts back.

'Gone for make money,' the woman translates.

'Where?' Luke asks.

The woman shrugs. 'Streatham, maybe.'

Luke doesn't know where that is but maybe he can catch a bus. He's got a map in his rucksack. Maybe he should make his way over there, see if he can spot her. Then again maybe he should stay here.

The figure under the blanket pokes out his head and vomits onto the floor. A pool of brown viscous liquid meanders towards Luke. The decision has been made for him.

The tube rattles and shakes as it passes through the belly of the capital. Luke has grown used to the way people avoid him. To be honest he would do the same, given that he hasn't had a bath in three days.

He can see now why tramps hunch in on themselves. It's the shame of being dirty, of being different. They don't want to be noticed.

He gets off at Balham and blinks into the daylight. Where should he start to look for Caz? The woman at the squat had said she'd gone to get some money. Most likely she meant begging.

He looks around the entrance of the station and catches sight of a man sat on a blanket, a teardrop tattooed under one eye.

'Spare some change.'

Luke shakes his head. 'Do you know Mad Caz?'

'Cocky Scouser?'

Luke laughs. 'That's right. Have you seen her?'

The man eyes Luke's dirty trainers and rucksack. Caz

has tried to make Luke understand the rules of the street. Never take someone else's spot, never move someone else's stash, and never give anyone up.

'If Caz wants you to find her, you will,' says the man.

Luke's desperate, he doesn't know what he'll do without her.

Perhaps it shows in his face, because the man's harsh eyes slacken – or perhaps that's just what Luke wants to think.

'I haven't seen you around before.'

Luke shakes his head in answer.

'Caz showing you the ropes, is she?' the man says to himself. 'I'll tell you what. You get a couple of tins from the Twenty-Four-Seven and you can wait with me. If she comes back this way you'll find her.'

Luke doesn't need to be asked twice.

'Tennent's Super,' the man calls after him. 'And make sure they're fucking cold.'

Luke scuttles across the road into the shop and heads for the freezer. He tugs at a can of Tennent's but it is held tight in plastic to another three. Maybe you can only buy them in packs of four. He left home with what his dad had given him for a new computer game and there isn't much left. Mum always goes potty, saying Dad should spend more time with them and less with his fancy woman, then he wouldn't feel the need to bribe them.

He did the maths in his head. The beer would leave him with six quid. Not much, not even enough for a McDonald's for him and Caz. Maybe he should leave it. Then again, the bloke at the tube would be pretty pissed

79

off if he came back empty-handed. Maybe he could say they wouldn't serve him. Luke watched a girl who looked about ten years old getting twenty Bensons and knew that would never fly.

'Do you want those?'

Luke realised the man behind the counter was speaking to him, although he was still having a conversation with someone else on the phone.

He took the money without touching Luke's hand.

The face in the mirror told the sorry story. Lines etched around the eyes, skin as colourless as the sky. Lilly hadn't been to bed the night before.

She picked up the phone and dialled. 'Is Sam there?'

'Nice to speak to you too,' said her ex-husband.

It wasn't so long ago that all their conversations went like this, each sentence tight with accusation.

'Sorry, David, bad night.'

His voice softened. 'I'm not surprised. I bet you can't stop thinking about what happened up at the school.'

Lilly's finger grazed Anna's file. 'Something like that.'

A silence stretched between them. David had never been comfortable with sadness or fear. In fact he was pretty useless with emotion full stop. When Lilly could no longer tolerate his affair with Cara and had kicked him out his relief had been palpable. He could have refused, promised to give up his mistress, but no, he simply couldn't bear a scene – and so had all but run away.

'I'll fetch Sam,' he said at last.

* * *

Lilly bought a large latte from the coffee shop on the High Street. She could see her mother's pursed lips, the click of her tongue at the extravagance of spending £2.10 on a drink when there was a perfectly good kettle in the kitchen.

'Needs must,' she whispered into the ether.

A quick chat with Sam had cheered her a little, and now she hoped to sneak into her office, hide under her desk and let the frothy milk do the rest.

As soon as she opened the door she knew her plan was doomed. Rupes and Sheila were both in the reception area, poring over the post.

Lilly's smile was weak. 'Hi.'

Rupes's face was impassive. If she knew about Lilly's trip to the police station she would be furious.

'Everything okay?' asked Lilly.

Rupes said nothing. Oh, this silent treatment was worse than a bollocking.

'You'd better show her,' said Sheila, and Lilly noticed how pale she looked. Maybe this wasn't about Anna.

Rupes handed Lilly a copy of the *Three Counties Observer*.

SCHOOLBOY MURDERED IN THE HEART OF ENGLAND
The TCO can exclusively reveal that Charles Stanton, 16, was shot in cold blood at his Hertfordshire school by a crazed gunman thought to be seeking asylum.

On and on the story went, with a grainy but still grisly photograph of the spot where Charles had been killed.

It was bad, truly awful, but it was the final paragraph that made Lilly's heart sink.

The police, who have made no comment until this point, have confirmed that a teenage girl has been arrested and charged and will be brought to court at the earliest opportunity.

'You should never have gone sneaking off to help that girl,' said Sheila.

'I don't know what you're talking about,' said Lilly.

'You had no business taking that case,' said Sheila. 'We don't even do asylum stuff.'

Lilly rounded on her secretary. 'For one thing, this is a criminal matter, not "asylum stuff", as you so nicely put it, and for another I have not taken on Anna's case.'

'So you went down the nick for a laugh, did you?' said Sheila. 'Didn't think about us, did you? More interested in some kid who ain't even from here.'

Lilly's face burned. Where was Sheila getting her information?

'She has a name and it's Anna,' she said. 'She came here to escape things you and I could never dream of.'

'Yeah, yeah,' said Sheila. 'And my granddad didn't get shot at in Normandy so we could give a home to everybody with a sob story.'

'What's the point?' said Lilly, and turned to leave. 'I'm not being told what to do by a bloody secretary.'

As Sheila opened her mouth for another tirade, Rupes pulled Lilly out of the room.

'It doesn't mention the firm,' said Lilly.

Rupinder held out a flyer. 'This was pushed through the letterbox this morning.'

We urge the people of Britain to stand up for what they know is right. Stop our precious resources dwindling away while our own old aged pensioners do without.
Refuse to support non-English shops and businesses.

'Bin it,' said Lilly.

'The other partners are worried that some clients might go elsewhere,' said Rupes.

Lilly shook her head. 'We can't bow to this sort of pressure.'

'I agree,' said Rupinder, 'but I'm not going to pretend that it isn't unnerving.'

Lilly hugged her boss. She smelled of cocoa butter. 'It's just racist crap.'

'I know that, but if you hadn't noticed, Lilly, I'm not exactly white.'

Both women laughed until Lilly's mobile rang. It was Milo.

'Thank God I've got you. I don't know what to do,' he said.

'What on earth's the matter?' asked Lilly.

He was breathing hard into his phone. It crackled into Lilly's ear. 'I'm at the court with Anna. There are lots of people here, shouting and screaming.'

'How's Anna? Is she okay?'

'She's terrified. She won't speak to anyone but you,' he said.

'Hang on.' Lilly looked at Rupes. 'I'll be there as soon as I can.'

Lilly didn't break eye contact with her boss and handed her Anna's file.

'Read this – and if you still don't want me to take on this case you can sack me.'

The Tennent's is thick and gloopy and it coats Luke's tongue. It doesn't taste like anything he's drunk before. He takes small sips and the can is still half full.

Tony pulls the ring on his second. He makes room for Luke on his filthy blanket and Luke gladly sits down. He ignores the brown stains, which may or may not be shit, just glad for the chance to be with another human being.

As the booze works into his system, Tony becomes chatty. He tells Luke he's from Wales but hasn't been back since he left the army.

'Why not?' asks Luke.

'Drugs, drink, prison,' says Tony. 'A full hand.'

Luke doesn't know how to respond. People on the streets talk openly about stuff like that, stuff that would make his mum have a fit. And Luke never knows what to say. He could just join in, that's what Tom would do, but these people would suss he was faking in a heart-beat. Like the time Caz asked if he needed any gear and he'd nodded, thinking she meant grass. When she poled up with a bag of heroin he'd tried to hide his shock and simply pocketed it, but Caz had laughed and called him 'a silly get'.

'They say I have a problem with my temper,' says Tony.

'Right,' says Luke.

Tony twists his mouth into a smile. His front teeth are missing. 'They say I'm unpredictable.'

'Better than being boring, I suppose.'

Tony's eyes close into two black slits. 'Are you taking the piss?'

'No,' says Luke, and searches for safer ground. 'Where did you serve?' he asks.

Tony takes a long swallow and bares his gums with an audible sigh.

'Bosnia, Macedonia,' he says. 'Would have been shipped out to the desert but they said my head was mashed.' He drains the last dregs and lets out a belch. 'Post Traumatic Stress they called it. Offered me counselling, like, but it didn't work. Once you seen them things you can't un-see them, can you?' He taps the side of his head. 'No matter how much bloody talking you do, it's all still in here.'

He closes his eyes and Luke's not sure whether he's wrestling with his demons or if he's just nodded off.

'Made yourself at home, I see.'

It's Caz, with her big toothy grin and grubby parka. Luke's heart swells.

She points to the remaining cans. 'Give us one, will you?'

Luke hands her one and she snuggles between him and Tony.

'How's business?' says Tony, his eyes still shut.

'Slow,' says Caz. 'But I got enough for today.' She turns to Luke. 'I need a shower after that lot.'

'Where?' he asks.

'There's a few places.' She nudges him with her elbow. 'You weren't planning on smelling like that forever, were you?'

He doesn't deny how badly he needs a wash. Even the foul stench of Tony's breath doesn't mask Luke's own body odour.

She pecks Tony on the cheek and scrambles to her feet. 'Thanks for looking out for him.'

Tony nods gently. 'Not a problem.' His eyes remain shut.

Caz presses the buzzer on a door in Peckham. It looks like it might be a village hall or something. Not that Peckham's a village. Luke's heard of it – well, everyone has after that poor little kid got stabbed on some stairs – but it's different to anywhere he's ever been in his life and he's been abroad loads of times.

The high street is lined with stalls selling fruit and vegetables. Gargantuan black women haggle over things that look like giant spring onions and bunches of leaves tied with string. Rude boys hang around, tracks cut into their hair and eyebrows, their accents dense. Sometimes Tom would put on a voice that he thinks sounds Jamaican. He says 'ting' instead of 'thing' and calls everyone in the dorm 'bredren'. The other boarders would laugh, but Luke thinks it makes him look like a twat.

He becomes transfixed outside a Caribbean takeaway, the smell of patties rooting him to the spot.

'On your way,' shouts the cook from behind the counter. They're not welcome.

Caz is impatient and presses the buzzer a second time. Luke can't believe they'll get a shower in here.

'Don't look like that, soft lad,' says Caz. 'Have I let you down yet?'

A woman opens the door, a fag between her lips. 'The lovely Caroline.'

Caz grins. 'All right, Jean.'

'And who've you got with you this time?' asks Jean, smoke causing her to squint.

'This is my mate, Luke,' she says. 'He's new.'

Jean nods and lets them pass.

The washing machine is hypnotic. Luke watches his clothes spin round and round. For the first time since he ran away he feels calm. It's not that he's forgotten about Anna and Tom and Charlie and all that stuff. It's more like it's pushed to the back of his mind. He's had a shower and has seized the opportunity to wash his jeans and hoodie. He offered to stick Caz's parka in but she declined.

'It's only the stains holding it together.'

'So, Luke,' says Jean, an unlit cigarette between her lips. 'Got everything you need?'

'Yes, thank you,' he says.

Jean pats her pockets until she finds a lighter and gives it a shake. 'Do you want something to eat while you're waiting? Make yourself a sandwich if you fancy it.'

He's not sure if he should. He's already had a shower and used the washer. His mum always says you shouldn't take advantage. But the woman seems to expect it.

Earlier, when two boys asked if they could take some milk with them, she just nodded and gave them one of the cartons out of the fridge. As for Caz, she's made herself right at home. Half a bottle of Radox in her bath, then she'd crashed out on one of the sofas in the common room. She's still in there, fast asleep.

'There's plenty of ham,' Jean says. 'Or cheese if you prefer it.'

'Thank you,' Luke repeats, and Jean laughs.

'Someone taught you good manners,' she says.

Luke blushes. He's not sure whether she's taking the piss. 'My mum says they maketh the man. Manners, that is.'

Jean just smiles and nods in the direction of the bread bin. Luke takes two slices and butters them. The bread's springy like it was bought fresh that morning.

'When d'you last see your mum?' asks Jean.

Luke grates some cheese. Red Leicester, his favourite.

'A few days ago,' he says.

'So you're still in touch?'

Luke gives her a puzzled frown, then realises Jean has no idea how long he's been on the streets.

'Don't worry, love, we don't have nothing to do with your parents unless you want us to. Nor the social or the police for that matter.'

Luke takes a bite but it's hard to chew. His mouth has gone dry at the mention of the police and all his fears come rushing back. What if the police have already arrested Tom and Charlie? And what if they're looking for Luke right this minute?

'What's your business stays your business. We're just here to help if we can,' she says.

Luke forces the lump of bread down his throat. 'I don't think anyone can help.'

Jean stubs out her cigarette. 'You'd be surprised.'

Kerry Thomson was fat. Properly fat. Not half-a-stone, jeans-a-bit-too-tight fat, but can't-reach-your-feet-to-pick-up-your-sandwich fat. Rolls of flesh began at her neck and fell down her body in waves. Her head seemed too small for the monstrous body, as if it belonged to someone else completely. And that was how Kerry liked to think of it, a pleasant – some said pretty – face that ought to have attached itself to a smaller person. Not necessarily a thin person, but not the hulk of blubber that was Kerry Thomson. She shunned full-length mirrors, preferring a pocket compact to isolate the one part of her body that she didn't hate. When had she started doing that? In her twenties when she last wore official sizes? In her thirties, when her periods dried up?

To be honest, she'd always been overweight. A podgy toddler wobbling around in her terry nappies making her brothers laugh, her sticky fingers outstretched for a custard cream. At school she didn't mind her 'puppy fat', at least not much, and in her mid teens she wore it quite well. While the other girls were all straight lines and right angles, Kerry had tipped into womanhood, breasts, hips and arse. It had been a window of opportunity and she'd used it to full advantage. Kerry had had more sex between the ages of fourteen and sixteen than she'd had in the rest of her life put together.

Some of her so-called mates had called her a slag;

others more kindly pointed out that Kerry was having a rough patch, what with her mum dying. Either way, Kerry had enjoyed those wet fumblings in the back of Ford Cortinas.

She looked at the clock and sighed. She'd zipped her way through six burglaries, four common assaults, two possessions and a pile of traffic including a drunk in charge of a bike. Only one case left, but the solicitor for the defence hadn't turned up yet. If they didn't get here soon the court would have to sit through the lunch break.

She felt in her pocket for a sweet.

A crowd had congregated outside the Magistrates' Court. The usual gaggle of smokers that gathered whatever the weather had been pushed to one side by a group of twenty or so dark-skinned men in checked shirts and women in headscarves. Lilly assumed they were Albanian. A hundred feet away a smaller group of white men shouted. One had a megaphone. Their suits were no disguise. WBA. White British Alliance. The swastika tattoos had gone but the sentiment remained.

Sandwiched between were the police, and watching with amusement were the press. Lots of them. Thank you *Three Counties Observer*. Lilly had no intention of shuffling past that little lot, and headed for the back entrance.

Inside the court, Milo was slumped in a chair. When he saw Lilly his face lit up. 'Thank you for coming.'

The noise of the megaphone filtered into the building.

Milo shook his head. 'Some of the Hounds Place

residents contacted their friends. I told them not to come, that it would do no good.'

'It won't,' said Lilly.

'But they're so angry,' he said. 'Anna was raped and yet she ends up in jail.'

Lilly put her hand over his. 'So let's try to get her out.'

Lilly slipped into the advocates' room and found Kerry Thomson building a glittering pyramid out of Quality Street wrappers. As always, Lilly noticed the hair sprouting from the doughy chin and wondered if Kerry knew she had polycystic ovaries.

'Hello there,' said Lilly.

Kerry scrunched the papers into her fist, a guilty secret.

'I'm here for Anna Duraku,' said Lilly. 'Conspiracy to murder.'

Kerry nodded to the lone file awaiting its fifteen minutes of fame.

'It's a load of old rubbish,' said Lilly. She knew that if it had been anyone else she would have ripped into them, but Kerry always seemed so vulnerable. Shouting at her would feel like bullying someone with Down's syndrome.

'Director of Public Prosecutions says it's good to go,' Kerry answered.

'The fact that she looked at it in person means there are people in the mothership with doubts,' said Lilly.

Kerry pressed both palms on the table and heaved herself to her feet. 'Let's get it into court and see what the magistrate says.'

As they made their way to court number three, Lilly didn't know which was louder – the rumbling from outside or that emitting from Kerry Thomson's stomach.

She could smell them before she turned the corner. Even if they hadn't been shouting she would have known they were there. Something about the food they ate and the clothes they wore gave off an odour. Not exactly unpleasant, just distinctly different.

No matter how many times the liberals and leftists insisted that these people were the same as us, Snow White knew it was not true.

Grandpa had travelled from Cairo to Soweto and back again, and he had declared the other races 'simply not cricket'. Today, watching this dark-haired horde screaming at the court house, she knew he was right.

'Terrible, ain't it?' said woman with a double buggy.

'Yes indeed,' Snow White answered.

'I thought there was a law against it,' the woman said, feeding her twins a packet of Cheesy Wotsits.

Snow White watched the toddlers turn their mouths and chins orange as they sucked the additives from their snacks.

'Sadly not.'

'It's the same on match day,' said the woman. 'The skinheads hijack the whole thing with their shouting.'

Snow White turned to defend the reasonable turnout of brothers that had come to make their feelings heard, but the woman had already pushed on to the bus stop.

At least these comrades had the courage to stand up

for what they believed in, however unsophisticated they might be in making their point. She had had some misgivings about involving them but, seeing them now, standing shoulder-to-shoulder against the enemy, the press documenting their every move, she knew she had done well. She wished she could join them but knew it wasn't possible. She used to resent having to keep her views secret, but now she realised it gave her an advantage. She could infiltrate, gather information and destroy the enemy from within.

The chanting reached a crescendo and a can was hurled at the foreigners.

The magistrate was the intelligent and intuitive Mrs Lucinda Holmes. Many wondered why she had spent so many years in the Youth Court; certainly she could have sought out promotion. Lilly had always assumed that, like her, she just loved kids.

'Before we begin,' Mrs Holmes fixed the advocates with a steely look, 'let's remind ourselves that Tirana is a minor and this is not an episode of *LA Law*.'

'Yes, Madam,' said Lilly.

'Now,' said Mrs Holmes. 'Do we need an interpreter?'

'No,' Anna shouted.

Mrs Holmes smiled at her, civilly but not warmly. 'We find things work better if you address the court through your solicitor.'

'Sorry,' Anna muttered.

'She neither needs nor wants one,' said Lilly.

Mrs Holmes made a note with a silver fountain pen. 'Then let's proceed.'

'This is a case of conspiracy to murder,' said Kerry. 'The prosecution say that the defendant went with Artan Shala to Manor Park Preparatory School, each with a firearm. The intention of both parties was to kill pupils at that school. They were unfortunately successful in their plan, fatally shooting Charles Stanton before Ms Duraku was disarmed and Shala shot dead by a police officer at the scene.'

'I gave the policeman the gun before Artan shot the boy,' said Anna.

Mrs Holmes frowned at Lilly. 'Miss Valentine, you must keep your client in check. This is not a free-for-all.'

'I'm sorry, Madam, but what my client says is true. She voluntarily handed her weapon to Officer McNally some time before Artan was killed. There is no question that he acted alone.'

Mrs Holmes nodded. 'That is for another tribunal to consider. Today I simply intend to transfer this case to the Crown Court. Nothing more.'

'What about an application for bail, Madam?' said Lilly.

Mrs Holmes replaced the top on her pen before laying it gently but deliberately on the pad before her. 'Do you intend to make one, Miss Valentine?'

Lilly thrust up her chin. 'Indeed I do.'

The magistrate opened her arms.

'I realise, Madam, that this is a serious matter and wouldn't normally attract bail, but this case is unusual in any number of ways,' said Lilly.

'Go on,' said Mrs Holmes.

'You may deny bail, Madam, if you believe my client is likely to re-offend.'

'Indeed I may,' said Mrs Holmes.

'Which is why I know you'll have worked out that re-offending in this case is impossible,' said Lilly. 'Anna is charged with a conspiracy with someone who is now dead. They could hardly plot anything else together, Madam.'

Mrs Holmes bit her lip. 'And what about the possibility that Anna might abscond?'

Lilly gave her best theatrical shrug. 'Where would she go? She has no living family and few friends. The Hounds Place hostel is her only lifeline.'

Mrs Holmes breathed evenly, clearly thinking things through.

'Who would supervise her at the hostel?'

'There are social workers on duty, Madam, and Milo Hassan visits every day.'

Mrs Holmes shook her head. 'There's insufficient continuity for my liking. One person needs to be in charge.'

Lilly looked over at Anna. Every molecule of her being looked terrified, and Lilly was consumed with guilt. If she had stepped in to prevent Artan taking the law into his own hands, Anna wouldn't be here now.

'She can stay with me,' said Lilly.

Everyone stared.

Lilly gulped. She'd surprised herself as much as anyone else.

'Stay with you?' Mrs Holmes repeated.

'Yes,' said Lilly. 'I will undertake to the court to supervise her in my home.'

'That's a huge commitment, Miss Valentine.'

Lilly gulped. It was huge. Bloody huge. Lilly pushed the implications to the back of her mind and nodded.

As they left court in Lilly's car, Milo rubbed Anna's shoulders. 'It's over.'

Lilly didn't speak but an old quote came into her head.

'This isn't the end. It's not even the beginning of the end.'

'Tell me this is a joke,' said Jack.

'Am I laughing?' said Lilly. She stared out at the field beyond her kitchen window. The earth was brown and hard. The harvest had been and gone and nothing would grow until spring.

'You can't have her living here,' he said.

'The court says I can.'

He groaned. 'It's madness.'

And of course it was. Sheer madness. Sam would hit the roof; David would apply to have her sectioned; and Rupes . . . Lilly shuddered at the very thought.

'I can't let them send her to prison.'

'But we're both involved in this case,' he said. 'Me in particular.'

Lilly felt a stab of guilt as to how much harder this would make things for Jack.

'She's just a kid,' she said.

He shook her gently by the shoulders. 'It's not your responsibility.'

'Then whose is it, Jack? 'Cos so far the "authorities",' she made speech marks in the air, 'have done a pretty piss-poor job of looking after her.' She rubbed his lapel. 'I owe her.'

'For what?'

'For not doing something before she got dragged into this unholy mess.'

At that moment Milo waltzed in and dumped a binbag of clothes on the floor. 'I'll bring the rest of her things later.'

Jack, eyes wide, watched him leave the room. 'Is that what's-his-name?'

'Milo,' she said.

'He seems at home.'

Lilly sniffed. 'I've barely spoken to him.'

Milo stuck his head back into the room. 'Dishwasher still working okay?'

Jack looked from Lilly to Milo and back again. Lilly opened her mouth to explain.

'Don't tell me you've finally got that dishwasher to work?'

It was David, carrying Sam on his back. He looked from Lilly to Jack to Milo and back again.

'Welcome to Piccadilly bloody Circus,' said Jack, and pushed his way out.

Lilly poured two glasses of Sauvignon Blanc and handed one to David.

'You look knackered,' said Lilly.

'Fleur's got colic.'

'Isn't she too old for that?'

David took a sip. 'I think she just likes crying.'

'She's a baby, that's her job,' said Lilly.

'I don't remember Sam being like that.'

Lilly laughed. 'Of course he bloody was. You just didn't notice 'cos I did all the dirty work.'

David opened his mouth to argue but stopped. 'You were always much better at sorting things out than me. You never seemed to mind the noise and the mess.'

'I thrive on a challenge.'

'I do wonder if you don't just love chaos,' he said.

'Don't be stupid.'

'Look at the facts, Lil: things were going well with you and Jack, so what do you do? Move a Bosnian refugee into the house.'

'Kosovan. And, anyway, it won't be for long. Once I can show the court she's not going to try to leg it I'll get her moved back to the hostel.'

'Sam's not a happy bunny,' said David.

Lilly forced a smile. 'He'll be fine.'

'He loves having you to himself,' said David. 'He hated sharing you with all those kids in care.'

'He shares you with Cara and Fleur.'

David finished his wine and grabbed his coat. 'I don't want to argue, Lil, I'm just pointing out the obvious.'

Lilly closed the door behind him and headed upstairs. 'Everything is going to be fine,' she said to herself. But who was she trying to convince?

In court, when the entire system – no, the world – seemed to be against Anna, she had jumped into the fray, thinking only of how she could help, how she could make amends. Now, as she smoothed her son's duvet over the slow rise and fall of his shoulders, drinking in his warmth, she questioned the sense of her actions.

Yes, the girl had been through hell, but did Lilly really need to bring her into her home? Sam's home?

As she moved down the hall she heard the sharp plink of a dripping tap and turned back to the bathroom. The tap needed a new washer, but judicious pressure normally did the trick. As she pulled it to the left she noticed a black tidemark around the basin. Not the usual ring of dirt but a slick line, almost purple. Had Sam been washing paintbrushes upstairs again? She'd have to have a word with him in the morning. Artistic license was one thing, but he brushed his teeth in here.

Then she saw the plastic tube in the bin. Hidden under a wodge of tissue, only the end peeped out. Lilly would have missed it but for the airbrushed picture of some impossibly glossy-locked model.

It was hair dye.

Since even Sam would struggle to find a use for a tube of dye, it must be Anna's. But why would a sixteen-year-old girl facing a murder charge worry about that? And why would she try to hide it?

She was still contemplating the tube when Anna came in. They both blushed.

'I once went green,' joked Lilly. 'Now *that* was a mistake.'

Anna didn't smile. 'This is my natural colour,' she said. 'Before I go grey.'

'Oh, you poor, poor girl,' said Lilly, and enveloped her client in her arms. Anna stiffened, but Lilly didn't let go.

Sometimes doing the right thing wasn't convenient, but that didn't stop it being right.

*   *   *

The landlord called time and Jack waved for another pint.

He'd overreacted again, stomping out of Lilly's like a Hollywood diva. He'd made himself look foolish in front of David and your man Milo, yet he hadn't been able to help himself.

He'd wanted to explain to Lilly that the shooting had crystallised his thoughts, made him realise that she and Sam were all he wanted. It had been so important to him to make her understand that. Instead he'd been faced with the usual maelstrom of Valentine mayhem. In what alternative universe did Lilly think it was sensible to have her client in the house? Surely she could see that it would ruin everything between them? Maybe she just didn't care enough about him to give his feelings a second thought. Maybe this whole relationship was purely one-sided?

He sighed and sipped his lager. He knew full well that that was not how Lilly saw it. She saw no choice between Jack and Anna – she simply saw a girl who needed help.

He drained his glass and knew he'd regret this last drink in the morning – that and not buying a loaf for breakfast.

The walls of the bridge smell of pee. It's so strong Luke feels like he can taste it at the back of his throat. Caz pushes a pallet against the wall and throws an old sheet over the top.

'Carry on camping,' she grins, but Luke can't even smile.

Ever since he left the Peckham Project he's been

thinking about the police and what they'll do if they catch him. Will the people in prison be like Teardrop Tony? Will they force him to have sex in the showers like people say, and will he be as frightened as the girl in the park?

He desperately wants to tell Caz, to ask her what he should do, but even though she's the nearest thing he's got to a friend here, so far from his home, he's only known her a few days.

She crawls into the lean-to and pulls her sleeping bag over her legs. Luke follows her in. A shiver runs down his back and he stuffs his hands in his pockets.

'Cold?' asks Caz.

He nods.

'Wait 'til January.'

But it's not the weather that is making his bones ache.

'Why are you here, Caz?' he asks.

'Because it's bleeding well pouring out there, and that Russian bitch won't let us back in the squat.'

'I mean why are you here, living like this?' he says. 'Why aren't you at home?'

She pulls an old tobacco tin from her pocket and unwraps her gear. A square of tin foil, a disposable lighter, a steel tube. And a bag of heroin. She says she's not addicted, that she just does it to pass the time, but Luke's seen the plastic sheen of her face in the morning.

'Do you really want to know?' she says.

He nods.

Caz sighs and sprinkles a couple of pinches of powder onto the foil.

'My stepdad was proper handy with his fists,' she says. 'Gave my ma some right beatings.'

She flicks the lighter and Luke sees the flint ignite.

'She always said he was as good as gold until he had a drink inside him.'

She puts the flame to the underside of the foil and makes a circular movement. 'Trouble was, most days he had a drink inside him.'

'Couldn't she leave him?' asks Luke.

Caz looks up from her fix and a wry smile plays on her lips. 'And go where, soft lad?'

He shrugs, an admission that he knows nothing of that sort of life.

She goes back to the foil. The powder is beginning to cook, bubbles popping.

'When she died he started on me.'

She puts the tube in her mouth and inhales the smoke.

'I stayed for a bit, for my little sisters, but when they got taken into care I legged it.'

'I'm sorry, Caz,' says Luke.

Her mouth has gone slack and her voice when it comes is a rasp. 'What about you? What brings you to the Costa del Shit Hole?'

He looks down at his feet and pulls the lace of his trainer. 'I got involved in something bad. Somebody – a girl, I mean – got something terrible done to her.'

'Raped?' asks Caz.

Luke nods, shame burning hot on his cheeks.

'Three of us took her into a park,' he says. 'She was terrified.'

'That's rough,' says Caz.

'I didn't help her,' he says. 'I did absolutely nothing to help her.'

Caz puts the flame under the foil again and chases the smoke around the edges.

'Do you hate me?' he asks.

'We all do stuff we're not proud of,' she says.

His eyes sting. 'But what I did is so disgusting.'

'Not for me to judge.'

He looks up at her, relieved by her words – but terrified her eyes will betray them as lies. He's glad when he sees her chin has gouched onto her chest.

Chapter Six

'Thanks for this,' said Lilly, and strapped Sam into the back of Penny's new Range Rover. 'Can I give you something towards the petrol?'

Penny crossed her arms. 'My husband is a hedge fund manager and I drive past your house on the way to school.'

'It's still good of you to take him for me.'

Penny shut the car door and turned her back so the children couldn't hear. 'You know it's no problem for me, but I'm still not sure this is a good idea.'

Lilly had had to confide in her friend when it occurred to her that she couldn't leave Anna alone during the school run, and she certainly couldn't take her back to what was effectively the scene of the crime.

'It's only for a week, two at most,' said Lilly.

'But this is your home,' said Penny.

Lilly touched Penny's hand. 'I know it seems like a step too far.'

'No shit, Sherlock.'

'But if you knew what Anna had been through you'd understand,' said Lilly.

'Don't be too sure about that.'

'It makes your foster kids look like they've been living with Jamie Oliver.'

Penny nodded. 'Just don't let anybody at Manor Park find out you're subletting to the opposition. Luella says there are hundreds of journalists still hanging around and you wouldn't want them finding out, now would you?'

When Penny started up the engine, Lilly tapped on the window and waved at Sam. He looked the other way.

'Tell me how you came to England.'

Anna looked startled, a fox in headlights.

'I can't defend you unless I know all about you,' said Lilly.

It felt strange to be conducting an interview in her kitchen, and Lilly wasn't sure she liked it. True, it was convenient to have a kettle and tea bags to hand, and she hadn't needed to pull on more than her jeans, but there was something uncomfortable about discussing murder in the place where she normally baked cakes.

Anna spread her palms on the kitchen table. 'My father paid a man.'

'Did you leave Kosovo with Artan?' asked Lilly.

Anna shook her head, slowly, deliberately. 'No. I left with my brother, Brahim.'

'What happened to Brahim?'

The words were flat, almost mechanical. 'We were separated on the journey. I don't know what happened to him.'

'Have you tried to find him?' said Lilly. 'Has he made contact with you?'

Again, Anna shook her head.

'And the rest of your family?' asked Lilly.

'Mother and sisters burned. Father missing.'

'So you have no one here?' asked Lilly.

'No one.'

Lilly thought of Artan's body sprawled on the ground, the whites of his eyes milky and still. If he was all Anna had left how must she feel now he was dead?

'Why did Artan do it, Anna? Why did he go to the school?'

The girl closed one eye and rubbed her brow bone with the fleshy part of her thumb. 'My head hurts,' she said.

Lilly could almost reach out and touch the terrors that had driven Artan to kill but she needed to know what Anna thought of his actions.

They sat in silence until the doorbell rang.

Lilly opened the door. Her hair was a crazy mass of curls.

'I come in peace,' Jack said, pulling a Yorkie from the inside of his jacket.

She eyed him coolly. 'Unimpressed.'

He pulled a Mars Delight from up his sleeve.

'Getting there,' she said.

And finally a Toffee Crisp from the back pocket of his Levis.

She threw her head back and laughed, the sound as welcome to him as spring.

'Come on through, we're in the kitchen.'

We? Jack thought. Surely not the ex-husband? Jack knew Lilly liked to keep tight with him for Sam's sake but the bloke turned up more often than the milkman. Please God, it wasn't bloody Milo, that would be worse still.

As he rounded the doorway he realised she meant the girl. God, he was some sort of eejit.

'Hello,' he said.

She didn't answer but got up from the table. 'I watch TV upstairs.'

Lilly nodded and they followed her tiny frame with their eyes as she backed out of the room.

Jack sat down and placed the bars on the table.

Lilly unwrapped the Yorkie. 'I know this isn't ideal, but I had to do it, Jack.'

'Did you?'

She snapped off a chunk. 'I didn't do it to be difficult, to make things hard for you.'

'I know,' he said. And he did.

Lilly was many things – impulsive, hot-headed, argumentative – but she never meant to hurt. He smiled, content in the knowledge that she did care for him.

They sat for a moment, Lilly eating her chocolate, Jack chasing stray grains of salt around the table with his thumb. Now he was here, he didn't know what to say. Or at least he couldn't find the words. How do you tell a woman that they make you feel whole? That without them you'd unravel?

'So how did Rupinder react?' he said.

'I haven't actually told her.'

Jack roared with laughter. 'Jesus, woman. If you thought I was pissed off you ain't seen nothing yet.'

Her fingers hovered over the keyboard. Every word seemed wrong. Should she grovel? Not Lilly's style. Should she resign and hope Rupinder wouldn't accept it? There was always the chance that she might.

When Jack had left he'd still been chortling over how Lilly was going to tell her boss that she was babysitting the defendant. Although Lilly had stuck her nose in the air and informed him she'd just give her a call, she hadn't, of course, actually dared to do it. An hour later she deleted the sixth email she'd drafted.

'There is problem?'

Lilly looked up at Anna.

'You make serious face,' she said, and screwed up her nose, which made Lilly laugh.

'I don't even know where to start,' Lilly said, and closed the lid of her laptop. She watched Anna fill the kettle with water and sighed. 'What I don't understand,' she said, 'is why *you* had a gun.'

Anna pressed the switch with a long, pale finger.

Lilly pressed on. 'I understand that Artan was disturbed. He'd been through too much and one day he cracked.'

Anna took two cups from the cupboard, her hands trembling.

'He told me that those boys had hurt you,' said Lilly.

Anna placed the cups on the counter.

'Did he kill that boy because he raped you?' asked Lilly. 'Was it revenge?'

Anna tilted the kettle, steam escaping from the spout.

'To be honest, I suspected he might do something,' said Lilly. 'But I never dreamt he'd involve you.'

The kettle slipped from Anna's hand and crashed onto the work surface. Hot, angry water splashed towards her. She screamed and jumped away, holding her hands in the air.

Lilly jumped to her feet. 'Are you hurt?'

Anna didn't speak but kept her hands in the air.

'Did you burn yourself?' Lilly asked. 'Anna, are you okay?'

The girl's body began to shake. A staccato jerking that progressed to violent convulsions until her legs buckled and she dissolved to the ground.

Lilly knelt down and took Anna's hands. She checked the palms and turned them over. They didn't seem to be burned. Lilly kept them in her own until Anna's shudders slowed.

'I know it's hard, but if I'm going to help you I have to know what happened. You have to tell me about the rape and why you had a gun if I'm to make people understand.'

'But how are you going to do that?' asked Anna. 'When I don't even understand myself?'

'Got anything for me, Posh?'

Alexia sighed. Would she be sitting here if she had?

Her boss breathed out his disgust in a plume of blue smoke, his frustration building like a boil. Any second it would burst and cover her in yellow poison.

Un-bloody-believable.

109

She'd been the only one inside Manor Park and got the exclusive before all the nationals. Yesterday she'd weighed into the scrum outside the court. What total bedlam that was. The skinheads on one side, asylum seekers on the other. She'd hoped for a bit of argy bargy, but they'd limited themselves to hurling abuse and the odd empty can.

Even so, she'd put together a fantastic piece. Steve was never satisfied.

'I got you the best fucking story this rag has ever had,' she said.

'Yesterday's news, today's chip paper.'

'So what do you want from me?'

'I want that girl.'

Alexia shook her head. He was being unreasonable. No reporting was allowed in court because the defendant was a child, so there was no way of finding out who she was or where she'd gone. A source in High Point, the nearest women's prison, had confirmed she hadn't gone there. The other women's prisons claimed to know nothing about her. The police had given the usual bullshit that said a lot but told absolutely nothing. 'Don't you think everyone from the *Guardian* to *Hello* is looking for her?'

'What about the lad's parents?' asked Steve.

'They're saying zilch.'

'Have you tried?'

Alexia fixed him with a stare. 'No, Steve, I left a message on their answer machine, and when they didn't get back to me I thought, "Ah well, I won't bother with that then."'

'What?!'

She shook her head in despair. 'Of course I tried. The number's been discontinued.'

'Probably done a deal with a tabloid,' he said.

Alexia smiled to herself. It wouldn't occur to her boss that the bereaved parents of a murdered teenager might prefer to keep a dignified silence.

Steve threw his fag end into a cold cup of coffee. It died with a hiss. He was cut from the same mould as her father. Pedantic and petulant. A bully.

'Maybe I should pop down to Noodles and Rice,' she said. 'Get us a Chinese.'

Her boss's penchant for greasy chicken floating in MSG made her stomach churn, but she hoped it might alleviate his temper.

'Maybe you should pop into the job centre on the way back.'

'Steve,' she looked him right in the eye, 'you're being a twat.'

He flared his nostrils. 'Find me that girl.'

'Everything all right?' asked Lilly.

Penny ruffled Sam's hair as he jumped out of her car and raced past Lilly without a word. 'He's seriously peed off about Anna staying here.'

'He'll come round,' said Lilly.

'Are you sure about that?'

Lilly gave a half-hearted smile. Penny wasn't exactly being supportive about Anna but, then again, why should she be?

'You don't think anyone could have guessed she's here?'

Penny shook her head. 'The papers all said that in a case like this she'd be remanded into custody.'

'Who tipped off the press?'

'Could be anyone,' said Penny.

'You wouldn't think parents would want their kids' school splashed all over the papers.'

'Maybe they think it will do some good.'

Lilly gave a hollow laugh. 'How?'

Penny shrugged.

'And in the meantime there's this.' She pressed a letter into Lilly's hands. It was from the school. A service was to be held for Charles Stanton.

Bloody marvellous. The mothers would be whipped into a frenzy.

Could anything else go wrong?

To: Lilly Valentine
From: Rupinder Singh
Subject: The Maudsley Hospital

As you know, the above is an establishment for the mentally ill and I am booking a place for you as I type, as I can only assume that you have lost your mind.

If you have another explanation you need to offer it before we open tomorrow.

Chapter Seven

'Here we are,' said Lilly, as they approached the office.

Anna nodded and smoothed her jacket. She had dressed as smartly as her few belongings would allow.

It was too cold to be without a coat and Lilly had tried to lend one to Anna, but the hugeness of it buried her and made her seem somehow even more pathetic.

'I think it would be best if you let me explain the situation,' said Lilly.

Anna laughed. 'I prefer I don't speak at all.'

Lilly took a deep breath and opened the door.

'Look what the cat dragged in,' said Sheila.

Lilly ignored the remark. 'Rupes in?'

'Yes indeed.' Sheila leaned back in her chair, hands behind her head, determined to enjoy herself. 'And she wants to know what the hell is going on.'

'Then I'll go and tell her,' said Lilly.

Sheila jumped to her feet and followed Lilly and Anna to Rupinder's office. 'This I gotta see.'

'Rupes,' said Lilly, and grinned so widely her cheeks hurt.

Rupinder placed her Dictaphone down at an exact right angle to her keyboard.

'Lilly,' she said.

'I know what you're thinking,' said Lilly.

'I think that unlikely,' said Rupes.

'Well, I can guess you're annoyed.'

Sheila snorted. 'That's an understatement.'

'Which is understandable,' said Lilly, 'but you have to see it from my point of view.'

'Do I?'

Lilly nodded. 'It all makes sense when you get where I'm coming from.'

'Lilly Valentine, I gave up trying to get where you're coming from years ago,' said Rupes. 'Your mind is an unfathomable place to me. A place of madness and chaos.'

Lilly hung her head. 'Is it really that bad?'

'Yes, it is.' Rupinder raised her voice, something she never usually did. 'You have taken on this case despite everyone telling you not to, and then you have agreed to have the client under your supervision.'

'It's worked out fine so far.' Lilly turned to Anna. 'Hasn't it?'

Anna nodded vociferously.

'In that crazy house you call a home that may be the case.' Rupinder was on her feet. 'But what about here? In the place we laughingly call your office? What on earth will you do with your client here?'

'She can help me,' said Lilly.

'With what?' asked Sheila; Lilly had forgotten she was behind her. 'We don't have much call for armed assassins.'

'Actually,' said Lilly, 'I was thinking she could make the tea.'

'Not bleeding likely,' said Sheila. 'She'll probably poison the lot of us.'

It was all too much for Rupinder, who roared like a panther: 'Get out of my room.'

Lilly pushed Anna outside and closed the door behind her.

'That went better than expected.'

Luke thumps the pinball machine. He knows they might kick him out but he doesn't care. It has rained on and off all day and some miserable bitch working in Topshop kicked him out of the doorway. He headed down to Chinatown, to the Golden Gate arcade, but got caught in a downpour. He spent the next hour wet and miserable, watching some rent boys play Motocross 3.

He pulls the neck of his hoodie over his mouth. It's dry now but it smells stale.

He remembers all the stuff he left at home, clean and hanging in his wardrobe. Jeans, trackies, a jacket from Quiksilver he'd nagged for and his mum said looked like an overpriced cagoule.

His mind is a tangle of thoughts, spinning round and round like clothes in a tumble dryer. Not looking where he's going, he bumps into a girl with dreads hanging past her waist.

'What's your problem?'

Luke is instantly ready for aggro, but it's someone he knows. Long Tall Sally, named not after her height but her tendency to stand at the top of bridges and multi-storeys to abuse the pedestrians below and spit on their heads. Despite this filthy habit she's always all right with Luke. Caz says she fancies him.

She smiles at him and reveals black teeth. 'What's up, mate?'

Luke shrugs. 'Pissed off, that's all.'

'Why's that?'

Why indeed? He could blame his mood on the shitty weather or the fact that he stinks, but he is used to both by now.

The real reason is Caz, of course. She's gone AWOL again. At about midday she'd gone off to score. Her usual dealer, Sonic Dave, was on the missing list. Some said he'd gone away for a six stretch, others that he'd been sectioned for climbing up the new statue of Nelson Mandela wearing only a loincloth and a pair of goggles. Either way, Caz said she would make her way over to some bloke she knew in Waterloo. She could have gone to any of the Turks who hung about on Oxford Street but she doesn't trust them.

'They cut the gear with vim and all sorts of shit,' she had said.

But she's been gone four hours now, and it doesn't take that long to go a couple of stops on the tube and back.

He doesn't feel frightened when she goes off any more, not like in the beginning when everyone and everything around him seemed overwhelming and dangerous. But he still hates it when she isn't around.

Maybe she has overdosed.

A couple of nights ago, Teardrop Tony had collapsed and no amount of slapping him and pouring water over his head could wake him up. Eventually someone phoned for an ambulance and they injected him with something that got him breathing again. Caz said it was adrenalin.

'Don't you lot think we've better things to do than keeping bloody junkies alive?' the paramedic had said.

Luke had tried to slink away but Caz had stood her ground, hands on her hips.

'Are you saying we should have just left him to die?'

The paramedic had strapped Tony onto a stretcher. 'Some might say you'd have been doing us all a favour.'

If Caz has overdosed today would there be anyone there to dial 999?

'You can't OD when you're tooting, only with needles,' she'd told him. But was that right?

'A gang of us are off to a squat party in Camberwell, why don't you come with us?' says Long Tall Sally. 'It'll cheer you up to get off your head.'

'Thanks, but I'm heading up to Waterloo to meet Caz,' says Luke.

Sally cocks her head to one side, her dreads shivering like snakes. 'I'm not sure she wants to see you right now.'

Luke frowns. 'Why would that be?'

'I'm saying nothing, mate, but we all have things we like to keep to ourselves.'

Luke watches her leave with a group of boys who already look halfway to being drunk. If he thinks about it, Long Tall Sally is right. Caz is obviously keeping something from him. The way she disappears with no explanation before or after. At first it made him sad, but now it makes him angry. They're friends, so why can't she trust him?

He's still racking his brain when he jumps the barrier at Leicester Square station.

'Oy,' roars the guard, and chases him down the steps.

Luke jumps them two at a time and races down the platform. A train is just about to leave. 'Please mind the gap,' warns the mechanical voice. Luke leaps into a carriage as the doors close and the guard is left slapping the glass with the palm of his hand.

People stare, so Luke pulls his hoodie back over his head and looks at the floor as the train pulls away.

Lilly poured herself a glass of Chablis. She was keen to draw a line under what had been a taxing day.

She had known Rupes would react badly to the current bail arrangements, but hadn't expected her to lock herself in her room. Lilly had felt the resentment seeping from under her door every time she crept past. Another round of bellowing would have been preferable.

Anna, on the other hand, had been a revelation, tidying Lilly's workspace and filing the snowstorm of loose papers. Sheila had tossed her tight perm and sniffed in disgust, but Lilly could tell even she was impressed.

It might have all ended relatively peacefully if the package from the CPS hadn't arrived. Lilly would have gladly slid the manila envelope into her bag and dealt with it at home but not today. No doubt it was to outshine their newest member of staff but Sheila insisted on following office policy. She opened the package with her knife and slid the photographs onto her desk to be date-stamped on the back.

As soon as Lilly saw what they were, she flung herself on top of them – but not before Anna had seen the corpse of Charlie Stanton.

'Autopsy,' said Lilly. 'Standard stuff.'

Anna nodded, her face as pale as the body in the photo. Then she vomited across the desk.

After that, Sam's tantrum about extra time on his Nintendo seemed almost to be expected.

'You never think about what I want,' he raged, and they both knew he wasn't referring to Super Mario.

Now, with Sam and Anna both in bed, Lilly would have a quick drink and get an early night herself.

Ring, ring. The doorbell.

'You've got to be kidding me.'

Lilly yanked open the door and found Milo standing in the rain. He held up a pink plastic rucksack. 'I found this in Anna's room.'

'And that?' asked Lilly, pointing to a box in his other hand.

'I shave your front entrance,' he said.

Lilly choked so hard that Milo dropped both items and clapped her on the back.

Lilly gasped for air, tears coursing down her cheeks. 'What did you say?'

'It's a lathe.' Milo knocked the warped door frame with his knuckle. 'I shave this so it opens more easily.'

Still coughing, Lilly ushered him inside and poured him a drink.

'I have spoken wrongly?' he asked.

Lilly wiped her face with the back of her hand. 'No, no. I just swallowed something too quickly.'

He smiled up at her, obviously relieved. His hair was damp and the curls on his forehead were more pronounced.

'That happens to me,' said Lilly. 'When mine gets wet.'

He touched his finger to his black coil. 'Kissing curls.'

He looked directly into her eyes, the green as startling as ever.

Lilly took a gulp of wine.

'Things are okay?' he asked. 'With Anna?'

Glad to be on safer ground, Lilly see-sawed her hand. 'I've got to get to grips with the evidence. Work out what our case is.'

Milo shrugged. 'She didn't do it.'

'I wish it were that easy.'

'It is simple. She didn't kill that boy.'

'Technically that's true,' agreed Lilly. 'But why was she there? Why did she have a gun? She can't give me any explanation for that.'

Milo put down his glass, his face thoughtful. 'Sometimes you just do what you're told to do.'

'What? Someone says here's a gun, now come with me, and you don't ask what's going on?'

Milo rubbed the stem of his glass. 'When I left Bosnia I spent eleven days in the container of a lorry. It was pitch black. I did nothing at all but sit there. I had put my life in the hands of the driver. I ate when the driver told me to eat, drank when he told me to drink. I even make toilet when he tells me.'

'Would you have taken a gun if he'd asked you?'

'My life was his to save or not.' Milo wiped his hands

across his face as if washing something away. 'I would have done whatever he asked of me.'

Without a second thought, Lilly leaned towards Milo and embraced him, one hand around his shoulder, the other around his head. She breathed him in as if she could inhale his pain. As she moved her hands through his hair she felt the distinct jolt of attraction and knew that if she did not move away she would kiss him.

'I'm sorry,' she said, and moved to the sink.

Milo laughed. 'Always you apologise. Do you think I mind when a beautiful woman tries to kiss me?'

'I didn't try to kiss you.' Lilly rinsed her glass. 'I was sorry for what had happened to you.'

'Not a kiss then,' he laughed. 'What you English call a mercy fuck.'

Lilly put her hands on her hips. 'First, what just happened then was not a . . . I mean, not even close to . . . not even in the same hemisphere as a . . .'

Milo got up to leave and smiled. 'And second?'

'Second, I would never, ever sleep with someone out of pity, and if you think that then you are a very poor judge of women.'

He paused at the door, amusement still playing around his mouth. 'So what would be a good reason?'

'For what?'

'To sleep with a man.'

Lilly's mouth opened and closed like a trout. 'I don't know.'

'Come on, Lilly, you have an answer to everything.'

'Okay, he'd need to be sexy and clever,' said Lilly. 'And funny.'

He went outside into the night and the rain. 'A tall order.'

'I'm choosy,' she said, and closed the door, thinking of all the men in her life who hadn't come even close to what she'd just described.

An hour later she was still shaken. She told herself that nothing had happened with Milo. He'd got the wrong end of the stick, nothing more. So why did it feel so deliciously dangerous? Please God, let David be wrong about her deliberately jeopardising her relationship with Jack.

She poured another glass of wine and forced herself to turn her mind to the case. What Milo had said about following orders rang true. When Lilly had last spoken to Artan he'd certainly been menacing. Perhaps Anna was afraid of him? But was she fearful enough to do whatever he asked?

Lilly needed to know what had been in Anna's mind. She ripped open a packet of peanuts with her teeth and emailed an old friend.

When Luke arrives at Waterloo it's dark and raining again. He swears to himself and sets off to The Black Cat, a café that lets the homeless hang out as long as they buy the crappy food and keep their fights outside.

There's quite a crowd, what with the crap weather, and the air hangs thick with condensation and grease.

'Either come in and shut the door or fuck off,' shouts the man behind the counter.

'Just looking for someone,' says Luke.

'Well, now you've looked, so make up your mind.'

Luke gives him the finger and leaves.

He heads over to the NCP. Most of the cars are gone by nine when the crack-heads and homeless take over the lower levels. Caz mostly steers clear at night.

'Can't bleedin' sleep with all that wailing and grunting,' she said.

'But isn't there safety in numbers?' asked Luke.

'Oh, yeah, soft lad, safe as houses with every psycho in London sleeping two feet away from us.'

But sometimes she makes an exception and goes over there when she's got something to sell.

A couple of fires are burning in old braziers but the place is still as gloomy as hell. Literally. It smells of piss and glue and the cold, catch-in-the-throat stench of crack.

Four boys suck on their pipes, eyes wide, shoulders stiff. They don't seem to have noticed the old man lying feet away in a pool of cheap cider. A woman sits on a roll of carpet, an aerosol tucked into her sleeve, its nozzle peeping out like a friendly mouse. She mumbles to herself, tears streaming down her face. Not long ago Luke would have been horrified by the concrete slap of her emotion. He would have looked the other way and passed quickly by. Tonight he just marches up to the poor woman.

'I'm looking for Caz,' says Luke. 'A girl from Liverpool.'

The woman looks up at him, her eyes red and hot. 'All the girls is up that end.'

He nods his thanks and peers down into the shadows.

Two figures are silhouetted in the firelight by the door

to the stairs. One is clearly a man, with tall, broad shoulders. The other is slight. Could it be her?

'Caz?' he calls.

There's no reply but it is her. He can see the dirty parka hanging off her shoulders.

'Caz!'

If she hears him she still doesn't answer. She's deep in conversation with the man. He is trying to pull her by the arm but she is shrugging him off. What's going on? Luke can't make out the words but they are definitely arguing.

As the voices become more heated the man manages to pull Caz into the shadows, out of sight.

'Stop,' Luke shouts, and starts to run. He splashes through the pools of water and knocks over a plastic crate acting as a table. Candles fly into the air and land with a hiss in a puddle.

A head peeps out of an overcoat, completely swathed in a scarf like a dirty blue bandage. 'Watch what you're doing.'

'Sorry,' Luke grabs the sodden candles and plonks them back on the crate. 'I think my friend's in trouble.'

'We're all in fucking trouble here, mate,' says the man.

Luke sets off again, swerving in and out of groups of addicts. At last he reaches the door but there is no sign of Caz.

His heart pounds in his chest. What if the man were trying to rob her? Caz would be just the sort of person to fight back. Luke's mum always says, 'If a mugger attacks you, give him what he wants. Nothing's worth getting killed for.'

Caz has hardly anything worth taking, but what is hers she will defend with her last drop of blood.

He hears a strange wheezing sound coming from the stairs. He can see them both now. The man is behind Caz, pushing her into the wall. Is he strangling her? Please God, she's still alive.

Luke lunges at the man and drags him backwards. He is much bigger but has been taken by surprise. Luke launches him back through the door and into the main body of the car park until the man hits the bonnet of a blue Porsche some city tosser has been too pissed to drive home. The alarm shrieks and the man slides to the floor.

The man is stunned, his eyes wide, but he has enough presence of mind to reach for his cock, which is hard and exposed, and tucks it back into his trousers.

Luke looks from the man to Caz, who is staggering after him, her knickers around her ankles, a skirt Luke has never seen before hitched over her bare arse.

Luke feels the fury spread through his body like liquid fire. The dirty bastard was raping Caz. His mind whips back to the night when that poor girl had laid there, shocked and terrified. Luke hadn't helped her. He was too scared, too pissed, too confused. But tonight he was none of those things.

Luke pulls back his leg and kicks the man in stomach. 'You fucker.'

The man shrieks and pulls himself into a ball.

Caz yanks down her skirt. 'What are you doing, Luke?'

Luke looks at his friend, so tiny and thin, and pulls back his leg. This time he aims at the man's head and feels the soft thud of his trainer as his foot connects.

'Stop it,' screams Caz.

'I'm going to kill him,' says Luke, and at that moment he means it.

'Don't be stupid,' she says.

'He's a rapist,' says Luke, and steadies himself to take another shot at the man, who is moaning softly. 'It's what they all deserve.'

'Oh, Luke,' she says, her eyes gleaming with tears. 'He wasn't raping me.'

'What?'

She looks down at the man, blood pouring from a gash above his eye. 'Come on, we have to get out of here.'

The familiar smell of Chanel No. 5 filled the air.

'Thanks for coming over,' said Lilly. 'You look fantastic.'

Sheba wrinkled her nose. 'I look fat.'

Admittedly Lilly's friend was heavier than the last time they'd met during a case at the Old Bailey, but she still retained her old-school glamour.

'How many months?' asked Lilly.

Sheba traced a ruby nail across her bump. 'Five.'

'It suits you.'

'No, darling, six-inch heels suit me, but it's kind of you to say.'

Lilly proffered the bottle of wine. 'A splash to be sociable?'

Sheba sighed. 'I suppose that's all right.' She picked up her half-empty glass and eyed it with suspicion and irritation. 'Six units a week and no fags at all, not really me, is it?'

Lilly laughed. She had to admit that it was strange not to see Sheba attached to a double gin and tonic and a Marlboro Light.

'Physician heal thyself.' Sheba swallowed the wine in one gulp. 'So what's this all about, Lilly?'

'I have a case.'

'Of course you do.'

Lilly sipped her own wine. 'A girl, an asylum seeker. She's been charged with conspiracy to murder.'

Sheba threw up her hands. 'Not the shooting at the boarding school?'

Lilly nodded.

'I've seen it all over the telly.' Sheba wagged her finger. 'You're going to be famous. Again.'

'They don't know her name or who's representing her.'

'Yet.'

Lilly winced.

'Hold on,' said Sheba. 'I thought you were steering clear of these cases? That you'd sold your soul for a new car and a set of fish knives.'

'I did, I have.' Lilly laughed. 'This one kind of fell in my lap.'

Sheba filled her glass from the tap. 'Snowflakes fall in your lap, Lilly, or apples at a push. Cases have to be accepted, you have to sign on the dotted line.'

She took a sip and seemed so disgusted by the water that she filled Lilly's glass with more wine. 'One of us may as well enjoy it.'

'The thing is,' said Lilly, 'I felt duty bound.'

'Are you sure you're not Jewish?'

'Catholic.'

'I rest my case,' said Sheba. 'Next you'll be telling me you're adopting this kid.'

Lilly looked up at the ceiling to the room above, where Anna was sleeping.

'You're not serious,' said Sheba.

'It's not for long.'

Sheba sloshed more wine into Lilly's glass. 'How *do* you do it?'

'It's a knack,' said Lilly. 'Like crashing cars and forgetting your tax returns. Not everyone is good at it, you know.'

'So what do you need?'

'Help.'

'No shit.'

'Professional help.'

Sheba nodded and pulled out her attaché case. Inside were reams of cream paper, held together with a paperclip. She laid out a sheet and smoothed it with her hand. The top right-hand corner was embossed with her initials.

Lilly scrabbled for a brown envelope and a biro.

'My client, Anna, came here from Kosovo. I won't tell you the whole story, but suffice it to say she lost her family and was smuggled to England.'

Sheba said nothing, her face impassive. Both she and Lilly had seen and heard a lot about human suffering in their careers.

'She took up with another refugee, a lad, and by all accounts he was pretty unbalanced,' Lilly continued. 'He was the shooter.'

'And where did Anna come in?'

'That I don't know. She had a gun but was quickly disarmed. She seems utterly traumatised by everything that's happened to her and terrified of the shooter. I can't be sure she had any real understanding of the situation.'

Sheba put down her pen. 'You think she lacked the mental capacity?'

'I think she may have acted without question.'

'That would be very hard to prove,' said Sheba. 'Crap things happen to a lot of clients, but that doesn't excuse murder.'

'But this is more than the usual horror story: this was a war.'

'It could be Post Traumatic Stress Disorder,' said Sheba. 'You'll need an expert.'

'Why do you think I asked you over? Your scintillating conversation?'

Sheba stuck out her tongue and wrote down a number. 'Give this woman a call. She specialises in this sort of thing.'

'Will she know where I'm coming from?'

Sheba emptied the rest of the bottle into Lilly's glass. 'She's a Kurd. She lost her husband in Iraq.'

Chapter Eight

Lilly swallowed three aspirins and pushed her hair off her face. Her hand felt clammy.

Sam scowled at his toast. 'I want some bacon.'

Lilly felt her stomach lurch. 'How about cornflakes?'

'I need protein,' he said. 'We've been doing it at school. It's what makes us grow.'

Lilly lowered herself into the chair next to Anna.

'William Mann is four inches taller than me,' said Sam, 'and his mum makes him bacon every day. And eggs.'

'William's dad is six foot two,' said Lilly.

'He probably had a cooked breakfast each morning.'

Lilly sighed and moved last night's empty bottle. The smell was enough to make her retch.

'Are you okay, Lilly?' asked Anna.

She wasn't about to admit she'd polished off nearly an entire bottle of wine on an empty stomach. 'I feel a bit off colour,' she said. 'Maybe it was something I ate.'

'Maybe you are pregnant,' said Anna.

Lilly was too shocked to speak.

'When women are sick in the morning they often have a baby,' said Anna. 'I saw it many times with my mother.'

'I'm not pregnant.' She turned to Sam, whose eyes were wide with alarm. 'I'm definitely not pregnant.'

Sam began to cry.

Lilly put her head on the table. 'Jesus.'

Anna put her hand on Sam's shoulder.

'Don't touch me,' he wailed.

Lilly held out a reassuring hand. 'I know this is tough, big man.'

'I don't want her here,' Sam wailed.

If Lilly's head were not pounding enough, her son's anguish was the tipping point. Why had she ever agreed to have Anna here?

Anna looked at Sam, nodded, and got to her feet.

Lilly caught her breath. If Anna walked out, she'd be in breach of her bail conditions and they'd both be up shit creek without a paddle.

'Anna, please don't leave.' Lilly turned to Sam. 'We can make this work, love.'

'I am not going to leave,' said Anna. 'I make the bacon for Sam.'

Sam wiped at his tears and watched Anna pull a plastic pack out of the fridge.

'Two pieces?' Anna asked.

'Yes please,' he whispered.

'How about you, Lilly?'

Lilly took one look at the raw rashers, the pink porkness of it all, and ran from the room.

*   *   *

Lilly wiped the sweat from her face into her hair. Not a good look. Her mouth still tasted of acid bile. She decided to have a lie down.

'You haven't forgotten, have you, Mum?'

Sam stood at the foot of her bed, his mouth greasy from his breakfast.

'I haven't forgotten your bad manners, young man,' she said.

He rolled his eyes. 'I meant the service.' He gestured to her dressing gown, the belt lost years ago and replaced by an old school tie of David's. 'You can't go like that.'

The school service for Charlie Stanton.

'It wouldn't be appropriate for me to go,' said Lilly.

Sam threw his arms around him like a windmill. Even watching made Lilly dizzy.

'But everyone's going. I can't be the only one whose mum's not there.'

'What about your dad?' asked Lilly.

'He's got to work.'

'So have I,' said Lilly.

'Cara's going to be there.' He turned to leave. 'She said you wouldn't go.'

Lilly's spine straightened at the thought of Botox Belle, the most upright she'd been all morning. 'I'll see you at eleven.'

This 40 message thread spans 10 pages
[1] [2] [3] [4] [5] [6] [7] [8] [9] [10] >>

<u>Wake Up and Smell the Coffee</u> Little Lamb at 5.30
I am so excited I can't sleep.

The shooting at Manor Park must finally alert the people of Britain to what these foreigners are really like.

Every paper and TV station is covering it!

Wake Up and Smell the Coffee Blood River at 5.50
I know exactly what you mean, Little Lamb.

The great Enoch Powell predicted this so long ago but the public wouldn't listen.

Wake Up and Smell the Coffee Fire Starter at 6.10
They were too busy listening to Red Ken and the rest of the liberal middle-class elite.

Wake Up and Smell the Coffee Blood River at 6.21
But now the immigrants have taken the struggle to them and bitten them right where it hurts, they can't ignore this problem any longer.

The leftist press, usually so determined to pretend that multicultural Britain is working just fine, has been forced to recognise that these interlopers are not just a threat to our culture but our safety as a nation.

Wake Up and Smell the Coffee Saxon King at 6.25
But we can't just sit and gloat or that poor kid will have died in vain.

We must keep the pressure on.

Wake Up and Smell the Coffee Little Lamb at 6.36
Agreed.

<u>Wake Up and Smell the Coffee</u> Blood River at 6.40
Agreed.

<u>Wake Up and Smell the Coffee</u> Fire Starter at 6.42
Agreed.

Snow White didn't have time to read the other posts but
was sure each one would pledge support. Their time had
come and each must play their part.

She clucked at the kitchen. The girls had left their
oily plates and discarded sausages on any available
surface. Grandpa had never allowed her to leave the
house until all was shipshape. He would have beaten her
for this unholy mess.

She would have a word with the girls when they
returned tonight. School discipline would sort them
out, as it had their elder brother, but in the meantime
it fell to Snow White to whip them into shape. Their
father was a good man but was far too soft when it
came to children. They would whinge and whine
and call her a nag, but they needed to learn about
responsibility.

As she wiped a cloth through a smear of ketchup she
turned her mind to her own responsibility to the
Stantons, and the cause. She held up her chin. She had
a duty to her town and country.

'You're a good man, Jack McNally,' said Lilly.

'I know.'

'A saint.'

'I know.'

Lilly rubbed a tea towel over her stiletto-heeled boots. 'Like Mother Teresa but without the headscarf.'

'Yep.'

'Or Padre Pio, without the bleeding hands.'

She was making light of the situation but knew he was placing his job on the line to help her. Sometimes she wondered how far she would be prepared to push him.

'You're a martyr,' she said.

'It's nice of you to say, but I'm still puzzled,' he pointed to her footless fishnet stockings, 'as to where you left the other half of your tights.'

Lilly wiggled her toes. 'I got them for a sixties party.'

'But you're going to a funeral.'

'Prayer service,' she corrected. 'And they're the only ones clean.' She pulled on her boots. 'Besides, you can't see my feet in these.' She zipped them up to her knees and smoothed down her skirt. Only a flash of fishnet showed in the split. 'Whaddya think?'

Jack whistled. 'I think you should skip the sermon.'

'Easy, tiger, you're here to babysit.'

Jack sighed and followed Lilly to the door. 'Is she upstairs?'

'Hardly comes down.' She kissed him on the cheek. 'But if she does I'm reliably informed she makes a mean eggs and bacon.'

She jumped in the car, started the car engine and wound down the window. Jack was inspecting the door frame.

'This seems better,' he said.

Lilly swallowed a sudden feeling of guilt. 'I think it's dried out.'

Jack frowned at the rain that had been pouring all night and showed no sign of stopping anytime soon.

Lilly was never on time. Her mum always said she'd be late for her own funeral. Well, not this one. She pulled into Manor Park with fifteen minutes to spare.

Her pulse fluttered as she passed the cameras and microphones at the gate but she reminded herself that they had no idea who she was. There was absolutely no need to panic. She would glide into the school.

'Fuck a duck,' she yelled. The place was already mobbed with cars parked right down the drive. There were so many 4 × 4s it was like an off-road rally.

She drove round the buildings, determined to find a place nearer to the chapel. For one it was still peeing it down, and for another she could barely walk in her heels.

On her second tour she spotted someone pulling out. 'Oh, baby, come to Mama.'

She pulled onto the gravel, ignoring the 'Teachers Only' sign. Surely today was an exception.

She hadn't even got out when the Amazonian figure of Mrs Baraclough loomed over the windscreen. 'You can't park here, Mrs Valentine.'

Lilly peered up at the headmaster's secretary, who seemed even taller and wider than usual in her grey suit. Why did the woman insist on calling her 'Mrs'? She knew full well she and David were no longer married.

'There's nowhere else,' she said.

'Back field has been designated for parents,' said Mrs Baraclough. 'All the way down to the ha-ha.'

Lilly imagined what a quagmire it would be on the

pitches stretching all the way down to the dip that had once kept wild animals out of the mansion house gardens.

'But I'll be late if I go back down there now.'

Mrs Baraclough raised one eyebrow and Lilly knew it was pointless to argue. She gunned the engine and pulled out, with the gargantuan woman's voice ringing behind her: 'The speed limit on school grounds is fifteen miles per hour.'

Lilly circled the drive, waited for Mrs Baraclough to go back inside and took back her place in exactly the same spot. She jumped out of the car. It was less than five hundred yards to the chapel. If she ran she would be bang on time.

With her head held high she strode off: 'Who pays the fees round here?'

With less than ten feet to solid ground, her heart sank as the grass gave way to something softer. Her feet sank low in the sludge, her heels making a gassy slurp with each step. She tried walking on her tiptoes but fell forward, only her hands stopping her from falling headfirst into the mud.

'There is no such thing as God,' she said out loud. 'And don't let anyone tell you otherwise.'

She heard tutting from behind and saw the chaplain and his wife huddled under their umbrella. They glared at her before passing.

At last she reached the school, her boots brown to the ankle, her hands desperately in need of a wash. She headed for the loos, but halfway down the corridor collided with Mrs Baraclough.

'You're late, Mrs Valentine,' she said.

'I need to . . .'

'No time for that.' Mrs Baraclough spun Lilly around and guided her into the chapel.

There was nothing else for it. When she thought no one was looking, Lilly opened her jacket and wiped her hands on the lining.

Alexia hung up her coat. A MaxMara wraparound she had got her father to pay for at London Fashion Week two years ago. It was soft and stylish, yet it felt dated. She'd never before had to wear anything for more than a season.

What she needed was something timeless. Dior or Yves Saint Laurent. She knew she need only pick up the phone and he'd have something sent over, but what would that achieve? All this hard work, this denial, this *poverty*, would be for nothing. He'd smile in that condescending way of his and congratulate himself that, once again, he'd been right all along.

Alexia couldn't bear to give him the satisfaction. She'd come this far and she'd stick it out. She'd prove to him that he was wrong about her.

She turned away from the coat and logged on. She'd spent hours in the racist chat rooms, ploughing through the vitriol to find any mention of the girl's whereabouts. There was a lot of speculation, some less sanguine than others, but no one seemed to know for sure.

She went into her 'favourites' and clicked on *The Spear of Truth*. How on earth had that become one of her most used websites? She didn't consider herself a left-wing person or anything – God, all that politically correct stuff got right up her nose – but she knew enough black people to know these Internet nutters were spouting a load of rubbish. She had shared a room in school with a girl from Saudi Arabia and was damned sure her parents weren't on benefits.

'What's happening, Posh?'

Alexia sighed and wandered over to Steve's office. Another day of his carping might drive her over the edge.

He sat on the edge of his desk and struck a match. Alexia pointed to the 'No Smoking' sign on the wall. 'Does the ban mean nothing to you?'

Steve blew a perfect ring that floated to meet the sign. 'It only applies to public buildings,' he said.

'And places of work.'

Steve took a deep drag. 'This is my home.'

Alexia looked around at the peeling woodchip, the framed clippings on the wall, a Kylie calendar stuck permanently open on May 2002.

'You do not live here,' she said.

'Tell my wife that.'

'I'll sue you if I get cancer.'

He dug into his pocket and slammed a fistful of change on the desk. 'Take it in advance.'

Alexia shook her head and headed back to her computer.

'Got anything for me?' Steve called after her.

She ignored him and went into the site. The forums were frenzied with hysterical predictions for an all-out race war. She scrolled down the page, hoping to find something – anything.

<u>Wake Up and Smell the Coffee</u> Snow White at 9.55
I truly believe that every one of us has a part to play in the bringing about of change to this great nation. We will all be called upon to fight, each in our own way.
   Today I am going to a memorial for the poor child whose death brought about this momentous battle, and I ask you all to offer your prayers.

'There's a service,' said Alexia. 'For the boy.'

'I've seen it on the telly,' he said. 'It's locked up tighter than Broadmoor.'

'That's why I'm not there.'

Steve ran his nicotine-stained fingers through his hair. 'I had thought you could get in this place?'

'In the dead of night, maybe,' Alexia rolled her eyes.

'If it were me,' Steve bared his yellow teeth. 'I'd at least give it a fucking try.'

Lilly looked up at the super-sized picture of the dead boy that hung from the rafters. Such a handsome boy. Such a waste. His mother sat on the first row, flanked by Luella, head to toe in black. She turned and glared at Lilly.

Mrs Stanton gazed into the middle distance, her face a portrait of anguish. That's how I would look if it were Sam, thought Lilly.

Charles's house master, a wiry man who Lilly had always suspected to be gay, spoke at length. 'We shall all remember him as a fine boy who gave of his best,' he said. 'A boy of whom this school and his family were rightly proud.'

He droned on and Lilly tried not to watch as his mother swiped at her cheeks with the back of her hand.

'I could think of a hundred things to say about him,' said the house master. 'But I think it better if I leave that to his best friend.'

He put out his hand and beckoned a boy to the stage. He was one of the boarders Lilly had seen at the shooting. He was smart in his house tie, and the lapel of his blazer gleamed with honours for football, rugby, swimming and athletics. His carrot coloured hair was smoothed against his skull, as befitted the occasion, yet he still walked with an undeniable swagger.

'I'm sure every teacher at Manor Park will tell you that Stanton was a fine pupil.' The boy's voice boomed with a clarity that belied his age. 'But I want to tell you about the real Charlie, a fantastic mate and a top man. The sort you could rely on, the sort who'd stand by you.'

He looked at the giant picture behind him and smiled. 'He was one of the lads to the end – and in an age where people change their opinions as often as their socks, his steadfastness is to be celebrated.'

Lilly stretched out her feet under the pew in front, her heels following the grooves in the oak-panelled floor. The boy clearly loved an audience and Lilly's backside was getting numb.

'And those who came here and snuffed out Charlie's

life probably thought he deserved it,' he gazed across the congregation. 'That he was just another posh kid with no idea about the world. But I can tell you, and them, that he knew perfectly well about what mattered in this world.'

He paused, holding every eye upon him.

'Because, ladies and gentlemen, Charlie Stanton had integrity.'

When the organist struck up the chords to the final hymn, Lilly sighed with relief. She was desperate to stretch her legs.

Everyone stood. Everyone except Lilly.

Her left heel was caught between two boards. She tugged at her foot but it was caught fast. She tried to reach underneath the row in front to release it but, short of crawling on her knees, she couldn't reach. When the man next to her glared she pulled herself upright, her right leg bent, her left still stretched in front of her.

'Amazing Grace, how sweet the sound,' Lilly warbled as she tried to balance.

At last, when she could hold her pose no longer, she gave a frantic pull that sent her prayer book into the air. Her foot came free, but only after she heard the snap of her heel.

The headmaster thanked everyone for coming and released the pupils back to class. The parents would be offered refreshments in the Great Hall. Lilly decided to wait until everyone left before hobbling back to her car. Marilyn Monroe had famously shaved off half an inch from one heel to achieve her famous wiggle, but Lilly was not a fifties film star and this was not half an inch.

Under cover of her bag and the pew in front, she eased off her boot to assess the damage. Too late did she notice Luella moving towards her.

'Is it true?' Her voice was shrill. She shrugged off the arm of another mother. 'I just want to know if what they are saying is true.'

Lilly felt all eyes upon her. 'That depends on what they're saying, Luella.'

'That you're representing the girl who murdered Charlie.'

Lilly took a deep breath. How the hell had Luella found out? 'I don't think this is the place.'

Luella snorted, her nostrils wide like a horse's. 'Tell that to Maddy, here.' She pulled the dead boy's mother from her seat. Her eyes were lifeless. 'Explain to her why her boy was killed.'

'I'm afraid I can't do that.'

Spit flew from Luella's mouth. 'But you can defend the monster who did it?'

'I really think we should all calm down,' said Lilly. 'After all, this is our children's school.'

'A place where they're no longer safe. Thanks to your client and people like her.'

'My work,' said Lilly, 'is a private matter that doesn't concern anyone else.'

'You're quite wrong. Charlie was one of our own, and this is a matter that is important to us all.' Luella drew a circle with her arm. 'Every single one of us.'

There were murmurs of assent.

Luella raised her chin. 'This isn't a time to sit on the fence. Charlie is dead and his friends are scarred for life.

Did you know Luke Walker hasn't been back to school because he's so disturbed?'

Lilly could say nothing in response. It stood to reason that some of the boys would be traumatised, but that was Artan's fault, not Anna's.

'We all need to decide where our loyalties lie,' Luella continued. 'And you have made it very plain where you stand.'

Her eyes challenged Lilly, willing her to dispute her case. 'I think you should leave,' she said.

With the eyes of the entire congregation on her, Lilly moved along the aisle and stood in front of her tormentor. Luella looked her up and down. Lilly's jacket had fallen open and revealed the thick smears of dried mud. A few flakes fell onto the bare toes of her left foot. The other boot, now two-toned, pushed her hip into an almost comical gait.

'Lilly Valentine, is this a joke?'

'I can't see anyone laughing.'

'Do you know the meaning of the word respect?'

'Yes, but if you're not sure I'll lend you a dictionary.'

Lilly heard Luella's slap before she felt it. The stinging crack of flesh on flesh. She put her hand to her cheek, heat burning her fingers.

Lilly turned to Charlie's mother. Her face was as white and dry as paper. 'I can't begin to imagine how you must feel,' she said. 'Please believe me when I say I meant no disrespect to you or your son by coming here today.'

Then she stalked out of the chapel with as much

dignity as she could muster, considering she was wearing one three-inch heel and a pair of footless fishnets.

Luke breathes hard through his nose, trying to quell the nausea that has gripped him for almost an hour. He tries to think of babbling brooks and lambs gambolling in fields, but to no avail. He bends from the waist and heaves, the contents of his stomach rushing to meet his mouth.

He's already purged himself of the cider he necked last night and all that is left is an empty pulling that hurts his muscles and brings tears to his eyes.

'You all right?' says Caz.

He wipes his mouth with the back of his hand. 'Do I look all right to you?'

She makes a small noise somewhere between a cluck and a tut and rubs his back. He shrugs her away.

He doesn't know what has made him so sick. Maybe the drink, though he's had plenty at parties before. Maybe the adrenalin from kicking that piece of shit, though he's had fights before. Or maybe it's the thought of Caz with her knickers round her ankles.

He groans and retches again.

'You need something to eat,' she says.

'Fuck off.'

'A bacon sarnie with plenty of sauce.'

He turns to Caz and shouts: 'I said, fuck off.'

She looks into the middle distance and sniffs like a sulky child.

'You don't get it, do you?' He shakes his head. 'You think it doesn't matter, that nothing matters.'

'I know what really matters, soft lad. Making money, staying alive, that's what really matters.'

'There are better ways than that,' he says.

She snorts through her nose. 'How about I walk into that shop over there and ask for a job?'

'What about begging? We make money that way.'

'It takes fucking hours to get a few quid, and when it rains we make nothing at all. I can make a ton in half the time and it keeps us going for a couple of days.'

Luke can't accept that it's the only way. He remembers the fat old man with his dick hanging out of his trousers. The filthy moans he made in the shadows.

If Caz is prepared to go with someone like that she must be the lowest of the low.

'What you did, what you do, it disgusts me.'

She eyes him coolly. 'Is that right?'

'It makes me sick.' He nods to the pool of bile at his feet. 'You make me sick.'

For the first time since he met Caz, she looks at him like he is a stranger. She opens her mouth to speak, but changes her mind. Instead she pulls the hood of her parka over her head and walks away.

Luke watches her tiny figure and is overcome by sadness. Caz has been his eyes and ears since he arrived. Without knowing anything about him she took it upon herself to watch out for him, and when she found out he was on the run it didn't matter. She stood by him.

When he told her what he'd done, what sort of scum he really is, she didn't turn on him.

It was never like this with Charlie and Tom. He's never had a friend like Caz and he's certain he never will again.

'Caz!' He legs it after her. 'Wait.'

She must have heard him but she doesn't stop.

'I'm sorry,' he calls out. 'I've been an arsehole.'

She stops but doesn't turn around.

'A total arsehole,' he continues. 'The biggest arsehole that ever lived.'

She swivels on her heel to face him, her hand on her hip, one eyebrow cocked.

'There never was a bigger arsehole in the history of the world,' he says.

She's trying to keep a straight face but he can see she's chewing her cheek.

'Or the history of the universe,' he says.

At last she laughs and Luke feels the weight of the world lift. He puts down his rucksack and leans his head on her shoulder.

'Fucking hell,' she says. 'You really stink of sick.'

Chapter Nine

Dr Leyla Kadir washed her hands at the sink in the corner of the consultation room, her slim brown fingers sliding through the water. She dried them carefully on a paper towel and covered them in hand lotion. Her precise movements creamed the area between each finger.

Her cream trouser suit was simple yet elegant against the bronze of her skin. When she sat down she slid open the jacket button so that its tailored lines remained unwrinkled.

She wasn't what Lilly had expected. But then how had she pictured a psychiatrist from Kurdistan? A full veil with a copy of Freud under her arm?

'Thank you for seeing me, Dr Kadir,' she said.

'Thank you for coming.' She motioned Lilly to sit in the chair at the other side of her desk, which was empty apart from a snow globe. Inside the glass dome a fairy cast its wintry spell. 'Where is the child?'

Lilly nodded towards the reception area outside, where Anna was flicking through a copy of *Grazia* magazine. Lilly wondered how much of it her client could understand, and whether the tribulations of a reality star's boob job held much fascination to a girl who had seen her family burnt alive.

The doctor pushed highlighted hair behind her ears. 'So?'

'It's difficult to know where to start,' said Lilly.

'At the beginning usually works well.'

Okay, smart arse, thought Lilly. 'My client is from Kosovo.'

'Yes.'

'She came here seeking asylum.'

'Yes.'

'And she's been accused of conspiracy to murder.'

Dr Kadir tapped her finger against her desk. 'I have read the papers you sent over, Miss Valentine.'

So not the beginning then. 'I was wondering if my client could be suffering from Post Traumatic Stress Disorder.'

'Naturally, I will need to assess her to make a diagnosis.'

Lilly's hackles began to rise. 'Naturally. But before I commit my client to that process, I wanted to know if this was a likely scenario or if I'm whistling in the wind.'

Dr Kadir wrinkled her nose. 'Guesswork is not how I do things, Miss Valentine. I'm a psychiatrist, not an NHS helpline.'

Lilly sat forward in her chair. She'd dealt with enough shrinks to know what she could and couldn't ask them to do. 'Listen, Doctor, I'm not asking for anything definite, just some theoretical discussion.'

The doctor opened her mouth to speak, but Lilly put up her hand. 'You know full well that the taxpayer will only give me one shot at a psych report, so I can't spend my money in the wrong shop.' Lilly waved at the door. 'I've a kid out there staring down the barrel of a life sentence, so I cannot piss about.'

Dr Kadir ran her finger over her snow globe. 'Okay then.'

Lilly sat back in her chair. 'Okay then.'

'Put simply, PTSD is a brain injury caused by a traumatic incident.'

'Such as?' said Lilly.

Dr Kadir opened her arms. 'An accident, a violent attack, a disaster of some sort.'

'A genocide?'

'Almost certainly.'

'And this disorder affects people how?' asked Lilly.

'There are many symptoms.' The doctor reached for a book from her shelves. 'This is the leading research study of victims from the Gulf War, which showed that veterans suffered in hundreds of different ways.' She ran her finger along a list that filled a whole page. 'Nightmares, flashbacks, depression, headaches, panic attacks.'

'Anna couldn't breathe at the police station,' said Lilly. 'The police doctor thought it might be a panic attack.'

Dr Kadir continued with her list. 'Chest pains, insomnia, detachment.'

'Detachment?' Lilly felt her heart leap. 'Tell me about that.'

'Patients are often overwhelmed by the symptoms

of Post Traumatic Stress Disorder, so they suppress their feelings about the trigger. They avoid all conversations about it, all contact with anything that may be a cue.'

'Does it work?' asked Lilly.

Dr Kadir gave a wry laugh. 'Of course not. They simply become detached from normality.'

'Delusional?'

'No. They become numb both physically and mentally,' said Dr Kadir. 'Many describe living as if on autopilot.'

'Anna says she has no idea why she went to the school with a gun,' said Lilly. 'I think most people will find that very hard to believe.'

Dr Kadir smiled. 'Most people don't understand PTSD.'

'Posh,' snarled Steve, 'this is genius.'

Alexia leaned back in her chair, hands behind her head, while Steve read the transcript she'd handed to him. 'Exclusive access to the service,' she said. 'I recorded the whole thing.'

Steve let out a cackle that would have frightened Lady Macbeth.

'Never mind the fucking prayers, what about the fight?'

Alexia couldn't resist a smile. That had been the proverbial icing on the cake.

When she arrived at Manor Park she'd assumed police would be patrolling the perimeter, but as the parents arrived, the other journos swarmed in with their microphones and flashbulbs – consequently the police's job was to surround the parents as best they could. It was an unedifying sight but it left Alexia's secret entrance entirely unguarded. As she slipped through, she was sure she would be spotted but the weather was foul and the parents dashed from their cars to the school.

All was nearly lost when an officious-looking woman demanded her invitation but then her attention was drawn to someone parking a Mini in the wrong place. Alexia had seized her opportunity and dived into the back row. When the head had announced refreshments she intended to leg it back to the car before anyone could ask awkward questions – but then the entertainment really started. One of the inmates from Camp Boden had accosted some woman about what she was wearing. To be fair, footless tights *were* a bold move best left to the fashionistas on Bond Street. Then, bosh, she smacked her so hard it echoed around the chapel.

A ladette with ten Bacardi Breezers inside her couldn't have done better.

Though it made for great copy, it had all seemed a bit of an overreaction to Alexia, but she recalled that her father had once fired someone for wearing the wrong coloured socks.

She finished the piece and mailed it to Steve. While the big boys were scrabbling around printing pictures of cars pulling into the school and conjectured pieces about what may or may not have been said, Alexia's story was the real deal. She could quote what was said about Charles Stanton in full tearjerking glory. And the cherry on top was the argument among the parents. Within seconds her inbox was alive.

To: Alexia Dee
From: Steve Berry
Subject: Not bad
Shame you didn't get a picture.

* * *

Lilly sang along to the radio all the way home. The drivetime chart music suited her mood. She had the beginnings of a defence, just a seed, but with Dr Kadir's help it had begun to germinate.

She reached into her bag and found half a tube of Rolos. Life was sweet.

When the front door glided open as if on wheels, she kissed its wooden frame.

'I thought I was the crazy one,' said Anna, and they both laughed.

'I can't see anything funny.'

Sam stood in the doorway, his hands on his hips, his beautiful face pressed into a scowl.

Anna evaporated up the stairs.

'Hello, big man,' said Lilly. 'Do you fancy making a cake?'

Sam narrowed his eyes.

'I've tons of chocolate.' She headed for the kitchen. 'Or carrot. That's a healthy option for my favourite footballer.'

She heard his heavy footfall follow her. Baking was definitely not high on his agenda.

'Everyone at school says you made a total show of yourself at the service.'

Lilly reached into the cupboard for flour. 'I'm in the mood for muffins.'

'The boarders called you a laughing stock.'

Lilly sighed and began to weigh the ingredients. 'Why don't you get the eggs?'

'Cara says you weren't even wearing shoes.'

Lilly pushed her hair out of her eyes, leaving a white powdery patch across her forehead. Why didn't the bitch from hell mind her own business? Jesus, Lilly hadn't even seen Botox Belle at the service.

'The heel snapped off my boot. Not the end of the world.'

Sam shook his head in utter disgust. 'Why does everything you do get so difficult?'

'Because there's only one of me, Sam.'

Luke shakes the shoe box and mentally counts the change. Just over eight quid, not bad.

Caz says the punters feel sorry for him, with his big eyes and floppy hair. Like he's someone nice who's just hit hard times. They don't even look at Caz. She says it's because she looks like this is the life she deserves. Luke thinks it might have something to do with the stuff she shouts at them.

His mum always insists on finding educational value in everything, and he wonders what she'd make of his newfound talent. Five games of Sonic the Hedgehog was proclaimed 'good for fine motor skills'. An hour reading the Arsenal programme was an 'excellent practice of foreign pronunciation'. What would she make of blagging money from total strangers? 'Ah, Luke, begging is just a form of advocacy. A great start for a budding lawyer or politician.'

His laughter gives way to a stab of guilt as he thinks of his mother worrying about her only son's whereabouts. Does she spend each night crying and ringing round the hospitals?

Though surely everything's come out about the girl in the park by now? She'll be glad he's disappeared. Francesca Walker cares what people think. She'd be mortified if Luke was on the telly or in the papers. And he certainly would be if the police caught him.

At first he'd been convinced they'd be searching for him and that every officer would have his old school photo tucked in their pocket. Now he realises the authorities don't give a shit about kids like him and Caz. There are hundreds like them on the streets, living in derelict houses, dossing in tube stations. The police don't even pull them in for begging. They might ask a few questions, but usually they just tell them to move on.

'But don't rely on it,' says Caz. 'You might get one with a cob on, like he's just caught his missus having it away with the next-door neighbour's dog. You might get away with a kicking . . . or worse, you might get nicked.'

Caz's instructions in the face of the latter are clear: 'Run like fuck.' She prides herself on seeing the inside of a cell only twice. On both occasions she convinced the coppers she was eighteen. Whether they believed her or whether they didn't care is unimportant. She got bail and they got rid.

Luke slides the coins into his rucksack and tosses the box into the gutter. A woman passing by with a toddler on reins tuts her disapproval. Luke gives her the finger and heads off to find Caz.

She pockets her share. 'Ta very much.'

'You're welcome,' says Luke, an automatic response that still makes Caz laugh. He always hands over half of whatever he gets, even though she doesn't reciprocate. She says she will but then she blows it all on smack. She's doing more and more and it doesn't come cheap. He doesn't care. He'd give her everything he owns to stop her doing the other thing.

They're off to the Peckham Project for a shower and some toast. To be honest, Luke can't be arsed going over there.

'It's part of my routine,' says Caz, as if her life runs on an orderly timetable.

Luke tells her that he likes the seamlessness of their days.

'Well, it's a bleeding holiday for you, soft lad,' she says. 'When your whole life's been nothing but a fuck-up, you start to fancy a bit of order.'

She's probably right.

On the wall outside the Project two men are playing cards. With their dark hair and leather jackets Luke can see at a glance they're Eastern European. They look up at Caz and stare.

'Problem?' asks Luke.

'Nah,' says Caz, but the breeziness has gone out of her voice.

'Caroline,' says one of the men, his words sing-song, his accent rolling the 'r'.

She ignores him and pushes the buzzer.

'Don't be like that,' he says. 'We just want to be friends.'

The other man laughs and shuffles the pack.

Caz keeps her finger on the buzzer. 'I know exactly what you want.'

At last Jean opens the door and Caz pushes past her to get inside.

'What the hell's going on?' she says, her usual fag dangling from the corner of her mouth.

Luke shrugs his shoulders but Jean's seen the men outside.

'Get out of here right now,' she shouts.

'Sorry,' says one. 'I don't speak English.'

Jean comes outside, her hands on her hips. 'Make yourself scarce or I'll call the police.'

The men speak in their own language and laugh.

'You've got five seconds,' she says.

One walks towards them and there's something in his manner, the way he holds his shoulders, that scares Luke.

'We don't break any laws,' says the man.

Jean stands firm. 'Go inside, Luke, and dial 999.'

Luke's heart is pounding in his chest and he can't move.

The man takes a step closer so he's almost touching Jean. A plume of smoke separates them.

'Tell them to send squad cars,' she says, 'and the immigration unit.'

The man kisses his teeth in Jean's face but she doesn't

157

flinch. At last he turns back to his friend and once again they laugh. They collect up their cards and head back towards the high street. Luke realises he's been holding his breath.

'Are you okay, love?' says Jean.

Luke nods. 'Are you?'

She laughs and ruffles his hair. 'It'd take more than that pair to bother me.'

Later that night, Lilly was chasing the last crumbs of a freshly baked muffin around a plate.

Sam sidled into the kitchen. 'Any left for me?'

Lilly said nothing, but opened the cake tin and poured her son a glass of milk.

'Sorry about earlier,' Sam said.

Lilly kissed his cheek.

Sam took a bite. 'I just worry, that's all.'

'About what?'

'You.'

Lilly was astonished. 'Me! But I'm fine.'

Sam wiped the crumbs from his chin. 'Bad stuff always happens to you, Mum.'

'I can't imagine what you mean,' she said.

'Dad left, for a start.'

Lilly exhaled. This was big stuff. 'Your dad and I couldn't live together, Sam – and you're right, it was pretty bad for a while.'

'You mean totally crap,' said Sam.

'Okay, it was indeed totally crap, but things are fine now. We haven't argued for a long time.'

Sam licked the muffin case. 'But what about Jack?'

'We can't see much of him at the moment.'

'And that's because Anna's staying here,' he said.

'It's not for long,' said Lilly.

'But why does she have to be here at all?' he asked.

Lilly enveloped her son in her arms. 'I know it's hard, but she'll be gone soon and then things can go back to normal.'

'Oh, Mum, when are things in this house ever normal?'

Lilly kissed the top of his head and breathed him in. 'Anna isn't as lucky as we are, Sam, and that's something we should never forget.'

He nodded and tucked his forehead into the crook of her neck.

She rocked him in her arms, humming gently, until the peace was shattered along with the window as a stone came flying through.

Chapter Ten

'That so needs fixing before the rain gets in,' said Sam.

Lilly hoisted up her skirt and climbed onto the kitchen worktop. 'Thanks, Einstein. I see my school fees aren't wasted.'

'I thought Dad paid them,' said Sam.

Lilly shot him a warning glance.

'Is there any chance you could help?' she asked, tottering precariously on the window sill.

'Don't get cross with me,' he said. 'I didn't break the bloody window.'

'Swearing is neither big nor clever, Sam.'

She ripped off a strip of tin foil and tried to stick it across the hole with masking tape. A gust of wind blew it back at her.

'Fuck a duck,' she shouted.

Sam went to find his school bag, whistling.

Anna floated into the room, her eyes as dark as her skin was white. 'You need to have this fixed, yes?'

Lilly tore off a second piece of foil and tried to push it into place. 'Another genius.'

'You are very grumpy this morning,' said Anna.

160

'In the face of this sort of mayhem I think I'm showing the patience of a saint.'

As the foil once again drifted back into the kitchen, Lilly gritted her teeth and pushed hard. Too hard. She felt the sharp, hot sting as a shard of glass cut into her hand.

'Problem?' asked Anna.

Lilly sucked the blood that was spilling down her wrist and prayed she wouldn't need a stitch. Frankly, she didn't have the time.

'Everything okay?'

Penny had arrived to take Sam to school.

'Oh, you know, smashed windows, lacerated fingers,' said Lilly. 'Another day in paradise.'

'You'll need to get it fixed as soon as,' said Penny.

Lilly closed her eyes and counted to ten.

'Mum,' Sam called from another room. 'That bloke from the hostel's here.'

'Jesus Christ,' said Lilly. 'Can a woman not bleed to death in peace?'

Milo walked into the kitchen, a green scarf perfectly picking out the colour of his eyes. Penny's own opened wide. 'And this is . . . ?'

'Milo,' said Lilly. 'He works at the hostel.'

Penny held out her hand. 'I'm Penny.'

Milo shook her hand and offered his most winning smile. 'So nice to meet you, Penny.'

'And you,' Penny breathed.

Lilly, still crouching on the work surface, wrapped her thumb in a tea towel printed with a map of the UK. 'Aren't you going to be late?'

Penny checked her watch and let out a girly squeal. 'Got to run.'

'I hope to see you again,' said Milo, still smiling at Penny.

Lilly sighed as the tinkle of the other woman's laughter followed her out to the car.

Lilly's thumb was throbbing, a red patch seeping across Birmingham. 'So what brings you here? Aside from ogling middle-class do-gooders.'

It was an unfair description of her friend, but Lilly was in no mood to be even-handed.

Milo ignored her and surveyed the window. 'This needs to be fixed.'

'I know,' Lilly roared, and thumped the work surface, causing another round of blood-letting that seeped down past Wolverhampton. 'What do you imagine I'm doing up here? A little light cleaning before breakfast?'

Milo looked bewildered and turned to leave.

'That's right, you bugger off and leave all this to me.' She swept her hand round, sending the stained tea towel flying across the room. 'When you need me to represent your residents, give me a call and I'm sure I'll jump to attention. But when I need a little help, don't worry yourself about it.'

Milo gingerly picked up the makeshift bandage between his thumb and forefinger and handed it back to Lilly. 'I was just going to the car to fetch my tools.'

Lilly held her mobile against her ear with her shoulder, her arms full of files. 'It was just kids.'

'Are you sure?' asked David.

Lilly motioned with her elbow for Anna to hurry up as she stalked towards the office. Her hand was still wrapped in the tea towel and it flapped like a flag.

'Why would they do it?' he asked.

'Who knows, David? It's Hallowe'en soon so maybe it was a prank.'

'A prank?'

'They were probably just messing about.'

She wished Sam hadn't told his dad.

'Smashing people's windows?' he said.

'They probably didn't mean to. Don't you remember what it was like being young?' She laughed. David had been born middle aged. 'Don't answer that.'

'I want to know if it was anything more sinister. The school service has made all the front pages.'

'That's to be expected.'

'The *Three Counties Observer* said there was a show-down between some of the parents.'

'What?'

How the hell had they found out about that?

'They say one mother slapped another in the face,' David continued.

'Do they mention any names?'

'No,' he said.

'There you go then,' Lilly sighed with relief. 'Nothing to do with me.'

'Cara said someone attacked you.'

'Cara exaggerates.' Lilly would kill Botox Belle one of these days. 'Look, I need to get to work.'

Lilly pocketed her mobile and stuck out her chin. A story in the local rag was nothing. Who read that rubbish anyway? And as for the window, it was just like she said. Kids. God, the middle classes had never got up to anything. She remembered her own childhood on St George's Estate. Long evenings spent smoking and flirting, punctuated by setting old tyres alight and rolling them across the waste ground. On one December night when they'd managed to get three, they'd split into teams and had a competition to see whose tyre would get to the disused tracks the quickest. Lilly's team would have won if a boy called Buggy, who'd sniffed far too much glue, hadn't run in front of their tyre thinking it was Santa's sleigh.

She laughed at the thought till she caught sight of Rupes outside in the street. She was looking up, above the door, and Lilly followed her eye-line. In red paint someone had daubed 'Rights for Whites'.

'So what are you gonna do about it?'

Sheila's eyes were wide. She reminded Lilly of Luella and she instinctively took a step back, not keen for another slap.

'I should think the best thing to do is ignore it,' said Lilly, and moved across the reception towards her office.

Sheila barred her way. 'We can't stick our heads in the sand. Things are getting serious.'

'Don't be so bloody melodramatic, Sheila,' said Lilly. She was tired and her hand stung. She knew this was unpleasant for Rupinder but she could well do without Sheila overreacting. 'It's just paint,' she said.

Sheila turned to Rupinder. 'Will you explain to her what's happening here?'

'We don't know for sure,' said Rupinder.

'Don't we?' Sheila replied.

'Know what?' asked Lilly.

Rupinder sighed, the circles round her eyes clearly showing her tiredness.

'We're worried, Lilly.'

'Who is?'

'The other partners,' she said.

'And me, I'm bloody worried,' said Sheila.

Lilly ignored her and looked straight at Rupes. 'And you?'

Rupinder sank into a chair and put her face in her hands. 'I'm worried too.'

Lilly sat next to her boss and put an arm around her shoulder. If Rupinder thought the tea-towel bandage odd, she didn't say so.

'I'm sorry,' said Rupes. 'I know you'll say I should treat it with the contempt it deserves.'

'Absolutely,' said Lilly.

'And I would if it were an isolated incident,' said Rupinder. 'But first there was the letter, and now this. The other partners are saying . . .'

'Saying what?' said Lilly.

Sheila felt no compunction to sugar the pill. 'That we shouldn't be representing *her*.'

'Nobody tells me who I can and cannot help,' said Lilly.

'It's not your bleeding firm,' said Sheila.

'Well, it's certainly not yours,' said Lilly.

Sheila pointed her finger. 'It's all right for you, you're never here, but what about the rest of us? What happens when they start pushing dog shit through the letterbox? Or putting the windows through?'

'What did you say?' shouted Lilly.

The phone rang and Rupinder answered it.

Sheila lowered her voice to a stage whisper. 'I said, we'll be in real trouble if they start smashing the windows.'

Lilly thought of her own home, glass strewn across the kitchen. 'Do you know anything about all this?'

'I beg your pardon?' said Sheila.

'She'll be there,' said Rupinder, and put down the phone.

Sheila turned to their boss. 'Lilly's accusing me of having something to do with this.'

'I didn't say that,' said Lilly. 'But, come to mention it, you've made your feelings on the matter very clear.'

'Shut up, both of you,' said Rupinder.

'You see,' said Sheila. 'She's trying to blame me.'

'What I actually said was . . .'

Rupinder jumped to her feet. 'And what I said was shut up. So which part were you lost on? The shut or the up?'

Sheila and Lilly fell silent. Rupinder almost never raised her voice.

'Thank you,' said Rupinder. 'I need to think very carefully about how to handle this. And to think I need some quiet, not a scene from *EastEnders*.' She picked up the post and handed it to Sheila. 'You deal with this little lot, and you,' she turned to Lilly, 'get yourself to court.'

'Where?'

'Luton Crown Court. That was them on the phone. Anna's case is listed at eleven-thirty for directions.'

Lilly flapped her arms around her. 'What sort of notice is that? I'll ring them and tell them we need more time.'

Rupinder put up her hand. 'I told them you'd be there.'

'But I haven't briefed a barrister,' said Lilly.

'You passed your exam, remember? You don't need one.'

Lilly was about to argue but Rupinder's raised eyebrow stopped her.

'It will help matters greatly if I can tell my fellow partners that you are at least making some money out of this unholy mess.'

Lilly swallowed her list of complaints. 'I'll get my robes.'

Row after row of cheap shoes. They looked bad and smelled worse.

Alexia read the label with disgust. 'Manmade sole and upper.' She sighed. There were no decent shops outside of London. There was the grubby Arndale Centre full of cheap chain stores where fat teenagers could buy glittery crop tops and plastic belts. Then there was the precinct, which seemed to act as a race track for the thousands of mobility scooters that infested Bedfordshire.

It was just as well there was nothing to buy. She had a mountain of debt since she'd cut herself free from the shackles of Daddy's obscene wealth. She sometimes wondered if the price she was paying for freedom wasn't too high.

Maybe Steve would give her a bonus this month. He damn well ought to. But he was just like her father, always moving the goal posts. No sooner had you met his last demand than he raised the bar of expectation.

She left the shoe shop and wandered up to work. Every window was decorated with plastic pumpkins. Cheap tat from China that would end up as landfill.

'You're late,' Steve growled.

She gave him the finger and collected her emails. Half a dozen from the nationals asking for information on the Stanton case, two from the radio and even one from the producers of *Richard and Judy*.

'Don't even think about it,' Steve leered over her shoulder.

She batted him away. 'Do you really think I'm that stupid?'

'Stupid, no,' said Steve. 'Ambitious, yeah.'

'You make it sound like a dirty word.'

He leaned back in so she could smell last night's pork balls on his unbrushed teeth.

'If you tell these people what you know and how you know it, they'll suck you dry then spit you out.'

Alexia logged on to *The Spear of Truth*. Steve was right. She'd managed two exclusives but she was still small change. Big names were not made on the back of a small hole in a fence. She needed more to prove what she was capable of.

She scrolled through the forums. There was no sign of Snow White, but Alexia's piece about the service had been uploaded on to the site. There were a lot of comments posted underneath. Most praised her brave journalism and surmised that the fight was about the fact that the defendant was an asylum seeker.

She'd been so excited about the fracas that she hadn't paid enough attention to what had actually sparked things off. She pulled out the tape she'd recorded at the school and plugged in her earphones. She'd had to move forward to make sure her machine could pick it all up. Some of the parents had mumbled about her lack of manners, but there was no way she was going to miss the action. The house master's speech was even more boring second time round. She fast-forwarded to the fight.

'Is it true? I just want to know if what they are saying is true.'

'That depends on what they're saying, Luella.'

'That you're representing the girl who murdered Charlie.'

Alexia stopped in her tracks and pressed rewind.

'That you're representing the girl who murdered Charlie.'

How had she missed it the first time?

She sat back in her chair, trying to absorb what this meant. The solicitor in the case was a parent at the dead kid's school . . . This was the stuff that journalistic wet dreams were made of.

She tried to recall the woman who'd been slapped. The first thing that sprang to mind were those bloody footless tights. But what else? Auburn hair, creamy skin.

She went back to the tape.

Mrs Boden was on a roll, her speech grandiose. It was real 'them and us' garbage, the type of noise all over the racist sites.

'I think you should leave.'

Then a pause, some scrabbling as her victim tried to hobble out of the pew.

'Lilly Valentine, is this a joke?'

Alexia punched the air.

'What you got, Posh?' came Steve's voice

'Gold dust,' said Alexia. 'Fucking gold dust.'

'What is Luton Crime Court?' asked Anna, trotting after Lilly.

Lilly heaved her files and bag across the car park, her robe thrown over her shoulder. 'Crown Court. It's the place where your case will be heard.'

Anna's eyes shot open. 'Today?'

Lilly balanced everything on the roof of the Mini and fished in her coat pocket for her keys. 'No, today's just for timetabling the case and ironing out any problems.'

Anna nodded, but Lilly could see she was both bewildered and frightened.

'It's nothing to worry about.' Lilly's tone was soothing. 'Trust me.'

'You'll be with me all the time?' asked Anna.

Lilly thought about how much time she might have to spend with the prosecution or in chambers with the judge. 'Let's collect Milo.'

'I'd forgotten how much I hate this place.'

Kerry Thomson looked up at the barrister, still muttering to himself over the papers. God, he was gorgeous. All doe eyes and olive skin. When she'd been told he was taking on the Duraku case she'd dashed out to Evans to buy a new skirt. The elastic chafed around her middle but she thought it looked nice. Well, quite nice. At least it wasn't summer when everything was floaty and short sleeved. She ran her thumb under the waistband. There was already a welt.

'It's better than the Youth Court,' she said. 'Which is where I spend most of my time.'

He looked up at her and smiled. 'Lord help you.'

Kerry nearly peed her pants.

'I thought you only took on defence work,' she said, hoping he'd be impressed that she knew something about him.

He shrugged. 'I do, or I did, until the powers-that-be pointed out that if I want to take silk I need to broaden my appeal.'

Kerry couldn't imagine anything more appealing than the man himself right now.

Jez fingered the pages of his brief and wished to God this was someone else's case. Late last night he'd considered handing it back. It was too late. At this stage any decent barrister to pick it up and run. Most would be champing at the bit.

Then he remembered the call he'd received the day before from the cocky new clerk who refused to wear a tie.

'Mr Churchill wants to see you.'

Jez's interest was piqued to be summoned by his head of chambers but he wasn't about to show that to the teenaged little oik on the phone.

'Tell him I'll pop in later.'

The clerk let out a snigger and Jez imagined him running his hand around his open collar. 'To be honest, mate, I think it would be in your interest to get yourself up there now.'

Jez fought back the urge to tell him to fuck off.

'Like I said, I'll see Ronald when I've got a second.'

He put down the phone before he said something he'd regret later, then raced upstairs to Ronald.

Ronald's office was the best in the building and it stretched across the entire top floor with huge windows looking out on to Embankment.

The boss himself leaned back in his chair and smiled. 'How the devil are you, my boy?' asked Ronald. 'Busy?'

'Certainly can't complain,' said Jez and took the seat opposite.

Ronald leaned over the table conspiratorially and Jez could smell whisky on his breath. 'I wonder if you could do me a little favour.'

Jez carved a smile across his face. 'Anything for you.'

Ronald nodded but said nothing further.

Jez sighed inwardly, he knew better than to hurry him. This was one of the greatest trial lawyers in the country and he lived to stretch the tension.

At last Ronald pushed a brief towards him. No doubt some relative had been nicked for drink driving and needed a decent barrister on the cheap.

Jez opened the pink string and laid it flat.

Regina v Duraku. He scanned the list of enclosures and saw the police papers.

'This is a prosecution case,' said Jez.

'It is,' said Ronald.

'I don't prosecute, Ron, you know that.'

Ronald winked. 'It's a murder. High profile. Done deal.'

'Which is great,' said Jez, 'but I don't prosecute.'

'Listen, Jez,' Ronald put his full weight on his fore-arms so that the table creaked. 'This chambers needs another silk and I'd like it to be you.'

'I'd like that too,' said Jez.

'You're bright, thorough and consistent.'

Jez tried not to grin. Ronald was old-school and hated gratuitous shows of emotion.

'Though I have heard it said that your practice is a little . . .' Ronald fished for the word. 'Lop-sided.'

Jez could feel his inner smile slipping. 'Lop-sided?'

'This defence work is all very admirable,' Ronald tapped the side of his bulbous nose. 'But you don't want people to think you're one of these bleeding hearts.'

Jez fingered the brief. He hated the idea of trying to get someone convicted, and of murder of all things – but he'd worked for bloody years to get this far. He wanted to get to the top. Hell, he wanted a big room with fabu-lous views.

'I'll take a look,' he said.

Today, in the cold light of Luton Crown Court, he wondered if he should just have told Ronald to bugger off.

Jez pushed his papers away. 'This case sucks.'

'The director thinks it's a runner,' said Kerry.

'She doesn't know shit from sugar.'

'Do you think we'll lose?' asked Kerry.

The barrister shook his head. 'No, I think we'll win, but not because we have a good case.'

'Then why?'

He sighed. 'Because a large section of the British public hate asylum seekers and won't be able to resist the chance to show this one what they think.'

'Maybe the defence will plea-bargain,' said Kerry.

'Depends who's for the other side.'

'A local woman,' said Kerry. 'Lilly Valentine.'

A grin broke out on his face, like the sun after a storm. 'Lilly Valentine.' He was laughing now. 'Lilly fantabulous Valentine.'

'It's nice to see you too.'

Jez saw the solicitor in the doorway, her hair tumbling to her shoulders, her blouse open just a little too low, the lace edge of her bra making a tantalising appearance. Things had just got a whole lot better.

Lilly hadn't seen Jez Stafford for over a year but he was still every bit as handsome.

'I didn't know you persecuted,' she said.

'Just stepping up to do my moral duty.'

She laughed. 'You mean you're up for your promotion this year and some media coverage won't do you any harm at all.'

He placed his hand over his heart. 'I'm wounded you think me so shallow.'

'Hello, Miss Valentine,' Kerry spoke up from the other side of the room.

Lilly smiled at her. 'Sorry to ignore you, but Jez and I are old friends.'

'We bonded over another murder case,' he said, still grinning cheekily at Lilly.

Lilly jabbed him in the ribs. 'Only that time you weren't on the side of the forces of evil.'

'What on earth?' Kerry pointed at the stained tea towel still wrapped around Lilly's hand.

Lilly reddened, pulled it off and stuffed it into her bag. 'Sorry.' Unfortunately, her hand now looked even less appealing with its deep gash and congealed blood.

'Ouch,' said Jez.

Lilly laughed. 'I must sack my manicurist.'

Kerry's smile was forced. 'So what is your client saying?'

'That there was no conspiracy,' said Lilly. 'She had no idea what Artan was going to do.'

'The gun didn't give her a clue?' said Jez.

Lilly ignored him. 'I'm going for a psych report today.'

'Who?' asked Kerry.

'Leyla Kadir,' said Lilly.

'Never heard of her,' said Jez.

'Well, you should have, Mr Hot Shot Prosecutor, she's one of the leading shrinks in PTSD.'

'Is that a brand of tampons?' he asked.

'Post Traumatic Stress Disorder,' said Lilly. 'Ask your sis, she recommended Kadir.'

Jez groaned and hid his face in his hands. 'Not Sheba. How the hell is she involved?'

'I asked for her help. She doesn't want to see a mis-carriage of justice.'

Jez leaned over to Kerry and stage-whispered behind his hand. 'When my sister and Lilly join forces, things often get out of hand.'

175

Kerry's smile became less stiff. 'We'll just have to do our best to stop them.'

'Indeed we shall,' said Jez, and Lilly noticed the thrill his proximity sent through Kerry's massive frame.

The two old friends headed down the corridor towards the robing room.

Lilly nodded back to Kerry. 'You've an admirer there.'

'What can I tell you?' said Jez. 'Women can't resist me.'

'Is that right?'

He threaded his arm through Lilly's. 'There was a time when you were quite keen, Mrs Valentine.'

'Stop right there,' said Lilly. 'You won't put me off my game by trying to embarrass me.'

'I wouldn't dare,' he laughed. 'So, which poor sucker have you instructed?'

Uh-oh, crunch time. 'No one. *I'm* going to conduct the case.'

'You!'

'I do have some experience in these matters.'

'As a solicitor,' he said.

'A solicitor with rights of audience in the Crown Court.'

Jez rubbed his hands together. 'This is going to be fun.'

Lilly strode across the foyer towards the consultation room where her client and Milo were hiding. Her black robes billowed around her and she felt faintly ridiculous.

Anna was tucked into the far corner, her head leaning

against Milo's shoulder. She looked every bit the child in an adult world.

'Where have you been?' she asked.

'Speaking to the prosecution,' said Lilly.

'The fat woman with a beard?' asked Anna.

Lilly let it ride. 'And their barrister, Mr Stafford.'

'I hope he's terrible,' said Milo.

Lilly smiled. 'He's not. He has years of experience, but in some ways that will work in our favour.'

Neither Milo nor Anna looked convinced.

'For one thing, he won't argue every irrelevant detail,' said Lilly. 'And for another, he's not out to crucify you.'

'You also have years of experience, yes?' asked Milo.

'I've defended hundreds of cases,' said Lilly, and led them into the courtroom where, for the very first time in her career, she would address a Crown Court judge.

The hearing had been sprung on her so quickly she'd hardly had a chance to gather her thoughts, and when she'd seen Jez she'd been too busy gassing to worry, but now Lilly's hands began to sweat. She rooted in her bag for a tissue. Naturally, she had none. Hoping no one would see, she wiped her hand across the stained tea towel.

'Ugh.'

Lilly saw Kerry pull her lips back from her teeth. She was beginning to reassess her views on Miss Thomson.

She tried to rearrange the papers on the table in front of her but her hands were trembling. Instead she turned to Anna and Milo, who were sitting on the bench behind.

'Okay?'

They nodded dumbly. At least they were more nervous than she was. Lilly gulped. The fate of that young girl was in her hands, and she wasn't sure she was ready.

Hell, Lilly knew she wasn't ready. She should never have allowed Rupinder to insist she come today. She needed a barrister. Someone like Jez. She should call a halt to this now, insist she be given time to instruct a QC.

To her left was Jez, cool and calm.

'All rise,' said the clerk.

Jez gave Lilly a wink.

His Honour Patrick Banks entered the room, his face impassive, his eyes as colourless as his wig. It was impossible to second-guess what sort of mood he might be in.

Jez leaned forward on his hands, a casual gesture that heightened Lilly's fears.

'Your Honour,' he said. 'I am here today for the Crown.'

The judge gave a chuckle. 'Prosecuting, eh? I suppose a man in your position needs to spread the old wings.'

Jez opened his hands. 'What's a man to do?'

Lilly gulped. If the camaraderie was meant to alienate her, it was working.

'And this,' said Jez, 'is my colleague for the defence.'

He nodded to Lilly, who scrambled to her feet. 'Good morning, Your Honour.'

The smile the judge had given to Jez turned quickly into a scowl as he appraised Lilly. 'I'm afraid I can't hear you.'

Lilly cleared her throat. 'I said, "Good morning".'

'I still can't hear you, young lady.'

Lilly felt her cheeks sting. Why was he calling her that? She was nearly bloody forty, for God's sake. 'Good morning, Your Honour.'

The judge shook his head. Was he taking the piss?

'I said, "Good morning".' Lilly was shouting now. 'And if you can't hear this then we've got a problem.'

The judge peered at her as if she were something unpleasant he'd found in his food. 'I am not deaf, young lady.'

So what the hell was all this about?

'You said you couldn't hear me, Your Honour.'

'And indeed I cannot while you are incorrectly attired.'

Lilly looked down at her gown. Not flattering, she had to admit, but it was the right one for court.

The judge sighed and made a circle around his head as if he were tracing an imaginary halo.

Lilly touched her hair. She'd tied it back neatly, so what was the old cretin going on about?

'Your wig,' whispered Jez.

'I haven't got one,' Lilly said.

'Exactly,' said the judge. 'Go and put it on immediately.'

Jez rose to his feet and laughed. 'Your Honour, perhaps I may be of some assistance.'

'I certainly hope so,' said the judge. 'Your friend doesn't appear to be able to keep up.'

Lilly pulled at her collar. She didn't know what was worse: the judge criticising her in front of her client or Jez coming to her rescue. She would kill Rupes for making her do this.

179

Jez smiled. 'My colleague is a solicitor and, as Your Honour will know, that precludes her from wearing the full courtly attire. In particular, the wig.'

Jesus, he made it sound like Lilly was missing out on free money. Still, at least the judge would have to apologise.

'Young lady,' said the judge. 'Why on earth didn't you say so in the beginning?'

Now Lilly was cross. The man had made her look like an idiot.

'Your Honour hardly gave me a chance.'

The judge frowned. He was clearly unused to being spoken to in such a direct manner.

Jez coughed. 'I think you and Ms Valentine were at crossed purposes, Your Honour.'

There was a silence while the judge glared at Lilly. She, in turn, refused to look away. Her mother had always told her to stand up to bullies and she wasn't about to stop now.

At last the judge turned to his papers. 'We've wasted enough time. Let's get on.'

'I believe', said Jez, 'that my colleague wishes to instruct an expert in this case. A psychiatrist.'

'For what purpose?'

Jez was about to reply when Lilly got to her feet. She'd already shown the judge she wouldn't be belittled. Now it was time to show Jez she wouldn't be sidelined.

'My psychiatrist will show the court how Post Traumatic Stress Disorder affected my client's ability to take part in the alleged conspiracy,' she said.

'Very well,' said the judge.

He stood to leave, then turned to Jez. 'Any press out there?'

'No, Your Honour. They are clearly unaware that this case was listed today.'

'Good,' said the judge.

'The victim's family and the school are very eager to avoid media intrusion so the police and the CPS have released only the most basic information,' said Jez.

'And the defence?' The judge didn't even look at Lilly. 'Are they managing to keep glory-seeking to a minimum?'

Lilly slapped the table in front of her. 'I assure you that the defence have no interest in seeing their case in the headlines.'

The judge gave a half-smile. 'Then you'd be one of the first.'

'Can I remind you that the defendant is a child,' Lilly stood erect, 'and as such she is entitled to full anonymity? I hardly think that the one person on her side would seek to erode her right to that.'

'I see,' said the judge, and left without so much as a goodbye.

'You shouldn't have answered him back like that,' said Jez.

'He was trying to make me look like a twat,' she said. 'Don't tell me you would have taken it lying down.'

Jez shrugged. 'Water off a duck's back. If you want to get on with the judiciary then you learn to play the game.'

'If that's what it takes, you can stick it.'

'Oh, Lilly, don't ever change.'

*   *   *

Back in their cubby-hole, Anna and Milo huddled in a corner, whispering.

Anna's eyes were wide with fear. 'He is very bad man, this judge.'

'He's not the easiest I've dealt with,' said Lilly.

'But you fought him like a lion,' said Milo.

Lilly couldn't resist a smile but Anna remained unconvinced.

'But he can send me to prison, yes?'

Lilly knelt at Anna's feet and looked up into her terrified face. 'It's not up to him. A jury will decide whether you're guilty or not.'

'They will believe her,' said Milo. 'They will understand.'

Lilly nodded to reassure Anna. But inside, when she thought about the gun and Charlie Stanton lying on the floor, she wasn't so sure.

Chapter Eleven

A couple of conversations with the Law Society confirmed that one Lilliana Elizabeth Valentine was on the roll of solicitors. She had qualified in 1992, was a member of the specialist Children's Panel and had rights of higher audience. She worked for a firm in Harpenden.

Alexia nabbed Steve's car keys and headed over there.

It was one of those towns that knew its place in the world and was terribly pleased with it. Yummy Mummies in last season's Uggs pushed Bugaboos, their children rosy-cheeked and nibbling organic rice cakes. Older couples, arm in arm, strolled to the library, safe in their inflation-linked bubble.

The brass plate outside Fulton, Carter and Singh reflected its middle-class glory. Or was it just the sun?

Alexia pushed open the door and the receptionist looked up.

'Can I help you?'

The voice and perm were pure Luton.

'I'd like to speak with Miss Valentine.'

The receptionist wrinkled her nose. A small gesture, but Alexia noticed.

'Lilly's in a meeting,' said the receptionist. 'Would you like to leave your number?'

Alexia knew there was no way the solicitor would ever call her back.

'I'll wait,' she said, and took a seat.

'She could be a long while,' said the receptionist.

Alexia smiled and picked up a magazine from the coffee table.

Ten minutes dragged by while she pretended to read *Country Life*. Eventually the receptionist scuttled out and returned with an elegant Asian woman. She glided over to Alexia, her sari barely rustling.

'I'm afraid Lilly may not return to the office today, but I'm sure I can assist you.' She held out her hand. 'Rupinder Singh. I'm one of the partners.'

Her fingers were cool and slender in Alexia's.

'I really do need Miss Valentine,' said Alexia.

Rupinder didn't release Alexia's hand. 'Please state your business here, Miss . . .'

Damn it. She couldn't lie.

'My name's Alexia Dee. I work for the *Three Counties Observer*.'

Rupinder's smile didn't slip. 'And what can we do for you, Miss Dee?'

'I understand Miss Valentine represents the alleged killer of Charles Stanton,' she said. 'And I wondered if you had anything to say about the case.'

'Bleeding hell,' said the receptionist.

Rupinder drifted past Alexia in a cloud of silk and voile and opened the door. 'Good day, Miss Dee.'

Alexia sighed and picked up her bag.

'You don't deny this firm is on record in that matter?'

Rupinder held her arm out into the winter sunshine. 'I have absolutely nothing to say on the subject, and if your paper prints anything without substantiating evidence we will, of course, sue you.'

Alexia unlocked the knackered Honda and slumped in the driver's seat. She needed something far more concrete than the taped argument at the school. She thought of the receptionist and the look of distaste that had passed over her at the mention of Valentine's name. She was obviously no fan. Perhaps she could get her hands on some paperwork showing Valentine was involved in the case.

Her father always said everyone had a weak spot. The trick was identifying and manipulating it. You can't con an honest man.

She peeped through the office window. No sign of the Asian woman. The receptionist was on her own.

She swept back to the desk, looked into the woman's eyes and put down her card.

The air was heady with blackcurrant as Dr Kadir made herbal tea.

'Are you sure I can't get you anything?' said the doctor, offering a box of individually wrapped infusions.

Anna shook her head.

Lilly could have killed for a coffee. There was Camomile Heaven and Summer Fruit Garden. There was even something called Ginger Zinger. Who in God's name would drink that?

185

'Try this.' Dr Kadir held one up. 'Peppermint. It's very good for the digestion.'

'I'm fine, thanks,' said Lilly.

Dr Kadir smiled and unwrapped it. The small string attached to the bag reminded Lilly of that on a tampon.

When handed the tea, Lilly blew on the pale green water and took a sip.

'Good?' said Dr Kadir.

Lilly swallowed. It tasted like hot toothpaste.

Satisfied, Dr Kadir turned to Anna. 'Tell me about the war.'

Lilly spluttered. The question was so direct, not at all what she'd expected. Surely a few moments of getting to know you was in order? Maybe this wasn't such a good idea after all.

Anna looked down at her hands. She seemed very childlike. 'I don't like to speak of it.'

'Of course,' said Dr Kadir. 'But all the same, I'd like to hear your story.'

Anna picked at one of her cuticles. Lilly could see it was raw and pink.

'It's all in her statement to the immigration department,' said Lilly.

Anna glanced briefly at Lilly, her eyes brimming with tears and gratitude. Dr Kadir looked less impressed.

'Perhaps,' she said, 'you could let Anna answer for herself.'

Lilly nodded and returned to her mouthwash.

'Were you offered counselling by social services?' asked Dr Kadir.

'I didn't go.'

'Why not?'

Anna sighed. 'I don't like to speak of it.'

Dr Kadir tapped her notepad with the nib of her ink pen. It left a sprinkle of blue marks like the dot-to-dots Sam had been addicted to as a three year old.

'What about your friend, Artan, did he go to counselling?'

'He said it was a waste of time.'

'Did he advise you not to go?'

'He said we shouldn't discuss these things. It does no good to look back.'

'How do you feel about Artan's death?' asked Dr Kadir.

Lilly watched her client closely. She had seen the only person she had left in the world shot at close range. How did that make her feel? Terrified? Angry?

'Ashamed,' said Anna.

Lilly spluttered out a mouthful of tea. 'Sorry. Went down the wrong way.' She could not have been more surprised by Anna's reply.

Dr Kadir studiously ignored Lilly and cocked her head towards Anna. 'Because he killed someone?'

'No,' said Anna. 'Because it should have been me.'

Lilly checked that her client was busy in the waiting room. 'What do you think?'

Dr Kadir smiled. 'More tea?'

Lilly willed herself to be patient. 'No, thanks.'

Minutes seemed to stretch into hours as Dr Kadir poured herself another cup. Her stainless steel Cartier watch reflected the light. Georgous yet understated. Just like the woman herself.

'I think', she said at last, 'that Anna is displaying symptoms of PTSD. She is clearly depressed and bewildered by all that has happened and will do anything to avoid thinking about it.'

'Why does she think she should have been the one to die?' asked Lilly.

'Survivor guilt is a very common symptom in such cases. No doubt she wonders why, when so many innocent members of her family have died, she should have been allowed to live.'

'So you think I have a defence?' asked Lilly. 'I can prove she was incapable of the conspiracy because of the PTSD?'

Dr Kadir warmed her hands around her cup. 'In order to make that assessment, I'm afraid I'll need to dig deeper, much deeper.'

Lilly sighed. 'You mean, whether Anna likes it or not, she's got to start talking.'

The information was bothering Snow White.

She'd baked a Victoria sponge, washed and dried two lots of hockey kit, helped the girls with their prep, yet it was constantly there, gnawing away. Like a seed in her tooth or an insect bite on her ankle.

Valentine was helping the girl.

It was obscene.

Snow White had never liked her. She was so disorganised, always running late and her holier-than-thou attitude made Snow White sick.

Something had to be done about her.

She checked the girls were asleep and began to type.

<u>Time to Take Action</u> Snow White at 20.50
I feel the time for words has finished.
    Can any brothers or sisters in Hertfordshire help
me take things to the next level?

<u>Time to Take Action</u> Blood River at 21.03
At your service, Snow White.

*　　*　　*

The mound of roast potatoes steamed, their skins tanned
golden against the white of the serving dish.

Jack rubbed his hands together. 'You know the way
to a man's heart.'

Lilly took the lid off the casserole. Chicken breasts
bubbled thickly in red wine with softened onions. Coq
au vin. Not some plastic stew but the unadulterated
French classic. Lilly breathed in the mellow thyme and
smiled as Jack tucked into an enormous plateful.

Still, she wasn't daft enough to believe it would keep
a man content in the long run. Her mother had made
a wicked steak and kidney pie that her dad loved. 'Elsa,'
he'd say, slapping his wife on the arse, 'if I die tonight
I'll be a happy man.'

It hadn't stopped him from buggering off.

And then there was David – he'd run off with a
woman who didn't eat, let alone cook.

'What are you thinking about?' asked Jack.

'My ex-husband,' said Lilly.

'Very romantic.'

Lilly laughed. 'I mean, how odd it is that I'm so happy.'

'Is it so odd?'

She put down her fork and struggled to make herself understood. 'When he left, I thought I'd never smile again – that my life had come to an end. Yet now, here, I wonder if it wasn't all for the best.'

Jack smiled and went back to his food.

'What about you?' said Lilly. 'What are you thinking?'

He pointed with his knife. 'That you're just like this spud.'

'Now that is romantic.'

'Bear with me.' He speared the potato with his fork and held it aloft. 'Firm on the outside, hard, even, but fluffy in the middle.'

He pushed it into his mouth and grinned while he chewed.

She spooned more chicken onto his plate. 'They're not hard, they're crisp.'

Later they settled on the battered sofa with a bottle of Shiraz. Lilly leaned lazily across Jack's lap, a glass of wine at her feet. A romantic comedy was playing on the television, something about a famous tennis player. Sam was in bed.

'Can you stay tonight?' said Lilly.

'I'm sure Angelina Jolie will give me the night off.'

Lilly sat up. 'I mean, are you allowed? What with the court case and everything?'

'I don't suppose it's a good idea, what with me being a witness and the defendant in the spare room,' he said.

Lilly was disappointed, but she understood he was still a copper, suspended or not. She took a sip of wine and changed the subject. 'What did you do today?'

Jack shrugged. 'Couldn't read the papers or turn on the telly without someone banging on about Charlie Stanton.'

'What are they saying?'

'Not a lot,' he said. 'They haven't got any real info, so they're having a field day guessing who our mystery shooter might be.'

'Oh, God.'

'Artan and Anna have turned into an Albanian drug gang and I've been described as a crack S.W.A.T. team,' he said.

Lilly shook her head. 'How can they print such crap?'

'My thoughts entirely,' said Jack. 'So I went for a run.'

'With all this exercise you'll soon disappear to nothing.' She tapped his leg for emphasis but it felt firm and muscular. She left her hand on his thigh.

He eyed her hand but didn't move it. 'What about you?'

'I had a date with the shrink. She made me drink molten Polos.'

'And how's the case going?'

'I thought we weren't supposed to talk about that.'

He nodded at her hand. 'We're not, but I'm trying to take my mind off other things.'

Lilly took another sip of wine. She'd thought a lot about what Dr Kadir had said and wasn't sure how best to proceed.

'Anna's suffering from Post Traumatic Stress Disorder.'

'Come again?'

'It's a mental disorder brought on by what happened in Kosovo. It's made her detach from reality.'

191

'Meaning?'

'I hope she wasn't mentally capable of being part of a conspiracy to murder.'

'You hope?'

Lilly shrugged. 'It's not that easy. In order to make a positive diagnosis, Dr Kadir needs Anna to talk about her feelings – but one of the symptoms of this illness is that she just can't do that.'

'A case of the chicken and the egg.'

Lilly nodded. 'I need her to open up to me and talk about what happened.'

It was so difficult. Most of her divorce clients treated her like a mother confessor and couldn't wait to get it all off their chests. If their story was worth telling once it was worth telling a hundred times. Oh, the irony of her current situation.

'If anyone can do it, it's you.' He traced the line of her jaw with his fingertip. 'You've a natural way with people.'

She turned her head and kissed his palm. Jack was right, she would get Anna to open up to her and create the defence she was looking for.

'Is there no chance you can stay?'

It was still dark when Jack set out for a run. There were few street lamps on the country lanes and dawn was still hours away, but a fat moon was beaming down through the bare trees.

After Lilly had talked him into staying he couldn't sleep. Well, talked him into it was a bit strong. She had given him every opportunity to refuse, but he hadn't taken it. He hadn't wanted to.

He smiled to himself at the thought of her, tangled in the sheets, her hair smelling like toffee. As he crept across the bedroom to find his trainers she'd leaned up on one elbow. 'Where are you going?'

He knew she would worry if he admitted that his nights were constantly broken by the sound of gunfire. So he'd kissed her head and winked. 'Go back to sleep.'

He heard the pad of his feet on the road, his breath regular and deep. The rhythm soothed him and gently pushed the picture of Artan's pale, dead face from his mind. Doctors should prescribe a jog instead of so many antidepressants.

Maybe he'd get Lilly to join him when she didn't have to babysit Anna. He could imagine them side by side, their steps in time. The sooner this case was over and they could all get back to normal, the better for all of them. He'd never been one for making plans, kind of took each day as it came, but when he pounded the pavement his mind was clear and he found himself looking to the future. It became obvious to him with each stride that he was never happier than in Lilly's kitchen or playing football with Sam in the overgrown garden. He wanted to feel like that all the time.

The new super-sleek, super-decisive Jack McNally turned on his heels and headed back to the cottage. He was going to tell his woman exactly how he felt. He'd tried before and ended up chatting about her work. Not this time.

He chuckled to himself. 'Get you, alpha male.'

When he rounded the corner to Appleyard Lane he saw the lights were on in the cottage and a figure was outside. It was Lilly, her hair still wild, a dressing gown wrapped around her. She was poking about in her car.

'You're up early,' he said.

She didn't speak but her eyes were as wide as an owl's.

'I didn't mean to startle you,' he said.

Then he looked from Lilly to the car and saw that it wasn't his presence that had frightened her. The windscreen was smashed, glass spewed over the dashboard.

'Not more bloody kids,' he said.

She pulled her gown around her and handed him the brick that had wrecked her car. It was wrapped in a single piece of white paper.

Jack placed a chipped blue mug of tea in front of Lilly.

'You have to report this,' he said.

She nodded lightly. 'I will.'

Jack eyed her with suspicion. 'I mean it.'

'So do I.'

She drank the tea and reread the letter.

A child has been murdered and the community must stick together.

The terrible people who committed this crime must be punished and those that side with them have no place here and will be forced to leave.

You have been warned.

'It mentions the community. Do you think it might be someone in the village?'

Lilly tried to keep her voice even but the thought of it made her feel sick. She was on pretty good terms with all her neighbours, wasn't she? Except, of course, the woman at Crab Tree Farm. Lilly had run over her cat.

'Could be,' said Jack. 'And if we get a couple of coppers over here, taking statements and poking around, that should put the fear of God into them. Or maybe it's referring to Manor Park.'

'That can't be right,' she said.

'Wasn't that woman at the service banging on about everyone being in this together?'

Lilly shuddered. The morning was brisk, but it was the memory of Luella glowering at her that made her cold.

'I don't think anyone at school would do something like this,' she said.

Jack didn't reply – but she could see he wasn't convinced.

Lilly got up and stretched. 'I have to go to court later. The judge wants to see me.'

At first she thought Jack was going to argue, that he'd say she was in shock and should spend the day at home. Instead he rinsed her cup. 'Take my car.'

'You'll make someone a very good wife,' she said.

He continued to face the sink. 'How about a husband?'

He held his breath, waiting for her reply. The silence roared between them. When he could stand it no more, he turned to face her.

The room was empty.

*   *   *

Snow White crept out of bed and checked her laptop.
<u>Time to Take Action</u> Blood River at 4.30
Mission completed.

Chapter Twelve

Caz is singing in the bath. Her tuneless rendition of the Scouse anthem 'You'll Never Walk Alone' carries into every room of the Peckham Project.

'God help us,' laughs Jean. 'She'll never make the *X Factor*.'

She hauls an enormous pumpkin onto the work surface and rummages in the cutlery drawer for a sharp knife.

Luke helps himself to a frosted-yellow glass and fills it with milk. He doesn't feel rude any more. All the kids that come here help themselves to whatever's in the fridge and stay as long as they like. They chat to Jean if they want to, or ignore her if they prefer. Sometimes she helps them with forms or reads letters out to them.

'You know those men the other day?' says Luke.

Jean stops what she's doing. 'Are they outside?'

Luke shakes his head.

'Good,' says Jean.

'Who are they?' asks Luke.

'Didn't you ask Caz?'

'She said they were pimps.' She'd also called them 'low cunt-scum', but Luke doesn't pass this on.

'To be honest, they can't even call themselves pimps,' says Jean. 'They're more like jailers.'

'What do you mean?'

Jean stabs the top of the squat vegetable, drags the blade in a rough circle, then levers off a fat disc of orange flesh.

'They smuggle girls into this country and force them to work as prostitutes,' she says, still engrossed in her work.

'Like slaves?'

'Yes, love, like slaves.'

Luke is speechless. He'd done all about the abolition of slavery at school – how it had led to a civil war in America. He'd got an A* for his end-of-year project.

'What were they doing here?' he asks.

'Occasionally one of the girls escapes, and it's been known for them to make their way here.'

'Why?'

'I make it known they're welcome,' says Jean. 'And I also make it known I won't tell the authorities.'

'Don't they just want to go home?' asks Luke.

'They'd just get picked up again,' she says and gouges out three more holes. 'Boomerang straight back to square one.'

Luke is appalled. 'That's absolutely terrible.'

'You're a lovely boy, Luke,' she says. 'And one day, when you're ready to tell me what you're doing here, I'll help in any way I can.'

'I can't talk about it,' says Luke.

Jean nods and pulls out one of those small candles his mum insists on calling a tea-light.

'You know where I am if you change your mind.'

He drains the last of his milk and washes out his glass. The others don't bother, but Luke feels it's only fair to Jean.

'There is something you could do for me,' he says.

'Go on.'

'Explain to me how I could get somewhere to live.'

He feels daft even saying it. No doubt Jean has heard the same thing ten times that morning. It never ceases to amaze Luke how often rough sleepers talk about 'getting a place'. No cider-fuelled gathering is complete without a boisterous discussion of who is just about to get the keys to a flat, how said person will decorate the flat and how the entire homeless population will be welcome.

'Do you have your name down on the housing list?' asks Jean.

Luke knows all about housing lists. Teardrop Tony has had his name down on one for six years. He pops down to see his housing officer at least twice a week, he says she's 'sound' and always lends him a few ciggies, but he's still number four hundred and two. Luke might be retired before his number comes up. Anyway, he can't go through the official channels or he'll be caught for sure.

'What about a private place?' he says.

'Most landlords want proof of earnings, references and what-have-you.'

'But not all?'

'There are always those who'll do it under the counter.' She fixes him with a stare. 'But I wouldn't have anything to do with them if I were you.'

Luke nods, but he's already wondering how he can get his hands on a deposit.

She reaches in her bag for her lighter, puts the flame to the candle and places it in the bottom of the pumpkin. The ragged gashes glow. 'What do you think?' asks Jean.

Luke looks at the ugly face she has carved out, his brows knitted in quandary.

'I know it's not perfect,' she laughs. 'But it's just a bit of fun.'

'I thought you were, you know, making soup,' says Luke.

Jean throws back her head and hoots in amusement. 'It's a Hallowe'en lantern, you wally.'

Luke is so startled he falls backwards, groping for the chair. When he finally feels the plastic under him he puts his head between his knees to stop the room swimming.

'You alright, love?' Jean is crouched at his side.

Luke pushes the heels of his hands in his eye sockets.

'I didn't realise,' he says. 'How didn't I realise it was Hallowe'en?'

Jean pats his hand in understanding. 'When you live this life, Luke, you lose your sense of time.'

He knows she's right. It's always been a big deal in the past, trick or treating until his mum said he'd got too old, then parties with Tom and the rest. Cocktails full of red cochineal and the odd slug of vodka sneaked in for good measure.

This year he'd missed it altogether, simply hadn't noticed.

'Come back later, have a bit of fun,' says Jean. 'You need to remind yourself what normal people do.'

What I need, thinks Luke, is that deposit.

'It's my fault, yes?'

Anna's voice was low but deliberate.

Lilly crunched the gears as she tried to park Jack's unfamiliar car.

'Not at all,' she said.

'They don't want you to take my case, so they do this.' Anna stretched out her arms to encompass the car and the whole mess with it.

'Maybe that's true, but that doesn't make it your fault,' said Lilly.

Anna cocked her head to one side, her face a blank.

Lilly mounted the kerb with the back wheel and sighed.

'There are some people – not many, thank God – who don't like what you are and why you've come to this country. They don't want me to help you so they're trying to bully me.'

Lilly didn't feel the need to point out that 'they' might not be some anonymous group of strangers but someone far closer to home.

Jack's rear sensor began to beep. Lilly looked in her mirror at the car behind. She was nowhere near it, for God's sake.

'What they don't know is that one thing I cannot stand, and I mean truly detest, is being told what to do.'

The beeping became more insistent, like a drill in Lilly's brain. She furiously pressed buttons on the dash to override the noise until at last the car fell quiet.

Lilly smiled in triumph and reversed. 'Silence is golden.'

The next sound was metal scraping metal.

Lilly looked from Jack's car to the gleaming Porsche 911 and back again. The bodywork of the two cars had melded like kissing cousins. 'Maybe no one will notice.'

She turned at the sound of laughter, a familiar throaty chuckle. Jez was standing with Kerry, admiring her handiwork.

'Stirling Moss strikes again,' he said.

'You always were hilarious,' said Lilly, and tried to straighten the licence plate. *PB 21*. Private registration.

Jez slid his hand along the car's silver flank as though along a silky thigh. 'At least it's just a pile of old junk.'

Lilly groaned.

'Not the owner's pride and joy,' he said.

'Jesus,' she said. 'How much do these things cost?'

Jez shrugged. 'Sixty, seventy grand.'

'For a car?' Lilly was incredulous. 'Who the hell can afford that?'

Jez threw his head back and laughed. Even Kerry let out a tiny miaow of a giggle. Lilly looked again at the license plate and sighed. PB. His Honour Judge Patrick Banks. Great.

Little Markham was a small place. The sort where everyone knew everyone else and everyone's business was common knowledge. It reminded Alexia of the village in Oxfordshire where her father owned a farmhouse. She had spent much of her school holidays rattling around the lanes on her bike, unchecked by the succession of au pairs who failed to teach her any French.

She entered the newsagent's and fingered the rack of greeting cards, all golf clubs and flowery verses. She could feel the gaze of the man behind the counter working up from her toes to the curves of her bottom.

'You're not from round here,' he said.

Alexia looked up as if surprised to be noticed, and flashed a smile. 'Visiting a friend.'

'Anyone I might know?'

Alexia licked her lips. 'I doubt it. Someone I went to law school with years ago.'

'A solicitor?'

'Her name's Lilly,' said Alexia.

'Oh, yes, I know Lilly,' he said. 'She pops in almost every day to stock up on chocolate.'

'She always did like her sweeties.'

'Well, I'm sure she'll be glad to see you.' He leaned across a pile of *Daily Mail*s. 'Now I'm not one to gossip, but she's been having a bit of trouble.'

'Oh, dear,' Alexia gasped. 'I do hope she's all right.'

The man tapped the side of his nose. 'I'm sure she'll tell you all about it when you get there.'

'I'll do whatever I can to help,' said Alexia. 'Which reminds me. It's been so long since my last visit, I wonder if you can point me in the right direction to her house.'

The room was supposed to be the informal chambers of the presiding judge, but to Lilly it felt no more relaxing than a library. Papers stood in neat piles, files proud in alphabetical order. The judge sat on the opposite side of his desk, hands clasped, as he glared at Lilly.

'I must say, young lady, that in all my years on the bench I have never come across anything like this.'

Lilly bit her tongue. She hated being patronised but thought it might be better to let him get it off his chest.

'I cannot understand how this happened.'

'Well, it wasn't anyone's fault. I wasn't used to it, you see,' said Lilly.

The judge shook his head. 'That, of course, is the crux of the matter. Lack of experience has brought you to this point, and I'm not sure it would be right of me to let you continue.'

Bloody hell, was he threatening to take away her driving licence? Could he even do that?

He leaned towards her, his eyes flashing. 'People's lives are at stake, young lady.'

Oh, please. Lilly knew a lot of men had a thing about their cars, but wasn't he over-egging the pudding?

'I think, Your Honour, that if you look closely you'll see that very little damage has been done. A minor incident, you might call it.'

The judge's mouth opened and closed like a fish in a bucket. 'Young lady, a life has been ruined.'

Something in Lilly snapped. This idiot had taken a dislike to her from the start, and now he was making some huge drama over a prang to his car.

'With all due respect, Your Honour, I think you're getting this entirely out of proportion. I've been driving for twenty years, and I'll admit I've had my share of accidents.'

203

Jez coughed.

'Okay,' said Lilly. 'Maybe more than average, but no one has ever been hurt. Except the boy I knocked off his moped – but I'd only just passed my test and it *was* dark.'

The judge was aghast.

'To be honest, it was partly his fault because he was far too close to the white lines,' Lilly continued. 'But I accept that he broke his arm and that must have been inconvenient, because you can't drive a moped when your arm's in a sling, can you? So, hands up, that was my doing, but it wasn't serious and his life wasn't ruined or anything.'

'Young lady . . .'

Lilly was desperate. She couldn't afford a ban, not living in a village where there were only two buses a day.

'The rest of the time it's just been cars that I've hit.' She was gabbling now. 'And lampposts. And I once knocked down a fence.'

The judge's face was scarlet. 'Young lady!'

'And I promise I will pay for all the damage.'

The judge slammed his fists down on the desk. 'Young lady, could you kindly tell me what any of this has to do with the subject of your client's bail?'

'Bail?'

'Indeed.'

'We're not talking about your Porsche then?' she said.

The judge fixed Lilly with a steely eye. 'And why would we be discussing my car?'

'Ah.'

She could only imagine the look on Jez's face.

'Well?' said the judge.

Lilly took a deep breath. 'I tapped your car. Nothing major, you understand.'

The judge seemed to be holding his breath.

'But, as you said, Your Honour, we're here to talk about life and death stuff, not tiny matters of car accidents.'

The judge clamped his jaw shut. Lilly could see the muscles on his mandibles working up and down. He still hadn't taken a breath. She knew she was making matters worse but couldn't stop herself. 'So, what was it you wanted to know about Anna's bail, Your Honour?'

'I wanted to know how on earth we got to the point . . .' The judge narrowed his eyes. 'Tell me there's not too much damage.'

Lilly made a small gap between her thumb and forefinger.

He winced. 'How on earth we got to the point where the defendant is living with you.'

'Oh, that?'

'Yes, that.'

'It was the only way, Your Honour,' said Lilly.

'The only way to do what?'

'Keep her out of jail,' said Lilly. 'The magistrate would only give her bail with twenty-four-hour supervision.'

'So you volunteered.'

Lilly nodded.

The judge sighed; the morning was clearly taking its toll. 'The problem is, young lady, you can't do it, can you?'

'I admit it's unusual,' said Lilly. 'But there's no law against it.'

The judge put his head in his hands. 'We are at crossed

purposes again. And, before we spend another hour having two different conversations, let me make myself abundantly clear. I am not saying you have breached any rule by agreeing to supervise the defendant. I am simply saying it cannot be done as a matter of practicality.'

Lilly stuck out her bottom lip. 'We've managed so far.'

'If that is the case, perhaps you would be good enough to explain exactly where she is now.'

'Ah.'

The judge raised his eyebrow. 'Ah, indeed.'

'She's outside your chambers.'

'Are you sure?'

Lilly began to panic. Anna had been as good as gold since she arrived, but what if she wasn't there? What if she had run off?

'I'm certain of it.'

'I think we'd better call her in,' said the judge.

Lilly slunk to the door, barely able to look. Please be there, Anna.

She opened it slowly.

Please be there, Anna.

Lilly's heart leapt into her mouth at the sight of her client and Milo sitting together, sharing a bag of salt and vinegar crisps. She beckoned them into the room.

'And who is this?' asked the judge.

Before Lilly could speak, Milo approached the desk with his hand outstretched. 'I am Milo Hassan.'

The judge had little option other than to take his hand.

'I work with Anna and Miss Valentine,' said Milo. 'I supervise bail whenever I am needed.'

It wasn't strictly true, but Lilly grinned nonetheless.

The judge pursed his lips. 'That was not stipulated in the conditions of bail.'

'Perhaps not,' said Lilly. 'But I'm sure the court envisaged a second string to my bow. Otherwise the arrangement would be unworkable, as you so rightly pointed out.'

The judge looked at Jez. 'This is all highly irregular. What do the prosecution have to say?'

Lilly glanced at Jez and bit her lip. Would he bring the whole thing crashing down and send Anna off to High Point?

'It is, as you say, quite irregular, and yet the defendant has attended court on each occasion requested. If Miss Valentine says the defendant is being properly supervised, then who am I to argue?'

The judge sighed and waved his hand, as if dismissing the whole affair. 'I shall change the conditions to incorporate Mr Hassan's name. But you have ultimate responsibility, young lady.'

'Yes, Your Honour,' said Lilly, and watched the judge scuttle off, no doubt to check his precious car.

Jez leaned in to Lilly. 'I didn't see the need to mention that your friend was nowhere to be seen when we arrived.'

Lilly mouthed her thanks and ushered Anna and Milo out of the court.

She patted Milo's arm. 'I owe you one.'

'How about dinner tonight?' He pushed back one of those gorgeous curls. 'I'll cook for you.'

A man this sexy who could cook, now that was textbook material. Lilly glanced at Anna. Having a murder suspect along on the date was a touch more maverick.

The cottage was much smaller than some of the grander houses in the vicinity, but it was chocolate-box pretty, with pots of herbs on the step and spectacular views over the fields behind.

What Alexia wanted more than anything was to get a job with a broadsheet and move back to London. Hoxton, maybe, or Notting Hill. But when she hit the big time she'd buy herself something like this for the weekends and bring down her friends to have barbeques in the garden. She'd string lights in the trees and lay Cath Kidson picnic rugs on the lawn for everyone to crash out on and watch the sunrise. Her father had always split his time between town and country and she would do the same.

A Mini Cooper was parked at the front. Something else Alexia would buy when she got some cash. Only she'd go for the supercharged model, and get a sunroof. Once again, her heart ached for her little Alfa.

She ordered herself to forget all about it. Her star was in the ascendancy – soon enough she would get the recognition she deserved and the trappings to go with it.

She sneaked around the back and found the kitchen window boarded up. Was this the trouble the newsagent had mentioned? And was it a coincidence or had others got wind of Lilly's involvement in the Stanton murder trial? Maybe those people were none too pleased. And if others knew, the nationals wouldn't be far behind.

She needed to get some evidence and get the story out there before someone snatched it from under her.

She crept back to the front and noticed the car windscreen was also smashed.

Now that simply couldn't be a coincidence.

The door opened and a man came out brandishing a dustpan and brush. Alexia dived behind a hedge, which provided her with some cover while being sparse enough to still allow her a ringside view. The man began to sweep out the glass from inside the car. Alexia could hear the swish of the brush against the carpet and the tinkle of glass.

Who was this? Husband? The title on the roll of solicitors was Miss Valentine, but that didn't mean much. Alexia never used her real name.

He was a good-looking chap. Scruffy as hell, but with soft eyes and the lean body of a man who liked to keep himself fit. At the sound of each passing car he looked up, obviously eager to see someone. If that someone was Lilly, she was a lucky woman.

When at last an estate stopped, he bounced on his toes.

'Easy, tiger,' Alexia whispered.

The driver got out and waved. 'Hi, Jack.'

It must be Valentine.

The man, Jack, grinned, and his cheeks flushed at the sight of the curly-haired woman getting out of the car. But his shoulders dropped and his smile cooled when the other passengers got out too. Alexia doubted it was the sight of the skinny girl that dampened his spirits, more likely the man with his arm around her shoulders.

With jet-black hair that slid down his forehead into the greenest eyes Alexia had ever seen, it was no surprise old Jack was feeling a bit disconcerted. Alexia strained to hear them speak.

'You didn't have to do that, McNally,' said Valentine, nodding at the brush, which was still in Jack's hand.

'No bother,' he said.

The green-eyed competitor laughed. 'You will make a very good wife.'

Ooh, there was no need for that. They might all be laughing but the gloves were off.

Jack smiled at the other man but there was open hostility in his eyes. Alexia wondered for a second whether he might punch him. Instead he played his trump card. He turned towards Valentine and slipped a hand around her waist.

'You look tired,' he said.

The intimacy was quiet, not showy, but unmistakable nonetheless, and the other man beat his retreat. When he got to the lane he turned and smiled, his emerald eyes glittering. He might be down but he wasn't out.

'I'll see you tonight, Lilly.'

When he was gone, Jack pulled his arm away and headed for the house.

'We're going to work on the case,' said Valentine, trotting inside after him.

When the coast was clear, Alexia crept back to her car and pulled out her phone.

'What?' Steve growled.

'I've found the lawyer.'

'Did you get a quote?'

'I haven't approached her yet,' said Alexia.

'What are you waiting for?' shouted Steve. 'A gold-embossed invite?'

Alexia took a deep breath. 'I'm going to follow her for a bit first.'

'You're a reporter, Posh, not fucking MI5.'

'I think there's even more to it,' she said. 'I can feel something big.'

There was a pause.

'Okay,' said Steve, and Alexia punched the air. 'But look sharpish, I want to run with this tomorrow.'

'Fair enough.'

'So what's this solicitor like? Stuck-up bird, is she?'

Alexia paused for a moment. What did she think of Lilly Valentine?

'She isn't Miss Popular, that's for sure.'

Steve grunted. He wouldn't exactly win any awards himself.

'Somebody has smashed her windscreen,' she said. 'And her kitchen window.'

'"Local unrest fuelled by greedy lawyer", I love it,' he said. 'What does she look like?'

'Redhead, late thirties.'

'A looker?' he asked.

'If you like that sort of thing,' she said. 'Which, judging by the two men I saw fighting over her, I think you probably would.'

Steve let out another bark. 'Get a picture.'

Alexia had already pulled out her camera. 'I will. In the meantime, do a bit of digging for me.'

'On the lawyer?'

'Yes, and on one of the guys I saw at her house. Probably the boyfriend. She called him Jack McNally.'

'"Sleazy defence brief in village sex scandal", he said.

'You're an evil so-and-so,' said Alexia.

'It takes one to know one.'

'I do my best,' she said.

'Your dad would be proud.'

Lilly didn't know why Jack had made a fuss. Not that he'd shouted or made a scene. That wasn't his style, but his tight lips and curt goodbye had made his point.

She'd explained that Milo was helping. That he'd agreed to share supervision of Anna. The fact that they were going to talk over dinner was nothing for Jack to get worked up about.

Most people cooked for their guests. It was a sociable thing to do. Something Jack, who could burn a Pot Noodle, would never understand.

He was being ridiculous.

So, why was she pouring almond oil into her bath, an inner voice asked her.

Now *she* was being ridiculous. She liked to feel soft. Her mother, Elsa, had always taken the view that there was no point keeping things for best. True, she was talking about crockery, but the same held true for skin, surely?

She swished the unctuous puddle with her hand and sank into the hot water. Long soaks were one of life's great joys. Like pasta and epidurals. She closed her eyes and smiled. She would slather herself in the matching lotion until she was as flawless as a butterfly's wing, then pour herself into the brown wrap dress that clung in all the right places.

A tiny knock came at the door.

'Yes,' said Lilly.

Anna opened it a crack. 'Phone,' she said. 'It is for you.'

Lilly sighed and heaved herself out of the bath. 'Yes?'

'It's me.'

Lilly wound a towel around her, her skin still steaming. 'Hello, Jack.'

'I'm being an eejit, aren't I?'

Lilly sat on the bed. 'A little.'

'I mean, it is only work, isn't it?'

She thought of the dress and the lotion. 'Of course it's only work.'

'So, I'll see you soon?'

Lilly shoved her brown dress back in the wardrobe and pulled out her jeans. 'Of course you will.'

Alexia followed Valentine at a discreet distance. In truth, most people didn't check their mirror often enough to know they were being followed, but it was better to be cautious. She'd once tailed the local MP all the way to a brothel in Watford. The poor idiot didn't notice her until she had a nice picture of him in the doorway.

She was glad to be moving, having been stuck outside the cottage for what seemed like hours. First someone came to fix the windscreen, then a Chelsea tractor pulled up and a young boy ran into the house. It must have been Valentine's kid. Funny, he looked nothing like the teenage girl. Seconds later, another man arrived.

He stopped and chatted to the driver of the 4 × 4, who called him David. From his pinkie ring to his hand-stitched shoes, Alexia could see he was public school. Takes one to know one, she supposed. He was handsome enough, with his blond floppy hair. This solicitor really had some appeal.

When Valentine left the cottage she had only the girl with her. Now, why was she taking her to a dinner date with Green Eyes? Alexia's instincts told her she was on to something interesting.

The Mini pulled up outside an old station house where Valentine and the girl were greeted by a group of adults and children. Lots of them were dressed in masks or wearing witches' hats. Valentine grabbed one and wedged it down onto her curls. Alexia humphed. Hallowe'en seemed such an American affair these days. When she was a kid the whole thing went largely un-noticed apart from the odd scraped-out turnip. Now it was just another money-making exercise. She'd seen that one of the teen mags her Dad owned was giving away free plastic fangs and plastic blood. He never missed an opportunity to make a killing.

She looked back up at the station house. What was this place?

Alexia got out of the car and crept around the back of the building. There was a tall gate marked 'Private'. She waited for a gaggle of torch-wielding ghosts to pass, undid the lock and slipped through.

The building itself was three storeys high, its brick-work clean but old. The window frames and doors were peeling and chipped. As a whole, it appeared tired and put-upon. There was a patch of grass worn thin by foot-balls and the patio was littered with recycling boxes.

Suddenly the back door opened and Alexia froze, pushing herself back against the wall. The smell of cooking filled the night air and soft voices broke through.

'So, how are things with you and Anna?'

It was the green-eyed man. She recognised his honeyed voice from outside the lawyer's house.

'We're managing,' said Lilly.

The man stepped outside and dropped a bottle into the box. Alexia held her breath, sure he would see her, but he didn't take his eyes from the woman inside. Thank goodness he found her so attractive.

'It must be hard on your son,' he said.

'He's trick-or-treating with his father tonight,' she said. 'Sam won't give up until he has collected every fun-sized Snickers in Little Markham.'

'But it must be hard for him to find a strange girl living in his house.'

So the girl wasn't her daughter.

'It's not ideal,' Valentine said.

'You have a very big heart,' he said, 'to help a client when everyone is against it.'

'Perhaps I'm just bloody-minded.'

The man moved back inside and closed the door.

Alexia tiptoed back through the gate and to her car. Her hands shook as she took out her phone. The girl was Valentine's client. Could it really be *the* client? Had she found the other shooter? Living with her solicitor?

'Steve,' she said into her phone.

'Why are you whispering?'

'I've just been spying on the solicitor.'

'Never mind that, Posh,' he said. 'I did that digging around you wanted, and Jack McNally's a copper.'

Alexia whistled. 'The policeman and the defence solicitor, now that's a nice angle.'

'Too bleeding right,' he said. 'I'm writing the headline now. Get back here with a nice picture for me.'

'Forget the picture, Steve, hold the front page,' she said.

'Are you fucking mad? This is the best story all year.'

'Trust me, you'll want to run this one.'

She heard the death rattle of his throat as Steve thought about it. 'This had better be good.'

Chapter Thirteen

The morning had gone so smoothly it was almost eerie. Anna had grilled them all sausages and tomatoes and they had gone through the contents of Sam's swag bag from the previous night. Eight bars of chocolate, ten packets of sweets, three satsumas (well, you can't win 'em all) and over five quid in change. Anna had oohed and ahhed at his loot and Sam had not been aggressive even once. Granted, he had dived into Penny's car without so much as a thank you for breakfast, but it was progress nonetheless.

When Lilly went to her wardrobe to pull out a work shirt she found all five washed, ironed and hung up. Anna had clearly been keeping herself busy.

She checked her watch. Eight-thirty and she was already at her desk – a record.

She cupped her cold hands around the latte she had collected on the way in and sighed contentedly. She'd been so early, she'd beaten Sheila and had been able to usher Anna down to her office without a barbed comment or glare. Honestly, you'd think a woman with three children of her own would be more sympathetic.

'So,' said Anna with a bright smile. 'I should help with the filing?'

Lilly glanced at the bare shelves that Anna had systematically cleared.

'I don't recognise the place as it is,' she said. 'Let's get down to some work.'

'I should make coffee then,' said Anna.

Lilly pointed to her steaming cup. 'I mean, work on your case.'

Anna's smile slipped.

'I know it's hard, but we can't keep putting it off. Dr Kadir said we need to talk.'

'I don't like this doctor,' said Anna.

'She's on your side,' said Lilly. 'And she may be the only person who can prevent you from going to jail.'

Anna flopped into the chair opposite Lilly and rested her chin on her hands. She could have been any teenager being forced to do what she didn't want to do. Only this one had suffered more than most adults could even dream of.

'So, what do you like to know?' she said.

Lilly shuffled the papers on her desk. She had reread Anna's statement to immigration at least ten times and it never got easier – but she needed more detail.

'When your mother and sisters were killed, how did you feel?'

Anna shrugged. 'Sad.'

'And what about when your father said you were to escape with your brother?'

'Scared.'

Her answers seemed flat, inadequate, but maybe that

was the point. Maybe there were no words to describe the horror of what had taken place.

Lilly tried a different tack. 'Tell me about your journey to the UK.'

Anna visibly squirmed.

'How long did it take?' asked Lilly.

'Many days.'

'Four, five, six?'

'Yes.'

Lilly groaned. 'Which was it?'

'Six, I think,' said Anna. 'I don't know exactly, it was very confusing.'

Lilly tried to imagine a child being smuggled across a continent in the midst of a war. Of course the days would blur into one another.

'And when you got here,' Lilly softened her tone, 'how did you feel?'

Anna furrowed her brow as if struggling to find the words. 'I feel as though it is living a dream.'

'Because you were so happy to get away from Kosovo?' asked Lilly. 'A dream come true?'

'No. Because it does not feel real. It feels like I am here but yet not here,' said Anna.

Detachment. Now they were getting somewhere.

Lilly opened her mouth to ask Anna if she had felt the same way at Manor Park, when the office door burst open. Sheila stood with her legs akimbo. Her perm had expanded to twice its girth. For a woman of five foot two she cut an impressive figure.

'I thought you two would be hiding in here.'

Lilly sighed. 'We're not hiding, Sheila, we're working.'

'Very cosy.' Sheila's eyes flashed. 'All tucked up in here away from prying eyes while I'm in reception dealing with the abuse.'

'What abuse?' asked Lilly.

Sheila snorted in disgust. 'It's just about to kick off, I can tell you.'

In a flash of turquoise silk, Rupinder appeared. 'Can someone tell me what's going on?'

'God knows,' said Lilly. 'Anna and I were down here going through her statement when Genghis Khan here started one of her rants about people abusing her.'

Rupinder frowned. 'I didn't know there had been any more problems.'

'There haven't been,' said Lilly. 'Sheila's being hysterical.'

'I'm hysterical?' Sheila prodded her chest with a square, white-tipped acrylic nail. 'Let's see how the clients react.'

Lilly was exasperated. 'React to what?'

'To that,' Sheila shouted back, and threw a copy of the *Three Counties Observer* onto the desk.

The picture was a nice one. Not the school picture that had been on every TV channel, but a holiday snap with Charles Stanton in board shorts, sticking out his tongue cheekily at the camera.

Rupinder read aloud. 'At least Charlie's family had the comfort of spending the summer with him in Cornwall where they have a second home. He spent his days surfing and his evenings with his many friends.'

Lilly tried not to look at Anna.

'He was a popular boy and a big hit with the girls,' Rupinder continued. 'His death is a tragedy which has sent shockwaves through the small Hertfordshire village where he lived and the £25,000-a-year Manor Park school where he was gunned down in cold blood.'

Sheila was incredulous. 'You spend twenty-five grand a year on that school?'

'Not my idea,' said Lilly.

'You obviously get paid too much,' said Sheila.

'Hardly.'

'Will you two shut up?' said Rupinder, and went back to the editorial piece on page five. 'As locals and class-mates alike have been attempting to come to terms with recent events, they will no doubt be horrified to learn that their neighbour and fellow parent has taken on the case for the defence. Lilly Valentine, a solicitor with Harpenden firm Fulton, Carter and Singh, has agreed to represent the asylum seeker charged with Charlie's murder, who cannot be named for legal reasons.'

'They've named the firm,' said Sheila. 'We'll have them queuing up to take shots at us now.'

Rupinder ignored her. 'A source close to Charlie's family described Miss Valentine as a disgrace. Some readers may find this harsh; after all, isn't she just doing her job?'

'The chance would be a fine thing,' said Lilly.

'But the *Three Counties Observer* has discovered that not only is Miss Valentine working for the defendant, she is letting her live in her house.' Rupinder glanced nervously at Lilly. 'While local people assumed the person suspected of an armed massacre was safely in custody, it turns out she is living happily only minutes from the school where the attack took place.'

They all looked at the picture at the foot of the page. Anna and Lilly chatting on their porch, Jack with his arm around Lilly's waist.

'Oh, Jesus, tell me they don't mention Jack,' Lilly said.

Rupinder cleared her throat. 'And what do the police make of this unusual state of affairs? No doubt they're affronted and demanding to have bail revoked. Actually, they're not, perhaps something to do with Miss Valentine's relationship with Sergeant Jack McNally, a child protection officer who is currently on a leave of absence.'

The telephone rang and Sheila automatically reached for it.

'Don't,' said Rupinder. 'Put the answer machine on.'

'But the clients,' said Sheila.

Rupinder sighed. 'The clients are the least of our problems today.'

Snow White read the report with a mixture of satisfaction and disgust.

She was pleased that the world could now see Lilly Valentine for what she was. A traitor. That she would sneak the foreigner into their very midst showed there were no levels to which she would not stoop.

Grandpa had always said it wasn't the advancing armies that troubled him. 'If you can see the buggers, you can shoot them.' It was the covert cells that frightened him. Silent, deadly. 'The enemy within.'

How right he had been.

This was it. The moment she had been waiting for. The moment when everything she had predicted finally came true. The enemy was within.

She needed to clear her mind and consider her next move.

Lilly put her head in her hands. She wanted to scream, she wanted to cry, she wanted to run away from the office, and this stupid case. The phone had not stopped ringing with requests for comment on the *Three Counties* piece. It would only be a matter of time before they were camped on the office doorstep.

'You okay?' asked Anna.

'Not really.'

'I will make coffee,' said Anna.

'Coffee,' Lilly repeated. How could the girl think about coffee at a time like this? It was as if she didn't understand the seriousness of what was happening. The papers, and therefore the world, knew Anna was living with Lilly.

'And we have chocolate,' said Anna. 'One bar or two?'

Lilly looked up at Anna. Her beautiful green eyes shone with an almost mystical phosphorescence.

'Things are pretty bad, Anna,' said Lilly.

Anna nodded. 'Before I come here, things were very bad, so this is an improvement.'

Despite herself, Lilly smiled. Anna was right. The situation might be difficult but it was nothing compared to what Anna had suffered in the past.

She reached into her drawer and pulled out a Picnic and a Curly Wurly. 'This is definitely a two-bar moment.'

Her mobile rang and she checked caller ID. Jack. She was ashamed to admit it but she couldn't face him. He'd told her not to take the case and warned that it would end badly. She'd call him later when she'd bolstered herself.

A moment later it rang again. This time it was David. Oh, God, she certainly couldn't talk to him right now. She could only imagine what he would say about Sam's home being splashed over the headlines.

It rang a third time and she switched it off. Cowardly, for sure, but necessary for mental health.

Seconds later her computer sprang to life with a message in her inbox. Lilly sighed. When she had started out as a lawyer she was armed only with a pager and she regularly forgot to put a battery in that. People didn't feel the need to be in touch twenty-four hours a day, and work got done, lives were lived.

Her mother, Elsa, never even had a landline, and when Lilly went away to university they stayed in touch by letter – one a week until the day Elsa became too ill to write. Lilly still had every one in a shoebox tied with the pink chiffon scarf Elsa had worn on the day she died. Couldn't do that with texts or emails, could you?

She opened her message.

To: Lilly Valentine
From: Jez Stafford
Subject: Eat your heart out, Mrs Beckham
I see that you have media coverage dear Victoria would be proud of. At least you look cute in the picture. Not so sure about Jack.

Anyway . . . the judge wants us round there now. He's tried to call the office but can't get through and your mobile's turned off. No doubt you're doing an interview with Richard and Judy.

J x

Lilly closed her eyes. Could she pretend she hadn't got the message? There was no way for Jez to know whether she'd read it, was there? She was sure she'd read that somewhere.

She quickly logged off and sat back in her chair. No phone, no mobile, no computer. It was disquieting.

She picked up her bag. 'Come on, Anna.'

'We go home?' said Anna.

'Afraid not.'

'Nice earrings,' said Jez.

Kerry felt the hot flash of pleasure at her throat. 'Thanks.' She'd bought them last weekend at a craft fayre. The stallholder said the topaz stones matched her eyes.

'I like your tie,' she said, forcing the squeal of pleasure from her voice.

He ran a hand down the yellow silk. 'Christmas present.'

She wanted to ask who from, but didn't dare. He seemed distracted, repeatedly checking his watch.

At last Lilly dashed into the robing room. Why did she always arrive like a whirlwind? And why did everyone smile? It wasn't professional to keep everyone waiting and then explode into their faces, thought Kerry.

'Who leaked the story?' asked Jez.

Lilly rolled her eyes. 'Someone who hates me.'

'No one hates you, Lilly,' he said.

Kerry sniffed. She might not hate the solicitor for the defence but she found her flipping annoying.

'You'd be surprised,' Lilly said. 'When the mothers at Manor Park read that little lot they'll be hiring a hitman.'

'And I don't suppose the judge is very pleased,' said Kerry. 'He's trying to attract as little media attention as possible.'

Jez laughed. 'There's no way he can blame you for this mess.'

'I wouldn't bet on it,' said Lilly. 'Anyway, let's get it over with. I've spent the morning avoiding men I don't want to speak to and I can't put it off any longer.'

She stood up and, to Kerry's annoyance, Jez jumped to attention. Kerry's own bulk precluded any sudden movements, but she refused to be rushed in any event. Just who did Lilly Valentine think she was?

'Great suit,' said Jez to Lilly as they swanned down the corridor.

Lilly looked down at her nylon jacket and laughed. 'Can't say the same for that tie,' she said.

Kerry sniggered to herself. Lilly had put her foot in it now.

'Sheba gave it to me for Christmas,' he said.

'What did you give her?' asked Lilly.

'A hostess trolley,' he said.

Lilly howled with laughter and Jez joined her. Kerry wondered why that was funny.

'My nan once gave me an ironing board,' said Lilly, wiping her eyes. I was twelve.'

'I can only imagine seasonal festivities in the Valentine household,' said Jez.

'Oh, they were hilarious,' said Lilly. 'My mum used to try to get everyone on our street to be more PC. When Mr Johnson at number twenty-two called his dog Nigger Boy, she gave him a copy of *Roots*. Then she invited him to Christmas dinner with the Patels from the corner shop. They all got pissed on Babycham and ended up trying to do a seance.'

Jez clapped his hands in mirth.

Kerry imagined his Christmas dinners to be a magazine glossy with at least twenty friends squeezed around a table heaving with champagne and smoked salmon. A far cry from Lilly's council-estate affair. Yet even that sounded more fun than her own. She usually visited her dad and his cat. They were all snoring by the end of the Queen's Speech. When they woke around seven, Kerry would drive back to her dark flat and eat a tin of Roses.

Judge Banks shook his head. He had the case file to his left and the latest edition of the *Three Counties Observer* to his right.

'This is most unfortunate.'

'Yes, Your Honour,' said Lilly. 'But at least this time I didn't crash into your car.'

'I hardly think this is a time for humour, Miss Valentine.'

Lilly threw up her hands. 'I'm not sure what else to do, Your Honour. This story is not my doing or that of my client. A reporter obviously followed me to my home and worked out that Anna was living there.'

'Something that is surely no longer tenable.'

Lilly thought he might try this.

'Your Honour, I don't see why not. The fact that this information has been made public doesn't change the risk posed by my client. It doesn't make her more likely to abscond and it doesn't make her more likely to reoffend.'

'Now everyone knows where she lives, the child herself may be in danger,' said the judge.

'You can grant a non-molestation order here and now, Your Honour, make sure they don't come to my office or my house.'

'That's one possibility but we will have the world's media breathing down our necks,' he said.

'The *Three Counties Observer* is hardly international,' said Lilly.

'Who knows where all this will end, young lady?'

On the way home Lilly couldn't help dwelling on Judge Banks's ominous words. As soon as Lilly had tried to take control of this case, disaster lay at every turn – the cottage window, the office, the car and now the press.

As she pulled up outside the cottage she craned her neck for photographers.

'No one is here,' said Anna.

Lilly realised she'd been holding her breath.

'The press have had their day and we'll soon be old news.' But she couldn't help wondering what might happen next, and – as the judge had also wondered – where it all might end.

Her phone beeped with an incoming text, answering Lilly's question. It was the office.

> *Just heard from Luton Crown Court that due to excessive media coverage, The Crown v Duraku has been transferred to CCC.*

She had her answer. The case was going to end at the Old Bailey.

Chapter Fourteen

Snow White pulled out onto the A5. Old Rusty screeched as she pushed the gear stick into second.

'Distracted, darling?'

Snow White smiled at her husband in the passenger seat. The car lurched forward and he moaned. He was hung over after a night out with the boys and needed a lift to the station.

'You should have called a cab,' she said. 'I have better things to do than chauffeur you around.'

He rubbed her knee and exhaled. Snow White could smell his breath. Scotch and mouthwash.

She shot over a roundabout, oblivious to the horns of the other cars.

'For the love of God,' he said. 'Keep your mind on the job in hand.'

She sneaked a glance at her husband. He was a good man but a simple one. He wasn't alive to the extreme danger in which they were living.

'I can't stop thinking about that girl,' she said. 'Something should be done.'

'Better not get involved,' he said.

'You're not having your nose rubbed in it every day.' She pulled up at the station, blocking in three taxis.

Her husband leaned over and kissed her cheek.

She watched him stagger to his platform and ignored the irate hooting of the minibus behind. A rag-head. Not even worth her contempt.

The fridge had looked bare this morning and she thought she might pop over to M&S before the parking places rose to golden-fleece status.

As she turned Old Rusty around she caught sight of red curls. It was the enemy. Snow White looked again, her heart pounding. She was with that anorexic girl, *the girl*, and they were obviously on their way to somewhere important.

Once again it was time to take action.

'What the fuck?'

Luke and Caz emerge from the tube at St Paul's, surprised at the sea of people. They push past some meat-head in an Adidas tracksuit.

'What's your problem?' the man snarls, his hand already drawn into a fist.

'Leave it,' says the man next to him, and Luke takes the opportunity to escape into the crowd.

They'd made their way over to do a bit of begging, as nine-thirty always meant hoards of office workers dashing to Cheapside, but this was manic.

'Crowds are good,' says Caz, but she doesn't sound sure.

There is something in the atmosphere, something tense. Luke had felt something similar once at a Gunners' match and his dad had insisted they left before the final whistle.

They can't bed down in their usual spot just inside the entrance, because a group of skinheads have congregated, talking and nodding, organising something.

Luke looks at Caz and she beckons him outside.

'I think we should get off,' she says.

He looks at the beads of sweat on her top lip. 'Don't we need some money?'

'I can get some,' she says, avoiding his eyes.

Luke feels a knot tighten in his stomach. Ever since he found out how Caz made extra cash he's tried to put it to the back of his mind.

'Let's give it a try here,' he says.

'I don't get a good feeling about this, Luke.'

He puts an arm around her. 'Like you're always telling me, one person's money is as good as the next's.'

She looks unconvinced, so he squats down on his heels and pulls her down with him. 'With this amount of people we'll have twenty quid in less time than it would take you to find a punter.'

She puts her head on his shoulder, too sick and needy to argue.

The men in the station start to emerge, still in groups but moving as one body.

'Spare some change?' says Luke to the nearest two.

One looks right through him but the other snaps his head. 'What did you say?' His clothes are expensive but his chipped teeth and earrings tell Luke he's spent his life on an estate.

Luke bends his head and feels Caz shrink into him, her hand gripping his upper arm.

'I asked what you said,' sneers the man.

Luke shakes his head and folds in on himself.

The man nudges Luke's leg with the toe of his loafer. 'Don't fucking ignore me when I'm talking to you.'

The other man laughs and is soon joined by others until Luke can feel the press of a group above him. The man nudges again, only this time it's more of a kick. 'Fucking junkie scum.'

Luke braces himself. The homeless get beaten up all the time. Especially after last orders. Someone once set fire to Caz's sleeping bag. And she was in it.

Luke imagines what all those boots and trainers will feel like raining down on him.

Another voice booms from behind, clear and authoritative. 'Lads, lads, let's not give anyone a chance to criticise us.'

'It's these dirty fuckers, boss, they do my head in, sitting here begging for money.'

'Not a pretty sight on the streets of this once great city, I'll grant you,' says the boss.

'Why can't they just get a job instead of dossing around in their own filth?'

The boss laughs, and it's hard, humourless. 'That's a very good question, Bigsy. Why can't they just get a job?'

He moves to the front and squats down in front of Luke and Caz. Luke can smell the sharp lemon of his aftershave.

'Tell me, son,' he says. 'Have you tried to get work?'

The way the man is nodding tells Luke not to point out he's a schoolboy from Harpenden.

'Let me guess, where you're from, all the jobs have been taken by the Poles. Plumbing, building, you name it,' says the man.

The group grunt their understanding.

Luke's only ever met one Pole and he was a consultant at the private hospital where his mum had an operation on her knee after a fall on a skiing holiday. But he nods his agreement.

The boss gets back to his feet. 'See, lads, this is what has become of the great white working classes. Reduced to poverty and despair by mass immigration.' He pulls out a twenty-pound note and brandishes it so everyone can see. Luke wonders if he's supposed to take it but his hands are shaking too much. The boss frowns as his note flaps in the wind. For a moment, Luke thinks he will put it back in his wallet but Caz snakes out her fingers and snatches it away.

With that, the boss leads his flock down towards the cathedral.

'I still think they're dirty cunts,' mumbles the first man, but he chucks three pound coins at them all the same.

As the men round the corner, Caz jumps to her feet and sets off to Waterloo, where the word is a dealer has just got fresh stash from Afghanistan.

Luke tags behind her and vows to find that deposit.

Lilly dropped her biro as she signed in at the entrance of the Old Bailey.

Anna took Lilly's hands in her own and blew on them. 'You are cold.'

Lilly smiled. She wasn't about to admit that she was terrified. Last night she had been through all the case papers and rehearsed exactly what to say. She'd gone to bed having drunk enough Sauvignon to sleep well but not enough to feel it in the morning.

She was determined to remain calm, and reminded herself that she appeared in court most days. This was nothing new.

She looked around the Central Criminal Court. The whole place sighed with a thousand life sentences and nausea growled in her stomach.

She left Anna with Milo and headed for the loos. A barrister was washing her hands, chatting into a Bluetooth headset. She looked so relaxed, as if she belonged.

Lilly appraised her reflection. Her hair was neat but not severe. Her black suit was freshly dry cleaned and Anna had pressed and starched a white shirt to within an inch of its life.

Her mother had always said, 'If it waddles like a duck and quacks like a duck . . .'

Well, here was Lilly, waddling and quacking for all she was worth.

'So, get your arse in gear, Donald,' she mumbled to herself.

Nothing could go wrong. She was prepared.

'Hello gorgeous,' called Jez as she came out of the toilet.

Lilly gave him a weak smile.

'Ooh, someone's nervous,' he laughed. 'It's only P and D.'

It might only be a short hearing for Anna to put in her plea and for the new judge to give yet more directions, but it would be in the grim auspices of one of the most infamous courtrooms in the world.

'Who've we got?' asked Lilly.

'Teddy Roberts,' he said.

His Honour Judge Edward Roberts. Lilly gulped. 'Didn't he once order a solicitor to spend a night in the cells?'

'It was only an hour and she was late.' Jez put his hand on Lilly's arm. 'He's a pussycat. Nothing can go wrong.'

They entered Court Four.

Nothing can go wrong, nothing can go wrong.

'Lilly,' said Jez. 'Where's your gown?'

Shit.

Lilly sank onto the bench and wondered what the food would be like in custody.

'Where's the judge?' Jez asked the usher.

'Coming down the corridor.'

Jez turned to Kerry. 'Do you have one?'

Kerry nodded and fished in her bag. Lilly snatched it and threw it around her shoulders. It was enormous and looked like a Victorian cape that skimmed her ankles.

'Thanks,' Lilly whispered and tied the bands that hung like a loose bandage around her collarbone. Everything smelled faintly of toast.

The usher opened the door. 'All rise.'

Lilly struggled to her feet like a black pair of curtains.

Jez leaned over and whispered, 'Tell me you didn't take a lump out of *his* car.'

'I'm ignoring you,' she said.

Judge Roberts entered court and raised a quizzical eyebrow at Lilly's attire.

'Miss Valentine, thank you for coming at such short notice.'

Lilly nodded and smiled. Maybe he *was* a pussycat.

'I have spoken with the *Three Counties Observer* and ordered them to release your address to no one. I have also made it abundantly clear that if they harass you in any way this court will deal with them most forcefully.'

Lilly beamed. Definitely a pussycat. 'Thank you.'

'But I should tell you now that I am most unhappy with the situation in respect of your client's bail.'

Maybe not.

Lilly cleared her throat. 'Your Honour, I know that in these circumstances a defendant would be remanded in custody, but the *Bail Act* makes it clear that the presumption is always for bail to be given . . .'

Judge Roberts put up his hand. 'Miss Valentine, I have been a judge for nearly twenty years, so you can imagine I've come across the *Bail Act* once or twice.'

'Yes, Your Honour,' said Lilly. 'I just wanted to explain how this particular arrangement came about.'

The hand came up again. 'Frankly, I'm not interested in the hows and whys. I just want to make it clear that I am not comfortable at all.'

'I can understand your apprehension,' she said. 'But if you revoke bail . . .'

The hand again. Lilly was beginning to feel like she was a car in traffic.

'Did I say anything about revocation, Miss Valentine?'

'Well, no,' said Lilly.

'Then let's move on,' said Judge Roberts. 'I've made

it clear I'm unhappy, but since your client is here today I can hardly complain she's a flight risk, can I? Now, are you ready to plead today?'

'Yes, Your Honour. My client will plead not guilty.'

'On what basis?' he asked.

'On the basis that she didn't do it.'

The courtroom erupted into laughter. Lilly felt her face burn.

'On what legal basis?' said the judge. 'Self-defence?'

'I intend to show that my client did not have the mental capacity to take part in a conspiracy to murder,' said Lilly.

'You have an expert?' asked the judge.

'Dr Leyla Kadir will say my client was, and still is, suffering from Post Traumatic Stress Disorder,' said Lilly, hoping to God that was what she would say.

'Very well.' The judge nodded curtly at Anna. 'Please make your way to the dock.'

Anna was led by the usher to the wooden box at the back of the court. She stared down the steps and Lilly wondered if she realised they led directly to the cells. The kid looked swamped by her surroundings, like a pixie trapped in the real world.

The clerk cleared his throat. 'Tirana Duraku, it is said that on 2 October you did conspire with Artan Shala to murder Charles Stanton. How do you plead, guilty or not guilty?'

Anna looked up at the judge, a semi-circle of white beneath each iris. She opened her mouth to speak when there was a huge bang behind her.

Lilly gasped and saw that the public gallery had been stormed by about twenty men, all shouting and clapping their hands, nylon sportswear stretched over their beer bellies.

The judge banged his gavel. 'This is a closed court.'

The men continued to jeer until a man pushed his way to the front. He was dressed from head to toe in black: suit, shirt, tie, overcoat. He leaned against the balcony railings and glowered at the judge.

'The public are not allowed to be present during this hearing,' said the judge, his tone thunderous.

'And why is that?' asked the man.

'I am not at liberty to explain,' said Judge Roberts. 'Now, if you would kindly leave.'

The man pointed at Anna. 'Is it because she's an asylum seeker?'

'Leave my courtroom,' said the judge, the steel in his voice sharpening.

'Is it because the likes of her get special treatment? Houses, social security, and now protection from the law?'

The men behind him clapped.

'If you do not vacate the gallery immediately, I will have each and every one of you arrested,' shouted the judge.

'And I suppose you'll sling us in the cells while this foreigner gets to live it up with her brief.'

The men erupted. Cheering, clapping and banging their fists against the balcony railings.

'England for the English,' the man shouted.

'England for the English,' screamed the rest, until it became a terrifying chant, each beat punctuated by stamped feet.

'Everyone into my chamber,' said the judge.

The usher, clerk, Kerry and Jez made for the door.

Anna didn't move. She was like a rabbit caught in headlights, glued to her chair, staring at the men.

'Anna,' Lilly shouted above the cacophony. 'Let's get out of here.'

But Anna was mesmerised by the sight of ugly and angry men spitting abuse. All directed at her.

The alarm sounded. The noise was ear-splitting.

Lilly ran across the courtroom to the dock. Milo followed closely. He stood on her robe, which was now dragging behind her, and they both tripped. Another roar came from the balcony.

Lilly shrugged off the gown and stumbled towards Anna. 'Quickly,' she said.

Anna didn't or couldn't move but continued to stare at the men.

Lilly pulled her client by the hand but she fell to the floor like a stone. Milo leapt into the dock and carried Anna in his arms towards the back of the court.

They hobbled towards the door. The men in the gallery dug into their pockets and began hurling the contents. Lilly felt something hit her back. Then her head. Then her cheek.

When they passed into the chamber they stood panting. Anna was still in Milo's arms.

Only then did Lilly realise that all three of them were covered in dog shit.

Steve Berry looked at the image of the skinheads being bundled into a police van and let out a hard rasp of a chuckle.

'Posh,' he said, 'this picture is genius.'

Alexia shrugged as if it were nothing.

'I still don't know how you got this.'

Alexia tapped the side of her nose. 'Instinct.'

She wasn't about to admit she'd received an anonymous tip-off. That morning, a woman had called. She said she'd just seen Valentine and the kid heading into London. 'Are you sure it was them?' Alexia had asked.

The woman tutted. 'Of course I'm sure, and I should say by the way they were dressed that something is interesting is going on.'

It could have been a crank, but something in the way the woman spoke told Alexia to investigate. The woman wouldn't give her name but there was something about her voice – she couldn't place it but she'd definitely heard it before.

Alexia called Luton Youth Court and was told the case had been transferred. She called the Crown Court who confirmed the same.

Then she got a call from the Bailey telling her in no uncertain terms that if she impeded the defence case again she would be arrested. Bingo. She knew exactly where the case had been transferred.

Alexia had grabbed her coat and jumped on the next train. She knew the hearing would be closed but she might get something. She'd need to be careful – she didn't want to end up in court herself. However, once she arrived and saw the racists filing in, she knew that it was going to be another bonanza news day. The top judge himself could try to arrest her but Alexia Dee was going to get this story.

*   *   *

Lilly had cried, thrown up and cried some more. Finally she ran a bath. It was time to wash the crap out of her hair.

She'd shaken the biggest lumps out and washed it as best she could at a sink in the ladies', but she could still smell it.

The police, to be fair, had been lovely. They'd driven Milo, Anna and Lilly all the way home and promised that the thugs would be charged. But it didn't stop Lilly feeling humiliated.

She held her nose and dunked her head under the surface. Had this been what it was like for Anna in Kosovo: had she been made to feel less than human? She hadn't spoken since they'd got back and had locked herself in the main bathroom. God knows what memories this had brought back.

A tap came on the bathroom door. 'Is anyone alive in there?' said Jack.

He opened the door, padded across to the bath and put his arms around her. She relaxed into his embrace, her hair dripping down his leather jacket.

'Are you still mad at me about the picture of you in the paper?' she said.

He didn't let her go. 'Yep.'

'Are you in trouble about being here with Anna?'

He buried his nose in her neck. 'Yep.'

'Oh, Jack, I'm sorry.'

'Yep.'

They stayed like that, clinging on to one another until the water grew cold.

At last Jack let her go.

'Are you all right?' he asked.

'I'll survive.'

'It's been a rough day.'

'Yeah,' she said. 'Pretty shitty.'

They both laughed, and Lilly pulled herself out of the bath.

'Here,' said Jack, and patted her shoulders with a towel. 'Let me.'

'Do you do this for all your women?' asked Lilly.

'Only those attacked by marauding mobs.'

He put a squirt of lotion onto his hand and began massaging it into her back.

'I could get used to this on a daily basis,' said Lilly.

'So, why don't you?' he asked.

She turned to him. 'What are you saying, Jack?'

He opened his mouth to speak when Sam waltzed in and pulled down his trousers.

'Sorry, Mum, but Anna's in the other bathroom and I'm dying for a poo.'

'Bloody hell, Sam,' Lilly said, and covered herself with a towel. She put on her dressing gown and looked at Jack. 'Let's continue this conversation downstairs.'

'Oh, Mum,' called Sam.

'Yes?'

'Dad's here.'

If Jack was prepared to put his anger aside, David was not. As soon as Lilly entered the sitting room she could sense the dark cloud above her ex-husband. The sight of him pacing reminded her of the bad old days.

'The rug's already threadbare,' she said.

'Very droll,' he replied. 'We need to talk.'

'Can it not wait?' asked Jack. 'She's had a terrible shock.'

David glared at Jack. 'When it comes to children, things can't be put on hold. You'll understand that one day when you have a son of your own.'

Lilly saw Jack wince. He loved Sam and had a great relationship with him, but he wasn't his father.

'I'll be off,' he said to Lilly, and pecked her on the cheek. 'Call me later.'

When she heard the door close she rounded on David.

'There was absolutely no call for that.'

David held his back straight. Elsa would have said he had a pole up his arse.

'I think there was every call. When I need to discuss my child with his mother, I won't be deterred by every Tom, Dick and Harry you've taken a shine to.'

'Jack's not just anyone, he's . . . he's . . .'

'What, Lilly? What is he? You're not married, you don't even live together, and as far as I can tell you've no plans for either,' he said. 'Not when you still want to flirt with your Bosnian friend.'

Lilly was stung by the unfairness of the comment. Yet was he so far from the mark?

She sighed and sank onto the battered old sofa. 'Let's not fight, David.'

'I need to know our son is safe.'

'He is,' she said.

David shook his head. 'You're making a lot of enemies with this case, and I won't allow Sam to get caught in the crossfire.'

'He's fine,' said Lilly.

'Fine?' David shouted. 'Journalists have been stalking you, Lilly, taking pictures of you outside the house. Sam's house.'

'The trial judge has taken care of that. Warned then to stay away,' she said.

'And you think they'll listen when this story is getting hotter by the day?'

'If they come anywhere near me or Sam I'll call the court.'

'Well, make sure you do.' David dropped his voice. 'Or I shall have to take steps.'

Lilly felt her heart begin to thud. 'What steps?'

'Sam will have to come and stay with me.'

'You can't take him away from me,' she said.

'I'll do whatever I have to,' he replied, and left.

Lilly stared after him, shaken by a mixture of fear and rage. Who did he think he was, making threats about Sam? Lilly wouldn't let him come to any harm. He was everything to her and David knew that. Hadn't he been so jealous of her fierce love for her son that he'd needed to seek attention from Botox Belle in the first place?

As for the stuff about Milo, well, she had been acting like a fool. There was an attraction between them, a spark at most, but nothing compared to what she shared with Jack. He was the one who had stood by her through this nightmare of a case, despite how much he had to lose. He was the one, she reminded herself, who had stood between her and a bullet. And if she wasn't completely mistaken, he had just, in his own inimitable fashion, asked her to live with him.

Chapter Fifteen

Dear Headmaster,

We are sure you share our concern that Charles Stanton's murderer is being represented by the mother of Samuel Valentine, a pupil in the preparatory school. Under normal circumstances we would be of the opinion that a parent's mode of employment should be of no interest to anyone but themselves. However, no doubt you will agree that the current circumstances are far from normal, and it would be in everyone's best interests if Samuel Valentine were asked to leave Manor Park. We should be grateful if you would bring this matter before the governors with the urgency it deserves.

Mr Lattimer looked at the list of parents who had signed the letter. The usual gaggle of overprotective helicopter mothers.

Mr Lattimer reread it and sighed.

. . . a parent's mode of employment should be of no interest to anyone but themselves . . .

If he and the governors didn't apply that strict rule across the board there would be no annual garden party, which was sponsored by a publisher of several racy magazines including *Pearl Necklace* and *Bottom Love*. Ditto the new drama studio, which had been paid for by the CEO of a cigarette company.

Mr Lattimer prided himself on his pragmatism.

He folded the letter and placed it in his top drawer. This issue wouldn't go away, but he could try to ignore it, at least until he had called Johnny Philips's mother and asked for a donation towards the cricket pavilion. She was the author of several trashy thrillers and always good for a few hundred.

'Tell me how you felt after the rape.'

They were back in Dr Kadir's office for the third time in as many weeks, and once again her questions shocked Lilly. The harsh simplicity of the words, the unwavering eye contact, seemed brutal. She had to remind herself that this was not a therapy session designed to heal Anna. This was a diagnosis under the cosh of a court timetable.

'I don't know,' Anna whispered.

If Dr Kadir was frustrated she didn't show it. Instead, she poured hot water over one of her endless herbal tea bags and filled the air with a strawberry-scented cloud.

'Did you feel dirty?' she asked. 'Used?'

Anna thought for a moment. 'I felt cold.'

Lilly sipped her tea. It smelled more fruity than it tasted.

'And Artan,' said Dr Kadir, 'was he cold?'

Anna shook her head. 'He was on fire.'

Dr Kadir cocked her head and waited for Anna to elaborate.

'Many times I have seen him angry, but not like this,' said Anna. 'He said it was the worst thing that could happen.'

'And what did you think? Was it the worst thing that could have happened?'

'Many, many things have happened, and all are bad,' said Anna.

While Anna busied herself with *TV Quick*, Lilly turned to her expert.

'So, what do you think?'

'I think you are under a lot of strain.'

'What?'

Dr Kadir smiled. 'I read the papers, you know.'

Lilly waved away her concern. 'What about my client?'

Dr Kadir's smile vanished. 'She is definitely suffering from PTSD.'

Lilly punched the air. 'Yes.'

'Hardly a cause for celebration,' said Dr Kadir.

'The way this case is going,' said Lilly, 'I'm almost tempted to throw a party.'

The doctor pursed her lips. 'It almost certainly started in Kosovo, but I would say the rape was the defining incident which pushed Anna's mind into freefall.'

'The straw that broke the camel's back?'

Dr Kadir nodded. 'From that point I think she disassociated from real life.'

'So she wouldn't have understood what Artan was doing with the gun?'

'Oh, no, she would have understood exactly what was happening.'

Lilly's heart sank. 'But I thought you said she was detached from reality.'

'Detached – yes. Divorced – no.'

'There's a difference?' asked Lilly.

'Think of it as a house detached from next door. You are not connected but you can still see your neighbours, hear them shouting.'

Lilly's mind was racing; she put her fingers to her temple. 'Let me get this straight. Anna would have realised what Artan intended to do.'

'I think so.'

'But could she have taken part? Could she have had the necessary intent to join Artan?' asked Lilly.

'It's possible.'

Lilly opened her mouth, but Dr Kadir silenced her with her left hand. Lilly noticed she still wore her wedding band.

'It's more likely that Anna simply went along on autopilot. That she never considered the consequences of what was going to happen.'

'She couldn't make the active decision to join Artan.'

Dr Kadir cocked her head in agreement.

'Then Anna couldn't have committed the offence,' said Lilly.

The doctor brought the bone-china cup to her glossed lips. 'You're the lawyer, Miss Valentine, you tell me.'

'So?'

Lilly gazed longingly at Rupinder's Tupperware box of samosas. She often brought leftovers to work that looked and smelled so much more appetising than a sandwich wrapped in plastic.

Rupes sighed and pushed the box in Lilly's direction. 'So, are you going to tell me where we are?'

Lilly bit into the pastry and her mouth filled with cumin-scented lamb and peas. 'These are fantastic.'

'Lilly!'

Since the débâcle at the Old Bailey, Rupinder had insisted on a daily meeting to discuss the Duraku case.

'You're a conveyancer, you don't know anything about criminal law,' Lilly protested.

'And you don't know how much aggravation I'm getting about all this,' said Rupes.

Lilly rolled her eyes. 'From Sheila?'

'And the other partners,' said Rupes. 'They weren't overjoyed to have our name in the press.'

'Consider it free publicity.'

'And the office being vandalised?' asked Rupinder.

'It was just a bit of graffiti,' said Lilly.

Rupes glared at her. 'Do you know how much it cost to get that filth removed?'

Of course, Lilly didn't so she changed the subject.

'These meetings are just a waste of time,' said Lilly. 'Time you and I could spend earning fees.'

But Rupinder was not to be diverted. 'Think of it as bonding.'

Lilly swallowed the last bite of samosa. 'There's nothing much to report.'

'No smashed windows at home? No journalists hiding in dustbins?'

'Everything's been quiet.' Lilly smiled. 'The judge was

pretty clear that anyone overstepping the mark would have him to deal with.'

'The *Three Counties* still ran the thing about the skin-heads at the Bailey.'

Lilly shrugged. 'There's not a fat lot he could do about that. The reporter didn't come anywhere near me or Anna and the photo was taken outside court.'

'Where do you think this Dee woman is getting all her exclusives?'

Lilly paused. She'd given this a lot of thought. Someone was definitely feeding her information. Luella? Or one of the other sour-faced parents up at the school?

'Who knows?' she said. 'But another story is bound to break soon. The Prime Minister will be found in a gay *ménage à trois* and we'll be yesterday's news.'

Rupinder allowed a small smile. 'And your defence?'

'Looking much stronger,' said Lilly. 'Dr Kadir will say Anna couldn't have taken part in the conspiracy, that she was incapable at the time.'

'That's good, isn't it?' asked Rupes.

'It's great,' said Lilly. 'But I'm still going to have to convince the jury that Anna is basically a decent person who wouldn't ordinarily go around the countryside waving a gun.'

'Do you think you can win?'

Lilly laughed. 'I bloody hope so. What with me taking a shit shower and David threatening to kidnap Sam, I'd better get something out of this.'

Anna popped her head around the door. 'I've finished cleaning your desk, Lilly, so I make tea, yes?'

Lilly's eyes pricked with tears. 'That would be lovely.'

If she was going through trauma, it was nothing compared to what Anna was going through.

Rupinder put her hand over Lilly's, her bangles jangling like sleigh bells.

'Sometimes we have to make sacrifices to do the right thing.'

Lilly smiled. 'Tell that to Jack.'

'Not a happy camper?'

'Let's just say he's counting the seconds until the trial,' said Lilly.

'And until then you're not allowed to see one another?'

'The Chief Super made it very plain that the photo in the paper was the last straw and that Jack should have no contact with Anna or me until this is finished.'

Rupes pressed the lid down on her box. 'And you're sticking to that, are you?'

Luke has a plan.

He's given it a lot of thought. In truth, he's thought of little else. It's amazing how much time he used to waste thinking about stuff that doesn't matter: what's on telly; will Arsenal win the double; does Lindsay Lohan give good blow jobs?

Although his current life is less comfortable, in many ways it's easier. It's as if he's cut through all the crap and knows what's important.

'I've been thinking,' he says.

Caz doesn't look up from the phone she's just bought from Long Tall Sally. 'Steady on, soft lad, you'll give yourself a nose bleed.'

'I mean about this,' he says. 'Us.'

She jabs at the buttons with a blackened nail. 'If this is your way of proposing then stop where you are. I've already said yes to Teardrop Tony.'

'I don't mean getting married,' he sighs.

But what does he mean? He wants them to make a different life for themselves, him and Caz. Maybe to her that sounds as ridiculous as a wedding.

'Do you ever wonder about what will happen to you?' he ventures. 'To me?'

'This is fucked,' says Caz, and throws the phone to the ground. 'She's robbed me.'

Luke picks it up and takes a look. 'Do you ever think about where we might all end up?'

'I can tell you where that thieving cow will end up,' she spits. 'Six foot under.'

Luke opens the back of the phone and wipes the SIM card against the leg of his jeans. 'Because we can't just live like this for the rest of our lives, can we?'

The phone springs to life and he hands it back to Caz. 'We can't stay here, can we?'

'I've no intention of staying here.' She pockets the phone with a toothy grin. 'I'm going to Peckham.'

Luke shakes his head and laughs. Caz might not be able to take it in, but he's got a plan for them. They're not an item, not even dating, but someone's got to look after Caz. He's going to get them somewhere to live.

'Got anything for me, Posh?'

Alexia sighed.

She knew what he wanted, but he knew as well as she

did that the story had run cold. No new evidence, no different angle to run.

They'd rehashed the hearing at the Old Bailey in at least ten different ways. They'd had comments from the local Chief of Police, councillors, human rights activists, and anyone prepared to give their tuppence ha'penny. Everyone had been forced to sit up and listen to the *Three Counties Observer* but now they had nothing else to say.

Alexia spent hours on *The Spear of Truth*. There was a lot of traffic, a lot of rhetoric, but nothing specific. Snow White had gone to ground.

'How about a piece on gun crime?' she said. 'We could get the stats. Ask an MP for a quote.'

'Bollocks,' he replied.

'Something on local gangs, then,' she said.

'I'm beginning to suspect you're a one-hit wonder,' he answered.

As she turned to flip him the finger, the phone rang.

'This is Snow White,' said the woman's voice. 'I have an invitation for you.'

In many ways the secrecy made things more exciting, and Lilly was flushed with anticipation as she dropped Anna at the hostel.

'I don't know what is making your cheeks pink,' said Milo, 'but it suits you very well.'

Lilly blushed even deeper. 'Just in a hurry.'

'Ah yes,' said Milo. 'A meeting at your office.' He checked his watch. 'Eight o'clock at night is a very strange time, no?'

'A client,' said Lilly. 'He works in the day so I agreed to meet him out of hours.'

Milo raised a suspicious eyebrow. 'So committed.'

Lilly waved and ran into the night to her car.

The office was in darkness, everyone having gone home hours ago. Lilly dropped her keys as she fumbled with the lock.

'Shit.' She felt around the step for it and then saw Jack coming out of the gloom.

'Can I ask what you're doing?'

'The limbo,' she said.

'What?'

She rolled her eyes. 'I've dropped my key.'

He fished in his pocket and pulled out a pencil torch.

'Aren't you a good little boy scout?'

He shone the beam around the step. 'Dib, dib, dib.'

The key was nowhere to be seen.

'I'll have to find it in the morning,' said Lilly.

'What will we do in the meantime?' asked Jack.

'Have you got your skeleton key with you?' asked Lilly.

'I can't use that, woman,' said Jack. 'I'm in enough trouble as it is.'

'You're right,' she said. 'Let's call this off and go home. You to yours, that is, and me to mine.' She patted her bag. 'What a shame you'll never find out what I have in here.'

'A nurse's outfit?'

'Better than that.' Lilly leaned close and whispered in his ear. 'A lemon and almond cake.'

'Sold,' he said, and opened the door.

* * *

255

'You'd be in heaps of bother if the Chief knew you were here,' said Lilly.

Jack sat on her desk and chased the last crumb of cake around a plate with his finger.

'Indeed I would.'

'Am I worth it?'

He looked up at her, his gentle brown eyes twinkling in the dark. 'More than you know.'

Lilly smiled at her own stupidity. Jack *was* the man for her. It was typical of her that she'd only discovered the fact once they couldn't be together.

'I can't do this very often,' she said.

'I know.'

'I have to get Sam looked after by David, and Anna looked after by Milo.'

'I know.'

'It's a bloody nightmare.'

'I know,' he said. 'Which is why we have to make the most of the time we've got.' He leaned over and kissed her. 'I've always wondered where defence lawyers keep their briefs.'

'This is a closed meeting.'

Alexia had arrived at the Turk's Head, a shabby pub in Tye Cross, the red-light district in Luton. Outside the pub, one buttock on a bar stool, was a hulk of a man with a bald head that seemed to melt in folds over his collar. He was eating a doorstep sandwich that dripped mayonnaise down his pink chin.

'I've been asked to attend,' said Alexia.

The hulk raised an eyebrow. 'I don't think so, love.'

Alexia was unsure of what to say next when another man appeared in the doorway. He was smartly dressed, in a well-cut black suit. His shirt, also black, was double cuffed. But something about him didn't fit. It was as if he were trying far too hard. As if he would feel far more comfortable in a nylon tracksuit.

He put a hand on the hulk's meaty shoulder. 'It's all right, Bigsy.'

Alexia squeezed past, close enough to smell the filling in the bouncer's sandwich, and followed the other man into the belly of the beast.

'Don't mind him, he's there to keep out troublemakers.'

Alexia looked around the dingy interior of the pub, packed with more tattoos and England tops than a Wembley final, and wondered who on earth they had in mind.

Men and women of all ages filled every inch of the saloon. Young skinheads at the back, top to toe in denim, laughing with their girlfriends over pints of Stella. Middle-aged men nodding their Burberry caps as they propped up the bar. Pensioners around the tables engrossed in games of dominoes.

'Thank you for coming, Miss Dee.' The man led her to the front of a makeshift stage. 'The Pride of England have been very impressed by your reporting on the Stanton boy.'

'I've tried to be fair,' she said.

He pointed to a chair that had been kept deliberately free with a well-thumbed copy of *Pride and Prejudice*.

'Take a seat,' he said, scooping up his novel, and he took his place on the stage.

He tapped the microphone. 'Testing, testing.'

The noise of the crowd began to quiet in anticipation, and Alexia slipped her hand into her pocket to turn on her tape recorder.

'Good evening.' His voice was low but clear. A home-made banner with the club name 'Pride of England: Luton and Dunstable Branch', daubed in red, hung behind him. Next to it was a surprisingly well-drawn outline of a British Bulldog. 'How are we all tonight?'

It reminded Alexia of how the stand-ups at Jongleurs warmed up their crowd, and she half expected a joke about George Bush. But this wasn't comedy.

'I know most of you know me.' He laughed at the whistles that rustled through the audience. 'But for those of you that don't, I go by the name Blood River.'

Alexia shivered.

'I assume that most of you have come to show your solidarity against the terrible murder of Charles Stanton.' Blood River waited for a mumbled assent before continuing. 'And the even more shocking treatment of his killer.'

'Scum,' someone shouted from the back.

Blood River put up his hands. 'I know all of you here ask yourselves every day why foreigners get everything they need when most ordinary, working-class whites face low wages and poverty. The question on each and every lip is why do we, the British people, allow that?'

'We're fucking mugs.'

Blood River chuckled indulgently. 'Let me tell you why. White Britons are basically a decent and generous bunch, so when the government tells us some poor souls are in trouble our instinct is to help. After the Second World War the Jews and the Russians came here, and we smiled and made room, never mind that the country was nearly bankrupt from fighting the Nazis. Then the Jamaicans and the Indians arrived by the boatload, so we budged up some more and nobody mentioned the decline in industry or the rising unemployment figures. And on and on it's gone, until day by day the incomers have taken over.'

'Scroungers!'

Blood River held up his hands again. 'To be fair, it's not their fault, is it?'

'Too fucking right it is.'

Blood River shook his head. 'No, lads, we asked them to come, bleedin' begged them to come. And you can't blame them, can you? If you were living in some shit-hole and one of the richest countries in the world, one of the kindest countries in the world, said all right then, come and live with us, we'll give you a job, a house and a good school for your kids, what would you do?'

A skinhead girl with a feather-cut and a ring through her lip stood up. Alexia wondered if it could be Snow White.

'The trouble is they've stayed, haven't they?' said the girl, but her voice was unfamiliar to Alexia.

'You're right.' Blood River nodded. 'What the government wanted was a short-term solution to labour problems, but what they've got is long-term social problems.'

He pointed to a table of old boys. 'Sid, Jim, I bet you've seen a lot of changes round here over the years.'

A white-haired man with frail hands and an inhaler poking out from his top pocket nodded. 'When me and Sid was kids the whole of Luton was white. Now my daughter is the only one in her block that's not one of these Muslims.'

'Don't get me wrong,' said the man next to him, presumably Sid. 'I like a Ruby Murray on a Friday night, but it's too much now, there's just too many of them.'

'You've hit the nail on the head,' said Blood River. 'It's the number that is the problem. Most of us don't mind a few foreigners here and there.'

'Speak for yourself,' shouted the girl.

'But it's when we become a minority in our own land that we can't stand it,' said Blood River. 'When we can't wave our own flag, the great cross of St George, at football matches, we have to say enough is enough.'

A cheer went up through the crowd. Blood River was on a roll.

'We do not like it when cheap Polish plumbers drive our lads out of business; when British nurses don't get a pay rise because so much is being spent on translators. We especially don't like it when half the people we allow into this country turn out to be criminals.'

While he waited for the fresh applause to die down, Blood River took out a white handkerchief and wiped the sweat from his face. Alexia watched, half appalled, half in awe. He really knew how to work a crowd.

When he went back to the mike he let his voice drop. 'People ask me why I hate the incomers, and I always say the same thing. I don't hate them, I don't hate anybody. What you see on my face and what you hear in my voice isn't hate – it's anger. Anger that a person who the decent folk of my country have allowed in, could throw it all in their faces and kill a child in his own school.'

His voice rose. 'Anger that this person who was given the best of everything: a free house, free money, medical care if she needs it . . . this person spat on the graves of every man, woman and child who lost their lives in the war.'

The room erupted, with the skins stamping their ten-holer boots and the chavs beating their fists on the bar. Alexia could feel the heat of passion in the room like a flash-fire. She was frightened yet intoxicated by the force of his words.

Once the din had settled, Blood River spoke again. 'And do you know what makes me angrier than anything else? It's the leftists, the liberals, the do-gooders. The social workers who queue up to sort out their problems, the solicitors who keep them out of jail.'

'Fucking Judases,' shouted the skinhead girl.

Blood River nodded solemnly. 'These are the people we must stop.'

Chapter Sixteen

Rats.

Luke is woken by the telltale scratching outside the lean-to.

It's the worst thing about sleeping rough. The cold and the damp he can survive, but he can't stand the vermin, with their black coats and long pink tails like fat worms. They say that in London you're only ever a couple of feet from a rat, and Luke can well believe it.

Teardrop Tony claims to have been bitten by one, but Caz points out he also says he's related to the Queen. Either way, Luke's not taking any chances and throws an empty can at the pallet, sending them scurrying back to their lair.

Caz stirs and snuggles closer. She smells of last night's chips but Luke doesn't mind. He likes watching her sleep, when her system isn't fighting drugs and trouble.

He casts his mind back to the girls at Manor Park, with their shiny hair and straight teeth. Here's Caz, with her hair scraped off her face in an old elastic band, her lips dry and chapped; yet asleep like this, peaceful, she's the prettiest girl he has ever seen.

She yawns and opens one eye. 'What you looking at, soft lad?'

'You,' he says.

She pulls her sleeping bag over her face. 'Well, don't.'

He laughs and crawls outside.

'Where you off to so early?' she asks.

He smoothes down his crumpled clothes and ties his laces. 'For a coffee.'

'Make mine a skinny latte with a double shot of hazelnut syrup.'

He laughs again. They both know the Black Cat only serves piss water with last night's milk floating in blobs on the top like cottage cheese.

'Do you know where I can get some money?'

Sonic Dave chews over both the question and his fried egg carefully. Reports of his incarceration have obviously been greatly exaggerated, for here he is, as mad and as greasy as ever.

'Where could you get some money?' He repeats the question as if it's an exam.

At last, he points his knife at Luke. 'A bank.'

Luke sighs. Sonic Dave was always going to be a long shot.

'What do you know?' asks Teardrop Tony, sliding in next to Luke, closely followed by Long Tall Sally.

'Young Luke here was just wondering where he might obtain some cash,' says Sonic Dave.

Teardrop Tony slaps two twenty-pence pieces onto the Formica tabletop. 'Don't spend it all at once.'

Luke smiles and pushes the coins back towards Tony. 'I need a bit more than that,' he says.

'How much?' asks Long Tall Sally, expertly rolling a few slivers of tobacco with one hand.

'A grand,' says Luke.

His audience nod sagely, though Luke knows between them they probably have less than a tenner in their collective pockets.

'The Boots up in Charing Cross has got a load of new perfume in,' says Teardrop Tony. 'You could get at least a fiver a bottle.'

Sally shakes her head, the roll-up attached to her bottom lip by saliva. 'It's totally on top. They've got at least three security guards.'

'And stealing two hundred bottles would seem a tad impractical,' says Dave, yolk running down his chin.

Long Tall Sally lights her scrawny cigarette, filling the air with the smell of paper rather than Old Holborn. 'It's no smoking in here,' shouts the owner from behind his counter, but he doesn't make any attempt to stop her.

'The lads at the Troc do all right,' she says.

Luke wrinkles his nose. Sally often hangs out with the rent boys who work the Trocadero on Piccadilly Circus. They're mostly young and mostly off their heads. The living dead who sell their arses for crack.

'I was thinking of a job,' says Luke.

The other three stop dead in their tracks as if hit by a taser.

'Work?' asks Sally, the novelty the idea of spreading a tidal wave through her dreads.

'Why not?' says Luke. 'This is the bloody capital city of England. There must be lots about.'

'I had a job once,' says Sonic Dave, a wistful look in his eye. 'It was 1985.'

'Doing what?' asks Teardrop Tony, suitably incredulous.

'Window cleaner,' he answers.

'I've always fancied that,' says Sally. 'Up on those ladders and that.'

Luke swallows his impatience. Conversations among the homeless veer off at tangents like puppies on their first walks.

'So do any of you know of anything?' he asks.

'Anything what?' asks Sonic Dave.

Luke banishes the tension from his voice. 'Jobs. Work.'

'Oh,' says Dave. 'No.'

'No,' says Teardrop Tony.

'No,' says Long Tall Sally.

Luke breathes deeply.

'You looking for work?' asks the owner, scooping the ash and fag ends along the table with a cloth.

Luke is so shocked he can only nod.

'Be here any morning at five,' says the owner. 'Sharp.'

'So where's my bleeding coffee, soft lad?'

Caz is in the doorway, her hood framing her face like a grubby halo.

Long Tall Sally makes room for her to sit down. 'Luke's getting a job.'

'Oh, aye?' says Caz.

'He needs a grand,' says Sonic Dave.

265

'What for?' asks Caz.

'I'm going to get us somewhere to live,' says Luke.

Caz winks at him in the way his mother used to when he said he'd seen a ghost or Batman.

'I am,' he stammers, feeling like a ten-year-old kid. 'I really am.'

Caz leans over and pats his hand. 'Course you are, soft lad.'

'Tell me again why we're doing this?'

Penny crushed a handful of pistachio nuts, sending at least half flying across Lilly's kitchen.

'We're making kulfi,' said Lilly, and stirred a panful of milk and ground almonds.

'Come again?'

Lilly sprinkled a generous spoonful of sugar into the pan. 'Indian ice cream.'

'But you're not Indian,' said Penny, brushing slivers of nuts off her alpaca jacket.

'We are a broad and catholic church,' said Lilly. 'Particularly when it comes to food.'

'Why can't we just stick to British traditions?' said Penny. 'It should be toffee apples for Bonfire Night, not this stuff.'

'Sam hates Bonfire Night so I'm adopting Diwali.'

'It just doesn't seem right,' Penny sniffed. 'Next they'll be telling us we can't celebrate Christmas.'

Lilly looked sideways at her friend. 'No one's saying that.'

'Don't be naïve, Lilly, there are some London boroughs where they have to call them *seasonal holidays* or some other nonsense.'

'That's just racist propaganda,' said Lilly.

Penny pointed to a pile of chopped pumpkin flesh. 'So what's that for?'

'Pie,' said Lilly. 'I'm incorporating Thanksgiving.'

Penny threw up her hands in exasperation. 'Anyway, why can't we just buy the food?'

Jordan, Penny's new foster child, whooped through Lilly's garden. They watched him through the window as he chased the leaves swirling in the wind.

'Because this is a celebration,' said Lilly. 'Not online shopping.'

'You're such a good mummy,' said Penny, with more than a trace of sarcasm.

Lilly nodded at Jordan, who was leaping around like a demented sheep dog.

'He's settled in nicely.'

Penny beamed. 'Poor little lamb. He's been through a lot but he seems happy with us.'

'And up at school?' asked Lilly. 'Does everyone hate me?'

'Course not.'

'Liar.'

Penny laughed. 'And you? It all seems quiet on the Western Front.'

'Indeed it is.'

'And is that good?' asked Penny.

'How can you even ask that?'

Penny eyed her through her fringe. 'The Lilly Valentine I know seems to thrive on drama and excitement.'

'Not this one,' said Lilly. 'This one likes a peaceful life.'

She reached into the cupboard for a bottle of rose-water. The smell reminded her of her nan. 'I've kept out of everyone's way at Manor Park, Sam's happy, and Anna's case is coming along.'

'So everything's in order?'

Lilly let a few drops of the pink elixir splash onto the surface of the kulfi and set it to cool. 'Just the way I like it. No trauma, no scenes, no surprises.'

'So who's that?' asked Penny, pointing through the window to the figure of a man crossing the lawn.

Lilly squinted at the silhouette. It was Jez.

'What on earth does he want?'

If Jez was embarrassed by Penny's flirtatious smile he didn't show it.

'Take a seat through there.' Lilly waved a sugar-encrusted hand towards the sitting room.

'Why am I not surrounded by gorgeous men?' whispered Penny when Jez was out of sight.

'You're married to a millionaire,' Lilly pointed out.

'I might give it all up and become a legal aid lawyer.'

'And do your own ironing?'

'Good point,' said Penny. She went to collect Jordan and headed for the door.

'What about the food?' Lilly called.

'I'll stop in Waitrose,' she said.

'Shop-bought!'

'I have better things to do.'

Lilly turned to Jez. 'I don't mean to be rude, but what are you doing here?'

'It's nice to see you too,' he laughed. 'Can't a man call in on a friend these days?'

Lilly poured Jez a glass of wine and eyed him suspiciously. 'We've known each other a long time and you've never seen fit to pop by.'

He took a sip. 'This is a great place. Very you.'

'I mean it, Jez, I'm starting to worry,' said Lilly.

Jez put down his wine and sighed. 'We go back a fair way, don't we?'

'I just said that.'

'Which is why I hope you'll take what I'm about to say in the spirit it's intended,' he said.

'Now I'm really worried,' she replied.

'This case we're involved in, Lilly, it's a tricky one, very tricky,' he said. 'The law on conspiracy is complicated.'

'My expert says there was no conspiracy.'

Jez put up his hands. 'I know that, but it doesn't mean the jury will buy it.'

'It'll be my job to convince them.'

'And I'm sure you'll do your level best,' he said. 'But this is a murder trial at the Old Bailey.'

Lilly felt her hackles rise. 'I wonder how I missed that.'

'Don't get shirty,' Jez sighed. 'I'm not saying you're not good enough.'

'It sounds that way.'

'I'm just trying to point out that this isn't your usual thing, Lilly.'

She felt her throat redden. 'I appear in court every day.'

'On family matters,' he said. 'Divorce hearings at Luton County Court are not in the same ball park.'

Now she was angry. Who did he think he was, coming into her home and telling her she wasn't up to the job?

'If you've come here to patronise me, Jez, I suggest you head back to London.'

Lilly stalked to the door and opened it, the clear indication being that he should walk through it.

He followed with a sad smile. 'Sheba said you'd react like this.'

'She's a genius,' said Lilly.

He put a hand on her arm. 'I truly didn't mean to upset you, Lilly, but I just wish you'd consider getting a silk.'

'You're not a silk!'

It was below the belt. Lilly knew Jez would be made up any day.

His smile didn't falter. 'Just give it some thought.'

Jez jumped onto the train back to London. He hoped Lilly would take his advice. He didn't want to annihilate Lilly but what choice did he have? He had been summoned yet again to an audience with Ronald.

The waitress leaned over to light the candle, revealing a generous portion of cleavage.

'How the devil are you?' asked Ronald.

Jez smiled across the table. He hated this place, with its red brocade drapes and leather banquettes. The air was hot and oppressive. 'I'm very well, Ron.'

The head of chambers reached into the humidifier and extracted a San Cristobal cigar. He ran it under his nose, his eyes half closed, then nodded for Jez to take one.

Jez had never seen the point of cigars. He liked the instant nicotine hit of a Marlboro Light, but even in a club like Campions the smoking ban applied to every-thing – except their own products at fifty pounds a pop.

He chose a cigar, bit off the end and lit up with the candle.

'I've been talking to Tobias about you,' said Ronald.

Tobias De Winters was the man who currently dealt with the applications to take silk. The gatekeeper of the brotherhood.

'All good I hope,' said Jez.

Ronald smiled through the cloud of smoke. 'He has no doubt about your abilities.'

Jez nodded coolly. 'And he knows I've taken some prosecution work?'

Ronald beckoned to the waitress to bring more whisky, a sherry-casked single malt that Jez thought tasted like strong cold tea.

'He has noted that you are happy to use your full skill set,' said Ronald.

Jez took a sip of the golden liquid and longed for a vodka tonic. He wasn't sure sending kids to prison was a skill he particularly wanted to hone but needs must and all that.

Ronald tapped his ash. He clearly had something else to say, but Jez knew better than to hurry him.

'He has one little concern.'

'Oh?' Jez tried to sound unconcerned.

'The Duraku case,' said Ronald. 'There is a worry that it may not be going as well as it could.'

Jez frowned. 'In what way?'

'Tobias feels you've been giving the defence an easy ride.'

Jez shook his head. 'I can't imagine what's given him that impression. We've only got as far as entering pleas.'

Ronald sat back in his chair, his jacket falling open to reveal his ever-increasing paunch.

'Come on, Jez, you've let the débâcle of bail slide without so much as a comment.'

'It wasn't worth the argument, Ronald. The girl's being well supervised.'

Ronald tipped back his head and blew a column of smoke towards the yellow ceiling.

'And it's got nothing to do with the redhead defending her?'

Jez feigned a laugh. 'If I didn't know that was a joke I'd be offended.'

'I hear that you and she have been somewhat friendly in the past,' said Ronald.

Jez thought back to the drunken snog he and Lilly had shared at a party, when she'd smelled delicious and tasted even better. It might have gone further if she hadn't thrown up.

'Who's been telling tales?' he asked.

'The criminal bar is a very small world,' Ronald shrugged. 'Not much stays secret.'

Jez shook his head. 'Whatever anyone's been saying about Lilly and me, it has absolutely no bearing on this case.'

'So at the trial you'll kick her from here to tomorrow?'

'And the day after that.'

'Good.' Ronald drained his glass and tamped out his cigar. 'This is high profile and all eyes are on you.'

Jez watched Ronald leave, picked up the bill and

sighed. If he wanted to join the big boys he was going to have to come out fighting.

On the train, Jez felt his tension ease as the landscape outside became more urban. He was back on his own territory. He had told Lilly to get a hired gun, the rest was up to her.

Lilly was still fuming when the kitchen timer pinged.

She glugged down her wine and pulled the kulfi out of the freezer.

Jez was being a total wanker.

She cut off a large block and grabbed a spoon.

He was trying to undermine her, a tactic used by a lot of coppers. She remembered one interview when a DI had told her she shouldn't try to comfort her hysterical thirteen-year-old client because it made her look unprofessional. Fortunately she had realised that this piece of 'friendly' advice was given in the hope that, without a reassuring arm around his shoulders, the boy would crack and admit to an assault he hadn't committed.

She hadn't fallen for that piece of male bullshit and she wasn't about to fall for this one.

She scooped a heap of pudding into her mouth, and the temple-aching sweetness instantly salved her mood. She took another mouthful and sighed. Perhaps Jez had a point. She'd never done a criminal trial in the Crown Court, let alone the Bailey.

Instructing a silk would be the most sensible thing to do.

'Something looks very good.'

Anna entered the room in her usual apologetic way. Lilly handed her a spoon and together they demolished the vast dish of ice cream.

Lilly undid her trouser button. 'What would you think of me hiring a barrister for your court case?'

'To assist you?' asked Anna.

'I doubt a silk would see it that way,' Lilly laughed. 'He or she would do the speaking for you in court.'

'Who would tell them about my case?'

'I would,' said Lilly.

Anna pursed her brow. 'So you would say to this person what it is they must say?'

'Something like that.'

Anna shook her head. 'What is the point? Why don't you just say it?'

Lilly sighed and licked her spoon.

'Cases like yours, very serious cases, are normally done by barristers that deal with this sort of thing every day of the week.'

'Lots and lots of cases?' Anna asked.

'Exactly,' said Lilly.

Anna's eyes filled with tears. 'So my case is just one in very big pile, nothing special to them. I am nothing important.'

'Oh, Anna,' Lilly put her hand over the girl's. 'You are important to me.'

Anna squeezed Lilly's hand hard, as if she were trying to hold on. 'Then promise that it is you who will speak for me in court.'

Lilly closed her eyes. 'I promise.'

*   *   *

274

'Our children have suffered enough.'

Mr Lattimer smiled politely. He'd known feelings were running high when he called this extraordinary meeting of governors and parents, but some of these women were almost hysterical.

'Luella,' he used her first name, hoping to add a human touch. 'I understand that your concerns lie with your children, but I can assure you I am on top of the situation.'

'You weren't on top of it when Charlie was shot,' said Evelyn Everard.

Mr Lattimer did not allow his rictus grin to slip. 'I think we all know that that tragedy was unavoidable.'

'Unavoidable?' Luella was on her feet. 'You make it sound like an accident.'

'What I meant to say was that no one could have foreseen that something so terrible would happen,' he said.

'I think some of us could have predicted this a long time ago,' said Luella.

'I don't see how,' he said.

Luella threw up her hands. 'How many times do I have to say it? Those people hate us.'

'I'm sure that's an over-generalisation,' he said. 'And anyway, we had no contact with the people at the hostel before this incident.' He tried not to think about the numerous maintenance men and kitchen staff who the school hired from an agency for less than the minimum wage.

Evelyn Everard got to her feet. Lord, her son looked just like her, with the same red hair, the same obsessive gleam in the eye, the same ability to take up every available inch of space around them.

'What matters here is not what has gone before,' – the same voice that demanded to be heard – 'but what happens now.'

'Indeed,' he said.

'And we parents feel that Mrs Valentine's presence at this school cannot be tolerated while she is representing the chief suspect in this murder.'

'I thought Sam was being brought in by another parent.'

'Yes, me.' Penny Van Huysan raised her hand.

'Well then,' said Mr Lattimer.

Luella almost threw herself over the chair in front. 'Penny's only doing that to spare the other children's feelings. I think she'd rather not do it.'

'Mrs Van Huysan?'

The woman blushed. 'It's pretty difficult.'

'If Penny were ill, what then?' Luella shouted. 'Or if Sam hurt himself? Lilly would have to come in then.'

'Aren't we getting ahead of ourselves?' asked Mr Lattimer.

'We are simply being practical,' said Evelyn Everard.

Luella jabbed her finger at the headmaster. 'The best thing for all concerned would be to ask Sam to leave Manor Park.'

'The pupil in question has done nothing wrong,' he said.

'That's not the point,' said Luella. 'His presence here is putting all our children in danger.'

'Is that what you want?' added Evelyn Everard.

Mr Lattimer sighed. 'Of course not.'

'Then why won't you take action?' Luella shouted.

'If I thought it would help, I would,' said Mr Lattimer. 'But I can't see how the action you're suggesting will have any positive effect.'

Luella pointed at Mr Lattimer. 'If the press were to discover that the murderer's solicitor had free rein to swan up here whenever she felt like it they'd have a field day.'

'I have taken every possible step to ensure that the good name of this school has stayed out of the gutter press.'

Luella gave a theatrical laugh. 'What about those stories in the *Three Counties Observer*?'

'Those were unfortunate indeed,' said Mr Lattimer, 'and showed none of us in our best light.'

At least Luella had the decency to redden.

'Are you afraid of what the papers might say?' asked Evelyn.

Of course Mr Lattimer was anxious to avoid any adverse publicity that might dissuade parents from enrolling their children.

'Absolutely not,' he said. 'I am merely upholding the time-honoured tradition of facing adversity with dignity and restraint.'

'Because that will be nothing compared to the mass exodus you'll face if nothing is done about this,' said Luella.

Mr Lattimer gulped. The crunch was already being felt. Four pupils had left to attend the excellent grammar school only four miles away.

Mr Lattimer glanced at the governors. They blinked blankly back at him.

He collected his papers into a file. 'I'll see what can be done.'

Chapter Seventeen

Jeremiah Stafford was not a bad person. He recycled the Sunday papers, tipped fifteen per cent in restaurants and visited his father once a month, even though the old folks' home invariably smelled of cauliflower cheese. Not a saint, obviously, but if pushed he would describe himself as essentially decent. Which was why he felt so uncomfortable making Lilly's life difficult.

He sighed and poured a handful of coffee beans into the grinder. They rattled like shiny black jewels and filled the air with the wonderful aroma of Jamaica.

He'd always liked Lilly. She was funny, clever and sexy. A single mum who spent a good deal of her time helping disadvantaged kids. What's not to like? Admittedly, she was also opinionated, difficult and pig-headed, but no one was perfect, were they?

He'd tried to make her see reason, to get an experienced barrister on board, but he should have guessed how she'd take it. Sheba had advised him against it. 'Come on, little brother,' she'd laughed, 'this is Lilly

Valentine we're talking about. Not some dozy little tart who hangs on your every word.'

'But this case will get very messy and I don't want to hurt her.'

Sheba had barked a gravelly laugh. 'I think she can give as good as she gets.'

He took a sip of his espresso and lit a Marlboro Light. The twin pleasures of caffeine and nicotine cleared his head of the swamp caused by last night's whisky. Sheba was right. Lilly was expecting a fight, and would feel patronised by anything less. The fact that reducing her to mincemeat would seal his bid for promotion was just an added bonus.

He pulled out his laptop and cobbled together an email. Then he swallowed down the bitter dregs of his coffee as his finger pushed 'send'.

Strawberry, black cherry, apricot and ginger. Kerry's fingers hovered over the pots of jam in her fridge.

Each morning she ate four slices of toast, each with a different topping. It was the first thing she did and her stomach growled in anticipation.

As her toast popped, her computer gave out its familiar ping. Email.

Kerry felt excited. Apart from spam and outstanding balances on her many catalogue purchases, Kerry received few messages. She waddled from the kitchen to her living room, a slice of toast dripping butter down her doughy fingers, and squealed when she saw who had got in touch.

Up until this point we have, I feel, been very fair to Anna Duraku and her lawyer, but it occurs to me that we should perhaps push a little harder.

While I do not intend to bully either lady, I am most certainly prepared to put up my most able fight.

Experience has taught me that in the law, as in boxing, preparation is everything, and so I propose that we go through the evidence page by page to ascertain any chinks in our opposition's armour.

Perhaps we could meet later for a working lunch to discuss how best to proceed?

Regards, Jez

Kerry squealed again. The most handsome barrister she had ever met was taking her out to eat. She scurried through to her bedroom, wondering what she should wear. Lilly Valentine had obviously fallen from favour; he hadn't even mentioned her by name.

She filled the basin with warm water and grabbed a clean cloth without a second thought for the rest of her uneaten breakfast, turning cold and hard in the kitchen.

The rape was the key to the case. Dr Kadir had confirmed it. Anna had suffered trauma in Kosovo, but '. . . the rape was the defining incident which pushed Anna's mind into freefall . . .'

To make a jury believe that Anna was incapable of murder, Lilly would need to show how pivotal the rape had been. To make them understand that such a thing would have been terrible for any woman, but for this girl it was the final assault that broke her mind.

She stretched her feet out under her desk, unaccustomed to the space Anna had made by returning Lilly's legal books to the firm's library. She kicked off her shoes, wiggled her toes and sighed.

In her years of experience she'd seen many witnesses giving their accounts of rape. She recalled one teenager telling the court how her attacker had left her to die in a canal. That she had dragged herself out and walked three miles to the nearest police station. The girl's quiet dignity was so appalling that Lilly had wept openly. She'd seen crime photos that had made her vomit and read doctors' reports listing injuries so severe she hadn't slept for days.

Sad as it was, these were the cases lawyers dreamed of.

On the other hand, Anna was probably the least jury-friendly victim she had ever encountered. Her recollections of both the genocide and the rape were hazy, with important details missing. What she could remember, she delivered in such a deadpan manner it was as if it had happened to someone else. Lilly knew this was partly due to the PTSD, but it didn't help their defence.

Anna opened the door with her foot, a tray in her arms laden with tea and biscuits.

'We need to go through the evidence,' said Lilly.

Anna placed a mug on Lilly's desk without looking up. 'I must take the drinks to the others,' she said.

Lilly reached for the plate of ginger snaps. 'This is more important.'

'The partners are waiting for tea,' said Anna.

'Sit,' said Lilly, her tone brooking no argument.

Anna slid into the chair opposite.

'Excellent,' said Lilly. 'I know going over this must be terrible, but we have to get it straight. The prosecution will go over and over the paperwork with a fine toothcomb. If there are any inconsistencies, Jez will find them.'

'He is a very nice man,' said Anna, a small smile playing on her lips. 'He likes you.'

Lilly snapped a biscuit in two, showering the desk in crumbs. 'Any friendly feelings he harbours for me will not be enough, trust me.'

Anna nodded that she understood.

'The boys you met on the high street,' said Lilly. 'Had you met them before?'

'No.'

Lilly nibbled on the rough edge of the broken biscuit. 'So why did you go with them?'

'They seemed nice.'

'You didn't think it might be unwise to go to a deserted park with three strangers?' asked Lilly.

Anna shrugged.

God, this was like pulling teeth.

'What did you do when you got there?'

'At first we talked very nicely,' said Anna, 'but one was getting too close, touching me.'

Lilly swallowed dry crumbs. 'Did you tell him to stop?'

'Yes.'

282

'What then?' Ginger stung Lilly's throat, or was it that she knew what was coming next?

'He pulled me to the ground and had sex with me.'

There it was – the horror of it – bald and simple. And yet Lilly knew it wouldn't be enough to convince a jury, not nearly enough.

'Did you fight him off?'

'He is very big,' said Anna.

Lilly nodded. 'But did you try?'

Anna shrugged.

'And the other boys, did they . . .' Lilly coughed, trying to clear her throat, 'did they have their turn?'

Anna shook her head. 'There was one very drunk, very frightened, I think.'

'And the others?'

'The one who is dead, he held my arms so other one could do it.'

'So you must have struggled,' said Lilly.

'Must I?'

'Yes,' said Lilly. 'Or why would they need to hold you down?'

Anna nodded slowly. 'And I screamed so he put his hand over my mouth.'

'What was he like? The one who raped you?'

Anna wrinkled her nose. 'Very big, with orange hair.'

'Anything else?'

'He has an ugly mouth, with a gap here.' Anna pointed to her front teeth. 'Horrible skin flap is peeping out.'

Shit. It was a bloody good description of the cocky so-and-so who had spoken at Charlie's service. And that lad was a dead ringer for his mother, one of the most prominent parents at Manor Park. If Anna's attacker was the son of Evelyn Everard, things were about to get a whole lot worse.

'The trouble is, people like her are little better than animals.'

Alexia cringed inwardly.

'She's from a part of the world where life is cheap,' Blood River continued, 'so one more death is nothing to her.'

Alexia nursed a warm tonic water and considered the man opposite. Once again he was impeccable. Head to toe in black. Even his cufflinks were onyx, and glinted in the harsh strip lighting.

He appeared supremely confident, at ease in his world. A joke with the barman as he ordered a Coke. A smile to one of the regulars, already worse for wear at lunchtime. Yet his eyes told Alexia that this man wasn't at peace. They darted at every movement around him like those of a hunter. Or were they those of the hunted?

'In a way I feel sorry for her,' he said.

Alexia raised a cynical eyebrow.

Blood River chuckled. 'I'm not a man of stone, you know, but you've seen for yourself how feelings are running high.'

Alexia wondered how much of the emotion was being stoked by groups like the Pride of England. The people at the meeting had indeed been inflamed, but would they simply go back to their ready meals and *Big Brother* without Blood River's manipulation and stirring words?

'I owe it to our members and the wider community to take their concerns seriously,' he said. 'Much like yourself.'

Alexia nodded. She couldn't care less what the residents of Luton thought, but she knew what sold papers.

'Will you continue to support us, Miss Dee?' Blood River asked.

'The *Three Counties Observer* doesn't take political positions,' she said. 'You know that.'

He chuckled again, but his eyes stopped wandering and focused entirely on Alexia. She felt the heat being drawn from her body.

'You've been sympathetic to our cause this far,' he said. 'I was just asking if you'll continue in that vein.'

Alexia was nervous. She didn't like the idea that her stories had been overtly racist, and she didn't like the way his eyes bored into her.

'I'll report the news as I see it.'

He nodded and broke eye contact, clearly satisfied with her reply.

The oily anchovy lay on its side, curled into a tiny 'c'.

Kerry poked it with her fork. It looked like a dead earwig.

She'd fancied the hot ciabatta with melted brie, but when Jez had ordered a Caesar salad she'd followed suit.

'The good thing about this case is that we pretty much know what the defence's case will be,' said Jez, and speared a piece of lettuce.

Kerry watched the crisp forkful make its way to his mouth. 'We do?'

'They won't deny she was there or that she had a gun,' he said. 'How can they, when Anna's lawyer witnessed the whole thing?'

Kerry nibbled on a crouton. They were the only thing in the slimy plateful that she liked, and there were only six of them. She'd counted.

'So what is there left to say?' asked Kerry.

Jez waved his fork. 'That Anna lacked the mental capacity to commit the crime.'

'I see,' said Kerry. 'And how will they support that?'

'They'll get their shrink to say she was suffering a breakdown as a result of her experiences in Kosovo.'

'Gosh,' said Kerry, as if Jez had just made an original and insightful discovery.

She knew full well what Lilly Valentine planned to say, and she'd already done some research into Post Traumatic Stress Disorder to try to refute it, but she hadn't read *The Rules* from cover to cover for nothing. In a date situation it never paid to be a smart arse.

'So what do you suggest?' asked Kerry, making sure Jez felt in control at all times.

'We trip them up,' he said. 'Their defence has only one leg to stand on, so we find something to kick it out from under them.' He leaned back in his chair and waved for the bill. Pudding was obviously off the agenda. 'Let's spend the rest of the day going through every scrap of evidence until we find what we're after.' He slapped down some cash. 'I'll do statements and you do forensics.'

Kerry watched him stride out of the door and beamed. Despite it being the worst lunch she could remember, she was a happy woman. She toyed with ordering the chocolate fudge cake but decided to go back to her desk. She was determined to show Jez what she was made of.

'I think Evelyn Everard's son raped Anna.'

'Tom!' Penny looked at Lilly in shock. 'You've got to be kidding.'

'Do I look like Russell Brand?' asked Lilly.

'Sometimes, when your hair sticks up,' said Penny.

Lilly punched her friend on the arm. 'This is serious. Anna described her attacker, and I'm almost sure it's him.'

The changing room at the gym was deserted, but Penny looked around anyway. 'So what are you going to do?'

Lilly pulled on her trousers for Tae Kwon Do and shook her head. What was she going to do?

'I should request an interview with him.'

Penny let out a low whistle. 'Rather you than me. Evelyn will go apoplectic.'

Lilly sighed. She could well imagine the rage with which Anna's allegations would be met. Hurricane Katrina would look like a blowy day in comparison.

'Are you ladies joining us?' It was the coach, his head poking around the door as if it were detached from his body. 'I'm sure your hairdressing appointments can be discussed at another time.'

'Hairdressing,' sighed Lilly. 'I would give anything for enough time for a cut and blow.'

'I shouldn't worry. You've got a great look going on.'

Penny ruffled Lilly's tangle of curls. 'For an oversexed stand-up comedian.'

Lilly bowed deeply and took her place on the mat. As they went through the rhythmic moves she felt some of her tension lift. Maybe she wouldn't have to interview the Everard boy. Maybe there was another way round this.

'Anything happening at school?'

Penny shook her head and continued with her warm-up.

Lilly punched forward and snapped her arm back. Once. Twice.

'Three times, Miss Valentine,' shouted the coach. 'One, two, three.'

Lilly performed the sequence again, counting each punch under her breath. She waited until he had begun to berate another paying member of his class and whispered to Penny.

'There were three boys there, the night of the rape.'

'And?' Penny continued her movement.

'Don't you see?' said Lilly. 'One was Evelyn's boy and one was Charlie Stanton.'

'The first you don't want to speak to and the second you can't.'

'Give me thirty press-ups.' The coach's voice floated across the room.

'Thank you, Lilly,' said Penny. 'I've known air-raid sirens quieter than you.'

They got down on their hands and knees and began hauling themselves up and down.

Lilly groaned. Her puny forearms were not designed to bear the full weight of her breasts and arse.

'But there were three boys there,' she wheezed. 'So all I have to do is track down the third.'

Penny finished her thirty and sat up, panting. Lilly had only got as far as eight.

'Luke Walker,' said Penny.

'What?'

'The third boy,' said Penny. 'I bet it's Luke Walker. Those three were in the same house and as thick as thieves. Apparently, Luke's been off sick since Charlie was killed.'

Lilly collapsed onto the mat. Her friend's ability to name every parent and child at Manor Park was a mystery. But then, it was a small school and very tight knit. Perhaps it was Lilly who was out of the loop.

The coach loomed above her like a storm cloud. 'You haven't given me thirty, have you, Miss Valentine?'

Lilly remained prone. 'No.'

'Why not?'

She dragged herself to her feet, leaving a wet smear of sweat across the rubber. 'I guess I'm just not built that way.'

The coach shook his head in disgust. 'Maybe you spend too much time in the hairdresser's, Miss Valentine.'

Lilly held his gaze, willing him to stop before she lost her temper.

'Maybe you spend all day watching soap operas, Miss Valentine, and the only use these get,' he lifted her right wrist between his thumb and forefinger, 'is flicking channels.'

He let her hand fall. And it would have fallen to Lilly's

side if she hadn't snapped it back to her waist and punched him in the mouth.

Her fist made a satisfying smack against the coach's lips and, although it wasn't a right hook Prince Naseem would have been proud of, it took the coach by surprise and he toppled backwards to the floor. Maybe she had learned something from the classes after all.

Everyone gasped except Penny, who choked down a laugh, and Lilly turned tail to the changing room.

'Where are you going?' Penny called.

'I thought I'd get a quick pedicure before *EastEnders*.'

* * *

<u>Most Muslim Men Are Paedophiles</u> Skin Lick at 17.04
Why else do Arabs and Pakistanis marry girls as young as ten?

Alexia sighed. She'd been trawling the racist chat rooms for over an hour. When Blood River spoke, most of what he said made perfect sense. Well, some of it anyway. The UK was full of foreign workers while there was still a substantial number of British citizens unemployed. Surely it was wrong to spend tax money on benefits while jobs were being scooped up by the Polish? And when there was so little social housing in the first place, did it make sense to give some of that provision to new arrivals, while those born here might have to wait years?

And yet . . . a slight scratch of the thumbnail on the

surface and the true face of these people bared its ugly yellow teeth.

Why Are the Nurses in this Country Paid So Little?
Fire Starter at 17.30
It's because half the NHS budget is spent on translators.

The other half is used to fight diseases that foreigners bring into the country.

Alexia sighed again. It would be laughable if it weren't so bloody depressing.

Why did Blood River and his followers feel so threatened?

'Luton's a ghost town,' Blood River had told her.

Alexia had thought he meant it was dead, but her time on the Net revealed that 'ghosts' were the white working class, and the term 'ghost town' alluded to the lack of white faces.

It was true that Luton was a mixed bag. Asians, Africans and Eastern Europeans had all made there homes there, but white people were evident in every shop and bus shelter – at least as far as Alexia could tell. As her father repeatedly explained, truth and facts are not as important as what people *perceive* to be truth or facts. She remembered the time he punched someone for taking his parking space. Not because there was nowhere else to park or because he particularly wanted that spot. 'But because my staff need to believe that I care about every detail,' he said.

Alexia clicked her fingers. That was it. She'd do a piece about the Pride of England. Not supporting their views, but explaining why they felt the way they did and how that translated into racism. She would show how the current government policy on immigration was nurturing such feeling, especially in a place like Luton where the indigenous population already felt threatened. Then she'd drop in the Stanton murder and highlight how such incidents fuelled the flames. Who said regional news couldn't be serious and hard-hitting? Together with the investigative stuff she'd already done, it would show her talents as an all-rounder. Then, it would only be a matter of time before she moved up the ladder. She could see it now, a comment piece in the *Guardian*, even a talking-head slot on the *Late Review*. She smiled at the rosy future that stretched out before her.

Lilly felt a wave of nausea sweep through her. Those bloody press-ups had left her weak. Admittedly, she'd only done a few, but it was on an empty stomach. No wonder she'd lost her rag and belted the coach.

She bought a tuna sandwich from a petrol station and took a bite. It was cold and flat, as if someone had forced it through a mangle before stashing it in the freezer. She washed it down with a can of Cherry Coke. The icy, fishy, fruity mouthful was odd but not unpleasant.

She pulled up at a modest new build just off the A5 and checked the address. According to the school class lists, this was where Luke Walker and his parents lived.

Lilly had assumed herself to be the only Manor Park mum without an Aston Martin and an offshore account. Obviously not.

'There are plenty of people who make sacrifices for

their children's education,' David had told her, rolling his eyes when she complained she was like the poor cousin up at school. She hadn't seen much sign of it until now, but she had to admit she had never really looked.

Lilly wasn't entirely sure how she was going to handle this. She knew nothing about Luke's parents or how they would react to her. Their son had been seriously affected by the shooting and they might well blame Anna for her part. Maybe they wouldn't want to help her and maybe Luke would refuse to speak to her. But if she could make them see that she needed to know what happened the night Anna was raped, perhaps they would be willing to assist.

She knocked on the door with trepidation and was shocked when it swung open almost instantaneously.

'Luke?' A woman thrust herself at Lilly, her face crumpling when she saw it was not him.

'Afraid not,' said Lilly. 'But I wonder if I might have a word with you about him?'

Mrs Walker led Lilly through to the sitting room, where she perched nervously on the end of the sofa. She didn't ask Lilly to sit.

'Are you here to give me bad news?'

'I'm sorry?' asked Lilly.

Mrs Walker looked up at Lilly, her eyes, already raw, welling with tears. 'Is he dead?'

Lilly was confused. 'Dead?'

Why would she think her son was dead?

'What then?' asked Mrs Walker, her voice scratchy and hoarse.

Something bad was happening and Lilly had no idea

what it was. 'Mrs Walker, I'm Lilly Valentine, the solicitor for Anna Duraku.'

'Oh,' cried Mrs Walker, showing no recognition of the name.

Blimey, thought Lilly, she must be the only person who hasn't read about me in the papers.

Mrs Walker jumped to her feet. 'I thought you were the police.'

Lilly shook her head. 'Not the police, no.'

Colour washed over Mrs Walker's ashen features and she threw her arms around Lilly's neck. 'Thank God.'

Lilly sniffed the box of Darjeeling tea bags. Her dad, who used to start each day with three cups of Typhoo and an Embassy Regal, would have shaken his head in despair. Was this the stuff you drank black? Or with a slice of lemon? She shrugged and slapped in some semi-skimmed and a heaped teaspoon of sugar.

'I'm sorry I frightened you, Mrs Walker,' said Lilly, handing her a cup.

'It's not your fault.' She clasped her tea protectively in both hands. 'I'm a nervous wreck since . . .'

Lilly's cheeks reddened. 'Charlie's death has made everyone very nervous.'

'Charlie?' Mrs Walker knitted her brow. Evidently something else was making her nervous.

'The shooting at the school,' said Lilly.

Recognition passed across Mrs Walker's face. 'Oh, that. Yes . . . it was absolutely terrible . . . I'm afraid I've been so preoccupied I haven't . . .'

She trailed off and stared out of the window into the night.

Lilly watched the other woman, whose mind was obviously working overtime, but apparently not about the death of Charles Stanton.

The loud crackle of fireworks echoed across the sky and Mrs Walker let out a scream. She dropped her cup, tea spilling across the carpet.

She put her hands to her ears. 'What is that?'

Lilly led her to the sofa and forced her to sit down. 'Just a rocket, Mrs Walker, it's Bonfire Night.'

'Oh,' the woman nodded. 'I hadn't realised. I've lost all sense of time you see . . .'

Lilly picked up the broken pieces of china and took them through to the kitchen. When she returned with a cloth Mrs Walker had returned to her place by the window.

'Why did you think I'd come here?' Lilly scrubbed at the tea stain. 'What made you think I was from the police?'

Mrs Walker didn't look directly at Lilly but ran a finger across the glass. Another person might have repeated their question, but Lilly knew Mrs Walker was deciding how to answer.

'Luke is missing,' she said simply.

Lilly was shocked. 'Everyone said he was staying at home because he's ill.'

Mrs Walker shook her head. 'That's what we've told everyone but it's not true. He packed some things a couple of weeks ago and no one has seen him since.'

'Have you told the police?'

295

Mrs Walker brought the cup to her lips but didn't drink. 'They say he's sixteen, he can leave home if he wants to. Apparently it happens all the time with boys his age.'

'But you don't think it's that simple?'

Mrs Walker's eyes cleared. 'Come with me.'

She led Lilly up the stairs to a bedroom. There was a typed notice stuck to the door with Blu-tack.

Absolutely no admittance.
And that means you too Jessie.

'Jessie?' asked Lilly.

'His younger sister,' said Mrs Walker.

Luke's room had all the trappings of a teenager. Arsenal duvet and pillow. Posters of Lindsay Lohan and Mischa Barton. But it wasn't the tip Lilly had expected. Nor did it have the usual smell of testosterone and footie boots.

'It's very tidy,' she said.

Mrs Walker ran her hand over his desk. 'He was never any trouble. And of course he boarded at school, so he wasn't here all the time.' She picked up a book left open next to the lamp and held it to her chest. 'I never wanted to send him away, but his father insisted.'

Lilly nodded. She'd been against prep school from the start, but David had bullied her into it.

'He said it would build character.' Mrs Walker's voice caught. 'He said it would toughen him up.'

Another flash of colour roared through the sky.

'Luke never liked the bonfire party up at school. He

said he preferred to stay home with a few sparklers,' she said.

'My son's just the same,' said Lilly.

Mrs Walker crumpled onto the bed and sobbed. 'Why didn't I listen to him? Why did I send my baby away?'

Lilly instinctively sat next to her and put an arm around the other woman's heaving shoulders. They felt bowed, as if even the woman's core were beaten down.

'His father thought it would be the making of him,' said Mrs Walker, 'but I should have stood up to him.'

Lilly vowed never to allow David to do this to her, however well-meaning his intentions.

'I keep thinking he must have been so miserable,' she said. 'He must have thought I didn't want him around.'

'I'm sure that's not right,' said Lilly.

'Why else would he run away, leaving everything behind?' Mrs Walker pulled open one of his drawers. 'His Nintendo, his iPod, everything.' She threw open his wardrobe and ran her hand through the rail of jeans and shirts with savage force. 'Why did he leave his clothes? He didn't even take a warm coat, just some stupid cagoule he begged me to buy. I told him it would never keep the rain out.'

She fell to her knees and sobbed. 'I keep coming back to the fact that he must have thought I was rejecting him. That this is all my fault.'

Lilly's heart ached. 'No, don't say that. He must have known how well-loved he was, but Charlie's death upset all the kids.'

Mrs Walker shook her head violently. 'It had nothing to do with that.'

'I know you blame yourself.' Lilly's tone was gentle. 'I'm sure I'd do the same. Hell, I'm a single working mum, I invented guilt.'

Mrs Walker smiled in spite of herself.

'But think about it logically,' Lilly continued. 'A shocking thing happened at your son's school. It can't have failed to have had an impact on him.'

Mrs Walker shook her head again, but this time she was sad and resigned. 'I know you're just trying to be kind, but I can promise you Luke's disappearance had nothing to do with Charlie's murder.'

'How can you be so sure?'

'Because he left the day before.'

Lilly reeled at the news. Luke had run away before the murder. She looked at the woman in front of her, bereft and empty: how would she feel if she knew Luke had potentially been involved in a rape? Lilly hadn't the heart to find out.

Lilly poured two glasses of Sauvignon Blanc, took a huge gulp from one and passed the other to Rupinder.

The silence of the countryside was cracked apart by an orchestra of bangs and screeches. Green and gold stars splashed into the night.

Sam was tucked up in bed, headphones screwed tightly into his ears blasting Amy Winehouse.

'That's bit depressing, big man,' Lilly had said, but Sam was a fan of anguished divas and loved to hum tunelessly along to 'Love is a Losing Game'.

'Thanks for coming over,' Lilly said to her boss.

'If the mountain won't come to Mohammed.'

'I thought he was with the other lot.' Lilly rummaged in the fridge and brought out the remnants of a left-over roast chicken and a tub of sour cream. 'Things are getting complicated,' she said to her boss.

Rupinder smoothed down her sari. The spotlights on the kitchen ceiling caught the silver flecks that darted through the jade silk. 'Straightforward is so last year.'

Lilly laughed and reached for fresh red chilli.

'You remember my shrink said Anna had PTSD?'

Rupinder nodded. 'And the rape was a catalyst.'

'Well, I'm going to have real trouble proving Anna was actually raped. The main protagonist will deny everything and the second is dead.'

'What about Anna? Can't she tell the story herself?'

Lilly tossed the chicken and chilli into the sour cream and snipped coriander over the top.

'Hans Christian Andersen she ain't,' said Lilly, and plonked the bowl on the table with a huge bag of nachos. 'There was another kid there, and I thought he might help us.'

'But?'

'He's had it away on his toes.'

Rupes raised an inquisitive eyebrow.

'He's run away,' Lilly clarified.

They sat in silence for a few moments, filling each crisp nacho with spicy dip and shovelling them into their mouths. For someone so elegant, Rupes could really put it away. Lilly wondered if Dr Kadir ate with such gusto. She hoped so.

Rupes licked each nimble finger. 'If you can't prove

the rape then you'll have to put your emphasis on what you can prove.'

'Kosovo.'

Rupes nodded and finished her wine. 'You have all the information to show exactly what happened to Anna during the genocide.'

'You're right,' said Lilly. 'That's something no one can dispute.'

The gun was Russian. Manufactured by Baikal as a harmless starter pistol, it had been smuggled into the UK and converted to take bullets. It had been dusted for fingerprints and two sets were found.

Kerry stifled a yawn. She had been at the paperwork for hours. File after file of photographs, autopsy reports and scene-of-crime maps sat at her feet. All that was left on her desk was the stuff about the gun.

She had so wanted to impress Jez. To find the one nugget of evidence that would blow Lilly Valentine's case out of the water. And she was hungry. She had toyed with the idea of going to the firework display at her local park. Not that she was a great fan of the pyrotechnics but she had fancied a hot dog or two. Or a burger. She was very partial to a burger, especially with cheese and lots of ketchup.

No doubt she'd missed the whole thing by now.

She went back to the papers. The first set of prints were Jack McNally's, the second were Duraku's. So what? She had never denied holding the damn thing.

Kerry stretched down for her bag and retrieved a menu for the Royal Bengali Restaurant and Takeaway.

If she ordered a chicken korma now, she could collect it and be home in twenty minutes. She might even treat herself to a portion of onion bhaji – after all, she'd virtually skipped lunch. And that couldn't be as fattening as burger could it? Onions were vegetables, after all.

As her hand hovered over the phone, her email pinged to life. It was from the database. Earlier that evening she'd requested confirmation that Duraku's DNA had never been previously recorded. She hadn't really expected a response, thought everyone would be out enjoying themselves. Obviously someone in records was as sad as she was, because here was the answer. Kerry was pretty certain that the girl would have no previous convictions, but you could never be sure.

She read the results as she dialled, making up her mind to get a peshwari naan while she was at it. When she got past the introductory paragraph her jaw dropped.

'Royal Bengali. Can I help you?' came the voice from the other end of the phone.

Kerry was speechless.

'Would you like to place an order?'

Kerry shook her head and hung up.

She reread the mail to make sure she hadn't gone insane, then pulled out Jez's card.

'It's been my life's ambition to be a barrister,' said the young woman, her eyes earnest.

Jez nodded sagely. She was the newest member of chambers, fluent in three languages, fresh out of bar school where she had excelled, having gained a first at Cambridge.

Jez wondered if she put out on a first date.

She stood on her tiptoes to slide the last Duraku file back onto the shelf. 'It's an honour to be asked to help you on this case.'

Jez had asked her to schlep through all the statements while he went to the gym.

He admired her pert little arse from behind. 'You've been a great help.'

'I'm afraid I couldn't find what you were looking for,' she said sadly.

Jez put a comforting hand on her shoulder. 'Sometimes the evidence is just against us.'

They looked at each other and Jez toyed with kissing her right there in his room. Maybe bending her over his desk . . .

His phone rang. He shrugged and answered it.

'I've got it,' came a strangled squeal.

'Who is this?' said Jez.

'Kerry,' she replied, her voice almost hysterical, 'and I've got exactly what we need.'

All thoughts of the pretty pupil were banished from Jez's head and he concentrated on what really turned him on. His career.

'Tell me.'

Kerry took a deep breath. 'I checked the defendant's DNA sample against the register, just to check she hasn't had any dealings with the police before.'

'And has she?'

'The readout shows that Anna Duraku has been arrested for soliciting over ten times.'

Jez whistled. 'So our sweet little frightened kid isn't nearly as sweet as she made out.'

'It's difficult to say.'

Jez laughed. 'Being on the game is fairly conclusive. Still, I know what you're saying – it doesn't mean she doesn't have PTSD and, knowing Lilly Valentine, she'll probably come up with an expert who'll testify that her client went on the game as a direct result of the war in Kosovo.'

'I think she'll have trouble getting anyone to do that,' said Kerry.

'You don't know Lilly.'

'But I do know that her client has lied about just about everything.'

'The report hardly says that.'

'It says Anna Duraku has previous for prostitution.'

Jez began to feel impatient. 'Which isn't the same thing as lying about everything.'

'It also says Anna Duraku killed herself three years ago.'

Jez was stunned into silence.

'Did you hear what I said?'

'Yes,' he spluttered. 'But how can that be right? There must be some mistake.'

'No mistake.'

'So who's our girl?' he asked.

'Good question.'

Chapter Eighteen

The smell of bacon wafted up the stairs and made Lilly's stomach flip. Normally she loved a fried breakfast but this morning even the thought of it made her shudder.

Anna looked up from buttering toast for Sam. 'You want something?'

'Just coffee.'

She watched Sam pile his plate high. He never spoke to Anna or looked her in the eye, but she quietly cooked for him and, in turn, he accepted her food.

Sam pointed with his knife at Lilly. 'Research has shown that people who eat breakfast perform their morning tasks more efficiently.'

Lilly wrinkled her nose at the yolk running down his hand. 'Fortunately my morning's tasks are minimal,' she said.

'We don't go to the office?' asked Anna.

Lilly shook her head. Even the smell of Nescafé was hard to bear.

'Nope. I'm working from home, doing as much research as possible into the conflict in Kosovo.'

Anna immediately looked away. Lilly reminded herself

not to be annoyed by the girl's aversion to discussing it. This was simply a symptom of PTSD.

'If I look on the Net I might even find other accounts from your village. What was it called again?'

Anna didn't answer.

'Your village,' said Lilly. 'What was its name?'

There was an uncomfortable silence finally punctuated by the phone.

'Hi Rupes,' said Lilly. 'Are you okay? 'Cos I feel bloody awful. Maybe the chicken was off.'

'What?' said Rupes.

'Do you feel sick at all?' said Lilly. 'Well, not sick exactly, just a bit queer.'

'No.'

'Must be a bug then.' Lilly looked towards her son. 'Anything going around at school?'

Sam shrugged.

'Listen,' Rupes interrupted. 'The Bailey have just called. They need you in court this morning.'

'For what?' Lilly roared.

'Don't shoot the messenger. The list office only told me to get you there ASAP.'

Lilly leaned against the worktop for support and pulled her dressing gown tightly round her. She felt lousy.

'I have to go to court.'

Sam pushed away his empty plate. 'Should have eaten some breakfast.'

'This is shit.'

Steve held Alexia's draft article between thumb and forefinger like a filthy pair of socks.

'I thought it would be good to show how local people are thinking,' she said.

'A handful of Nazis saying they hate asylum seekers.' Steve snorted his disgust. 'It's hardly a surprise, is it?'

Alexia stood her ground. 'A lot of people feel the same way. The Net is full of this stuff.'

'The Net's full of folk who believe they've seen aliens. It depends what you fucking tap in, doesn't it?'

Alexia stared him down, hands on her hips. 'It's interesting.'

'It's blather,' said Steve, and filed her copy in the bin.

She sighed and sank into her chair.

'Listen, Posh, that just isn't news.' Steve lit a cigarette and Alexia couldn't even be bothered to tell him off. 'The skinhead angle's not bad, but they haven't done anything, have they?'

'Apart from trashing the solicitor's car.'

'We can't prove that.'

'What about throwing dog crap all over the courtroom?'

He waved his arm, showering ash across her desk. 'Yesterday's fish and chips.'

Alexia wrinkled her nose at the grey flakes peppering her laptop. She knew he was right. She needed some action.

'So what do *you* suggest?'

'Get yourself down the Bailey,' he said. 'Find some idiot in the list office who'll tell you what's happening on the case.'

Luke's fingers are numb and his back is killing him. He's been picking tomatoes since six-thirty without a break.

He had finally plucked up enough courage to turn up at the Black Cat. He thought he would be washing up, sweeping floors and emptying the bin. Instead he was given a blue raffle ticket and told to wait. He sat in the corner and peeped at his number. Thirty-six.

The café was full. Not customers, although a few were drinking tea, but young men, laughing and chatting in a foreign language.

A woman walked in with a clipboard and a hush settled over the crowd. She had yellow hair that Luke's mum would call 'bottle-blonde', and eyebrows pencilled in in a much darker brown.

'Numbers one to twenty outside now,' she shouted. 'The vans are over the road.'

The men showed one another their tickets as if to confirm where they should be.

'I ain't got all day,' the woman barked. 'If you want a day's work, get in the vans now.'

The men tumbled forward and out of the door. She watched them disappear into the back of two vans and went back to her list.

'Numbers twenty-one to thirty-five, outside now.'

Another fifteen shuffled outside. There were only four men left in the café.

'Sorry,' said the woman, sounding anything but. 'There ain't nothing more today.'

She turned to leave.

'Can you fit me in?' Luke asked.

The woman raised her chocolate eyebrows. 'You English?'

Luke ignored the question. 'I'm number thirty-six. Can you fit me in? Please.'

She shouted over to the man behind the counter. 'This the one you told me about?'

The owner nodded but didn't take his eyes off the griddle he was scraping.

'All right,' she said to Luke. 'But only because your manners is so nice.'

He couldn't contain his smile.

'It's not a luxury cruise I'm offering,' she said.

'I don't care,' he answered.

All Luke's life he'd done as he was told. His mum wanted him to do well in exams so he'd revised. His dad wanted him to board so he'd packed his trunk. Tom wanted him to play sidekick so he'd laughed at his crap jokes and endless torments. His life was mapped out and he'd followed the dotted lines. Well, no more. Luke had taken control. By Manor Park standards his life might look a mess, but for the first time he was the one calling the shots. And that felt good.

The farm is somewhere in Kent, about an hour's drive out of London. It seems to be in the middle of nowhere with row upon row of polytunnels. The smell inside is overwhelming. It reminds Luke of the time he went on a school trip to Provence and Mademoiselle Townsend insisted they visit a typical French market. The stalls were piled high with wrinkled black olives and bunches of basil. But it was the smell of the tomatoes that filled the air. Mountains and mountains of them, attached to their vines in little bunches of three and four.

He rubs his hands against his jeans, leaving red smears

on his thighs, his fingers cramping from the relentless repetition.

'Okay?' asks the man beside him.

Luke was given strict instructions not to speak in front of the owner. 'Just nod,' the woman with the yellow hair had said. 'That way he'll think you're one of them.'

Luke scouts around. It's just the two of them in the tunnel. And thousands of cherry tomatoes.

'They tingle,' he says, and wiggles his fingers like a puppeteer.

'Do like this,' says the man, and blows on the tips of his own.

Luke does as he's told and the man nods.

'You English,' he says. It's not a question.

'You?' asks Luke. 'Where do you come from?'

The man goes back to the plants, twisting each fruit from its stem and laying it in his box. 'Ukraine,' he says.

'Do you do this every day?' asks Luke, his eyes following the endless rows to the horizon.

The man shrugs. 'Some days this, other days not this.'

'I bet you prefer the other days.'

'This better than fish factory,' says the man, and empties his full box into a crate.

'Less talking and more working,' shouts the owner from the entrance. He strides down towards them, his belly straining against the buttons of a polyester cardigan.

The Ukrainian points to the crates brimming with tiny red balls. 'We do very well, mister.'

'You'd do better with less chat.' He bares uneven brown teeth. 'Understand?'

'Yes, mister.'

'And your friend?' snarls the owner.

Luke doesn't know what to do. He's not supposed to speak.

The Ukrainian pats his arm. 'He understands.'

'Are you going to tell me what's going on or do I have to beat it out of you?'

'Let's discuss this in private,' said Jez, and led Lilly up the stairs of the Old Bailey to the robing room. He sat down and patted the chair next to him. 'Take a pew.'

'I'm fine.' She towered over him. 'This had better be important.'

'It is.'

'I mean bloody important,' she snapped. 'The sort of important that justifies dragging me away from my work at a second's notice.'

'I really think you should take a seat, Lilly.'

'This had better not be about me standing down from the case because if it is I might just punch you.' She clenched her fists. 'And I should tell you that the last man I punched was a black belt and he still ended up on his arse.'

If Jez was worried he didn't show it, which only incensed Lilly more.

'Here's the thing,' he said. 'Your client isn't who she says she is.'

'What are you talking about?'

'The name she's been using belongs to a girl who committed suicide three years ago.'

Lilly shook her head. 'It's a coincidence. Maybe Anna Duraku is as common as Joe Bloggs in Kosovo.'

'With the same date of birth? I don't think so.' He handed Lilly a print-out. 'This is all the information we have on the real Anna Duraku. It accords exactly with what your client's been telling everyone. Right down to the name of her brother.'

'It can't be right,' said Lilly, scanning the information.

'I'm afraid it is,' said Jez. 'Your client has been using someone else's identity.'

Lilly wandered back to her client as if in a trance. Anna had been lying from the very start. She had not escaped a brutal war. Her family had not been burned alive before her very eyes.

'Something is wrong?' said Milo.

Lilly almost laughed at the ridiculousness of it.

'Anna Duraku is dead,' she said.

No one spoke. No one seemed to breathe. Lilly looked from Anna to Milo and back again.

'The girl who came to this country to seek asylum died three years ago.'

Tears welled in Anna's eyes and ran down her cheeks as if in slow motion.

'Which begs the question,' said Lilly, 'who the fuck are you?'

'This is a matter of the utmost seriousness,' said Judge Roberts.

No shit, Sherlock.

'It affects every aspect of the case,' he continued. 'Do you have instructions, Miss Valentine?'

Lilly looked back at her client, huddled in the dock,

weeping. She hadn't uttered a word since Lilly had told her what she knew, and ten years' experience had taught Lilly that there was no point pressing.

The judge turned to Jez. 'What do the prosecution say?'

Lilly expected Jez to wring every drop out of the situation, but instead he rose slowly to his feet and coughed as if embarrassed.

'My friend will need time to address this,' he said. 'As you say, Your Honour, it affects every aspect of this case.'

The judge nodded and sighed. 'I will give you a week, Miss Valentine, during which time I expect you to thrash out with your client what on earth is going on.'

'I'll try,' said Lilly.

'And in the meantime we must address the issue of bail,' said the judge.

Lilly's stomach lurched.

'The current position is now untenable,' he continued. 'Your client must be remanded into custody.'

Lilly jumped to her feet. 'Your Honour, can we not let things stand?'

The judge removed his glasses and peered at Lilly. 'Miss Valentine, neither you, nor I, nor indeed anyone in this courtroom, have the slightest idea as to your client's identity. Do you seriously propose that I allow her just to leave the building?'

'But she's with me all the time,' Lilly blurted.

The judge shook his head.

'I wouldn't let her out of my sight,' Lilly shouted.

The judge put up his hand. 'You are not a character in a Jodi Picoult novel, Miss Valentine.'

'She won't run away, I promise.'

'Not another word.'

He signalled for the guards to take Anna down.

Alexia sidled onto the bench, next to a man with the worst case of adult acne she had ever seen.

'Tell me all about yourself, Mick,' she purred.

'It's Mark,' he said.

She let out a tiny tinkle of a laugh and smoothed a hand over a skirt that grazed her thighs. 'Of course it is.'

A scarlet stain flushed down from the man's prematurely balding temples to his pitted and infected chin.

Thank God for fishnets, she thought. Whoever had invented them should be canonised.

'So tell me, Mark,' she said, trying not to focus on a particularly large boil on his upper lip, 'is your job very interesting?'

'Not really,' he said, the angry lump moving up and down as he spoke.

Alexia sighed. After her argument with Steve she'd jumped onto the next train to London and raced to the Old Bailey determined to find a lead. She needed to find out what was going on and fast. One of the ushers had appeared with a face like a relief map of Africa and she'd dragged him off to El Vinos on Fleet Street.

'I bet you get to hear lots of juicy cases,' she said.

Mark rubbed his boil with the edge of a beer mat. 'Not many.'

'No murders?' she asked.

Mark shook his head.

'That's a shame.' Alexia licked her liberally glossed

lips. 'I find all that stuff exciting.' She leaned close enough to smell his antiseptic cream. 'Very exciting.'

He looked Alexia up and down, taking in every inch of her. She stretched out a slender wrist and picked up her glass. Gotcha.

'You from the papers then?'

Alexia spluttered on her drink. 'What makes you think that?'

''Cos if you ain't, I'll be off.' He stood to make his point.

'Sit,' she hissed.

He appraised her again, and this time Alexia could see the predatory look in his eye.

'You want to know about the asylum seeker?'

Alexia nodded.

'Five grand,' he said.

'Five thousand quid!' Alexia shouted. 'I'm from the *Three Counties Observer* not the *News of the World*.'

'Take it or leave it.' Mark sniffed. 'The *Sun* will give me double that.'

She thought quickly. Steve would never give her the money but then again, if the story was good enough, maybe she wouldn't give it to Steve. Maybe she could freelance it.

'Well?' asked Mark.

'Done,' she said. 'But this is an exclusive.'

He put his hand on her thigh. It felt clammy through her fishnets. 'Maybe this could be the start of something regular.'

She put her hand over his. 'Tell me what you've got.'

He looked around as if checking no one was listening.

'She ain't who she says she is.'

'What?'

'They've checked the DNA and everything. She's been using a false ID.'

Alexia was bowled over. She hadn't seen this coming. 'So who is she?'

Mark shrugged. 'She ain't telling.'

Lilly's mind was a blur. She couldn't get it straight. Anna wasn't from Kosovo. Anna wasn't an asylum seeker. Anna wasn't Anna.

'Let's walk,' said Milo, and led her outside.

The streets, restaurants and shops were teeming with life and noise, but Lilly felt as though she were viewing it all from the wrong end of a telescope. St Paul's was a mere speck on the horizon.

'Where did they take her?' Milo asked.

Suddenly the world changed perspective and the cathedral loomed in front of them, obliterating the sky.

'Prison,' Lilly muttered.

Her last client to be sent down had been a fourteen-year-old girl. With her mother dead, she was alone in the world and Lilly had fought like a cat for her. Until moments ago she'd felt the same about Anna.

'How could she do it?' asked Lilly.

'We don't know how desperate she was,' said Milo.

They walked without thinking past the cathedral and into the gardens where a group of nuns were eating sandwiches and taking photos in the crisp November day.

'I didn't suspect for a moment,' said Lilly. 'I just took her at her word.'

Milo stepped around one of the sisters who was taking a photograph but Lilly stood directly in the shot. 'We all just accepted everything she told us,' said Lilly.

Milo pulled Lilly to one side and looked at her. Something in his eyes brought Lilly up short.

'You knew?'

He shrugged. 'Not exactly.'

'But you suspected?'

He shrugged again and turned.

Lilly caught his arm. 'Why the hell didn't you tell me?'

The nuns looked up from their wholemeal rolls and frowned.

'She's made a fucking idiot out of me,' Lilly hissed. 'And you let her.'

'This is a place of God,' said the nun, waving her Olympus 9000. 'Please don't use profanities.'

Milo waved an apology. 'Maybe Anna didn't run away from the Serbs, but she was running away from something.'

'A parking ticket, probably,' said Lilly.

Milo shook his head. 'She left everything and everybody behind. This is more serious than a parking ticket.'

Lilly squeezed her eyes closed. Milo was right. Of course he was. People didn't just up sticks and take on false identities unless something was very wrong.

Her phone beeped. It was a text from Rupes.

How did things go in court?

Lilly sighed. Her boss was going to hit the roof.

Alexia felt uneasy about what she had set in motion.

After she'd left Mark with promises of money and

sex, she knew she was on to something. The story was a good one, but Alexia had not lived so many long years with her father without knowing that you could never be complacent. When the going was smooth you didn't lie back and pour a margarita, you worked harder, pushed harder.

The story was a good one, but she would make it a great one.

Sitting here now, in the thick of Blood River's hatred, she wondered if she had made the right choice. Alexia knew she was playing with fire and was anxious that it wasn't her who would get burned.

She had told him the news. The girl was a fake.

He had reacted calmly and asked her to meet him in the Turk's Head.

'I'm sure you'll agree that the time for words is over,' he said.

'What do you have in mind?' Alexia asked. 'A demonstration?'

Blood River gave a cold smile and pulled out his phone.

'Some of our brothers have it in hand.'

He dialled and laid his mobile on the table. It was an iPhone. Whoever was at the other end was filming a street in Harpenden.

'Oh, Rupes, I'm so sorry,' said Lilly. 'I begged you to let me keep Anna's case, and look where it's got us.'

She watched her boss calmly packing away her things. Lilly sometimes swept the day's detritus into her desk drawer but, more often than not, left everything exactly where it was. If she was out of the office for a few days, the half-eaten apples, sandwich crusts and cold cups of tea would begin to decompose and she would return to a scene out of *Great Expectations*.

'What I don't understand,' said Rupinder, 'is how she thought she could get away with it?' She poured the remainder of her Evian into the small vase of white roses that her husband sent every week. 'She must have known someone would find out eventually.'

Milo's words came back to Lilly. 'Maybe she was desperate.'

Rupinder pushed in her chair and put on her coat. 'How long have you got to sort this out?' she asked.

'The judge gave me a week.'

'Better get on with it then.'

They locked up and went out into the street, where it was already dark. The November rain was lashing down in harsh, stinging strips. Naturally, Rupes had an umbrella. Naturally, Lilly did not.

'I'll walk you to your car,' said Rupinder.

The streets were fairly empty, the few pedestrians marching purposefully with their heads down. Maybe that was why Lilly heard the men.

From the small screen on the phone Alexia could see two women huddled together. About twenty feet behind them were two men, one small, one huge. Alexia recognised the unmistakable bulk of Bigsy.

'What are they doing?' asked Alexia.

'Watch,' said Blood River.

'They're not going to hurt them, are they?' Alexia's voice was shrill.

Blood River responded with low menace. 'I told you to watch.'

Lilly unlocked her car and pecked Rupes on the cheek.

'Why can't you take on some nice conveyancing, Lilly?'

Lilly smiled but she didn't reply. She was watching three men over her boss's shoulder. Two of them stood together, seemingly oblivious to the downpour. The third was holding something in front of him. A phone?

'Let me give you a lift home,' said Lilly.

'I'm tempted, but this is the only exercise I get.' Rupes patted her bottom.

Lilly nodded her head at the men. 'I don't like the look of that lot.'

'Oh, Lilly,' Rupinder laughed, 'you spend too much time in Luton.'

'So what's the one at the back doing?'

'I don't know. Trying to get a signal?' She pushed Lilly into her car. 'This is Harpenden. Nothing exciting ever happens here.'

Lilly started the engine. Rupinder was right. The events of today had unsettled her, making her see trouble where there was none.

She pulled out and waved at her boss as she passed.

When she got to the junction she checked her rear-view mirror. There was Rupes walking along. There were the men behind her. Were they getting closer?

Lilly adjusted the mirror. It was dark and wet, difficult to make out. They were definitely getting closer.

In seconds they were right behind Rupes. On her heels. She turned towards them.

Alexia couldn't breathe. She was horrified. Terrified.

'I would never have told you if I'd thought . . .'

Blood River held her chin, his eyes glittering. 'Just do your job.' He turned her face to the screen.

The image was grainy, but she could see perfectly well as Bigsy raised his fist and punched the Indian woman in the face.

Lilly was out of her car before the second blow. She left the engine on, the door open, and raced towards Rupinder.

She could hear screaming. Her own? Rupes's?

Rupinder fell to the floor among the puddles, her sari splattered in mud and dirty water. The smaller man pulled back his foot and kicked her. Lilly heard the sound as it connected with Rupinder's head. A wet thump. A guttural groan.

'Shit-eating Paki,' he shouted, and pulled back for another kick.

Lilly closed the gap and leapt at the man.

'What the fuck?' He spun around, Lilly attached to his back. She clawed his face, feeling her nails tear his skin.

'Get her off me,' he screamed.

The bigger man grabbed at Lilly's leg but she punched away his hand. He roared at her, took hold of a handful of her hair and pulled. She was propelled backwards, clattering to the ground.

With his hand still entangled in her hair, he banged her head back hard against the concrete. The shockwave raced through her body. Her vision filled with points of light.

He lifted her head for a second time and Lilly braced herself for the slam.

'I've called the police,' she shouted. 'They'll be here any second.'

The man stopped in his tracks and looked at his companions. 'Let's get out of here.'

She was bleeding.

Even in the half-world of the iPhone, Alexia could see blood pooling under the Asian woman's head.

She was perfectly still, her neck at a strange angle.

The other woman was by her side, screaming directly into the camera, her face contorted. It was Valentine.

'You fucking scum.' Spit flew from her lips. 'You fucking animals.'

The screen went blank.

There seemed to be a vacuum of silence as if the very air had been sucked away. Alexia felt the weight of it on all sides, pressing down on her. Blood River had misjudged the situation. This time he had gone too far. Maybe he had no idea that his men would do such a horrible thing.

He turned to her slowly and whispered in her ear.

'You got exactly what you wanted. Now write the fucking story.'

Chapter Nineteen

The back of the van stinks of sweat and stale tobacco. Luke doesn't care. He squeezes into the far corner – happy to have been picked for another day's work.

The Ukrainian nods his head in acknowledgement and Luke smiles back. The journey is hot and cramped. At least fifteen of them are crammed in, squatting on the floor. Luke imagines how horrified his mother would be. She doesn't even let him sit in the front seat because she read some article about air bags setting on fire.

The men chat quietly. Though Luke can't understand what they say, he can tell by their glances in his direction that he is the main topic of conversation.

'They want to know why you're doing this,' says the Ukrainian.

Luke shrugs. 'I need the money.'

The Ukrainian translates to an eruption of laughter.

'They mean this type of work.' The Ukrainian smiles. 'Why not do with papers?'

Luke closes his eyes. He can't explain that he's wanted for rape. That he'll be arrested on the spot if he does anything official.

'It's complicated,' he says.

The Ukrainian nods. 'Life is always complicated.'

Luke keeps his eyes tight shut. Sometimes his situation makes his head feel like it might explode. Sometimes he's wondered if he'll just go mad. He's seen plenty of people on the street who've totally lost their grip on reality. They lurch about, deep in conversation with unseen demons. A year ago Luke might have laughed at them; now he wonders if he'll end up the same way.

'You haven't time for a meltdown, soft lad,' says Caz. 'Not now you're a wage slave.'

'You won't take the piss when I get us somewhere to live,' says Luke.

Caz cocks her head to one side like a tiny bird. 'You're serious, aren't you?'

'I've never been more serious about anything in my life.'

And it's true. Exams, footie matches, arguments with his mum, they all seem trivial now.

'I'm going to take care of you,' he says.

'I can take care of myself,' she replies. 'I've been doing it since I could walk.'

Luke kisses her gently on the cheek. 'Now it's my turn.'

The van comes to an abrupt stop and Luke is propelled into the Ukrainian's lap. The doors are thrown wide and Luke tries to untangle himself.

The Ukrainian clambers outside and groans.

'What's up?' asks Luke.

The Ukrainian points to the grey building belching smog from a handful of chimneys.

'Fish factory.'

Luke breathes in the stench of dead prawns and smiles. He's on a mission.

'You've got a bleeding nerve.'

Lilly exhaled loudly. She'd been at Luton General most of the night, pacing the corridors while her boss had emergency surgery. Rupinder's husband, Raj, had finally convinced her to go home at four, but she'd come straight back after Sam had left for school. She was exhausted. Her scalp screamed where her hair had been wrenched. She just didn't have the energy to deal with Sheila.

Ignore her. Ignore her.

'I said you've got a bleeding nerve.'

Lilly walked slowly around the irate secretary and made for the ward sister's desk.

'Can I have an update on Rupinder Singh?' she asked the nurse.

'Are you a relative?'

'No, she ain't,' Sheila shouted.

Lilly sighed. 'I came in with her yesterday evening.'

'I'll see what I can find out,' said the nurse, and disappeared into the office behind.

Sheila pressed in against Lilly, wobbling on unsteady heels. 'I hope you're pleased with yourself.'

'One of my closest friends is critically ill and I had the shit kicked out of me,' said Lilly. 'Out of interest, why do you think I'd be pleased?'

'This is your doing, this is.' Sheila spread an arm around the ward as if Lilly had personally caused the accident of every patient in there. 'This is all your fault.'

Ignore her. Ignore her.

'I warned you this would happen,' Sheila snorted. 'I told you that we shouldn't take on that bleeding case.'

'We don't know that this has got anything to do with Anna.'

Sheila threw back her head and laughed. The sound was hollow.

'That's what you said about the letter. Then you said it again about the graffiti.'

It was true. Despite niggling doubts, Lilly had denied a link. She hadn't wanted to believe there was one.

'I didn't think we were in any danger.'

Sheila shook her head. 'You didn't bleedin' care.'

Lilly opened her mouth to object, but the nurse returned.

'Mrs Singh is still in theatre,' said the nurse. 'Perhaps you could come back in an hour.'

Lilly nodded and shuffled to a row of chairs. Sheila hovered over her, every muscle in her body rippling with anger.

'And what are these nutters going to do next?'

Lilly put her head in her hands. She felt crystalline, as if she might shatter at the slightest touch.

'What are they going to do when they find out the little cow has been lying all along?' Sheila persisted.

'It's confidential,' said Lilly.

'No, it bleeding ain't,' roared Sheila, and threw a copy of the *Daily Mail* onto Lilly's lap.

The woman couldn't resist being the bearer, or more accurately hurler, of bad news.

Lilly read the headline.

Lilly felt her chest constrict and the words on the page began to swim. She ran for the exit.

Alexia smiled at the headline. It was fantastic copy. She would rather have sold it to a broadsheet, but in the end she had a choice between the *Mail* and the *Express*. They were the only two willing to stump up the money she'd promised Mark and pay a reasonable sum for the article. Her dad had always said you had to own the news, not write it, to make any cash.

They'd fiddled with it a bit. Well, a lot. More emphasis had been put on the outrage of the false claim for asylum than she had originally intended, and the beating of Singh and Valentine had been reduced to two lines – but still.

She opened her desk drawer and started to pack up her equipment. Steve hadn't said a word but his face told the story.

'I had to do it,' said Alexia. 'It was too big for us. A story like that needs national coverage.'

He didn't speak, just handed her a cardboard box.

She carefully placed her mug and pencils at the bottom.

Why was she so sad? She'd always known she was too good for this place. Too serious to work on a provincial rag. But her plan had been to stay for two years, learn all she could.

Steve snatched the drawer out of its runner and

upturned it, spewing the contents everywhere. Alexia felt panic rise in the pit of her stomach. He was a difficult old sod but he was one of the best hacks in the area.

'Can't we work something out? she asked.

'You're on your own now, Posh.'

Lilly leaned against the skip and threw up. She hadn't eaten since yesterday lunchtime and fourteen cups of hospital tea hit the deck.

How the hell had the *Daily Mail* got hold of the story? Her mobile rang deep in the recesses of her pocket. She fumbled for it and it fell to the floor.

'Shit.'

Lilly fished it out of the pool of tan-coloured bile. She cringed at the slime against her ear. 'Hello.'

'Miss Valentine,' it was the unmistakable voice of Dr Kadir. 'You are supposed to be here this morning.'

Lilly nodded. She vaguely remembered an appointment at ten for Anna. But Anna was . . .

'I'm sorry,' she said. 'Things have been a bit tricky at this end.'

'I've seen the papers.'

Lilly supposed she should be relieved. At least she didn't have to explain herself. Dr Kadir would understand that the case was in tatters.

'I think you should come,' said Dr Kadir.

'What?' Lilly exclaimed. Hadn't the woman understood that they'd been wasting their time?

'Anna is in prison.'

'I said *you* should come.'

Lilly was about to argue when she caught sight of Sheila stomping towards her, hair on end, eyes wild.

'Give me twenty minutes.'

'Tell me what has happened.' Dr Kadir steepled her fingers.

Lilly sagged into her chair. 'It's pretty much what they said in the paper. Anna isn't who she says she is. As far as I know she isn't from Kosovo or an asylum seeker. She isn't even called Anna.'

'I mean to you, Miss Valentine,' said Dr Kadir. 'What has happened to you?'

Lilly rubbed the crown of her head. She could still feel thick fingers pulling her scalp. 'My work colleague and I were attacked last night.'

Lilly's ears were ringing.

'You feel ill,' said Dr Kadir. It wasn't a question, no doubt the answer was bloody obvious.

'Headache,' said Lilly.

'Nausea?'

'Yeah,' Lilly nodded, the movement increasing the cacophony in her skull.

Dr Kadir got up and flicked the switch of her kettle. Not another herbal brew.

'I don't think essence of nettle is going to help,' she said.

Dr Kadir selected a tea bag and poured boiling water over it. A spicy steam ballooned around her.

'Ginger Zinger,' she said, and placed the cup in front of Lilly. 'Drink.'

Lilly took a sip and smiled weakly.

Dr Kadir leaned back and folded her arms. Clearly the discussion wouldn't continue until Lilly had finished. She took a deep gulp, feeling the liquid warm her throat, then her stomach. The latter immediately calmed. She took another drink. No more lurching. In fact, she felt hungry. She greedily drained the cup.

'More?' asked Dr Kadir.

'Yes, please.'

The other woman went back to her kettle. 'So Anna lied about how she came to be in the UK?'

'Yes,' said Lilly. 'I'm sorry.'

Dr Kadir gave a puzzled smile and passed the cup back. Lilly fell on it like it was the elixir of life.

'Not your fault,' said the doctor.

'I know,' said Lilly. 'But so many people went out of their way to help her. And you, most of all, must feel angry that she made it all up.'

'Why?'

Lilly reddened. They had never directly referred to Dr Kadir's past in Iraq.

'You know what it feels like to be caught up in tragedy,' Lilly said. 'To be torn from your family.'

Dr Kadir looked out of the window. Lilly thought she could feel the woman's sadness, tangible and real.

'I don't judge,' the doctor said, her eyes still on the horizon.

'The paper crucified Anna,' said Lilly. 'There'll be a public outcry. There's only one thing people like less than an asylum seeker and that's a bogus asylum seeker.'

'It's easy to point a finger from the sofa,' said Dr Kadir.

'But you and Milo know the truth. You've seen the suffering first hand, yet you still don't criticise.'

'Maybe it's because of what we have seen that we don't criticise.'

They sat in silence for a few seconds.

At last it was Dr Kadir that spoke.

'How is Anna?'

'I don't know. I haven't been to see her.'

'You'll go today?'

Lilly shrugged. 'My friend's seriously ill in hospital.'

Dr Kadir cocked her eyebrow.

'And I don't even know if there's any point in visiting Anna. Maybe everything's a lie. Maybe there was no rape. Maybe she knew perfectly well what she was doing on the day of the shooting,' said Lilly.

'Then I suggest you find out.'

Lilly scraped back her hair with her hands. She winced when her fingers touched her crown. 'Maybe I don't care any more.'

Dr Kadir reached into her box of tea bags. Her fingers went deftly through them like a secretary with a Rolodex.

'Why did you take this case, Miss Valentine?'

Lilly looked down at her own hands, cuticles ragged, varnish chipped. 'She was a frightened kid with no one else to help her.'

Dr Kadir pressed three Ginger Zingers into Lilly's palm. 'What's changed?'

Once you've got the hang of it, the job isn't hard. The heads are sliced off the prawns by huge choppers that leave the rest of the shells loose. The trick is to remove and discard those before the prawns drop off the end of the conveyor belt into huge vats.

Luke is ankle-deep in shells. He shakes them off the tongue of his trainers. God, he won't half stink later.

When the vat is full a siren sounds and the belt comes to a halt. When he'd first arrived, Luke had assumed this was to give the workers time for a break, but the Ukrainian had thrown a broom at him.

'You sweep, I wipe.'

Now Luke understands it's the signal to clean away as much debris as possible before the next ton of shellfish arrives and the evil choppers beat down once more. He collects armfuls of shell, juice and roe seeping through his fingers, and dumps them into a skip. The Ukrainian pushes a dishcloth along the belt.

'Next time,' says Luke, 'you sweep and I'll wipe.'

The silver Mini Cooper shot down the motorway. Spurred on by Dr Kadir, Lilly was determined to get to the prison by two.

It was usual to give forty-eight hours' notice to secure an appointment with a prisoner, but the judge had personally phoned the governor to ensure Lilly had access to her client all week. Such judicial interference might have been resisted, but the recent spate of suicides at High Point meant the governor was bending like Madonna in a Pilates class to accommodate anyone connected to the Home Office.

The prison sat in majestic solitude, crowned on all sides with razor wire. The car park was huge and, as usual, almost deserted. So much space would normally fill Lilly with gratitude, but she had once been attacked in the cavernous expanse and parked as close to the prison entrance as possible. Last night's attack had made her feel even more nervy and she marched to the doors with a military stride.

The guard at reception had a wandering eye. The right one stared straight at Lilly but the left danced somewhere over the rainbow.

'Who are you here for?' she asked.

Lilly made a concerted effort not to follow the wayward eye-line and looked deeply into the guard's face.

'Anna Duraku,' said Lilly, her forehead wrinkled in concentration.

'Can't seem to find her,' said the guard, then, noticing Lilly's mad stare, took a step back. 'Do you know which section she's in?'

Desperate not to even peek at the rogue pupil, Lilly shook her head.

'Are you okay?' asked the guard.

'I'm fine,' said Lilly without blinking. 'Absolutely fine.'

The guard nodded nervously and rechecked her list.

'It's possible she used a different name,' said Lilly, her eyes boring into the guard's face.

'And what name would that be?'

Lilly's eyes were beginning to sting with the effort. 'I don't know.'

'Ok-ay.' The guard nodded slowly as if Lilly might be insane and picked up the phone.

'Have you got a Duraku?' She turned her body so

that her shoulders were shielding her from Lilly. 'I think her brief's simple.'

At last Lilly was given the all-clear and shunted through to see her client. She arrived at the visitors' centre and scanned the crowd. The noise of shouting, laughing and screeching kids was like a wall. There was no sign of Anna.

She passed her papers to the guard at the door who was picking up a family bag of M&Ms that had spilled under her desk. On her knees, she slammed a fistful of Day-Glo pellets onto the plastic top.

'She's not in here.'

'I can see that.' Lilly nodded to a table in the corner. 'Can I wait there?'

'Not much point.' The guard shrugged and wiped her hands down her thighs. 'They won't bring her in here.'

Lilly sighed. Why were these people so difficult? They must know she was just doing her job.

'There's a court order in force,' she said. 'You have to let me see my client.'

A toddler with skin the colour of white chocolate raced past, spraying a packet of Skips in his wake.

'Jesus.' The guard brushed pink scraps off her jumper.

An argument erupted in the far corner between an inmate and what looked like a visiting husband. 'Filthy, two-timing cunt,' the prisoner roared. She threw her chair behind her and squared up to the man, who was twice her size.

'Simmer down,' the guard shouted.

The woman stood her ground, skinny arms wind-milling around.

'He's only got my sister pregnant,' she yelled. 'My fucking sister.'

As one, the room turned on the man, and insults, cigarette ends and sweets rained down on him. He shielded his face and head with a puffa jacket and ran for the door.

'I'd give next week a miss if I were you,' said the guard, missiles whizzing past her nose.

With the enemy in retreat and the noise dropping to riot levels, Lilly tried again. 'I really do have to see Anna Duraku.'

The guard mouthed her words as if Lilly were both hard of hearing and stupid. 'They won't bring her across here.'

'Why not?'

The guard shoved the paperwork under Lilly's nose and tapped Anna's name with an insistent finger. Marked in red biro were the words 'Vulnerable Prisoner'.

Something wasn't right.

Lilly checked the paperwork again. Why was Anna classed as a VP?

'Surely there's a mistake.'

The guard rolled her eyes and led Lilly to a door at the far end of the visitor's centre. On the other side lay a room separated from the centre by reinforced glass.

'Reception said you weren't the full ticket.'

Lilly would have argued but she was too concerned

as to why her client had been classified as a Vulnerable Prisoner. While the title might have seemed fitting for a kid in her predicament, the truth was the VPs were the most hated of all prisoners. Child killers, sex offenders, nonces. Segregated for their own good. Identified by a coloured bib wherever they went.

'I don't understand,' said Lilly.

The guard jangled a set of keys and unlocked the room. Lilly stepped inside and looked out. The inmates and visitors all watched her.

It was like being in a fishbowl.

'Why is she a yellow?' asked Lilly.

'She killed a boy, didn't she?'

'Actually, she didn't.'

'Nobody in here ever has,' said the guard. 'Every last one of them is innocent.'

Lilly smiled. It was true that no one in jail ever admitted to anything. 'I mean she wasn't the one who actually shot the boy.'

The guard wiped her nose along her sleeve, evidently unimpressed with Lilly's explanation.

'And anyway,' Lilly continued, 'he was about the same age.'

The guard nodded absently, still underwhelmed. 'To be honest, the main reason she's on the VP wing is nothing to do with what she's in for.'

Lilly felt colour rise at the base of her neck. 'What is the reason?'

The guard looked over her shoulder through the window. 'The girls don't really like her sort,' she said. 'It's better to keep them out of the way.'

At last, Anna arrived. Her hair was pulled off her face, the skin of her temples wrenched taut. Her tiny face and lips were colourless.

She sank into the chair opposite Lilly, her yellow bib crumpling around her.

'Nice to see you, Lilly,' she said. 'Everything is okay?'

Out of nowhere Lilly felt furious. Of course everything wasn't okay.

'Apart from the fact that a boy is dead and you may go to prison for the rest of your life?' she said.

Anna looked down in her lap. 'I'm sorry.'

'For what, exactly?' Lilly's tone was sharp. 'The fact that you went to my son's school with a gun? Or the fact that you've lied to me from the very first moment we met?'

Anna didn't look up. 'I'm sorry you are angry with me.'

Lilly sagged. Why was she being so judgemental? Couldn't she at least try to be like Milo and Dr Kadir?

An inmate passed the window and leered in. 'Go back to where you came from,' she shouted, and spat at the window.

Lilly watched the saliva slip down the glass.

'I'm trying to keep calm,' Lilly took Anna's hand, 'but I really need some help here.'

'I will do what I can.'

Lilly squeezed the girl's fingers, half the size of her own. 'Then tell me what happened. How you really came to this country.'

Anna pulled back her fingers and pushed her hands between her thighs.

Lilly felt her irritation return. She tried to swallow it back down.

'Anna?'

'It is very difficult.'

Lilly took a deep breath. They'd played this game before: Anna reluctant to divulge details, Lilly putting it down to the trauma she'd suffered. But none of that had been true, had it?

'I can't help you unless you tell me,' she said.

'I know,' said Anna, and stood to leave.

Lilly felt helpless. Had the girl given up?

She heard the clunk of iron in the lock and the door opened. Before her client could be swallowed into the darkness, she called after her.

'Tell me your name.' Lilly stretched out her hand. 'At least tell me your name.'

'Catalina.'

The horn sounds.

Luke has been waiting, his muscles flexed. He leaps towards the cloth and waves it above his head like a flag.

The Ukrainian laughs. 'You funny boy.'

Luke grins and nods at the broom. 'You sweep, I wipe.'

The man holds up his hands in mock surrender and bends down for the brush. He pushes the shells into piles, still tittering and shaking his head.

Luke drags the cloth along the black belt and removes the worst of the debris. He throws a prawn head onto the floor, the black beads of its eyes winking under the fluorescent lights.

'You missed a bit,' he says.

The Ukrainian picks it up and tosses it back onto the belt. It rolls towards the choppers.

'You missed a bit.' Luke flicks it with the edge of the cloth but it rolls further still. 'Now look what you've made me do.'

'You should stick to sweeping, my friend.'

'Not a chance.'

Luke leans over to grab it. Too late he hears the siren and the belt rumbles into life. Almost in slow motion he sees the chopper fall hard onto his outstretched hand.

Lilly's head was pounding. Not just the crown where the roots were still too tender to be touched, but her temples throbbed as well. The strain of the day coursed along with her blood.

She pulled the Mini up outside her cottage, killed the engine and laid her forehead against the steering wheel. Everything had gone shit-shaped. The case, the press, the attack on Rupes. Everything.

Lilly didn't even have the energy to get out of the car.

The day had disappeared and shadows loomed around the porch. The bulb had popped in the outside light. Over a month ago and she still hadn't fixed it. God, she really was useless.

At last, she hauled herself out of the car and lumbered towards the cottage. She fished into her bag for the door key, groping through old tissues. She pulled out three broken biros and sighed. Sam was always telling her to get a key ring. He'd even made one for her in DT. A phallic design in yellow plastic.

'A banana,' she'd laughed.

Sam had fixed her with one of his looks. 'It's an "L".'

Whatever it was, she wished she had the bloody thing

now, rather than scrabbling in the back pockets of her briefcase where no human hand had been in years. She winced as her fingers came up against something soft.

She was so engrossed in her search she almost missed the figure darting across the road. Almost.

It was properly dark now, like only the countryside can be when autumn turns to winter. She craned her neck. 'Is someone there?'

The figure seemed to be almost at her gate. It was so difficult to tell in the gloom. She rummaged frantically. Where was that key?

Could it be the press? They'd been well and truly warned to stay away by the judge but they were a slippery lot. Alexia Dee seemed to slither wherever she wanted to go.

Could it be the attackers from Harpenden? Could they have tracked down where she lived?

She felt panic rising in her throat. The figure was almost upon her. It was in outline but she could see it was definitely a man. He'd come to finish off the job.

She decided to run to the car. She could jump inside, lock the doors, and run the bastard over if she had to. With the key in her hand, she threw herself at the Mini. Aware that the man was almost upon her, she wrenched the door open and dived inside, knocking her knee hard and bumping her head on the roof.

'Jesus,' she screamed, as sickening pain attacked from all angles. She reached for the handle and pulled the door towards her.

It didn't give.

Someone had hold of it.

The man had hold of it. His thick fingers gripped the top of the window.

Lilly looked around in terror for something to defend herself with. She had only the pens she was still holding so she lashed out with one with full force. The man gave a gratifying scream as she dragged the jagged plastic across his fingers.

She pulled back her hand, ready to go again. No one fucked with Lilly Valentine.

'Mary Mother of God,' screamed the man.

That's right, thought Lilly, cry like a baby.

Then she stopped. Something in the voice was familiar. Very familiar.

Gingerly, she peeped around the car door, and there he was, clutching his hand to his mouth, sucking his knuckles.

'Jack,' she said.

'Why in the name of God did you do that?' he shouted.

Lilly burst into tears.

Jack poured the tea and placed a chipped mug in front of Lilly.

She gulped back a sob. 'Sugar?'

'Three,' he nodded.

She blew over the rim, enjoying the steam against her lips. 'I didn't think you were allowed to come here,' she said.

'If I'd known you were going to try to kill me I'd not have bothered.'

'I panicked.'

He wiggled his fingers. The flesh across his knuckles was ragged and bloody. 'I'm in two minds as to whether to give you this,' he said, and tossed a family-sized bar of Dairy Milk at her.

She ran her finger along the first two chunks and snapped the chocolate.

'Mum,' shouted Sam, and barged into the kitchen. 'You left the door open!'

When he saw Jack at the table he stopped in mid-rant and smiled.

'Long time no see, wee man,' said Jack, and held up his hand for a high five.

Sam rolled his eyes in mock derision but he slapped it all the same.

'She left it wide open,' he told Jack. 'Anyone could have walked in.'

'The old woman's had a pretty rough day,' Jack replied. 'And to be honest I was the last one in, so technically it's my fault.'

Not easily appeased, Sam eyed Jack suspiciously. Lilly was not yet off the hook.

'Hungry?' Jack asked. 'I was always starving when I walked in from school. My ma used to hide all the treats so me and my brother couldn't wolf the lot before tea.'

Sam laughed. 'Did you ever find them?'

'Course we did. Sweets in the bread bin, biscuits in the washer.'

Jack reached over the table and grabbed the Dairy Milk. 'I'd get some of this lot down you, before Charlie Bucket here scoffs the lot.'

Lilly watched Sam shovel four chunks into his mouth and felt relief. Jack was a life-saver.

'Do you fancy a bacon sandwich, Jack?' Sam asked through brown teeth.

'I'm sure that would be grand, but your ma's probably a bit knackered.'

Sam waved a dismissive hand. 'Ask Anna. She makes them better than Mum anyway.'

Lilly felt her shoulders tense again.

'She's not here, love,' she said.

Sam looked at his mother accusingly. Something in her tone had obviously alerted him to a problem.

'What's happened?' he asked.

'She's had to go away for a bit,' she said.

Sam stuck out his bottom lip. He looked every one of his nine years. 'Did she kill someone else?'

Lilly's mind did a somersault and landed flat on its arse.

'Listen, wee man,' said Jack, an arm around Sam's shoulders. 'What do you say we let the old woman make the food and you thrash me at Gran Turismo?'

Lilly was grateful as Jack led Sam out of the kitchen. She pulled some bacon out of the fridge and stuck it under the grill. Cheeky devil – no one made a bacon butty better than she did.

Jack popped his head around the door.

'Everything all right?' asked Lilly.

'He decided I was fecking useless so he's playing against himself.'

Lilly laughed. 'You're a saint, McNally.'

'The Chief Super doesn't think so.'

'Tell him from me, there's a special place in heaven for you,' she said, 'right next to Mahatma Gandhi.'

Jack wrinkled his nose. 'Is there no room next to Marilyn Monroe?'

'Sorry, love, fully booked.'

Lilly slipped the salty rashers between slices of soft white bread.

'I'll take it up to him,' said Jack.

'There's still no room next to Marilyn.'

'I'd settle for Diana Dors.'

She took his hand and he winced as her fingers brushed against the raw flesh of his knuckles. But he didn't pull away.

Chapter Twenty

The throbbing is unbearable. Caz had encouraged him to drink half a bottle of Thunderbird last night.

'Nothing hurts after you've necked this stuff.'

And it had worked. For a few hours, anyway. But now the pain was back with a vengeance: it felt as if Luke's hand had grown to twice its size and the blood was squeezing itself through his veins.

He stuck the offending limb out of his sleeping bag and hoped the icy morning air would numb the pain. People say it doesn't get properly cold anymore, with global warming and everything; well, they should try spending the night, all night, outside. And it's nothing like the camping trip Luke did with the Duke of Edinburgh when they all had double-lined tents and those special sleeping bags from Millets.

But this morning he's glad it's freezing because his hand feels like it's on fire.

When the chopper had first gone in he hadn't felt the pain. Just a huge pressure bearing down. It was when the blades came back up, sucking his hand with them, that the burning started. A massive white heat from his fingertips to his wrist.

He can't remember if he screamed but he supposes he must have done. He knows he was rooted to the spot, staring at his hand attached to the machine.

It was the Ukrainian who saved him from being chopped again. He'd leapt from the skip, prawn shells raining like pink confetti, and hit the emergency button.

An alarm had sounded and the cutters ground to a halt.

Luke simply stood there, open-mouthed, his arm shaking.

The Ukrainian shouted something Luke didn't understand and the other men came over, shaking their heads and whispering. There wasn't any blood, not then, and Luke noticed his hand was a ghostly white.

At last the foreman arrived. He was a thin man, with a thin moustache over a thin top lip. He had a permanently worried expression. He looked at the blade embedded in the top of Luke's hand.

'Jesus Christ.'

'We need a doctor,' said the Ukrainian. 'You call a doctor, yes?'

The foreman took a step back in shock. His lips disappeared as if removed by some surgical process. 'No doctors.'

The crowd of men murmured in dissent.

'He needs help,' said the Ukrainian.

'Listen to me,' said the foreman. 'If I bring in anyone from outside, what do you think will happen?' He ran his hands through his few strands of grey hair. 'I'll tell you what will happen,' he said. 'I'll lose my job. Do you understand that? I've got kids, a mortgage . . .'

'But this is not good.'

'And what about you and all your friends here?' The foreman waved an arm around the factory, full of illegal workers. 'A doctor will have the immigration here as quick as a flash.'

'I don't know,' said the Ukrainian, visibly wavering.

'You'll all be sent back to where you came from.'

The Ukrainian glanced at Luke's hand. 'He hurt very bad.'

'No,' the foreman shook his head, 'not very bad.'

'Not very bad,' the Ukrainian repeated.

The foreman snapped back his head and spoke directly to Luke.

'What about you, lad? Do you want me to get a doctor?'

Luke was terrified. If a doctor contacted the authorities surely they'd involve the police? Luke would be arrested, taken to prison. And what about Caz? Who'd look after Caz?

'No doctor,' he whispered.

'Right then,' said the foreman, and ran back to the office. For a moment Luke wondered if he intended just to leave him there, attached to the machine, but at last he scurried back, a first-aid kit in one hand, a bottle of Dettol in the other.

He turned to the Ukrainian. 'When I pull, you pour this over. Understand?'

The Ukrainian nodded, his eyes round with fear.

Before Luke could ask any questions the foreman wrenched his hand from the blade and the wound was doused in disinfectant.

Luke couldn't have described the agony that ran up his arm and through his body. It knocked him off his feet. Literally. He lay on the floor, convulsing.

Above him, he could see the faces of the other workers, cringing, scowling or turning away. He could feel his hand being tightly wrapped but he daren't even look.

'There you are,' said the foreman, and pulled Luke to his feet.

Luke plucked up the courage to check his hand. It was swathed in a bulky, uneven bandage, a red stain appearing through the gauze. The sight of it made him feel sick and his knees buckled. The foreman caught him.

'You're in shock, lad.' He led Luke towards the office. 'A cup of tea and you'll be right as rain.'

As they climbed the metal gantry the foreman called to the men who were still muttering to one another.

'Show's over,' he said. 'Get back to work.'

Now Luke checks his watch. It's 4 a.m. and he's in agony. No way can he get back to sleep. Caz is beside him, her breathing even. He puts his head inches from her shoulder, close enough to feel her heat. It's uncomfortable in this position but he likes to lie like this, next to Caz, almost touching. Anyway, he's got to get up soon for work.

Lilly checked the clock. Four a.m. and she was wide awake. After Jack had left she'd fallen into sleep like a stone, but her eyes had shot open half an hour ago and she'd been worrying about Rupes ever since.

She padded down the hallway, past Sam's room. She could hear his even breathing.

'The sleep of the righteous,' her mother used to say.

She was right – only babies and the mentally unsound could rest so easy.

Other mothers would tell their kids they had to 'grow up'. Not Lilly – she hoped her son remained in the bliss of childhood for as long as he could. A Peter Pan for the Xbox generation.

She opened the fridge. A large tub of ricotta winked at her seductively. She spooned it into a bowl, drizzled honey on top and took a fat, sweet mouthful. As she felt the cool blandness against her tongue, she phoned the hospital.

'Rupinder Singh,' she said. 'How is she?'

'There's been no change,' the nurse said. A mechanic, rehearsed reply.

'Is that good?' Lilly asked. 'Does that mean she's going to be okay?'

She heard the nurse's muffled sigh. 'It means there's been no change.'

Lilly shivered. She'd hated hospitals ever since her mum died. During Lilly's last year at university Elsa's health had deteriorated. She'd had emphysema. Years of work in a sewing factory had filled her lungs with crap.

'Feels like I've swallowed one of their bloody pairs of tights.'

As Lilly prepared for her finals, Elsa had been on Raven Wing at Leeds General, hooked to an oxygen mask.

Lilly had sat by her bedside revising the *Police and Criminal Evidence Act*. When Elsa could no longer take solids they'd shared ice-lollies, taking it in turns to have a lick.

On the day of her graduation Lilly arrived on the ward in her cap and gown and the nurses had taken photos.

'Will you be all right, Mam?' asked Lilly, on her way out to catch the train.

'Course,' Elsa had said. 'There's plenty of folk in the cemetery wish they were as healthy as me.'

Back then Lilly had forced a smile; now, she allowed herself the luxury of a single tear, then swiped it with the back of her hand. She could hear her mother as clearly as if she were in the room. 'Time on your hands, mind on yourself.'

Lilly smiled and pulled out a well-thumbed recipe book. Double chocolate brownies sounded just the ticket.

The lights come on at six. Every light in the whole prison.

The change from pitch black to bright white is disorientating.

A guard raps on the door with her stick then opens the cell with a clank of iron.

'Name?' she barks.

'Anna Du . . .' She stops herself. 'Catalina Petrescu.'

'Make your mind up,' says the guard, and slams the door shut. The clang bounces off every wall.

There's another bang as she performs the same routine in the cell next door. Then the next. Then the next.

'D wing present and accounted for,' the guard bellows, somewhere down the corridor.

What do they think? That someone might have escaped in the night?

Catalina doesn't really care, she is still reeling from saying her name. She puts her finger to her lips as if the words might still be there, words she hasn't used in an eternity.

'Catalina Petrescu,' she says again.

It sounds all wrong. That's the name of another person. A girl who lived another life. A life left long ago.

She pulls on her uniform. A pair of brown dungarees and a sweatshirt. Ugly clothes that hang off her. At least they're warm. Catalina hates to be cold.

The door opens again and another prisoner puts a tray on the table. She's in the same clothes but has a red band around her arm, like the captain of a football team.

'Thank you,' says Catalina.

The woman only nods and the door is slammed again.

There are no plates on the tray but three compartments are moulded into the white plastic. One contains a slice of toast, slightly burned at the edges, another has baked beans. A carton of orange juice lays in the third beside a plastic knife and fork.

Catalina sits down to eat. The food looks bad, but she has been hungry too many times in her life to waste it. She bites into the toast and hopes Lilly has cooked Sam his bacon and eggs. She smiles at the thought of him. Such a gorgeous boy.

Maybe Lilly won't have time. She's always so busy, running from here to there, her hair standing on end.

This morning she'll come to the prison. She'll plonk her papers and folders onto the table and demand answers. She's angry about all the lies. She wants the truth. But Catalina doesn't want to tell the truth. She doesn't even want to think about it. It hurts so much.

'Catalina, Catalina.'

Mama shouts up the stairs from the kitchen. She's drunk again.

'Catalina, Catalina.'

The babies look at their big sister, eyes wide. Mama will want another bottle and that will mean nothing for them to eat today.

Elena starts to whimper.

'Shush,' says Catalina, 'I'll sort this out.'

But she knows she can't. The last time she tried, Mama slapped her so hard the mark lasted two days. She looked like Fat Bobo in the post office who has a port-wine stain across one of his cheeks.

'Catalina, Catalina.'

She can't wait any longer. Mama is not a patient person. Not since Papa died. Catalina scurries into the kitchen. The empty bottle is upturned on the table.

'Why do you always take so long?' Mama slurs. 'Are you deaf?'

'I was putting on my shoes,' Catalina lies.

Mama lurches to the cupboard and pulls out her purse. She empties the coins into Catalina's outstretched palm.

'Spend whatever's left on food for the babies.'

Catalina can see there will hardly be enough for a loaf of bread. She pleads with her eyes. The babies are hungry.

'What are you waiting for?' Mama snarls, and Catalina runs out of the door without putting on her coat.

The wind is biting and she's numb by the time she reaches the shop. Her feet are wet from the grey slush. She passes the shelves stacked with potatoes. When her father was alive, Mama made *bigos* every weekend. Catalina can taste the stew now, thick with cabbage and as much pork as they could afford.

At the counter, Mrs Cirescu smiles hello. If she feels sorry for Catalina she hides it well, always happy to take the cash.

'Vodka?' she asks.

Catalina nods and puts the coins down, praying there will be enough left over for a loaf.

On the way back she slips on an icy patch. Her shoes are worn bare and as smooth as glass, so she tumbles into a snow drift. Her heart bangs in her chest. Has she broken the bottle? Mama will kill her if the vodka is lost. She scrabbles towards it and brushes off the ice crystals. It's fine, not a crack. The bread, however, has fallen out of its paper bag and is lying wet and dirty by the side of the road. Catalina stuffs it back in the bag. The babies will eat it all the same.

By the time she gets home, Catalina is breathing hard and soaked to the skin. Her teeth are chattering.

'Mama,' she calls. 'I'm back.' She takes off her sodden shoes and steps into the kitchen. She'll leave the bottle and then peel off her clothes.

To her surprise, she finds another woman is sitting at the table, whispering to Mama. The neighbours used to come by all the time to swap stories and drink tea. But not now. Not since Papa died. It's as if they're afraid the bad luck will rub off.

This woman isn't a neighbour. She's a stranger, dressed in a thick wool coat and good boots. Her hair is dyed yellow like the women in Hollywood.

'You must be Catalina,' she says.

Catalina nods. The woman's mouth is smiling but not her eyes.

'She's a quiet girl,' says Mama. 'Never smiles.'

'Quiet is good,' says the woman. She takes the vodka and pours it. Catalina notices she has only a finger for herself but she fills Mama's glass to the top.

'Kids today don't understand the world,' says Mama, her eyes rheumy. 'They want too much.'

The woman sips her vodka. 'I blame the television.'

Catalina can't understand that. She has only ever seen the TV in her friend Rina's house, and she's never invited any more.

'My mother had nine children under Ceauşescu,' says Mama. 'And four were sent away.'

Catalina has heard the story many times. How the youngest of Mama's brothers and sisters were taken from Granny and put in a state orphanage. She often wonders what happened to them, these unknown uncles and aunts.

'We were poor.' Mama stabs her chest with her thumb. 'Most of the time we went hungry.'

The woman nods to the soggy bread disintegrating in Catalina's hands. 'You're a lucky girl.'

'You see I love my children.' Mama begins to cry.

The woman pats her hand. 'Of course you do.'

'It's just been very hard since my husband was taken.' Tears pour down Mama's face and her mouth goes slack. 'I ask God every night to help me,' she says. 'Why won't he help me?'

The woman pours more vodka. 'He has sent me.'

Mama obviously has no idea what she's talking about and the woman sighs.

'The job,' she says. 'I've come to offer the job.'

Catalina's heart leaps into her mouth. She can scarcely believe it. A job for Mama. She's worked here and there, of course, she's had to keep the wolf from the door, but there's never been anything regular.

'What do you think, Catalina?' asks the woman.

Catalina beams. 'I think it's great. I'll do everything I can to help so that Mama can go to work.'

Mama shakes her head and snorts with laughter. 'Not me, you stupid child. Who would employ an old hag like me?'

'But I thought she said she'd come about a job.'

Mama rolls her eyes and nudges the woman. 'I told you she wasn't the brightest.'

The woman laughs but turns to Catalina. 'The job's for you.'

Catalina is incredulous. She's twelve years old and has hardly been to school. 'A job for me?' she says. 'Doing what?'

'A nanny,' says the woman.

'What's that?' asks Catalina.

'You see,' says Mama. 'Not the brightest.'

The woman ignores her. 'It's someone who helps women with their house and their children.'

'Why do they need help?' asks Catalina.

The woman shrugs. 'Because they are rich and lazy. Can you cook?'

'A little.'

'Clean?'

'Of course.'

'Look after babies?'

Catalina smiles. 'I have four little sisters.'

'There you go then,' says the woman. 'You're perfect.'

A week later, Catalina is standing at the foot of the stairs, a small grey bag by her feet. The babies are crying but she's trying hard not to.

'Stop all this,' says Mama, but her voice is softer than usual, like the old Mama. 'Your sister is doing this for the family. For all of us.'

The woman with the yellow hair has arrived to take Catalina to her new home. She is wearing a different coat with shiny black buttons. Catalina will buy one just like it when she gets her first month's wages.

The woman hands Mama some money. 'An advance', she calls it.

'See,' says Mama to the children. 'We'll go straight to town and fill up the cupboards.'

'I bet there's enough for some sweets,' says Catalina, and the babies whoop, their tears forgotten.

'Come on now,' says the woman, and picks up Catalina's bag. 'We've a long way to go.'

Catalina kisses each soft head and hugs Mama.

'I'll write every week,' says Catalina.

Mama nods but turns away.

The prison walls close in and Catalina fights to catch her breath. She can't do it. She can't remember that world, so many lifetimes ago. Maybe it would just be better to stay here and rot.

'Brownies?' Sam's eyes and smile were wide. 'For breakfast?'

'If you'd prefer muesli . . .' said Lilly.

Sam laughed his answer and grabbed one in each fist. Lilly took one herself and picked up the phone. She wanted to leave Dr Kadir a message to call her as soon as she got in.

To Lilly's surprise, Dr Kadir answered on the first ring.

'Hi,' said Lilly. 'You're up with the larks.'

'I don't sleep well,' said Dr Kadir.

After a moment's uncomfortable silence, Dr Kadir coughed. 'Can I help you, Miss Valentine?'

'Oh, yes.' Lilly stumbled over her words. 'I went to see Anna yesterday – actually, she's called Catalina.'

'That's a very beautiful name.'

'Yes, it is,' said Lilly, realising how well it suited her client.

'How is she?'

'Okay – well, I think okay,' said Lilly. 'She didn't say much at all.'

'That's to be expected.'

'The thing is, I need her to tell me everything.'

Dr Kadir laughed. 'Catalina has protected her story for so long it's unlikely she will dismantle her defence mechanism overnight. It will take time.'

'I don't have time, Dr Kadir. The court gave me a week to sort this out.'

'I'm sure you've represented enough damaged children to know their problems can't be timetabled.'

Lilly did know. She'd acted for hundreds if not thousands of kids over the years. They kept their abuse locked tight in themselves, denying it air or freedom. When the time came to speak they were often too frightened. And Catalina was locked more tightly than any client Lilly had encountered.

'I understand exactly what you're saying,' Lilly sighed. 'But if I can't construct a defence for Catalina there's a good chance she could be convicted and spend the rest of her life in jail. I can't let that happen.'

Dr Kadir didn't answer but this time the silence was thoughtful. At last she spoke.

'You need to do this in a sideways manner. Don't dive in like a dog at an oasis. You'll just make the water brown.'

Lilly laughed. The description was apt.

'Don't ask about her,' Dr Kadir said. 'She'll clam up.'

'I don't have time for small talk.'

'I understand that, but if you approach this softly you may at least get some information you can use,' said Dr Kadir. 'If you go straight to the heart of the matter you'll leave with nothing.'

Lilly raked her fingers through her hair, avoiding the tender spot on her crown. 'What do you suggest?'

'Ask about Artan. 'She may tell you his story, which will give you a way into hers.'

Lilly waved Sam off and grabbed her bag. If she set off now she should arrive at High Point for the start of visiting. The more time she had, the slower she could take things.

Her mobile rang. She toyed with ignoring it but it could be news about Rupes.

'Hello,' she said, the phone balanced between chin and shoulder.

'Lilly.' It was David.

'I'm on my way to see a client,' she said. 'I'll call you later.'

'I'd rather speak now.'

Uh oh. He didn't sound happy.

'Okay,' she said, and let the engine idle.

He cleared his throat, alerting her that this was a pre-rehearsed speech. He'd done it throughout their marriage, whenever he was sure Lilly wasn't going to like what he had to say.

'Sam's welfare is always at the top of my priorities.'

'I know that,' she said.

The old Lilly would have felt compelled to point out that shagging a stylist half his age and decimating their family life was probably not the best thing he had ever done for his son. New Lilly had moved on.

David coughed again. 'I think he should come and stay with us while this case is ongoing.'

'With you and Cara?'

'And his sister.'

358

'Has he said that's what he wants?'

'He was very worried about the window and the car, and of course there's what everyone's saying at school now the whole mess is public knowledge.'

'Has he said he wants to stay with you?' Lilly asked, thinking of her son in their untidy kitchen with his fist full of brownies.

'Not in so many words.'

Lilly pulled on her seat belt; she hadn't got time for this. 'So not in any words, as a matter of fact?'

David's voice was cold. 'You can dismiss this if you want, but I have to consider what's best for Sam.'

'I do that every day of my life,' she replied, and snapped her phone shut.

It's hard to pick tomatoes with one hand but Luke is doing his best. He tries to pinch off the fruit with his thumb and forefinger, but without the other hand to keep the plant still it bends towards him like a sniffing dog.

He arrived at the Black Cat at the usual time and stuffed his bandaged hand in his pocket. The woman was already there, her hair pulled atop her head in a palm-tree effect, one of her drawn-on eyebrows slightly smudged.

She gestured for him to go to the van. Obviously no one had mentioned the accident in the fish factory. Or perhaps she simply didn't care.

He pushes his injured fist against the stem, but even that pressure is agony.

'You okay?' asks the Ukrainian.

Luke nods, but they both know it's a lie.

'You have medicine?'

Luke shrugs and the Ukrainian shakes his head.

Luke inspects the dressing, already grey from a night on the street, peppered with tomato seeds and splashes of juice. There is a brown stain covering the top of his hand. But brown is good, right? It means the blood is old, that the wound is closing over?

The owner enters the tunnel, his cardigan buttons straining. He checks the trays. 'Bit slow this morning.'

Luke keeps his hand hidden in the leaves of the plants. If the owner realises he can't work properly he'll be sent home for sure.

The owner eyes Luke. 'I ain't paying you to stand around.'

The Ukrainian and Luke exchange looks.

'My friend needs toilet,' says the Ukrainian. 'Bursting.'

The owner scowls at Luke. 'Go on then. Outside.'

Luke pulls his hand into the folds of his jacket and makes his way out.

'Be quick about it,' the owner shouts after him.

Luke waits at the entrance until the owner has moved on to the next tunnel. Today is going to be very long.

'Tell me about Artan.'

Catalina looked puzzled. No doubt she was expecting Lilly to demand her life story.

'What do you want to know?'

Lilly relaxed into her chair as if it hardly mattered. 'Where you met. How you became friends.' Lilly shrugged. 'Just a general picture.'

Catalina closed her eyes to think. Her eyelashes rested at the top of her cheeks like black feathers. Lilly thought she looked beautiful yet fragile – like an ornamental doll.

'I met him on the day I left home.'

Lilly wanted to shout out 'Why did you leave home?' and 'Where did you come from?', but she followed Dr Kadir's advice and reined herself in.

'What did you think of him?' she asked.

Catalina opened her eyes and gave a slow, sad smile. 'That he knew how to take care of himself.'

'Were you frightened?'

'Yes.'

'Of him?'

'Of everything.'

'Did he tell you about his background? Where he was from?' asked Lilly.

Catalina shook her head. 'Not then.'

'Later?'

'Yes. He told me about his village and his family.'

'That must have been very harrowing for him.'

Catalina looked away. 'Yes. He lost everyone.'

'Were you boyfriend and girlfriend?'

'No,' said Catalina. 'Just friends.'

'He must have been very glad to make a friend like you.'

'Maybe,' Catalina shrugged. 'Or maybe he asked himself why he got stuck with a silly girl who can't look after herself.'

'I doubt that,' said Lilly. 'I know if I were all alone in the world and I met someone as warm as you, I'd be bloody grateful.'

Catalina looked at Lilly as if they were strangers. As if she had no idea who her solicitor was. Or perhaps she was wondering if Lilly had any idea who she was. Lilly was certainly asking herself the same question.

'It is me that should be grateful,' she said.

'For what?'

Catalina again looked away. 'Many, many things.'

Lilly covered Catalina's hand with her own, but the girl pulled away and walked to the window. The sight of her raised a chorus of jeers from the visitors' centre. Someone threw a sweet, which clipped the reinforced glass with a tiny pop.

Lilly stood next to her client and touched her shoulder. It felt lost in the folds of her uniform.

'Tell me what he did,' said Lilly.

The door behind them opened.

A guard leaned her weight on one hip and chewed a mouthful of gum. 'Time's up.'

'You've got to be kidding,' said Lilly. 'We've only just got started.'

The guard blew a bubble and let it pop.

'I haven't even had an hour,' said Lilly.

The guard transferred her weight onto her other hip. 'Should have got here on time.'

'I did,' said Lilly. 'Or I would have, but I had to take a call.'

She'd kill David when she next got hold of him.

The guard shrugged and gestured for Catalina to leave.

Lilly had to think quickly. 'I'll come back first thing tomorrow, Catalina, and you need to tell me some more about Artan. Maybe you could write it down for me tonight?'

'I don't have paper,' said Catalina.

Lilly tore her legal pad in two and held out one half.

'You'll have to get that checked,' said the guard.

Lilly was about to point out that a woman had recently been caught smuggling six wraps of heroin and a flick knife into the prison. In comparison, a few sheets of lined A4 were hardly going to pose a safety threat. But she knew it was wasted energy.

'Fine,' she said, and headed back to reception.

'You need to get that sorted, soft lad.'

Caz is peering at Luke's hand. It has swollen to twice its size. Each finger is hard and smooth.

'That's fluid, that is,' says Caz, pressing his thumb with her own.

They've made up the lean-to early tonight and are huddled inside around a single candle. An angry wind rages outside, blowing newspapers and chip cartons along the street. Luke is exhausted from his day's work but he knows he'll never sleep.

Caz unhooks the safety pin and starts to unravel the bandage.

'It's the Return of the bleeding Mummy.'

After two layers, the gauze won't come away and Caz has to tug. With each round of bandage the tug becomes less gentle. At last his hand is free, apart from a square of surgical lint, now black and rancid. It's stuck fast.

'That's got to come off,' says Caz.

'It hurts,' says Luke.

'All the more reason for it to come off,' she argues.

Without warning, she rips it away. Luke feels the white heat shoot up his arm again and roars. 'Why didn't you tell me you were going to do that?'

Caz ignores him and inspects the damage.

Luke can't look. 'Is it bad?'

'Minging.'

He forces himself to take a peek. 'Jesus.'

The two welts where the blades went in are full of blood-tinged pus.

'It needs cleaning up,' says Caz.

Luke looks around the damp and dirty space they call home, littered with McDonald's boxes and burnt tinfoil.

'With what?' he asks.

'Teardrop Tony always has bleach,' she says.

Luke imagines their friend's mud- and shit-caked clothes, his hair that hasn't seen shampoo in years.

'What the hell does he do with bleach?' he asks.

Caz rolls her eyes. 'To clean his works, soft lad.'

She scrabbles to her feet, heads out into the night and leaves Luke to chase after her.

They find Teardrop Tony at Charing Cross station, nursing a bottle of Lambrini.

'Look at this for us,' says Caz, and thrusts Luke's hand under Tony's nose.

He nods as if this is exactly what he was expecting.

'Got any Domestos?' asks Caz.

Teardrop Tony wanders over to the disabled toilet. 'Step into my office.'

'I reckon we squeeze the gunk out of it, then put the bleach right into the cut,' says Caz.

Teardrop Tony nods.

Luke's heart lurches. His hand is killing him, but the alternative sounds infinitely worse.

'Won't that hurt?' he asks Tony, in the hope he might lie.

'Indeed it will.'

Caz searches through her pockets. 'Here,' she says, and holds out two fluff-covered pills. 'Get these in your gob.'

Luke washes them down with Lambrini. 'What are they?'

'Mogadon.'

'Will they numb the pain?'

Caz gives him a wink. 'No, but you won't remember anything about it after.'

Luke takes another long swig of the sweet, fizzy wine. It's a bit like the champagne his mum lets him drink on Christmas mornings.

They hold his hand over the sink and press.

Luke screams from the depths of his lungs.

'I knew a man in Iraq who had his ear blown off,' says Teardrop Tony. 'He screamed like that.'

Luke begins to feel woozy. Whether it's the sickening pain or the tranquillisers kicking in he doesn't know, but the world has gone blurry around the edges.

'You men are all the same,' says Caz. 'I cried less than this when I was having a baby.'

Luke's field of vision is covered in Vaseline, then he passes out.

*   *   *

Hours later he wakes up in the lean-to. Everything is moving slightly, floating. He wonders for a second if he's on a boat.

'All right, soft lad,' says Caz.

'Hello,' he manages. His voice sounds gooey, syrupy.

'Try to go back to sleep,' Caz smiles. 'Let the pills do their job.'

Luke sticks out his tongue. He wants to speak but it feels huge in his mouth.

'Baby?' he manages.

She holds his freshly wrapped hand against her cheek and kisses it. 'Sleep.'

Chapter Twenty-One

Lilly jumped off the scales. She felt round and flabby. Even her pyjama bottoms felt tight.

She knew she'd put on some weight but the truth was shocking.

She got back on slowly, easing herself toe by toe, leaning against the sink to distribute her mass. Same result.

She exhaled in disgust. She'd always had a womanly figure. Even as a kid her dad used to say you could use her arse as a tray. But half a stone in the space of a few weeks was going some.

She pulled on her dressing gown and looked in her wardrobe. A nice double-breasted jacket and a black polo neck should cover a multitude of sins.

The phone rang.

'How did you get on?' asked Dr Kadir.

Lilly checked her clock. Seven-thirty. Blimey, the woman hadn't lied when she said she couldn't sleep.

'Slowly,' said Lilly.

'Excellent.'

Lilly held the phone in the crook of her neck and

fished in a drawer for some tights. She found a pair with ladders and some red leg-warmers.

'You might think so, Doctor,' she said. 'But I need answers.'

'Patience, Lilly, time is your friend.'

Lilly sat on the bed and tried to pull on a pair of pop socks. Christ, she could hardly reach her feet.

'I'm going back to the prison this morning. I want to push her a little more.'

'Not too hard,' said Dr Kadir.

'I know,' said Lilly. 'I know.'

Lilly called into the hospital on the way to High Point, expecting nothing more than an update from the nurse on duty. Like every hospital Lilly had ever been in, this one had the heat ramped up to Sahara levels and she pulled at the neck of her jumper.

'You can see her,' said the matron. 'For a few minutes.'

Lilly crept into the room and nearly collapsed.

There were tubes in Rupinder's hands and nose, and she was still, so very still. But it was Raj who stopped Lilly's heart, half-asleep in the chair next to the bed, his head lolling to the side.

He began to rouse and Lilly cursed herself for intruding.

'Hi.' He scratched his beard, his voice a raw rasp.

'Hi,' said Lilly. 'How is she?'

Raj turned to his wife and ran a gentle finger across her wrist. 'They managed to stop the bleed on her brain but there's still a lot of swelling.'

Lilly chewed her lip. 'She'll be okay.'

He nodded but didn't reply.

Lilly hovered above Rupinder, horrified by the size of her head, which seemed bloated and tight. Her eyes began to flicker but were so swollen the lids couldn't lift.

'Lirry,' Rupinder whispered, without moving her horribly deformed mouth. 'Lirry? Rat you?'

Raj took his wife's hand. 'Yes, Lilly's here.'

Lilly looked at her friend, broken and in pain, and felt overcome with guilt. She need never have taken Anna's case, need never have put Rupinder in harm's way.

'I'm sorry,' she said, and ran out of the room.

Catalina sucks the end of her pen.

She has spent all night thinking about Artan.

In her desperate refusal to relive the past she realises she has lost him. Artan may be dead, but if she denies that other existence does that mean he is also forgotten?

On that first day, when she was numb with cold and terror, he had reached out to her. Given her everything he had.

'Here,' says the boy, holding out a dry hunk of bread. 'Take it.'

Catalina snatches it and rips some off with her teeth.

It's a lie, all of it. She knows that now. The job, the money, none of it is true. She didn't want to admit it and clung to the promise of a better life like a totem pole. An au pair. The words are ashes in her mouth.

She left Mama and the babies and went with the woman with her yellow hair, shiny buttons and tight smile. She said her name was Lavinia.

Catalina had got in a car that smelled of sour milk. Lavinia said she was taking her to her 'new family'. They had driven for hours and hours. At first Catalina had been excited, but soon she was lulled to sleep by the endlessness of the passing landscape.

'Wake up.' Lavinia had shaken her roughly.

Catalina had blinked. It was dark outside. 'Where are we?'

'Bucharest.'

Catalina had felt a thrill snake through her body. During the time of the communists, soldiers from Bucharest had been to their small town. Her granny had told her all about them.

'Naughty boys,' she'd laughed, her pink gums gleaming in the black of her mouth. 'Such naughty boys.'

Was she going to work here? In Bucharest? She knew there were rich people here.

She had scrambled out of the car after Lavinia, who, she'd noticed, walked with a limp. The house in front of them was old, grey and tired. Catalina was disappointed. She'd hoped she was going to live somewhere fancy.

She had followed Lavinia through a hallway as bare as their own at home. Male voices spilled from the kitchen.

'Answer only when spoken to,' said Lavinia. 'Got it?'

Catalina had nodded and clutched her little grey bag to her chest.

Three men sat around a table, smoking and playing cards. A bottle of vodka sat in the middle. They didn't look up from their game.

'I have a good one here for you, Costel,' said Lavinia.

The man at the far end lifted his head. One of his eyes was half shut, encircled with a half-moon scar.

'Come over here,' he said to Catalina.

She was frightened. Was this the man of the house? The boss? But where was the lady, the lazy woman who needed help?

'Come here,' he had repeated more gruffly.

Catalina shuffled forward.

'She's a pretty one,' said Lavinia, her voice nervous.

'Skinny, more like,' he said.

'She's a good girl,' said Lavinia. 'She won't give you any trouble.'

Costel snorted. 'That's what you always say.'

He took a mouthful of vodka from the bottle and went back to his cards.

Lavinia had bundled Catalina out of the kitchen and into the room next door. The walls were flaking and there was no furniture. The floor was strewn with blankets and old curtains. Lavinia had opened a packet of cigarettes and lit one. Her hands were shaking.

'What's wrong, Lavinia?' Catalina asked.

'Nothing.' Lavinia exhaled a blue plume of smoke. 'Costel is a difficult man to do business with, that's all.'

'He scares me,' said Catalina.

Lavinia picked a loose piece of tobacco from her tongue.

'I want to go home,' said Catalina.

Lavinia sucked on the cigarette, her cheeks collapsing on each side of her face.

'Don't make a fuss,' she said. 'It will be the worse for you if you do.'

Catalina blinked away tears. 'I don't want to stay here.'

Lavinia took a last drag, ground out the dog-end on the floorboards and left Catalina in the room. From the other side of the door she heard the lock banging shut.

Catalina had stared at the empty room. What was she doing here? Why didn't they take her to her new family?

A snuffling sound came from the corner and one of the blankets moved. Mice. Then another blanket moved, then a curtain.

Catalina screwed up her eyes. It was dark in the room but she could definitely see movement. Sudenly she realised she wasn't alone. She gulped back her panic and peered into the shadows. Fingers, toes and eyes peeped out from the makeshift bedding on the floor and Anna felt fear sweep through her. The room was full of children.

From his hiding place under an itchy brown rug came a boy, about her age, with a thin, torn shirt and a scab on his lip. He held out some bread.

Catalina lies on the floor with the others and asks him his name.

'Emil,' he whispers.

'Why are we here, Emil?' she asks. 'They said I was going to work in a house for a rich lady. Why am I here?'

Emil puts his finger to his lips and she lets the tears come.

'Don't cry,' says Emil. 'Costel gets very angry if we cry.'

Catalina stuffs the back of her hand in her mouth and chokes back her sadness.

*   *   *

The letters scrawl under the lines and ink is smudged across the page. Her English is terrible, the words spilling onto the page in the wrong order.

Her pen flashes across the paper.

She is telling Artan's story. What he did for her.

Her fingers ache and a lump is growing on the side of her forefinger, but she can't stop. This is for Artan.

Alexia checked her inbox and her voicemail but both were empty. It wasn't that she thought she'd be inundated with offers, but after the piece in the *Mail* she had anticipated some interest.

She looked around her flat. It was a new build that the developer hadn't been able to sell. Even with a brand new MFI kitchen and a residents-only car-parking permit it had lain empty for so long that Alexia got a six-month contract at a knockdown price.

Still, without any money coming in she couldn't afford even that rent. Steve hadn't paid her much but it was regular.

Then there was the credit card bill.

She thought of the penthouse in Chelsea Harbour that her father had let her use, with underground parking and a private roof terrace. It would be so easy to pick up the phone. One word from him and she could have any job she wanted.

Her hand hovered over the buttons.

She could have a maid, a concierge. Anything she wanted. Free.

She put the phone down. As her father never tired of saying, nothing in life was free. If Alexia took her father's handouts there was always a price to pay and a heavy one at that. For a life of luxury she had to submit to his control. Her mother had realised this when Alexia was five years old and had run off with the assistant manager of a DIY store. They lived in Crawley in a tatty semi and her mother trained as a beautician. Alexia remembered she had lovely nails and a dog called Oliver.

She sighed and headed out to the Turk's Head. As a freelancer she would need another story to sell.

'Did you manage to write anything down?' Lilly hoped to God she had.

'I didn't get the paper,' said Catalina.

Lilly wanted to scream. She had two more days before the court expected a full report.

'Couldn't you have asked for some?'

Catalina shrugged. 'I didn't think about that.'

Lilly closed her eyes and counted to ten.

'I need you to understand how important this is.' She took Catalina's hand. 'If I can't get the information I need, I can't help you.'

'I do understand.'

The door behind them opened. It was the same guard as yesterday, her cheek full of gum.

'Time's up.'

Lilly groaned.

'You were late,' said the guard. 'Again.'

'My friend is in hospital,' said Lilly.

The guard pulled her gum into a thin strand that dangled between her teeth and fingers like a pink washing line.

'Forget it,' said Lilly.

When she got to reception she was greeted by the guard with the lazy eye. After the débâcle of their last meeting, Lilly's new tactic was not to look at the other woman at all. She put down a pad of paper and mumbled into her chest: 'Could you make sure my client gets this?'

'Another lot?' said the guard. 'Is she writing *War and Peace*?'

'She didn't get it yesterday,' said Lilly into her chest.

'I took it to D Wing myself.'

Lilly shook her head. God, it was difficult making your point without eye contact.

'I can assure you she didn't get it.'

'And I can assure you she did,' said the guard.

Lilly was about to lose her temper when her mobile rang. She turned her back on the guard.

'Bloody rude cow.'

Today was going badly, very badly. If this was David, calling to threaten her again, he was going to get very short shrift.

She stabbed the answer button with her thumb. 'What?'

'Miss Valentine?'

It was a man's voice. Not David's, but familiar.

'Who is this?' Lilly barked.

'Edward Roberts,' he said.

Lilly's heart sank. She had just snarled at the bloody judge.

'Hi,' she said. 'Can I help you?'

'I am looking at my lists,' his voice was icy. 'And I find I am over-committed on Friday.'

Yes. Lilly punched the air. He was going to adjourn the hearing until next week, and that would give her another couple of days to prepare.

'These things happen,' she said.

'Indeed they do,' he replied. 'Which is why I will require the parties to attend on Thursday.'

'Have you got a moment?'

Alexia's tone sounded breezier than she felt. She slipped onto the stool next to Blood River. He didn't look up from his book. She watched his even breathing, his nostrils flaring as he inhaled.

She had always suspected the man was off-key, and now she knew the truth. He was a wild animal, out of control, and sitting so close to him filled her with fear.

At last he folded the corner of his page. 'I saw your piece in the *Mail*.'

'What did you think?'

His eyes were diamond hard. 'Why did you leave the *Three Counties Observer*?'

Alexia shrugged and took a nervous sip of her tonic water.

'It was a big story,' she said. 'It needed national coverage.'

He shook his head. 'Loyalty is everything, Miss Dee.'

'Information is everything,' she answered.

The corner of his eye twitched. Blood River did not like being challenged.

'It's better for all of us if we reach a larger audience,' she said. 'My boss at the *Observer* understood that fully.'

Blood River acknowledged the ground she had given with a nod.

'What do you want?' he asked.

'I want to keep up the momentum,' she said. 'I wondered if you have anything else planned.'

She didn't really care who else he intended to give a beating to, but thought she'd better show interest.

'I have many things in the pipeline,' he said grandly. 'But I can't share them with you.'

'Of course not,' she said.

'Especially not now you're just another government arse-licking Trotsky hack.'

They sat in silence until Alexia wondered if she should just leave.

'What do you have planned, Miss Dee?' he asked. 'Any projects you'd like to develop?'

Alexia smiled. Blood River didn't smile back.

'Actually, I have,' she said. 'I'd like to interview the solicitor. Get her reaction to everything that's happened.'

'Do we want to give the enemy a platform?'

Alexia wanted to tell him that she didn't see Lilly Valentine as the opposition, that she hadn't taken a side, but she knew Blood River's world view was strictly black and white. If Alexia wasn't with him she was definitely against him, and she had seen how he dealt with people like that.

'I think she'll expose herself for what she is,' said Alexia.

Blood River nodded. 'So why don't you knock on her door and ask her some questions?'

'I don't think she'd open it to me.' Alexia laughed.

'Nor me, Miss Dee.'

'I'm pretty certain she'd refuse to speak to the pair of us.' Alexia leaned towards him. This was why she had come. 'But I think you may know someone who can help.'

Lilly nearly wrenched the fridge door off its hinges and grabbed pancetta, eggs and cream. Only spaghetti carbonara could soften a day like today.

Thirty-six hours was all she had to prepare. Thirty-six hours to visit her client, get the story straight and cobble together a submission to the court. It was impossible. Utterly impossible. Even if she could get to High Point before visiting began, there wouldn't be enough time to go through everything. She could only hope Catalina was making detailed notes. She had impressed upon her client how imperative this was, and the girl had seemed to understand.

Lilly reached for the parmesan and a grater.

'Hello, Lilly.'

It was David – he had let himself in with his old key.

She looked down at the pile of shredded cheese. This had always been his favourite dish.

'Are you psychic about this stuff?'

He didn't laugh. Lilly could see his face was grey.

'You didn't come for your tea?'

He shook his head. 'You know why I'm here.'

Lilly sighed. In the panic of the new hearing date she'd forgotten all about David and his threat to take Sam to stay with him.

'This is ridiculous,' she said. 'You are ridiculous.'

David raised himself up to full height. 'I am doing what's best for Sam.'

'Get out of my house,' she said.

'I will not leave without our son.'

Lilly let out a snort of laughter and pulled David's hand behind his back.

'Ow,' he yelled. 'That hurts.'

Lilly applied more pressure until his fingers grazed his shoulder blade. 'Oh, just shut up,' she said, and led him to the door. 'You're a total idiot,' she said, and pushed him outside.

He stood on the porch and rubbed his wrist.

'I won't let this go, Lilly. I will be back.'

'Not without a court order,' she said, and slammed the door in his face.

As soon as day breaks Catalina and the other children get up. They have slept in their clothes and only have their shoes and boots to pull on.

It might be hours before Costel unlocks the door, but they know to be ready the second he arrives.

They take it in turns to pee in a bucket. On the first morning Catalina was embarrassed, but when her bladder began to ache and a trickle of urine stung her leg she had no choice.

Four days later she doesn't care.

'I hope he picks me today,' says Nicolae, one of the little ones whose front teeth are just starting to show.

'And me,' says another.

Catalina and Emil exchange glances.

Each morning Costel opens the door and takes three or four of the children away. They don't come back.

The little ones wonder aloud about their fate.

379

'Do you think he takes them home?'

'Maybe another family takes them in.'

Catalina and Emil say nothing.

At the sound of the bolt sliding in the lock, Catalina's heart starts beating hard in her chest. What would be worse? To stay here, hungry and cold, or to go with Costel?

The door opens and Catalina can smell him before she sees him. Sweat and vinegar and cigarettes.

'You and you.'

He points at Emil and Nicolae.

'And you.'

His tobacco-stained finger wags at Catalina.

They follow Costel out of the house and through the city streets. Catalina has never seen so many people, so much traffic. Everyone and everything is moving.

Suddenly an idea strikes her. What's to stop her running away? She could run and run until she finds someone to help her. Her eyes dart down the side alleys, taking in possible dead ends.

'If he catches you he'll kill you,' says Emil, as if he can read her every thought.

Catalina looks at Costel, with the scar around his sleepy eye, and knows Emil is right.

They move north until they reach the Gara de Nord and Costel stops beside a kiosk at the entrance selling newspapers, cigarettes and chewing gum.

'Who's here?' Costel asks the owner, and slams down some coins.

The man hands Costel a packet of cigarettes. 'Gabi and Stelian.'

Costel grunts and leads the children to the side of the station. 'Don't move.'

Two men and two women are already there. Costel greets the men, and the women shiver in the snow. One has a purple bruise on her cheek. Both have dead eyes. By their short skirts and see-through shirts Catalina knows what they are.

Costel opens the packet of cigarettes and offers them to the men. They each take one and light up. They huddle together and laugh.

Out of the station come some kids. Despite the cold they are in T-shirts; some have no shoes. Most hold a plastic bag to their mouth.

They point and laugh, nudging each other.

'Fuck off, if you know what's good for you,' says Costel, and they move away, but not out of sight.

'So what do you say, Gabi, are you buying?' asks Costel.

The man he is speaking to, Gabi, nods, his face almost hidden in a cloud of smoke and hot breath.

'I'll take those two,' he gestures to the women 'for Moscow.'

The third man rubs his hands together, obviously pleased with his deal.

'And I'll give you two hundred for the boys,' says Gabi. 'My brother is setting up a dipping gang in England.'

Costel spits into the slush. 'That's an insult and you know it.'

Gabi shrugs. 'Why would I pay more when I can get them for free under the station?'

'It would take you two weeks to get them off the glue, and most of them are mad.'

'Okay, okay,' says Gabi. 'I'll give you three.'

'What about my girl?' asks Costel.

'She's too young,' says Gabi.

Costel laughs. 'I thought your punters liked them fresh?'

'She looks like a skinned rat,' says Gabi.

Costel laughs but he gives Catalina a murderous look. She's terrified. She doesn't want to go back to the house without Emil.

'Take her with us.'

Catalina realises it is Emil who's spoken.

The men look at him with incredulity. Costel raises his hand to slap him.

'Hey,' Gabi shouts. 'Not yours to damage any more.'

'Take her with us, mister,' Emil repeats. 'We're a great team. The best.'

'You've done dipping before?' asks Gabi.

'Practically every day,' says Emil.

Gabi turns to Catalina and she nods furiously, though she has no idea what dipping is.

'It's a good pitch,' laughs the third man.

'And when her titties grow you can sell her on,' says Costel.

Gabi puts up his hands up in mock-surrender. 'Three-fifty for all three, and that's my final offer.'

Catalina puts down her pen and rubs her wrist. That was the first time Artan saved her. But not the last.

Chapter Twenty-Two

'Did I hear Dad last night?'

Sam was pushing his cornflakes around the bowl.

'Uh huh.' Lilly tried to sound distracted.

'Why didn't he come up and speak to me?'

Lilly took a deep breath. Sam loved both his parents
unconditionally, and whatever crap she and David had
been through, Lilly had always avoided saying negative
things about him to his son.

'We thought you were asleep, big man.'

Sam pushed away his breakfast. 'I heard shouting.'

'Must have been the TV,' she said.

He narrowed his eyes. 'Are you sure?'

'Sure I'm sure.' She ruffled his hair. 'Now brush your
teeth.'

To signal the conversation was over, Lilly turned her
back to Sam and poured the soggy cereal down the waste
disposal. The orange sludge made her gag.

'You look terrible.'

Penny had waltzed into the kitchen to collect Sam for
school.

'Thanks,' said Lilly.

Penny put a hand to Lilly's forehead. 'Are you ill?'

'Just under a lot of pressure.'

'What's happened now?'

'Rupinder is in a terrible state.'

'And?'

'And my ex-husband is being a total shit.'

'And?'

'And the judge has brought the hearing forward and I still haven't got anything out of Catalina.'

'And?'

'And,' Lilly's eyes filled with tears. 'I don't have time for this self-pity right now.'

Penny rubbed her back soothingly. 'You need to give this case to someone else.'

Lilly pushed the heels of her hands into her eyes and inhaled through her nose. 'What I need,' she grabbed her car keys, 'is to get to High Point.'

Luke's head is swimming. The shrimps go in and out of focus as if he's messing about with a camera lens.

He'd managed another day's tomato picking with the help of half a tranq every two hours. He'd bought a handful from Sonic Dave, and by the time they'd bundled him into the back of the van he could barely keep his eyes open.

The men had glanced at him and muttered under their breath.

At last the Ukrainian had spoken. 'We know you are not well.'

'I'm okay,' Luke had slurred.

The Ukrainian had looked embarrassed. 'But we cannot cover for you tomorrow.'

'I don't know what you mean.'

The Ukrainian had shrugged, unwilling to expand. He didn't need to. Luke knew he hadn't been working fast enough, that the others had taken the slack.

It's his hand. It's still excruciating. Without the Mogadon he's barely able to stop himself crying out with every movement, but with it he's incapable of doing anything. It's like his head has been folded in a blanket and everything is soft and warm.

This morning when they arrived at the fish factory the Ukrainian patted him on the back. 'Today you will be fine, yes?'

Luke smiled and nodded because that was all he could do. His mashed-potato brain could not command his mouth to speak.

The foreman looked shocked to see him again.

'Hand all better, is it?'

'All better,' Luke mumbled, and took his position on the assembly line.

The foreman pursed his brow and pulled back his thin lips. 'You'd better go on quality control,' he said, and nodded to the end of the line.

'This is much better job,' said the Ukrainian. 'You watch shrimp, spot one with shell and take off.' He pushed Luke into a chair. 'Easy.'

And it should be easy. Hundreds and thousands of shell-fish trundle past him and ninety-nine per cent are pink and naked. The odd one that has missed its unveiling is obvious. The trouble is, Luke's mind keeps shutting down.

He sees himself as if he has stepped out of his body. He's sat on a chair and it's one of those swivelly ones. In front of him are lots of shrimp. Lots and lots of shrimps. Is it shrimp or shrimps?

'What the hell . . .'

The foreman appears in front of Luke, his arms waving like the bare branches of the trees outside.

Luke lifts up his hand. 'All better.'

The foreman hits the emergency button and the conveyor belt grinds to a halt. He reaches into a pile of shrimp.

'This one still has its shell.' He holds the offending fish between his thumb and forefinger. 'And that one.' He nods to another. 'And over there.'

Luke knows he should say something but he can't engage his brain.

'Is there a problem?' asks the foreman.

Luke tries to shake his head but the movement knocks him off-balance and he falls off his chair.

The foreman calls over to the Ukrainian. 'What's wrong with your friend?'

The Ukrainian looks away. 'He not my friend.'

Catalina thought Bucharest was busy, but London is ten, twenty, a hundred times worse. The noise is like a wall and it never stops. At night it dies down a little, but it never truly stops.

And the smell. The smell is disgusting. The people eat all day, even when they're walking down the road. Fried potatoes, meat and chicken. The air is thick with dirty cooking fat and smoke from the cars.

'I feel sick,' says Nicolae.

Catalina ignores him. They all feel sick. They have done since the horrific journey from Romania. Ten of them hidden in the back of a truck. No air, no light. Swaying from side to side for days, maybe weeks.

'I'm hungry,' Nicolae wails.

Emil checks what they've made. On days when the work's been good he might take a note from one of the wallets and buy them all some food. Gabi and his brother Daniel would beat them if they found out, but sometimes the hunger makes them take the risk.

'We don't have enough,' says Emil, and Nicolae begins to cry.

Honestly, that boy is becoming a pain.

'Let's do another one, then,' says Catalina.

They head down into Leicester Square underground station and watch. At this time in the morning the place is packed with workers and shoppers pounding through the ticket machines. Emil nods at a woman by the map. She's wearing an off-white coat, the colour of sleet, and a thick brown scarf that looks so soft Catalina is tempted to run her cheek against it. The woman is checking her journey, running her finger along the red streak of the Central line.

The ones who don't know where they're going are always the best. The easiest to distract.

Nicolae approaches.

'Help, please,' he says, his arm outstretched. 'I lost.'

He hasn't asked for money but with any luck she'll subconsciously touch the pocket or bag where she keeps her purse.

'Where's your mummy?' she asks, a gloved hand hovering over a patent black shopper.

Nicolae's eyes become glassy with tears. 'Help, please.'

Emil closes in on the bag, while Catalina blocks the view of any nosy passers-by and keeps a lookout for the police.

'Are you here on your own?' asks the woman. 'Is there an adult with you?'

Emil nods that the job is done and walks towards the exit. Catalina follows suit.

'Mummy,' says Nicolae, and points to the exit.

The woman looks over and nods. She can't see anyone but she's just glad to be rid of this dirty, cold little boy. That's London for you.

'It's full,' says Emil, holding open the red wallet full of crisp twenty-pound notes.

Catalina looks up and down Charing Cross Road. There's no sign of Daniel or Gabi. 'Let's get some food.'

Calm, calm, calm.

Lilly breathed in through her nose, out through her mouth.

As soon as her client arrived empty-handed, Lilly could feel the panic swell in her chest.

Calm, calm, calm.

'Did you get the paper?' Lilly asked. 'I handed in more and had a bit of a spat with the guards about it.'

'I got the paper.'

So where the hell was it?

'Did you do what I asked?' Lilly smiled at Catalina

and tried to control her increasing fear. 'Did you write down everything you could remember about Artan?'

Catalina rubbed her finger.

'Tell me you did,' said Lilly.

A silence stretched between them, as dark and cold as an ocean.

'I'm sorry,' said Catalina.

Lilly shook her head as if to discard what her client had said.

'I can't go to court tomorrow with nothing.' Lilly's heart was pounding. 'I just can't.'

Catalina's eyes filled with regret. Lilly had never seen anything more pitiable.

'I'm sorry,' Catalina repeated.

When Lilly got back to the car park she locked herself in the Mini, turned the heat up and let the tears come. Her shoulders heaved as the sobs wracked her body. She cried for Rupinder; she cried for Charlie Stanton; and she cried for Artan Shala. But most of all she cried for Catalina. Poor Catalina was locked in her own private hell and Lilly had failed to find the key. The kid would end up serving years for a crime she hadn't committed.

Her misery was interrupted by her mobile.

'How are you?' said Jack.

Lilly's voice cracked. 'Terrible.'

'What's the matter, Lilly?'

'I miss you, Jack,' Lilly wailed. 'I miss you.'

* * *

He smoothed her hair off her face and wiped her snotty nose. Trust Jack to be the sort of man who would drive twenty miles to meet Lilly in a prison car park.

'Thanks for coming,' she snivelled.

'Sure, I was bored with Keira Knightley. Yap, yap, yap.'

Lilly sniffed.

'And her cooking,' he said. 'Don't get me started on her cooking.'

Lilly smiled in spite of herself.

'That's better,' he said. 'So why don't you tell me what this is about?'

'I have to go to court tomorrow and tell the judge I have no idea how or why Catalina came to be in this country or why she was calling herself Anna Duraku.'

Jack shrugged. 'Not your fault.'

'I know, but it won't make the fact that she has to stay in jail any easier.'

'Like I said – not your fault.'

Lilly threw back her head and laughed. Her lips were so dry they cracked.

'You make it sound so easy.'

He kissed her gently.

'It *is* easy. You say you tried your best, but your client isn't playing ball.'

He was right. She knew he was right. And yet.

'Perhaps I can ask for another week.'

Jack shook his head. 'Now that I'd like to see.'

Chapter Twenty-Three

Alexia couldn't believe it. Every newspaper, radio station and TV channel was running with the story.

It was a disaster.

200 DEAD AND FEARS FOR 100 MORE
Screeched the *Independent*.

LOCKERBIE 2
Roared the *Mirror*.

Despite the upping of airport security around the UK the day everyone predicted had finally arrived – a British Airways 747 bound for Washington DC had exploded over the Atlantic.

Early reports suggested a terrorist cell working as baggage handlers at Heathrow had hidden a bomb inside the kennel of a pet stored in the hold.

It was indeed a disaster. Alexia had no money to get out to the States to cover it and the Stanton story, *her* story was of no interest to anyone.

She balled up the front page and threw it across the room. She would have put her head in her hands but they were inky, the fingertips smudged and black.

She sighed and went over to the sink. As the cold water ran onto her palms her temper began to cool. This was a setback, nothing more. Yes, the terrorist attack was ferociously exciting and the public would gobble up as much information as they could but as soon as the police and the authorities launched their ubiquitous enquiries the public would be angry. They would need to vent that anger. And who better than an illegal immigrant who had killed a schoolboy?

Alexia needed that interview with Valentine.

She had swallowed her pride and her better judgement and asked Blood River to help her. All she wanted was a number.

'I can't divulge the personal details of any of our members,' he'd said.

Alexia had wheedled and flirted, she'd practically begged, but Blood River was immovable.

'I'll pass on yours,' he said, and went back to his novel, their conversation clearly at an end.

She toyed with going to see Blood River again, but didn't want to appear desperate and, frankly, he frightened her.

The letterbox rattled and she sighed. More bills. Her credit card bill was overdue and she didn't even have enough for the minimum payment. And the rent; she didn't even want to think about the rent.

She plucked the pile of buff envelopes from the doormat and tossed them onto the kitchen surface. She wished she were the sort of person who could ignore them, hide them in a drawer like a dirty secret, but she was too much her father's daughter.

She decided on a hot drink before the torture began and snapped on the kettle. To her disgust she was down to her last teaspoon of coffee, and not even a heaped one at that. What sort of life was it when she couldn't even stretch to a mug of Kenco?

Alexia supposed some people, probably lots of them, lived like this all the time, but she'd had everything she'd ever needed without ever needing to ask. A pony; a princess party; a walk-in wardrobe of designer clothes. She tried not to think about the approach of Christmas, the parties she would miss, the trips to Courchevel.

She sipped her weak coffee and reached out for the bills. Credit card, telephone, electricity.

Her hand wavered over the last envelope. It was brown like the rest, but it was handwritten.

Dear Miss Dee,

A mutual colleague has informed me that you wish to discuss the solicitor Lilly Valentine.

I am not sure that I can be of any assistance but I am agreeable to meet on the assurance that it is in the strictest confidence.

You may not reveal my identity, nor may you quote me in the press.

On the assumption that this is acceptable, I shall be in Dunstable library at 3 p.m. sharp.

Snow White

Alexia pushed away her mug and smiled. The game was on.

Lilly had awoken with a feeling of trepidation that rippled through her entire body. She'd had cramp in her hands and feet, and her legs felt feeble, as if they weren't strong enough to hold up her torso – which might very well have been the case, considering how huge she felt.

Jack had advised her repeatedly that there was nothing she could do about this morning's hearing. Catalina's refusal to give instruction was not Lilly's fault. It was, of course, true in the strictest sense, but Lilly hated to feel powerless. Loathed it.

'Sometimes, woman, you have to accept that you cannot control everything,' Jack had said, his hands on her shoulders.

Lilly wished he were here now, but he couldn't even stay the night. If he was caught with Lilly again he would lose his job.

'I can't believe we still go to court,' said Milo, pointing at the hazy photograph of the fatal aeroplane.

Lilly looked up at him. She had almost forgotten he was there. He'd arrived at her house as promised. As reliable as ever.

'The world keeps turning,' she said.

He cocked his head to one side, his hair falling over one ear. 'Not for those poor people.'

She looked at the list of names of those who died but felt totally disconnected.

'I have absolutely nothing to tell the judge,' she said.

'You will think of something.'

Lilly shook her head. 'I wish I had your faith.'

They get up, they steal, they sleep.

Up, steal, sleep.

Weeks have gone by like this.

Catalina has no idea how many, she has lost all track of time.

At night, when they are huddled under an old coat, she wonders if they will live like this forever.

'Will they let us go when we are grown up?' she whispers to Emil.

He shrugs.

'When you are a man, they will have to set you free,' she says. 'When I am a woman . . .'

'Listen,' Emil looks deeply into her eyes. 'There are worse things than this.'

'Like what?'

He turns over and burrows into the itchy grey wool. 'Go to sleep.'

Catalina pushes her hair out of her eyes. Her scalp itches and she rakes it with her nails. She is cold, hungry, and she is sure she has nits. What could possibly be worse than this?

In the morning, Daniel throws open the curtains and the room floods with light. 'Get up,' he says, and gives Catalina a nudge with his foot.

She and Emil drag themselves to the sink and splash water over their faces. Nicolae is whining. Honestly, that boy never learns.

'I can't,' he says. 'My head is hurting.'

Daniel throws off the threadbare towel that Nicolae uses as a blanket and pulls the little boy to his feet.

'Don't ever answer back,' says Daniel.

Nicolae begins to cry. In fairness, he does look sick. His face is covered in pink blotches and his hair is dark with sweat.

Daniel looks at him as if he were a rat.

'Come here,' Emil pulls Nicolae to the sink 'A wash will make you feel better.'

Daniel grunts and walks away, leaving Emil to wipe a cloth over the back of the younger boy's neck. Nicolae sways on his feet. Catalina can feel the heat radiating from him.

In the back of the car, Catalina tries to read the road signs. Deptford, Greenwich, Rotherhithe. Somewhere in London, she doesn't know exactly. Nicolae is slumped next to her, his breathing ragged, his shoulders heaving. She glances at Emil. They know better than to tell Daniel or Gabi.

They are dumped in the centre, near Tottenham Court Road underground station. This is a good place for dipping, along with Leicester Square and Oxford Street. The children rotate so there is less chance of getting caught.

Nicolae leans heavily against Catalina. She shrugs him off. 'Stand up, will you.' Emil shakes his head at her and puts his arm around Nicolae. They can both see how ill he is, but Catalina can't be like Emil. Pity and compassion have been sucked from her, leaving only fear and self-preservation.

'Let's get on with this.' She heads down into the station.

They choose their mark instantly. A man in his late

396

sixties, his bald head crusted with warts and freckles, his veined hands leaning on a stick.

'I don't think I can do this,' Nicolae sniffs.

'Get on with it,' says Catalina, and gives him a shove. 'Then we can all have a hot drink,' she adds, not wanting to seem like a total bitch.

Nicolae wipes a hand across his face and staggers towards the old man. 'Help please.' He holds out his hand.

The man turns a kind eye to the boy. 'What's that, my son?'

'Help please.'

Catalina and Emil close in, but Nicolae begins to sway violently, his head rolling back.

'Are you all right?' asks the old man, a hand on Nicolae's back.

Before he can answer, the little boy has collapsed at the old man's feet. 'Hey,' the old man waves his stick in the air. 'We need help over here.'

Soon a crowd has formed around them and a guard pushes his way through. 'Get an ambulance,' says the old man. 'This child needs a doctor.'

Catalina's eyes are wide. She can hear her blood pounding in her ears.

'Come on,' says Emil, and takes her hand. 'We need to leave.'

Lilly left Milo on a bench outside the courtroom and headed up to the café where she blagged some hot water and waited for Jez.

She sipped her Ginger Zinger. It was the last one that

Dr Kadir had given to her and she would need to hunt down a box of her own after the hearing.

At last he arrived, stopping at the counter to grab breakfast and flirt with the lady at the counter.

He took the seat opposite Lilly and peered into her cup.

'What's that?' Jez wrinkled his nose.

'Don't ask.'

Jez picked at the edge of his blueberry muffin. 'What's your client saying?'

'Don't ask.'

He smiled and rubbed dry crumbs through his fingers. 'Someone's star has lost its twinkle.'

'I'm afraid that, like the music, mine died a long time ago.'

'It's terrible, isn't it?' he said.

'Yes,' she said. 'My case is terrible.'

'I meant the plane crash.'

Guilt flooded through Lilly. 'Of course.'

'Is your client here yet?'

Lilly shrugged. 'Don't know.'

'You can't take this personally,' he said. 'You win some, you lose some.'

Lilly finished her tea and pushed back her chair.

'But I'm not the one who's going to spend the rest of her life in jail.'

She went to fetch Milo, his usual patient smile intact, and together they descended the stairs to the cell area. The huge door swung open like the entrance to a cave and the corridor lay ahead, grey and bare. By now even Milo had lost his smile.

Catalina was in cell three. She jumped up from the bench. 'Hello.'

Milo greeted her with a hug and whispered words of encouragement in her ear.

Lilly stood back, her arms folded.

'When we go up to court, I'm going to be asked who you are,' said Lilly.

'You know who I am,' said Catalina.

Lilly leaned against the cold stone of the wall. Her whole body felt leaden.

'Your name is not enough,' she said. 'They want to know where you're from, why you came here.'

Milo opened his arms. 'This is not a simple task.'

'I know that,' said Lilly. 'Which is why I asked Catalina to write it all down for me.'

Catalina sank back onto the bench.

'Why didn't you do that for me?' asked Lilly.

Catalina rubbed her finger. 'I try.'

The guard thumped the door. It was time.

'Not hard enough,' said Lilly, and turned away.

'This is what happens,' says Jean.

Luke shakes his head. It's full of cobwebs.

'We came for a clean bandage,' says Caz. 'Not a bleedin' lecture.'

Jean nods and reaches into a cupboard for a blue Tupperware box full of plasters and tubes of Savlon. The smell of disinfectant intrudes into Luke's mind.

'I'm just pointing out that this life pulls everyone down eventually.'

Caz sneers at Jean and slopes off to the bathroom.

Luke can feel his hand as Jean wipes it clean. It grumbles at him. The pills must be wearing off.

'There's a rule of thumb,' says Jean. 'If we can help kids like you within six weeks we can really do some good.'

'What happens after that?' asks Luke.

Jean pours TCP onto a ball of cotton wool. 'Drink, drugs, glue.'

'Is that all?' Luke laughs.

'Violence, abuse, prison.'

Though she doesn't know it, Jean has hit home. The fear of prison has been what brought him here in the first place.

She dabs the ball onto the wounds and Luke can definitely feel the sting. He wonders if Caz has any of the ketamine left that she swapped for an iPod this morning.

Jean lifts up his hand and inspects it closely. 'How on earth did you do this?'

Luke can see no reason to lie. 'I was working in a factory.'

She wraps his hand back up. The new bandage feels clean and firm. His wound should now at least stand a chance of healing.

'I hope it was worth it,' she says.

And for the first time Luke realises that he hasn't been paid a penny.

'All rise.'

Lilly's rubber knees almost gave way as Judge Roberts entered court. When he gestured for everyone to sit, Lilly gladly fell back onto the bench.

'I'm sorry we have had to come to court on such a tragic day,' said the judge. 'But the bench have taken the view that we will not be cowed by these criminals. The wheels of democracy and justice must prevail.'

'Indeed they must,' said Jez.

Lilly nodded feebly.

'We all know why we're here today,' said the judge. 'So I suggest Miss Valentine addresses us.'

Lilly sighed and heaved herself to her feet.

'I'm afraid, Your Honour, that taking instructions has been difficult.'

'I myself ordered High Point to ensure you had access to the defendant,' he said.

Lilly nodded slowly. 'Access was not the problem, Your Honour.'

The judge looked over his glasses and waited.

Lilly gulped back her distaste. Betraying a child was anathema to her.

'My client has not been forthcoming.'

'Please expand,' said the judge.

'She has been unable to answer my questions,' said Lilly.

'Because she doesn't understand them?'

Lilly shook her head. 'Because they are too painful.'

'Is she from Kosovo?'

'I don't know.'

'Is she a refugee?'

'I don't know.'

'How did she come to use the name Anna Duraku?'

Lilly sighed. 'Your Honour, I don't know.'

The judge removed his glasses and leaned forward.

'Do you know anything at all, Miss Valentine?'

'My client's real name is Catalina Petrescu.'

'And she would tell you nothing further?' asked the judge.

'No.'

The judge looked directly at Catalina. 'This is most unhelpful.'

'I am sorry,' she said.

Jez rose to his feet. 'Your Honour, I'm wondering if my friend feels that she must withdraw from the case.'

'I'll give you ten minutes to think about it,' he said, and waltzed out of court.

'What are you talking about?' Lilly hissed.

Jez led Lilly into the corner. 'It makes perfect sense, Lilly. You've been out of your depth from the start.'

'So you've said.'

Jez waved away her anger. 'This way you get to bow out gracefully and no one can criticise.'

Lilly glanced over at Catalina, engulfed in her prison dungarees.

'You can't help her,' said Jez, and Lilly knew it was true.

Alexia hated libraries. It wasn't the books that bothered her, it was the people. 'The great unwashed' her father called them, and he avoided places where there was any danger of interacting with the public. Strange then, that he had made so many millions publishing the rubbish they wanted to read. Of the hundreds of magazines and newspapers he published around the world not one of them had anything of importance to say.

She fingered a copy of the latest Booker Prize winner. 'A quiet, beautiful novel,' announced the blurb, 'about the everyday life of a zoologist.'

Alexia yawned. Maybe she was more like her father than she wanted to believe.

'Miss Dee.'

Alexia looked up at the woman she instantly recognised as Snow White. 'We meet again,' said Alexia.

Snow White walked past her until she found a private space between Large Print and British History. Alexia followed her.

'I'll get straight to the point.' Alexia sensed this woman was not the type to waste time or words. 'I want to interview the lawyer, Valentine.'

Snow White stood erect, chin up, shoulders back. 'What makes you think I can help?'

'You know her,' said Alexia.

The other woman didn't speak, but stood thinking, her face framed on all sides by titles on the Second World War.

'Assuming I do know her, I still don't see how I can help.'

'You can introduce me,' said Alexia. 'She'd be more likely to trust me if she met me through one of her own.'

Snow White's nostrils flared. 'That woman and I have nothing in common.'

'I still think it's worth a try,' said Alexia. 'Imagine the impact a story like that will make.'

Snow White fixed Alexia with an icy glare. 'Your fortune would be quite made.'

Alexia didn't flinch. 'And your cause would be head-line news. Again.'

'I don't understand,' said Catalina.

They were back in her cell: the girl and Milo side by side on the bench, Lilly hovering above like an irritated wasp.

'The prosecution, and probably the judge, think I should stand down from this case,' she said.

'And who will speak for Catalina?' asked Milo.

Lilly threw up her arms. 'I don't know, another solicitor, someone she can work with.'

'Another solicitor?' Catalina looked horrified. 'I told you before, I want you to do this for me.'

'How can I, Catalina?' shouted Lilly. 'When you won't tell me anything?'

Catalina began to cry. 'I told you what happened in the park.'

Lilly sank to her knees and knelt at the weeping girl's feet. The floor felt hard and rough through her trousers. As difficult as it had been for her, Catalina *had* told Lilly about the rape.

'I trusted you,' said Catalina. 'Artan trusted you.'

Lilly gasped. Artan had come to her for help and she had let him down. Now Catalina was begging and here was Lilly trying to wriggle away again.

She put her arms around Catalina. 'I will not let you down.'

'Do you have instruction, Miss Valentine?' asked the judge.

Lilly drew herself up to full height. 'My client is

adamant that she wishes me to continue representing her.'

Jez exhaled audibly beside her.

'And you are comfortable with that?' asked the judge.

Lilly shrugged. 'It is what it is.'

'How do you propose to defend your client if she will not give you the salient details?'

Lilly thought of the rape. How Catalina had struggled to give her account.

'I know everything I need to know, Your Honour.'

'Then you will have no objection if I list this case for trial immediately?'

Lilly felt as if she had been thumped in the stomach. 'What?'

The judge's gaze fixed her to the spot. 'You said you have everything you need.'

Lilly fought to catch her breath. 'I need more time, Your Honour.'

'For what?'

Lilly floundered. 'For one thing, I need to check my expert is available.'

'My clerk has taken the liberty of contacting her,' said the judge. 'Dr Kadir is, as they say, good to go.'

Lilly looked at her client. What was she waiting for? Would the case be any stronger in a month's or even six months' time?

'Fair enough, Your Honour.'

'Monday it is then,' said the judge, and rose to leave.

Jez leapt to his feet. 'If I may interject, Your Honour?'

The judge turned and lifted a weary eyebrow.

'The prosecution would be interested to know the defendant's age,' said Jez.

'I am eighteen,' said Catalina.

Lilly pushed her papers onto the floor. 'Bloody hell.'

'Why is this so important?' asked Milo.

Jez rubbed his hands together with glee. 'For one thing, the reporting restrictions no longer apply.'

Catalina rereads what she has written. It doesn't feel like any of it happened to her, yet every word has been scratched down as if in her own blood.

The paper is nearly full. No matter. The story is almost finished.

Catalina opens one eye. The other is still swollen shut.

'Emil,' she whispers. 'Are you awake?'

He nods his head then groans. His back is still brown with bruises.

They have both paid a high price for losing Nicolae.

She puts her finger to his lips and gestures to the door. Daniel and Gabi are in the kitchen with a third man.

'The boy knows nothing,' says Gabi, his voice blurred by vodka.

'He could lead the police back here,' says Daniel.

'Rubbish,' says Gabi. 'He has no idea where we are.'

'Make up your minds,' says the third man. 'I haven't got all night.'

'Those two are good little earners,' says Gabi. 'I don't want to get rid of them.'

'Easy come, easy go,' says the third man.

'He's right,' says Daniel. 'And I don't want to take any risks.'

'Okay, okay,' says Gabi. 'But I want a decent price for them.'

'I'll give you two hundred for the boy,' says the third man.

'What about the girl?' asks Gabi.

'My brother works a strip club in Luton, he'll give you top dollar for her.'

'She's young,' says Gabi.

The stranger barks with laughter. 'He likes to break them in himself.'

Catalina and Emil look at one another. They both know there is nothing they can say to make it better; instead they cling together, oblivious to their bloody mouths and broken ribs.

Chapter Twenty-Four

Lilly was too exhausted to sleep. The weekend had passed in a storm of research and preparation, and Lilly had polished off a two-kilogram tin of Heroes.

This was the first criminal trial she had ever conducted in the Crown Court. It was at the Bailey. It was for murder.

At least things couldn't get any worse.

Her mobile rang.

'Hello Jack,' she said. 'How did you know I'd be awake?'

'Call it a copper's hunch.'

'What are you up to at five in the morning?'

'Watching the news,' he said.

'Why?'

'Switch it on.'

She picked up the remote control and snapped on the TV. The Old Bailey was still in darkness, lit only by the orange glare of lampposts. At this time of the morning it should have been deserted, but it was already as busy as Harrods on Boxing Day. The press were out in force.

'Shit.'

* * *

'Time to get up, soft lad.'

Caz shines a torch in Luke's eyes. 'Move your arse.'

'What?'

Caz pulls on her boots and scrambles out of the lean-to. It's still dark. Not the usual gloom of the bridge, but night-time.

'What time is it?'

'Crack of sparrows,' she says. 'Five o'clock.'

Luke groans and lets himself flop back in his sleeping bag.

He used to have no trouble with early mornings at Manor Park and was always the first one out of bed in the boarding house. To be honest, he wanted to be first in the showers, before they got gunged up with pubic hair and plasters.

Today is different. Today he can hardly raise his head. No doubt the three cans of Special Brew he necked with a handful of jellies haven't helped.

'I'm not doing this for the good of my health,' says Caz. 'And I'm bleeding well not going on my own.'

'Going where?'

Caz shakes her head. 'Stop caning the frips and frills, they're messing with your mind.'

Luke feels the criticism is a bit rich coming from someone who does as much gear as Caz, but he doesn't want to fight.

'We agreed last night to go down to the Black Cat and get what you're owed.'

Luke vaguely remembers a conversation fuelled by strong lager and bravado. He struggles to his feet. 'I don't feel too good.'

'All the more reason we need that money.'

When they get to the café the men are climbing into the vans. Luke catches the Ukrainian's eye and nods. The man doesn't acknowledge him.

Caz pushes Luke towards the woman with the yellow hair, which she has pinned back in an elastic band.

'What do you want?' She looks Luke up and down and wrinkles her nose. 'I've got no work for the likes of you.'

Luke is nettled by her remark. 'What do you mean "the likes of me"?'

'I took a chance on you because you seemed like a nice lad, but you turn up to work off your head.'

'My hand was hurting,' says Luke.

'My heart bleeds,' she replies. 'Now sling your hook.'

Luke turns to leave but Caz steps in front of him, her chin jutted towards the yellow-haired woman.

'He doesn't want your poxy job,' she says. 'He just wants his wages.'

The woman laughs. 'You've got to be kidding me.'

'I'm not even smiling,' Caz replies. 'He did four days' work and he wants paying.'

The last man gets into the van and the woman slams the door behind him.

'He was asleep for one of them.'

'Alright,' says Caz. 'Three days.'

'Listen to me,' she hisses. 'Your friend here nearly got us all nicked. He's lucky to get out of this without a kicking.'

Caz stands her ground. 'We just want what we're due.'

The woman thumps the side of the van and it speeds off into the distance.

'I had to pay off the foreman at the factory so I'm already out of pocket,' she says. 'So if I were you I'd crawl back under your stone.'

When they can hear snoring from the kitchen, Emil crawls from under the old coat.

'What are you doing?' Catalina whispers. If Daniel or Gabi catch them they'll get another beating for sure.

'We're leaving,' says Emil.

Catalina is petrified. 'They'll kill us.'

'I'd rather that than what comes next.'

Catalina thinks for a moment. She is rooted to the spot with fear, yet she knows that first thing in the morning she will be taken away. She will never see Emil again.

She nods at him. They creep to the door and prise it open with their fingernails.

Daniel and Gabi are both slumped over the table, an empty bottle between them. Emil points at Daniel's pocket. They know the door will be locked, and that is where he keeps the key.

Catalina slinks in his direction, her bare feet silent on the cold tiles. Gabi lets out a fart and shifts in his chair. Catalina holds her breath, afraid even to move her chest.

When his breathing is even again she slides her hand towards Daniel's pocket. As she slips her fingers in she looks at Emil. He smiles at her. This is it.

She can feel the hard smoothness of coins, a Zippo lighter and a phone. Where is the key? She presses further until she is at the pocket seam. She traces the rough ridge until she finds a hole. The key must have slipped into the lining.

Like a worm burrowing into an apple, her finger searches. At last she can feel metal. She has the key.

She extracts it from the pocket and holds it up for Emil to see. He gives her a silent round of applause.

She takes one step away from Daniel and then a hand grabs her waist.

'What are you doing?'

Catalina looks down into his face, ugly with anger, saliva still dripping down his chin. His hand around her waist is hurting, digging through her skin.

She shakes in terror. He's going to kill her.

She waits for the fist to break open her skull, but it is Emil's hand that darts through the air. He grabs the bottle from the table and brings it crashing down on Daniel's head. There is a smash, a scream, and the air is filled with glass and blood. Daniel falls to the floor.

Gabi wakes with a start. He sees his brother bleeding and his face contorts. 'You little bastards.'

He flies at Catalina. 'Emil,' she screams. 'Emil!'

Once again the air is filled with glass and blood, as her friend drives the broken bottle into Gabi's face.

For a second Catalina watches in horror as Gabi whirls around, his eyes gouged, his cheeks ripped.

'The key,' shouts Emil, and they race to the door. Catalina undoes the lock and throws herself into the cold night air. They run and run and run. They don't stop until daylight breaks.

The guard opens the cell. 'Ready?'

Catalina nods. She has packed her things in a transparent plastic sack.

Calm, calm, calm.

Lilly breathed in through her nose and out through her mouth. Who had suggested this yoga crap? It didn't work.

She lugged her papers up the escalator at St Paul's and headed to court. Her breath crystallised in front of her face in the chill.

Her mobile rang. Caller ID told her it was David.

'I really don't need an argument right now,' she said.

'Have you seen the news?'

She rounded the corner to Old Bailey. 'I think I'm just about to become the news.'

The pavement was crowded with journalists and photographers and cameramen. When they saw Lilly they began shouting and screaming.

'Miss Valentine, can you confirm your client will offer a plea of insanity?'

'Is it true she's currently being held in a mental institution?'

'Bloody hell, Lilly, I can see you on the telly,' said David.

'At least I'm wearing my good coat,' Lilly replied.

A man with a sound boom pushed it into her face.

'Is it true she was removed from your custody because she threatened your son?'

Lilly shielded her eyes from the barrage of flashes and pushed her way into court.

'This is serious, Lilly,' said David. 'Even they think she was a danger to Sam.'

'You never did have a sense of humour, did you?' she said.

'And that's my point,' he said.

Lilly shrugged off her coat and jacket as she prepared to go through security. 'So you do have one then? You didn't call to wish me luck?'

'My point is you laugh everything off when you need to consider things properly,' he said.

Lilly sighed. 'Can we not do this again, please?'

'Look at that lot outside court and tell me I'm wrong,' he said. 'Tell me honestly that Sam wouldn't be better with me right now.'

Lilly turned her head towards the crowd waiting outside and a hundred cameras clicked and whirred.

'If I don't agree you'll take me to court, won't you?'

'You know I will.'

Alexia stamped her feet against the cold.

She'd arrived at 6 a.m. and was nowhere near one of the first. She wasn't sure what she was doing there really. Every television network and radio station had the trial covered. Every national had sent a staffer. There would be no need to buy anything from a freelance reporter. And it would all be pushed to page three or four. What an absolute waste.

She'd hoped she might sneak in and get a chat with Mark, but the press were being kept strictly out of the body of the court. They could sit in the public gallery like everyone else, but no cameras or recording equipment were allowed.

Alexia didn't know if she fancied a whole day taking notes. She was thinking about nipping off for a coffee when the sight of a familiar face changed her mind. Snow White had come along for the ride.

The jury looked expectantly at Lilly. Jez had introduced himself and now it was her turn.

She cleared her throat and smiled. No one smiled back. Was that normal? Did they hate her already? Were they like dogs and could smell her fear?

'I am Lilly Valentine, and I represent the defendant, Tirana Duraku.'

Jez gave a small cough, almost a hiccup.

What had she forgotten? She checked her robe was correct and that her skirt wasn't tucked in her knickers.

'What?' she whispered.

'You called her Tirana.'

Lilly felt the heat seep up her neck. 'As my friend so rightly pointed out, my client is, in fact, Catalina Petrescu.'

The jury mumbled to one another, no doubt appalled that the defence lawyer couldn't even remember her client's name. Lilly sat back down before she could make matters worse.

Jez got to his feet and beamed at the jury. Two female members positively simpered back at him.

'Ladies and gentlemen, I won't bore you with a lengthy

opening today; frankly, I don't need to. The facts speak for themselves.' He twisted his body towards Catalina. 'Quite simply, the defendant went with her friend to a school in Hertfordshire. It was an ordinary day and ordinary things were afoot. The under-tens were playing a football match and some of the seniors had come out to cheer them on.'

Jez turned back to the jury, his face grave. 'Alas, the uneventful afternoon was shattered by the arrival of the defendant and her friend, who were both carrying guns.'

He paused to allow the gravity of the situation to sink in.

'What they didn't know was that a police officer was on the scene, and he was able to disarm them both, but not before a child was murdered.'

Jez put his hands together to make a mock gun.

'The defendant and her friend had a plan to kill that day, and, tragically for Charles Stanton, they succeeded.'

Jez nodded solemnly and sat down. Lilly wondered if the jury might give him a round of applause.

'I thought you weren't going to bother them with an opening,' Lilly whispered through the corner of her mouth.

'Oh, Lilly,' he said. 'Didn't I say you were out of your depth?'

'Fancy seeing you here.'

Alexia slipped into the gallery and took the seat next to Snow White.

The other woman frowned. 'Are you following me?'

Alexia laughed. 'I hear there's a big trial on, or something like that.'

Snow White smirked.

'Have you thought about my offer?' asked Alexia.

'It was hardly an offer, Miss Dee, more a request on your part.'

'I thought we agreed we'd both benefit.'

Snow White opened her arm around the courtroom. 'There seems to be no shortage of publicity.'

'But they're not on your side, are they?' said Alexia. 'Most of the press are very PC.'

She could see by the twitch at the corner of Snow White's mouth that she had struck a chord.

'Get me an interview with Valentine and we'll both get what we want.'

Jack sat outside Court Four and waited. Another witness sat opposite, a slender woman, probably a Middle-Eastern woman, her hair pinned up in one of those French bun things. Jack ran his hands through his own wayward mop. The woman was engrossed by her laptop, caramel fingers tapping. Jack opened his paper and tried to read. He crossed and uncrossed his legs, unable to settle.

Giving evidence was always one of the worst parts of the job, with defence lawyers doing their damndest to trip you up and make you look a twat. Even the most honest coppers came out looking like diehards from the West Midlands Serious Crime Squad, and the fact that it was his woman who would be doing the questioning offered no solace. If need be, Lilly would chew him up and spit him across the room.

At last, the door to the court opened.

'The prosecution calls its first witness, Officer Jonathon McNally.'

Jack groaned. He never used his full name.

He walked stiffly to the witness stand and took the oath.

'Could you give your full name please?' said Jez.

'Jonathon Christopher McNally.'

Lilly stifled an hysterical laugh with a coughing fit, and Jack felt himself turning crimson.

'Officer McNally, were you at Manor Park School on the day of this terrible event?' asked Jez.

Jack nodded. 'Indeed I was.'

'Were you on duty?'

Jack turned his body away from Lilly. 'No, I was watching my friend's son play football.'

'I see,' said Jez. 'And at what point did you realise the defendant and her co-conspirator were not merely supporters?'

'My friend noticed them first, and I noticed her noticing them, if you know what I mean?'

'I think I understand,' Jez laughed. 'And when did you notice they were armed?'

'As soon as they reached the pitch I saw they both had guns.'

Jez nodded at the jury. 'They *both* had guns.'

Lilly got to her feet. 'Your Honour, I doubt anyone here is deaf.'

'Indeed,' said the judge. 'Please don't repeat the testimony, Mr Stafford.'

Jez went smoothly back to his questions. 'Did you ask them to put down their weapons?'

'I did,' said Jack. 'And the defendant did give me hers.'

'Immediately?'

Jack thought back to Anna's hand gripping the gun. Her hand had been shaking. 'Not immediately,' he said.

'But Artan Shala wouldn't be disarmed and you had to shoot him?'

Jack shifted on his feet. 'I didn't have any alternative.'

'I'm sure no one blames you for the action you took.' Jez's face was a mask of concern. 'No doubt you fully believed that Shala was going to kill another child.'

Jack knew the barrister was faking his concern. He didn't care less what might have happened next, how Jack's life had nearly fallen apart.

'I believed Shala was still a risk.'

'Just a couple of questions.' Lilly looked up at Jack as if they were strangers. He knew she was at work but it was disconcerting all the same. 'It was definitely Artan that killed Charles Stanton?'

Jack nodded in what he hoped seemed a businesslike manner. 'Most definitely.'

'And it was Artan who you thought might shoot someone else?'

'Yes.'

Lilly glanced at the jury. 'Not the defendant?'

'She gave me her gun before Stanton was shot.'

'Definitely before?'

Jez rose. 'My friend seems to have caught the habit of repetition for which she showed so little tolerance only moments ago.'

'Apologies,' said Lilly.

Jack gave a tight smile. 'It was definitely beforehand.'

The court rules might have prevented Lilly from gaining mileage but Jack couldn't resist making the point for her.

If Lilly was grateful she chose not to show it and levelled Jack in her gaze.

'Officer McNally, at any point before you disarmed her, did you believe the defendant was going to commit a murder?'

Jack took his time. He knew what Lilly wanted him to say. He knew what Jez wanted him to say.

'In all honesty, I don't know.'

Lilly sat down, her face impassive. He had told the truth, nothing more.

The whole thing was a travesty. A mockery.

Charlie Stanton was dead and Snow White could see his killer from here.

In any other country the girl would be locked up, the key well and truly thrown away. Or, better still, she'd be hanged.

Instead, a game of cat and mouse was unfolding, with Valentine as the central player.

Why were they even having a trial? The girl was not British, so what right did she have to British justice?

The reporter was just as bad. Poor little rich girl, showing her parents she could make it on her own. Snow White could see through her like a plastic bag.

She was right about the press, though. The liberal,

leftist rags would bleat about poor treatment of asylum seekers and the lawyer would pounce on that.

The guilty must be punished.

'Right then,' said Snow White. 'We'll rendezvous in Little Markham at 9 p.m.'

The reporter couldn't hide her glee. 'You won't regret this.'

Indeed I won't, Snow White thought, but Valentine surely will.

'How's it going?' asked Sam. 'Are you going to win?' Lilly had phoned him as soon as she got back from court. 'If you do, will she come back to live with us?'

Lilly poured hot water over her Ginger Zinger. The bloody stuff was more addictive than good wine and she had tramped the length of Fleet Street to track another box down. 'I don't think you'd like that, Sam.'

'Where will she go?' he asked.

Lilly ached with sadness for her client. 'I don't know.'

'I don't hate her, Mum, I just didn't want her in our house.'

'I understand that.'

'And I don't hate you, I just wanted to get away from it all.'

Lilly felt a lump in her throat. 'I know that.'

'I've got to go, Mum, supper's ready.'

'How's Cara's cooking?'

Sam groaned. His dad's girlfriend was currently following a macrobiotic lifestyle.

'For tea tomorrow we're having lentil and cauliflower curry.'

'That sounds . . .' Lilly searched for the right word. 'Healthy.'

'When the trial's over we should do something kind for Anna,' said Sam.

'That would be lovely, big man.'

'We should cook for her,' he said.

'That's a great idea.'

'Where is she from, Mum?'

Lilly sipped her tea. 'I only wish I knew, big man, I only wish I knew.'

'What are they doing here?'

Alexia nodded at Blood River and Bigsy, who had just stepped out of the shadows.

'We didn't like your idea of a cosy Q and A,' said Snow White. 'So we thought we would confront Valentine ourselves.'

'You can get it all down,' said Blood River. 'Take a few pics.'

Alexia shook her head. 'That wasn't the deal.'

Snow White snorted. 'There never was any deal.'

Alexia was furious. This was a golden opportunity. Platinum-plated, as her dad would say. It would give her the break she needed. She wasn't prepared to let a bunch of idiotic Nazis ruin everything.

'I don't know what rubbish you've got planned, but I want my interview first.'

'Shut up,' spat Blood River.

Alexia stood her ground. 'I want that interview.'

Blood River pushed her hard and she fell to the ground. It was hard and wet under her hands. He stood

422

over her, his malevolent face filling her field of vision. 'Which part of "shut" and "up" do you not understand?'

He turned on his heel and Snow White led him to the solicitor's cottage.

Alexia scrambled to her feet, shaking dead leaves from her coat.

'Fine.'

Lilly pulled out her weighing scales and packets of currants, sultanas and raisins. Each year, at about this time, she and Sam made the pudding ready for Christmas. In the depths of dark November, when half term was long finished, it reminded them that a whole week of eating, present unwrapping and slumping in front of the telly lay ahead.

Sam might not be with her tonight but Lilly was buggered if she wouldn't make sure Christmas was as much fun as every other year.

And, let's face it, there was no way she would sleep tonight so she may as well fill her time making something delicious.

She grated orange and lemon zest over the dried fruit and, as the air filled with their citrus tang, Lilly's mind turned to the case.

The prosecution had closed, the entire case wrapped up in a day. No doubt Jez had wanted to make more of it, but Lilly had accepted most of it. She didn't dispute that her client was there with a gun. The argument rested on her state of mind. Could Catalina have had the requisite intention, or had her reasoning been impaired by the rape?

Lilly poured over rum, barley wine and Guinness.

The smell made her nose wrinkle. It was a standing joke with Sam that Lilly would usually polish off any leftover alcohol but tonight she didn't fancy it. Tomorrow she would open the case for the defence and that was making her stomach churn.

Alexia's heart was pounding. Her anger had dissolved to fear as Blood River and Bigsy approached the porch. These men had smashed windows and cars. They had thrown dog mess in court. They had kicked and punched two women.

'What are they going to do?' she hissed.

Snow White waved the enquiry away like a fly.

'That poor woman has done nothing wrong,' said Alexia.

'You didn't give any thought to her wellbeing when you posted her picture all over your torrid little newspaper.'

Alexia felt winded. It was true. She had hidden in the bushes like a dirty, sneaky thief and revealed to the world that Petrescu was living with her lawyer. She'd even used a picture of the boyfriend, a decent, honest copper, who had got himself entangled in a mess he didn't deserve.

'This is all wrong,' she said.

Snow White ignored her, rapt with her racist friends.

Alexia shuddered. The woman seemed almost turned on.

They watched the men creep to the side of the house, whispering to one another.

'Not more smashed windows,' said Alexia. 'The noise will frighten her son.'

424

One look at Snow White's face told Alexia she couldn't care less who was in the cottage.

The two men shuffled on the spot, retrieving something from a rucksack. Not another brick, please. Alexia craned her neck to see, but Blood River was almost swallowed by the darkness. She could see almost nothing but his outline until he lit a match, its yellow flame dancing around his face.

Too late Alexia saw the milk bottle, a rag stuffed in the top.

Too late she saw the material catch, fire licking the air.

Too late she saw Blood River throw the bottle and watched it explode through an upstairs window.

'Stop,' Alexia screamed. 'She has a little boy in there.'

The house was burning. Too late.

The noise was tremendous. An ear-ripping crash followed by a whoosh. Her immediate reaction was that there had been another terrorist attack.

Lilly had been stirring the mixture, making wishes, one for herself and one for Sam, when she heard it, dropped her spoon and ran upstairs. She threw open her bedroom door and saw a riot of colour. Oranges, reds and yellows.

Too shocked to move, Lilly watched the flames flash across the curtains, the walls and the ceiling. With a frightening speed the room was engulfed. Water, she needed water. She ran to the ensuite bathroom at the furthest end of the room and ran a towel under the tap. She tried to lash out at the flames, damp them down but now the room was filled with black smoke that tore at her eyes and made her choke. She needed to get out.

Which way was the door? Which way was out?

Both left and right was blocked and Lilly backed up until she was trapped against the wall.

'Give me your hand.'

Lilly couldn't breathe, couldn't see. She could feel herself fading.

Through the miasma she caught the faint outline of a hand.

Was it a hand?

She held out her own as the blackness started to take her.

'That's about it, love.' The fireman patted her on the back. 'It could have been a lot worse.'

Lilly looked at her cottage, the walls stained black with soot, water dripping off every surface.

'You reckon?'

He gave a sympathetic shrug. 'Got somewhere to stay?'

Lilly closed her eyes. She couldn't go to Jack's, he'd be fired on the spot. She didn't dare tell David what had happened, at least not yet.

'She can come back to mine.'

It was the woman who had dragged her out of the house. She had stayed while they revived Lilly with oxygen and while the police asked a million questions.

'Thanks,' said Lilly. 'But who are you?'

The woman held out her hand. 'Alexia Dee.'

'Jesus,' said Lilly. 'You're the woman who took my bloody photo.'

*   *   *

Alexia pulled two beers from the fudge and handed one to Lilly.

'Don't suppose you've got a Ginger Zinger?' asked Lilly.

'Sorry?'

'No worries,' said Lilly. 'Beer's fine.'

She looked around Alexia's flat. The generic prints of ballerinas seemed at odds with the glamorous young woman in her expensive shoes.

'I still don't understand why you were there.'

'Do you want the truth?' asked Alexia.

'It usually works for me.'

'I wanted to interview you and I asked someone to make the introduction.'

Lilly cocked her head. 'You thought I'd be swayed by a firebomb-throwing xenophobe?'

'One of them is a parent at Manor Park.'

Lilly was stunned. 'You're joking?'

'I wish I were.'

'And you had no idea what they were going to do?'

Alexia threw up her hands, sending bubbles spiralling across the carpet. 'God, no,' she said. 'I would never have agreed to something like that.'

Lilly nodded. 'Then thank you.'

'For what?'

Lilly laughed. 'For saving my life.'

'Don't say that.' Alexia's eyes filled with tears. 'If I had acted as soon as I suspected something was wrong, I might have been able to stop them.'

Lilly collapsed onto the sofa. It was brown and uncomfortable.

'That's exactly how I feel about Charlie Stanton,' she said. 'Artan Shala came to me after Catalina was raped and I knew what he was going to do.'

'He told you?'

'Not in so many words,' said Lilly. 'But I could sense it would be bad.'

'But you can't blame yourself,' said Alexia.

Lilly raised her eyebrows. 'Can't I?'

'That's why you've got so involved in this case.' Alexia pointed her bottle at Lilly. 'You're trying to make amends to the girl.'

'Thank you, Dr Freud.'

'Do you think it was the rape that sent them over the edge?' asked Alexia.

'Yes, I do,' said Lilly. 'But I'm going to have one hell of a job proving it.'

Chapter Twenty-Five

Drip, drip, flipping drip.

Luke watches the endless rain. Last night it poured relentlessly and it hasn't stopped this morning.

The weather wasn't something he used to give much thought to. If it was cold, Mum turned up the heating; and the boarding house was always stifling. He'd known Tom to mooch around in his shorts in February. When you were homeless it was different. You got damp right to your underwear and there was nowhere to dry your clothes, so everything began to smell of mould.

He can't even hang out in the Black Cat, because the owner is really annoyed that he messed up in the factory after he'd been the one to put Luke on to it.

'You stacking?' he asks Caz. It's not that he needs it, but getting off your head just makes days like this go so much quicker.

Caz shakes her head and wipes her nose with her sleeve. She's grumpy too.

'Got any cash?'

He empties his pocket and shows her the collection of five- and ten-pence pieces.

They'll have to go out begging.

He peers out into the downpour.

Great.

'Try this.'

Alexia held out a black jersey wrap dress. It was elegant and stylish. It was a size eight.

Lilly burst out laughing. Last night's clothes were black and acrid and there was no way she could wear them to court.

'Have you got anything bigger?'

Alexia went back to her wardrobe. 'I have this for when I'm premenstrual.'

Lilly took the blue silk skirt. It was floaty, the waist elastic. It would do.

'What about a top? It needs to be white.'

Alexia pulled out a white T-shirt with 'LA Lakers' emblazoned across the chest. 'You could wear it inside out.'

Lilly wasn't convinced.

'You'll have your robe thing over the top.'

As Lilly turned the corner to Old Bailey, her mobile rang.

'Right on cue, David.'

'I can see you on telly again,' he said. 'I've got to ask what on earth are you wearing?'

Lilly ignored the camera pointed directly under her chin.

'There was a fire at the cottage.'

'Bloody hell, Lil, are you okay?'

'Sort of.'

'Is there anything I can do?'

Lilly checked her reflection in the rain-spattered glass of the door to the court.

'Buy me a black suit.'

'What size?' he asked.

'Twelve.' She patted her stomach. 'Better make that a fourteen.'

She climbed the stairs and met Jez at the top, where he was stood with Kerry Thomson. Jez looked her up and down. Kerry sniggered into her hand.

'Don't say a word,' said Lilly.

Jez swallowed a laugh.

'Not even half a word,' said Lilly.

'Good morning,' a voice boomed from behind.

Lilly turned to see Teddy Roberts sauntering towards them. Out of his robes and ridiculous wig he was a handsome man. His hair was flecked with grey, his jaw distinguished.

He appraised Lilly in much the same way as Jez.

'My chambers. Now.'

Judge Roberts peered over his glasses at Lilly. 'There is an explanation, I presume.'

Lilly shrugged, as if a peasant skirt and a T-shirt worn inside out were everyday attire in the Crown Court.

'I didn't have access to my clothes this morning, Your Honour.'

'And why was that, Miss Valentine? An all-night party, perhaps?'

Lilly stuck her chin in the air. The pompous bugger had no right to make assumptions.

'Actually, Your Honour, my house was firebombed by racist thugs.'

The judge's mouth fell open.

'My things are in disarray,' she continued. 'But my ex-husband has kindly agreed to purchase something suitable and deliver it to me at court.'

'I'm so sorry, Miss Valentine,' said the judge. 'Surely you will want an adjournment?'

'Of course,' Jez spluttered. 'The case must be adjourned.'

'That won't be necessary,' said Lilly.

'Are you sure?' asked the judge.

Lilly held her neck quite straight. 'My mother taught me never to give in to bullies.'

When she had left the room, Teddy Roberts shook his head. 'She's a hell of a woman.'

Jez let a smile spread across his face. 'Indeed she is.'

Alexia headed down Fleet Street towards the West End. There was nothing to be gained by hanging out at Old Bailey. The story was well and truly covered.

She buried her head under her umbrella against the rain and looked longingly at the black cabs that sped past. Being skint was such a bummer. Then she thought about Lilly's cottage, charred and smoking, and how she'd just got out in time. Now was not the time for self-pity.

Lilly's commitment to Petrescu made Alexia shame-faced. With her world literally in ashes, Lilly hadn't wept for her home and possessions; instead she'd been more bothered about trying to prove her client had been raped.

When Lilly was finally asleep, Alexia covered her in a blanket. She pulled out her recorder and played the tape. There it was, an exclusive interview with Lilly Valentine. Guaranteed front-page material. She sighed and tossed it in the bin.

She had done a lot of selfish things in her time but had never felt guilt the way she did now. She had led a gang of dangerous thugs to this poor woman's door, and for what?

She felt angry with herself and sick at the same time. She had to make amends; do something to help. She could use her journalistic skills to help Lilly's case.

When she got to Theatreland she checked in her pocket and pulled out a photograph of Manor Park Year Eleven. Two rows of teenagers stood on the steps and squinted into the sun. There was Charles Stanton, a pretty boy with great teeth. Next to him was a bigger boy with wild red hair and bad skin. On the other side Lilly had circled a boy's face. This was Luke Walker. He had witnessed the rape and was the key to Catalina's salvation.

Alexia would bet her Vivienne Westwood platforms that he was in London. Didn't every kid think the streets were paved with gold? And when they discovered their error, a lot of them ended up here.

'The defence calls their first witness, Dr Leyla Kadir.'

Lilly wrapped the robe around her. She had borrowed it from a friend of Jez's and hoped it covered most of the madness she was wearing beneath.

Dr Kadir looked the epitome of sophistication in a beige jacket that perfectly complemented her dark skin.

Her hair was tied in a chignon, not a strand out of place. As was so common for witnesses, she had hung around all day yesterday without being called, yet she hadn't complained once. She had just worked on her laptop, smiled and worked some more.

'Dr Kadir,' said Lilly. 'Could you tell us what you know about Catalina Petrescu?'

'I know she is a very damaged person,' said the doctor.

'How have you come to that conclusion?'

'I have read the case papers and had numerous interviews with her,' said Dr Kadir.

'Have you been able to make any diagnosis?'

Dr Kadir nodded once. 'I think she is suffering from Post Traumatic Stress Disorder, which has affected the balance of her mind.'

'Dr Kadir,' Jez dazzled her with his most charming smile. 'Tell me a little more about this syndrome. What did you call it – PMT?'

The jury tittered.

The doctor clucked at him as if he were an errant schoolboy. 'PTSD, Mr Stafford, and you know perfectly well what it is. No doubt you were up all last night researching it on the Internet.'

Jez gave a cheeky grin. 'I may have been up all night, Doctor, but I most certainly wasn't working.'

The jury laughed at his brazen flirtatiousness.

'Your Honour,' Lilly jumped to her feet. 'Do we really need the theatrics?'

The judge banged his gavel to bring the mirth to an end. Jez put up his hands in apology.

434

'Dr Kadir,' he continued. 'Could you enlighten me as to the symptoms of PTSD?'

'Anxiety, sleeplessness, paranoia . . .'

'All nasty, I'm sure,' said Jez. 'But nothing that would make a person start shooting people.'

The doctor eyed him coolly. 'If you had let me finish, I was going to explain that one of the main symptoms in patients with PTSD is detachment.'

'And that would make a person load up their gun, would it?'

'It could mean a patient is so dislocated from reality that he or she may enter into such an action without fully comprehending the implications.'

'Are you serious, Doctor?'

She nodded gravely. 'When I myself was suffering with this condition I drove my car into a brick wall. I have a steel rod in my spine, but to this day I do not recall how it happened.'

The jury gasped.

Jez was visibly shocked, but collected himself quickly. 'What would cause PTSD, Doctor?'

'The clue is in the name,' she answered. 'A trauma.'

'Such as an accident – a plane crash perhaps?'

Lilly frowned at Jez's calculated use of recent events. 'Indeed.'

'And many Gulf War veterans are suffering with PTSD, are they not?'

Dr Kadir smiled. 'So you *were* up all night doing research, Mr Stafford.'

Lilly covered her mouth with her hand. Dr Kadir was a consummate professional.

'And you made your diagnosis of the defendant while she had us all believing she suffered her particular trauma in Kosovo?'

'I made my diagnosis at that time, yes,' said Dr Kadir.

'Well, given that was a lie, Doctor – that there was no trauma in Kosovo – how do you think this defendant got PTSD?'

Lilly sucked in her breath and crossed her fingers. This was such a vital point. One with so much mileage for Jez.

'It has always been my contention that the incident that triggered Catalina's condition was not necessarily the war in Kosovo,' said Dr Kadir.

Jez ratcheted up the pressure. 'Tell us then, Doctor, what else could possibly excuse the defendant's wicked actions?'

'It is not for me to say whether Catalina's PTSD excuses what happened.' Dr Kadir turned to the jury. 'It is for the jury.'

'Just so,' said Jez.

She levelled him in her sights again. 'But, as I said, it has always been my contention that the factor which pushed Catalina into detachment was not Kosovo but the rape.'

Noise erupted from the gallery.

Jez played to the crowd and somehow managed to address Dr Kadir, the jury and the gallery at the same time. Lilly wished she had even half his skill.

'Ah, the alleged rape,' he said. 'The unreported rape?'

'Thousands of rapes go unreported every year, Mr Stafford.'

'But we are only interested in this one,' he replied. 'And how can we expect intelligent men and women to believe it without any evidence whatsoever?'

Lilly pushed herself to her feet. 'Your Honour, that is a ridiculous question. How can Dr Kadir answer for the jury's expectations? She is a psychiatrist, not a palm reader.'

The judge wagged his finger. 'It was clumsily put, Miss Valentine, but it is valid nonetheless. Dr Kadir must substantiate the basis of her diagnosis.'

'I cannot say that the rape was real or not real. I was not there,' said Dr Kadir.

Jez turned to the jury with open palms. Lilly was almost expecting him to say, 'Told you.'

'However,' said Dr Kadir. 'My medical opinion, my *expert* opinion, remains the same.'

She gestured first to the jury and then to Catalina, ensuring each eye fell on the pathetic creature in the dock.

'This girl is suffering with PTSD, and my instincts as a professional say to me that it is as a result of a brutal rape.'

Six lousy quid.

Luke kicks the box aside in disgust.

They've been begging for hours and have hardly got enough for a Happy Meal, let alone what they really need. It's been impossible to find a spot with the police crawling around everywhere, some of them armed.

Caz is by his side, shivering, her nose running.

There's a reason they call it 'doing your rattle' – every bone is shaking inside her, like coins in pockets.

'I can't take this,' she says.

He scoops up the change. 'Let's get a coffee.'

'I don't want any coffee.'

Luke knows what she wants, but they don't have enough.

'I'm going to get some money,' she says.

Luke turns away. He can't bear the thought of it.

'Don't,' he whispers.

'C'mon, soft lad, it'll only take half an hour.'

'Please.'

She pleads with her eyes. 'I've got to get some gear, Luke.'

He pushes his hand through his hair. It is slick with grease and rain.

'Let's try to get the money I'm owed from the Black Cat,' he says.

Caz shakes her head. 'That bitch won't give you a penny.'

'Then I'll have to make her.'

'It's going very well.'

Milo smiled at Lilly as they descended to the cells.

'As well as I could expect,' said Lilly. 'Given the circumstances.'

'The doctor says Catalina has a problem with her brain,' said Milo. 'The jury will have to accept it.'

'The jury don't have to accept anything, Milo.'

'But she's a doctor, an expert.'

Lilly waited for the guard to swing open the door. 'The jury will make up their own minds.'

* * *

Catalina was standing in the far corner of her cell, the only colour against the grey bricks.

'You're going to have to take the stand,' said Lilly.

Catalina pressed against the wall as if she were trying to dissolve into it.

'You have to tell your story,' Lilly continued.

'I don't think I can.'

Lilly went over to the bench and sat. Her robe fell open, revealing the bizarre outfit underneath.

'There's no other choice,' said Lilly. 'I have to make the jury believe you were raped, and I have no evidence at all.'

There were signs of the homeless in every doorway. An empty bottle of cider, a dirty sleeping bag. But catching one of them was like shooting rabbits – as soon as you approached, the buggers scarpered.

Alexia managed to corner one man who was too drunk to run away, but he wouldn't even look at the photograph and buried his head in his jumper.

What she needed was some money. Anyone could be bribed to tell you things with ten-pound notes, particularly if they were cold and wet and desperate.

The trouble was, she had exactly eight pounds in her purse and her cashpoint card had been swallowed.

She thought about everything that had happened in the last few weeks. The lying and cheating. She had left home to make something of herself, to prove she was not a trustafarian with more shoes than brain cells. She didn't want to be a stylist, or to work in PR. She wanted to be a journalist. She wanted to make her father proud.

She pulled out her mobile.

'Daddy, it's Lex,' she said. 'I need some cash.'

Catalina took the Bible in her tiny fingers.

'I promise to tell the whole truth and nothing but the truth, so help me God.'

Lilly looked at her client, dwarfed by the courtroom, ludicrous in her dungarees. The only person who could tell her story was Catalina. It was up to her.

'Tell me about the night you met three boys from Manor Park School.'

Jez flew to his feet. 'Objection. My friend is leading her defendant as if she were a horse in a circus.'

'He's right, Miss Valentine.'

Lilly shrugged. 'I apologise, but I just thought we should cut to the chase.'

Catalina glanced at the jury, then at Lilly. Her face was pink with shame.

'I met them in the village and we went to the park,' she mumbled.

The members of the jury craned their necks to hear her. Lilly could have advised her to speak up, but decided it was better coming out in Catalina's own sorrowful way.

'Everything was fine until . . .'

'Until what?' asked Lilly.

'One of the boys pulled me to the floor and raped me.'

'How did that make you feel?'

Catalina buried her head in her chest. 'Like an animal.'

'And afterwards?'

'It was as though everything wasn't real. Like I was

there, but not there.' Catalina shook her head as if it were a puzzle to her. 'I felt like a robot.'

Lilly took a deep breath. This was the crux. 'On the day of the shooting, did you still feel like that?'

'Yes. It felt like a dream.'

'Miss Petrescu,' Jez leaned on his elbow as if she were hardly worth the effort. 'Do you seriously expect this court to believe you didn't know what you were doing when you obtained a gun and went to a school with it?'

'I didn't think about it.'

Jez laughed. 'Surely it seemed a little out of the ordinary?'

'I didn't think about it,' she said. 'I'm sorry.'

'Don't apologise to me,' said Jez, inferring that there were others more deserving of her excuses. He leafed through his papers and Lilly sighed. Jez would know every letter in those files, he was simply putting Catalina under the scrutiny of the jury's glare.

'You say you were raped, Miss Petrescu.'

Catalina nodded.

'Yet you didn't go to the police?'

'I didn't think they would believe me.'

'Why not?' he asked. 'They can perform tests, make notes of your bruising.'

'They were rich boys, English boys,' she said. 'I thought they would say I was another lying asylum seeker. Just like you say I am lying.'

'I don't infer you made this up because I am a racist, Miss Petrescu,' he said.

'No?'

441

Jez shook his head. 'Not at all. I am simply going on your track record.'

'I don't understand.'

Jez tore off a sheet of paper and handed it to Catalina. 'Do you recognise this?'

'Yes.'

'Of course you do.' Jez tapped it with his finger. 'This is the statement you gave to the immigration authorities. Do you recall what you said?'

'Not word for word.'

'Then let me refresh your memory.' Jez snatched back the statement. 'You called yourself Anna Duraku. You said you were from Kosovo and that your family had been murdered by the Serbs.'

Catalina hid her face in her hands.

'It's a tissue of lies, isn't it?' roared Jez.

'Yes,' Catalina whispered into her fingers.

'I'm sorry, I didn't catch that,' said Jez.

'Yes,' Catalina wailed.

'Then answer me this.' Jez lowered his voice. 'If you were lying about that, why should we believe you about the rape?'

'Not you two again.'

The woman with the bleached hair is letting the workers out of the back of a van.

'Just give me what you owe me and I'll never come back here again,' says Luke.

'Piss off,' she says.

'I worked hard.' Luke sees the Ukrainian. 'He'll tell you that I did a good job.'

'You need to leave,' says the Ukrainian. 'You have caused enough trouble.'

Luke's eyes fill with tears. If he can't get the money, Caz will let some disgusting old man do it to her and he can't bear it. It's too much.

'If you don't give it to me I'll go to the police.'

Everyone stays very still.

'That's right,' Luke says, 'I'll tell them what you do. That everyone here is illegal.'

A rustle runs through the men. Many of them don't speak much English, but they know about the police.

'That's enough, Luke,' warns Caz.

'You think I won't do it, but I will,' says Luke, tears streaming down his face. 'I've got nothing to lose.'

Someone shouts at Luke, the words foreign, the tone universal.

'You'll all be sent home,' screams Luke.

The Ukrainian grabs Luke by the neck. 'No one is going home.'

'He's joking,' says Caz. 'Ha ha, hee hee, get it?'

'It's not funny,' says the Ukrainian, his eyes boring into Luke's.

'Stick him in the back of the van,' says the woman. 'Teach him a lesson, the junkie scum.'

The Ukrainian drags Luke towards the van. He's going to get the kicking of his life, and he's terrified.

Without warning, Caz darts forward and aims a kick to the Ukrainian's groin.

'Ooph.' He doubles over and lets go of Luke.

'Leg it,' shouts Caz, and they pelt down the road.

'Little bitch,' roars the Ukrainian, and chases them.

Luke's breath is loud in his chest. He used to be so fit. Football, hockey, cross-country runs. All he does now is sit about and get off his head. Caz is even worse, trailing slightly.

They run towards the main road, at least five men seconds behind them.

Luke has never been so scared in his life.

He dives through the traffic, ignoring the horns, the cyclists' shouts.

Caz has stopped to catch some air.

The men are right behind her.

'Caz,' Luke yells. 'Quickly!'

She glances behind her, her eyes round as she sees how near their pursuers are. She runs into the road.

The car screeches to a halt but the thud is sickening.

Luke stands in the rain as the driver leaps out and hovers over Caz, her body bent and bleeding.

The Ukrainians melt away.

'Do you know this boy?'

Alexia shoved the school photograph under the girl's nose. She had dreadlocks down to her waist and kept spitting out the side of her mouth.

'No comment.'

Alexia brandished fifty pounds like a fan.

The girl checked around as if MI5 might be watching and snatched the money.

'His name's Luke. He hangs with Mad Caz.'

'Where will I find him?'

The girl shrugged.

Alexia sighed and handed over another tenner.
'Most days they go to the Peckham Project.'

'I did okay?' Catalina brushed Lilly's hand.
'You did great,' said Milo. 'Just great.'
Lilly gave a small smile. Her client's testimony had been exactly what she'd anticipated. 'Tomorrow I will give my closing speech and then the jury will make up their minds.'
'You will persuade them, Lilly,' said Milo.
'Let's hope so.'

Alexia took the bus to Peckham and rang the doorbell of what looked like a community centre.
A middle-aged woman answered in a cloud of smoke. 'Sorry,' she said. 'This is a resource for children.'
'I know.' Alexia waved away the fog. 'I need to speak to you about one of them.'
The woman went to shut the door. 'Our policy is "no involvement with the authorities".'
'I'm not the police, social services or immigration,' Alexia laughed. 'To be honest, I don't even have a job right now.'
'So what do you want?'
Alexia pushed the photograph under the woman's nose. 'I'm trying to find this boy.'
'Is he in trouble?' the woman asked.
'Not that I know of.'
The woman paused as if deciding what to do.
'I'm Jean. You'd better come in.'

* * *

Alexia warmed her hands around the chipped mug of tea. 'What do you do here?'

'Whatever we can,' Jean lit another cigarette. 'We offer everything from filling in forms to washing socks.'

'And what do you do for Luke Walker?'

Jean touched the photograph. 'He's not like most of them, I could see that from the start.'

'How?'

'Some of these poor buggers, most of 'em really, never had a chance in the first place. Parents couldn't give a damn about them.'

'But not Luke?' asked Alexia.

'He'd obviously come from a nice home,' said Jean. 'And I don't mean money. I hoped I could help him get back to his mum. Is that why you're here?'

'Sort of,' said Alexia. 'Luke witnessed a rape, and I need him to give evidence about what he saw.'

Jean laughed. 'Good luck with that. Most of these kids would sooner gnaw off their arms than get involved in a court case.'

'I understand that,' said Alexia. 'But a girl's life depends on it. Another kid who never had a chance in the first place.'

Jean leaned back in her chair and blew smoke at the ceiling.

'He hasn't been in today, but when I next see him I'll tell him you're looking for him.'

'That might be too late, the trial finishes tomorrow.'

The doorbell rang.

'I can't do more than that.' Jean got up to answer it.

A tiny boy, no more than ten, came rushing in. He pointed to Alexia. 'Who's that?'

'She's leaving,' said Jean.

Alexia smiled her thanks and moved towards the door.

'Guess what, Jean?' the boy squealed. 'Mad Caz got run over. She's in St Bart's.'

Alexia let herself out.

'How's it going?'

David passed her a Harvey Nichols bag.

'Not great.' She pulled out a Prada trousersuit. 'I don't think the jury believed she was raped.'

'I meant you,' said David.

She wasn't ready to think about the fire. Not yet.

'Fine.'

She held the jacket against her. The tailoring was exquisite.

'Do you like it?' David asked.

'I can't afford designer stuff.'

'Cara says you get what you pay for.'

Lilly smoothed her hand over the soft fabric. 'Except she's never the one paying.'

Her mobile rang.

'I've found the boy,' said Alexia.

'Have you spoken to him?'

'I thought that would be better coming from you.'

Lilly stuffed her £900 suit back in the bag. 'Don't let him out of your sight.'

Lilly shuddered as she entered the hospital. She felt sick at the thought of Rupinder still attached to all those tubes, and the smell always reminded her of Elsa's last days – the tang of disinfectant attempting to mask decay and death.

'He's in there,' whispered Alexia, and pointed to a teenage boy sitting by a bed. He was filthy and pale. His eyes were sunk into his face, but it was definitely Luke Walker.

'Luke?' Lilly approached the bed.

He didn't answer. He was transfixed by the patient in the bed, both arms encased in bandages, the face so swollen it was impossible to say if it was a boy or a girl.

'Luke?' Lilly repeated.

This time he looked up, his eyes guarded.

'Do I know you?'

Lilly see-sawed her hand. 'My son attends Manor Park.'

She saw his eyes flicker around him as he looked for an escape route.

'You're not in any trouble, Luke,' she said. 'In fact, I've come to ask for your help.'

'What do you want?'

Lilly moved towards him as if he were a wild animal that might take flight.

'I represent Catalina Petrescu.'

She could see the name meant nothing to him.

'Anna,' she said. 'The girl in the park.'

Luke sprang up, his chair flying behind him. 'I didn't do anything. If she says I did, she's lying.'

Lilly put up her hands. 'She's not saying that, Luke. She's never said that.'

Luke backed away. 'What do you want?'

'It's a long story, Luke, but I need you to go to court and say she was raped.'

'I'm not going near any court.'

Lilly nodded. 'I know you're frightened, but if you don't do this Anna will go to prison for something she didn't do.'

'Just leave me alone,' Luke shouted. 'Leave us alone.'

A nurse arrived and put her hand in the small of Lilly's back.

'I think that's enough, don't you?'

Chapter Twenty-Six

Jez let out a whistle. 'Looking foxy, Miss Valentine.'

Lilly did a small twirl.

The Prada suit was fantastic.

'Shame your case isn't up to the same standard,' he said.

Lilly batted him around the head.

He was right. The case was hopeless. Catalina was going down.

Her mobile rang.

'You look gorgeous,' said Jack.

Lilly laughed. 'Are you spying on me?'

'Are you fecking kidding, woman, I've been stalking you all morning.'

'Are you in court?' she asked.

'Just want to see the verdict. I just want to know that this is all over, one way or another.'

Lilly too was glad the trial would soon be over, that she could then see Jack again, that Sam could then come home – or as soon as she could get the decorators in. But the thought of Catalina spending years locked away made her heart turn to dust.

*   *   *

Luke had lain by Caz's bed all night. Some of the other patients and their visitors had made rude comments about the smell, but he didn't care.

He puts his cheek next to hers and breathes her in.

'You need to brush your teeth,' she says, her voice barely audible.

He can't even smile. He looks up and down her broken body and blinks away tears.

'Why did you do it, Caz?'

'I was being chased by a gang of mad Russians,' she says.

'I mean, why did you look after me?' he says. 'You don't know anything about me.'

She lifts her finger and rubs his hand. 'I know what I need to know, soft lad.'

A memory flutters past. Tom, Charlie and Luke are wandering down the lane from the school to the village. It's a cold night and spider webs lace the hedges. Tom is showing off and Charlie is laughing. Why did he go with them that night? Why didn't he just tell them to get lost and finish his prep?

He kisses Caz's head. 'You are my best friend in the world.'

'You are my only friend,' she answers.

'When you get better I'm taking you back home with me,' he says.

'I think your ma might have something to say about that.'

Luke shakes his head. 'I don't care. You can have my bed and I'll sleep on the floor.'

'Sounds nice.' Her voice trails away.

'You can have a hot bath every day,' he says. 'Twice a day if you fancy.'

Her eyes flicker shut.

'Caz?'

He can't feel her breath on his cheek.

'Caz?'

He shakes her gently at first, then harder. 'Caz!'

'What a bitch.'

Snow White looks up from the pan of cheese sauce bubbling on the Aga.

Her son is watching the news.

'The slut that killed Charlie is saying she did it because she was raped.'

'She's said a lot of things,' says Snow White.

'She shouldn't be allowed to get away with it.'

Snow White is proud of her son. He has a clear sense of right and wrong.

'They will find her guilty,' she says.

'Now that I'd love to see,' he replies.

Snow White pours the sauce over cauliflower. It was Grandpa's favourite. 'Righty-ho,' she says. 'You can come to court.'

'Really?' he laughs. 'Take a day off school?'

'Some of the other mums are taking their boys,' she says. 'You're all old enough now to understand that we each have to take responsibility.'

Calm, calm, calm.

Lilly tried to stop her hands shaking. This was it. Her last chance to make the jury understand what her client had been through.

The atmosphere in the courtroom was electric. The

public gallery was packed. She could even see Manor Park parents and pupils dotted among the press.

She glanced at Catalina in the dock. The girl gave a small smile.

Calm, calm, calm.

'Ladies and gentlemen of the jury.' How Lilly wished she had something positive to give them. 'You have now heard all the evidence that is to be put before you, and I would like to say a few things on behalf of my client.'

Lilly paused. What could she say? *Please believe my client, even without any evidence that she's telling the truth.* This was hopeless.

The door burst open and Alexia fell into court.

'Who let this person in?' roared the judge, and a very spotty usher slunk to the back of the room.

'I'm sorry, Your Worship,' said Alexia. 'But I have something important for the defence.'

'You can't just burst in here,' said the judge. 'There is a trial going on.'

Alexia turned to Lilly. 'He's here.'

'What?'

'He's outside now.'

'Can someone tell me what is going on?' asked the judge.

'Your Honour, we have a last-minute witness,' said Lilly.

Jez jumped up as if scalded. 'It's too late, the defence have closed their case. My friend had already started her final speech.'

'Come on,' said Lilly. 'I didn't say a fat lot.'

'Nevertheless,' said the judge. 'Mr Stafford is correct.'

'Your Honour,' said Lilly. 'This whole case has turned upon whether or not my client was raped, and I now have someone who will say that it did happen.'

A shocked whisper ran through the court.

'He's here now,' said Lilly. 'Can we really say that without him Catalina Petrescu has had a fair trial?'

The judge bit his lip, no doubt weighing up the unorthodox nature of Lilly's request against the country's media breathing down his neck.

'I'll allow it.'

'Is your name Luke Walker?'

The boy in the witness stand squirmed. His eyes were red, his hair matted. He had obviously not slept. At last he nodded.

'Can you tell the court what happened to my client in the park?' said Lilly.

Luke flicked a look at Catalina.

'She came with us for a drink.'

'With who?'

'Me and Charlie Stanton and Tom Everard.'

'And what happened?'

'We were just having a bit of a laugh, you know, chatting her up and that. We had some cider.'

'Sounds like harmless fun,' said Lilly.

'It was at first.' Luke worried his lip with the edge of his thumbnail. 'Then things turned nasty.'

'In what way?'

'She started dancing around and that, acting all crazy,'

he looked at her again. 'Then Tom dragged her to the ground.'

'That's a lie!'

Lilly looked up to the gallery. Tom Everard was on his feet, his nasty gums on show. 'You're lying,' he shouted, before someone pulled him back into his seat.

Luke ignored him. 'He pulled her down and forced himself on her.'

The judge leaned over to Luke. 'That is a very serious accusation, young man.'

'He raped her,' said Luke. 'I was there.'

'I understand you've been on the run, Luke?'

Jez was smiling at him. Lilly sensed danger.

'I understand you've been living rough?'

'Yeah,' said Luke.

'Drinking, I suppose?'

'Yeah.'

'Taking drugs?'

'Sometimes.'

'Has it made things hazy? A little less sharp?' asked Jez.

'I know what I saw.'

'Perhaps your memory is fading,' said Jez. 'Or perhaps you misunderstood?'

'There is no mistake. Tom had sex with her.'

Jez nodded slowly. 'Is it possible that they did have sex, but that it was consensual?'

Luke stopped in his tracks.

Lilly gulped. Oh, no. Please, no.

'Is that possible, Luke?' asked the judge.

Luke looked at Catalina, then up to the gallery where

Tom Everard was leaning over the balcony, flanked by other Manor Park boys. Lilly saw Jack was sitting up there too.

'Luke?' Jez prompted.

'No,' said Luke. 'It wasn't consensual.'

'Do you know what that means, Luke?' asked Jez.

Luke snorted. 'Of course I know what it means. Just because I'm dressed like this, because I'm a bit of a mess, it doesn't mean I'm stupid.'

'I wasn't implying . . .'

Luke stood tall. 'You think you can dismiss me just because I've been homeless?'

Lilly had never before seen Jez Stafford flummoxed.

'I was simply questioning your memory of events,' he said.

'Well, don't,' said Luke. 'Because I know exactly what happened.'

In the gallery, Tom once again struggled to his feet. 'Shut your mouth, Walker.'

Luke pointed at the other boy but didn't take his eyes off Jez. 'You think because he's rich and goes to a nice school that he should be believed?'

Jez was speechless.

'He put his hand over her mouth because she was screaming,' said Luke. 'And Charlie held down her arms.'

A shockwave ran through the court.

'You fucking grass,' shouted Tom.

'He thought she didn't matter,' said Luke. 'That she was nothing.'

'You're a traitor,' spat Tom.

At last Luke looked up at his old school friend. 'You

456

treated her like an animal, but she is just as important as you and me.'

Tom roared at Luke. 'We're supposed to be friends.'

'My only friend is dead,' Luke held his old school mate's glare. 'You and I were never friends.'

The gallery erupted and Jack dragged Tom out of court.

'Tom Everard, I am arresting you on suspicion of rape. You do not have to . . .'

'This is preposterous,' said Mrs Everard.

'Tom can have his say at the station,' said Jack.

'You can't take that boy's word, he's clearly deranged,' said Mrs Everard. 'The family he's from are not the right sort.'

A woman Jack knew as Luella screwed up her nose. 'She's right. They're just not one of us.'

Jack bridled. One of us? What century were these women living in?

Jack took Tom by the arm and began to lead him away.

'We'll have our solicitors on to you like a shot,' said Mrs Everard.

'And the papers,' said Luella.

'I'm already here.' Alexia bounded up.

'Then you should get this down,' said Luella. 'Police harassment.'

'Oh, please,' said Jack.

'Why don't you people spend your time solving real crimes?' said Luella.

'What,' said Alexia, 'like burning down Lilly's house?'

'Lilly's house has been burned down?' shouted Jack.

'It was firebombed by Nazis two nights ago,' said Alexia.

Jack was stunned. 'Is Sam okay?'

Alexia nodded. 'Not that those bastards cared less about that.' She turned to Luella and Mrs Everard. 'But I suppose his family are just not the right sort for you to care.'

'Do you know who they are?' asked Jack.

'Oh, yes,' said Alexia. 'And I know exactly who helped them.' She stared at Luella and Mrs Everard.

'You're not saying this pair were involved?' Jack replied.

'Nah,' said Alexia. She gestured to Luella. 'She's a small-minded idiot but she'd never dare do anything other than talk.' Then she pointed at Mrs Everard. 'But if you check *her* computer you'll see she's a very busy bunny under the name "Snow White".'

Jack grabbed Mrs Everard's arm. 'You are so nicked.'

Alexia whooped with delight and dialled the number for News International. What a story.

Lilly faced her client in the cell.

'Now everyone knows I was raped,' said Catalina.

'Yes,' said Lilly.

'But will it be enough?'

Lilly looked at her client intently. Luke's testimony had been electrifying. The stuff of Hollywood.

'I don't know if they'll be able to get past the lies about where you came from.'

Catalina nodded as if this was exactly what she had suspected. She seemed strangely calm. Calmer than Lilly.

'I want to give you something,' she said.

She rifled through her bag of belongings, retrieved a tattered sheaf of paper and pressed the dog-eared bundle into Lilly's hands.

Lilly locked the toilet door and sat on the lid. She knew that she needed to be alone, and in the mania of the Bailey this was the only place.

She looked at the crumpled pieces of paper covered in childlike writing, each word pressed heavily with a pencil, and began, at last, to discover who her client really was.

Lilly ran the cold tap over a wad of toilet paper and pushed it against her eyes. Milo and Dr Kadir had been right all along. Catalina had had every reason to do what she did. But could a jury forgive all those lies?

Her mobile rang.

'Lirry.'

'Rupes?'

'Are you okay?'

Lilly could imagine the swelling to Rupinder's lips and it made her wince.

'What do you mean, am I okay? How the bloody hell are you?'

'Sore,' said Rupes. 'But on the mend.'

Lilly's knees began to tremble with relief and she leant against the sink for support.

'How's it going?' asked Rupes.

'Who knows, mate?' said Lilly. 'I'm about to close.'

Rupinder chuckled. 'Sock it to 'em.'

*   *   *

Court reconvened, and Lilly took her place once again.

'Ladies and gentlemen of the jury,' said Lilly. 'I know I started this speech before . . .'

The jury laughed politely.

'What I didn't know then was what on earth I was going to say.'

Lilly shot another glance at Catalina's 'statement'.

'In truth, I still don't.'

She turned to her client. 'What I do know is that Catalina Petrescu is an amazing person. She escaped a situation that most of us couldn't imagine in our worst nightmares.

'And, yes, she lied about where she came from and took on a false identity, but I for one am not going to judge her for that, for who am I to say what I would have done in her situation.'

Lilly scanned the jury, hoping to see a glimmer of understanding.

'To most of us, the way she was living, in a hostel, shunned by polite society, might not seem that great, but to Catalina Petrescu it was all she wanted because she was safe.

'Then, one night, even that was taken from her.'

She pointed to the witness stand as if Luke were still in it.

'A brave young man came forward and told us what happened. How Catalina was forced onto the ground and brutally raped. For most of us that would be a trauma we might never recover from but, for my client it was that last abuse, that last betrayal of her humanity, that pushed her over the edge.'

460

Lilly took a drink of water. God, she wished it were a Ginger Zinger.

'Her mind took a path of its own and stayed there. So, on that fateful day when she went to Manor Park School, she had no comprehension of what was about to unfold. Now, given what you've seen and heard in this courtroom, is that so difficult to believe?'

Chapter Twenty-Seven

'Mr Foreman, have you reached a verdict upon which you have all agreed?'

'We have.'

The judge nodded. 'And how do you find the defendant, Catalina Petrescu – guilty or not guilty?'

Lilly squeezed her eyes shut.

'Not guilty.'

Lilly threw her arms in the air. 'Yes!'

'What happens now?'

Jack was driving Catalina and Lilly to the station.

Lilly pushed her client's hair out of her eyes. It was streaked with grey.

'You'll be interviewed by immigration,' he said. 'Maybe you can make an application for asylum.'

Catalina shook her head. 'I'm from Romania.'

'She was sold by her mother to a pickpocketing gang,' said Lilly. 'And they trafficked her to England.'

'Jesus,' Jack muttered.

'She escaped with Artan and they bought new identities,' said Lilly.

Catalina nodded. 'We bought new papers for fifty pounds. No one cared about a few dead refugees. That way we could stay here, make a life for ourselves.'

Lilly thought about the pair living in Hounds Place, with no money or future. Was that a life? Maybe for them it was enough.

'What will happen now?' asked Catalina.

Lilly's heart lurched. 'I expect you'll be deported.'

They drove in silence for a few miles. Lilly knew full well that there was every chance that as soon as Catalina landed, the traffickers would pick her up again. Catalina knew it too.

Jack pulled into a petrol station. 'Let's get some chocolate.'

'Get me a Twix and a Bounty,' said Lilly.

'Why don't you come and choose it yourself?' he said, and got out of the car.

Lilly watched Jack saunter to the shop. He was the best man that ever lived. The best.

Slowly, Lilly took out her purse and pressed it into Catalina's hand.

'You don't have to,' said Catalina.

Lilly nodded. 'There's about a hundred quid in cash and I'll cancel the cards tomorrow.'

A silent moment stretched like elastic until Lilly knew she had to let go.

'It's been a pleasure knowing you,' she said.

'Give my best love to Sam,' Catalina replied.

Lilly thought of her son – his sunny life with two parents that adored him – and, not for the first time, she questioned the lottery of life that gave some children all the luck.

'He will make a very good big brother I think,' said Catalina.

Lilly opened her mouth but nothing came out.

Catalina smiled and patted Lilly's rounded stomach, acknowledging something she herself had been studiously avoiding.

Lilly burst into tears. 'Be happy,' she said, and ran to the father of her unborn child.

Read on for an exclusive extract from Helen Black's new novel, coming in 2010.

Prologue

I watch Yasmeen sleep, her breath shallow, her mouth slightly parted.

She is so beautiful.

Wherever she goes people stare at those eyes, heavy lidded, flecked with amber.

At mosque she takes her place, her hijab secured tightly under her chin and I can see her lips move. They are red as Carmelite as she murmurs her prayers.

Here, on the bed, I am dazzled by her all over again and I nearly change my mind. There's still time. I could call an ambulance and they would inject her with drugs, attach her to machines.

I pull out my phone and my finger hovers over the number nine.

But no, I have made up my mind.

There was a time when I would have done anything for this girl and she would have done the same for me. In this cruel world we stood shoulder to shoulder against those who would torment us. When I lost hope she held my face in her hands.

'God will provide.'

I wonder then why she has chosen to wreck everything. To bring this family to its knees. To crush me like a can.

Her chest rattles and I picture myself sitting here in Yasmeen's bedroom watching this girl I have loved so well. Watching her die.

Do I still love her?

With all my heart. Yet I am immobile as her life creeps away.

She lets out a tiny gasp and a pink bubble forms on her lips.

When it bursts I know it is over and I whisper into her ear.

'Salaam.' *Peace.*

Chapter 1

'Un-bloody-believable.'

Lilly Valentine leaned against the wall and sighed.

'I paid for this system to be up and running last week and I still can't make outgoing calls.'

The telephone engineer was laid on the floor, unscrewing a socket.

'There must be a glitch in your system,' he said.

'A glitch?'

'That's right,' said the engineer. 'There are often problems with the fibre optics.'

'Listen mate, I'm trying to run a law firm not sit for a degree in telecommunications.' Lilly heaved her backside into a chair. 'Can you fix it?'

'I'll need a new circuit board,' said the engineer. 'Can I come back tomorrow?'

Lilly shook her head in despair.

'Try not to worry,' the man laughed. 'Teething troubles are routine.'

Lilly smoothed her hand over her pregnant belly and looked around at the new offices of Valentine & Co. Unopened post was spewed across the door mat, files

469

littered every seat, the espresso machine still needed a plug and the potted plant had already died.

'Trust me,' she said. 'Nothing in my life is ever routine.'

When the engineer had left Lilly put her feet on her desk. Her ankles were swollen to elephantine proportions. She felt like an overstuffed cushion, all lumpy and uncomfortable. She didn't remember being like this when she was pregnant with Sam. Then again, that was nearly ten years ago.

When the door opened she remained in the same undignified position. Perhaps the engineer would hurry up if he could see what dire straights she was in.

'Are you open?' A young Asian man asked, looking at her doughy toes.

'Not exactly,' said Lilly and struggled to get upright.

'Oh,' he said but didn't move.

'Can I make an appointment for you?'

Lilly scrabbled around for the diary she'd bought especially. It was leather bound and had a whole page for each day. Her plan was to colour code clients. Red for family, green for property. Where had she put the damn thing?

She grabbed a biro and a ticket for the dry cleaners.

'Next Tuesday?' she asked.

The young man stroked his goatee. Lilly could see now that he was in his late teens. A boy really.

'Thing is, I've got my Mum in the car,' he said, 'and we really need to talk to someone.'

'I don't want to be unhelpful,' Lilly smiled and opened her arms to encompass the chaos, 'but as you can see we're not quite up to speed.'